Presented to the
Tulsa City-County Library
by
tulsa
LIBRARY TRUST

The Librarian of Burned Books

The Librarian of Burned Books

A Novel

Brianna Labuskes

wm

WILLIAM MORROW

An Imprint of HarperCollins*Publishers*

This is a work of fiction. Names, characters, places, and incidents are products of the author's imagination or are used fictitiously and are not to be construed as real. Any resemblance to actual events, locales, organizations, or persons, living or dead, is entirely coincidental.

FIRST EDITION

Designed by Diahann Sturge

Library of Congress Cataloging-in-Publication Data has been applied for.

ISBN 978-0-06-325925-6
ISBN 978-0-06-329712-8 (hardcover library edition)

23 24 25 26 27 LBC 5 4 3 2 1

To librarians, the guardians of books

The Librarian of Burned Books

New York City
November 1943

The telegram regretfully informing Vivian Childs that her husband had died in battle arrived before his last letter.

When Viv saw the familiar scrawl on an envelope two weeks after that baby-faced sergeant had knocked on the door, her knees gave out. She hit the marble floor of the entryway with a sharp crack that she distantly knew should hurt but didn't.

Edward.

For one desperate second, Viv thought that terrible telegram must have been a mistake.

But no, that couldn't be. This was a ghost, the words of a dead man who didn't yet realize his fate.

Viv's heart beat painfully against her wrists, her throat, and time passed, the ticking of the grandfather clock matching the throbbing at her temples. The comforting numbness that had protected her for the past two weeks had lifted and the pain she'd been holding at bay rushed in to every hollow space in her body.

It was almost a relief when the knob of her wrist connected with the edge of the table as she groped for the letter above her. That kind of pain she understood.

She stared at her name on the envelope, touching it and then his gently before slipping her nail underneath one corner.

My Viv,

I cannot tell you how grateful I am for your letters. Please keep them—and updates about your amusing feud with Mrs. Croft and her smug poodle—coming. All the men are as invested in the outcome of the blue-dye incident as I am.

You never think of war as dull, and yet there is nothing but monotony and sand and then moments of terror that leave you shaking for the long hours until all that wears off and what's left is monotony once more. Your stories keep us entertained more than you can know.

On that front, we may have more relief coming, thank goodness. The army has launched an ingenious initiative wherein they ship us poor, bored boys small, portable books to keep us entertained and distracted from all the bombs that are landing inches from our heads.

Forgive my dryness. But truly, the books have been a godsend to us. I managed to nab a copy of Oliver Twist, *and it makes me think of Hale. My brother is too proud to have ever accepted what he would have thought of as charity from me, but I do wish I had figured out a way to help him more when we were children. Thinking of him struggling when I had so much . . . well, the guilt makes it harder to sleep, doesn't it? War is good at that—making you remember everything you wish you'd done differently.*

I know this letter pales in comparison to your lively ones, but please don't punish me for my lack of stories by withholding your own. Give Mother my love.

Yours,
Edward

Viv ignored Edward's mention of his brother Hale as much as she ever could. A flash of hot summer nights, sticky cotton-candy lips, a teasing smile, and calloused hands came and went, a lightning strike in the dark night of her grief.

Why think about something she could never have?

Instead, she reread the letter, and for the first time in two weeks let herself picture Edward. Every time she had tried before, she had only been able to see a bruised and broken body, ripped flesh and blood, charred earth and flames. Now, she imagined him in front of a fire, but a gentle one, at night, surrounded by his brothers-in-arms. He cradled a book in his hands, calling out favorite passages to the others, pausing to listen as they did the same.

She clung to that image, basking in its comforting warmth.

After the fourth time through, Viv lifted a hand to her face and felt the corners of the first smile she'd allowed herself since Edward had died.

Chapter 1

New York City
May 1944

Viv pressed her spine against the brick wall of the alley as she split her attention between the back door of the ritziest steakhouse in Manhattan and the curious rat that was getting bolder by the second.

In Viv's mind, this escapade had played out with less garbage and more intrigue and she was starting to wonder if her plan was fundamentally flawed. As she pondered the possibility of retreat, the dishwasher she'd been waiting to bribe finally appeared. Her head went a little light in equal parts excitement and terror as she slipped the boy the bill she'd folded up just so.

The stench of days-old cabbage receded once she stepped into the restaurant's kitchen. Her confidence returning, Viv donned the femme fatale persona she'd been channeling all morning in preparation for this wild scheme. She'd even deliberately dressed the part, having paired her black skirt with matching garters and precious stockings with seams that hugged the backs of her calves. She'd pinned her hair into perfect victory rolls she usually didn't have the time to bother with, and she'd carefully slicked on a cherry lip that should have clashed with the red tones in her blond hair but never seemed to.

She wound her way past stoves that belched smoke and men who belched curses, the remnants of both curling around her so that she might as well have been walking through the docks on a foggy morning after having just killed a lover. Her hips swayed at the thought, her shoulders straightening.

It mattered, this feeling. It bolstered her resolve, helped compensate for her trembling hands.

Because Viv would have only one shot at this, and she could not mess it up.

Senator Robert Taft was headed back to Washington, DC, in the morning, and he didn't have a strong track record of answering her letters. This confrontation had to happen in person and it had to be today.

When she stepped out into the steakhouse's dining room, Viv spotted Taft easily. Before she'd met him months earlier, she'd pictured him as a small man, with a frame that curled in on itself. Pictured mean eyes and pinched features. A weak jaw. The personification of his petty personality.

In reality, he towered over his lunch companions, the candlelight glinting off his bald head. He took up space in that way powerful men seemed naturally able to, his arm spread along the back of the circular booth.

Viv had been right about the jaw, though.

And the personality.

A guard stopped Viv before she got to the group, melting out of the curtains beside the booth, a dangerous shadow she should have anticipated. She had, really. She'd just thought he would have been stationed by the entrance and directed to keep her out.

After all, Viv had been nothing but a thorn in Taft's side for the past six months. He wanted to avoid this conversation as much as she wanted it to happen. Hence the kitchen and the dishwasher and the bribe.

"Senator, if I could have a moment of your time," she called out, going for broke.

The chatter at the table died as everyone tensed. It was a strange moment in history to be a politician, when you were sending the nation's boys to their death while enjoying steak and whiskey lunches on the taxpayers' tab.

Taft's fingers drummed an uneven beat on the rich leather beneath his hand, likely trying to figure out how big of a scene she would make. He wasn't the only diner in the restaurant, after all, and he was nothing if not aware of his image.

Viv even noticed out of the corner of her eye a *New York Post* reporter whom she'd worked with before. As the publicity director for the Council on Books in Wartime, Viv had become friendly with a good number of journalists in the city. The man raised his glass and his brows in a salute, looking far too amused not to already be plotting to include an item about this encounter in the anonymous gossip pages.

The gesture must have caught Taft's attention because his lips flattened into a tight line as he stared at the reporter. Then Taft waved for Viv to take a seat, the other men shuffling out so that Viv was left sliding in far closer to him than she would have liked.

"Mrs. Childs," Taft said on an exhale as if she were a naughty child, called in front of the school principal. "What can I help you with?"

Viv nearly laughed at that. As if he didn't know why she was here.

Without answering, Viv reached into her purse and pulled out the slim books that were at the heart of her crusade against this man. She tossed one on the table in front of him.

"*The Adventures of Huckleberry Finn,*" Viv said, keeping her eyes locked to his. She wondered if he had ever even seen an Armed Services Edition. She sent him copies of the paperbacks in the mail, but his secretary—the same one who'd clued her in to this lunch—had let her know that any messages from Viv or the council got immediately repurposed as scrap paper. There was a ration on, or else they probably would have ended up in the fire. She threw down the second one. "*Grapes of Wrath.*"

"Mrs. Childs, I don't know what you think this stunt is accomplishing, but let me assure you—"

She was on a roll, though. "*Candide. Yankee from Olympus. The Call of the Wild.*"

With each title, she slammed one of the green books down on the table between them.

"All of those books will be banned from our Armed Services Editions program under your new censorship policy," Viv said, sitting back and folding her arms to try to contain the bright, sharp anger coursing through her. "Shall I keep going? There are plenty."

"It's not a censorship policy, Mrs. Childs," Taft said in that supremely rational tone that had her clenching her teeth. "All I'm requiring is that your little council doesn't use taxpayer money to send to our troops books that are lightly veiled political propaganda." He slipped a toothpick between thin lips and rolled it from corner to corner. "There are hundreds of well-written, enjoyable books out there that don't touch on politics. Please feel free to include any number of them in your ASE program."

"The language is too broad." Viv prayed he didn't notice the slight tremor in her voice. Part of her realized she'd let this all become too personal, as if the ASEs and Edward's final letter were entwined for her now. But she refused to let Taft dismiss her as a hysterical woman, as just another grieving war widow in a country full of them. "If you truly drafted the legislation in good faith, the wording should be changed. Right now, all the ban is doing is crippling our ASE initiative."

They both knew acting in good faith had never been important to him. His main goal had always been to hurt the council without looking like he was hurting the council.

But she had to try.

"This issue has been debated by the United States Congress and has been decided. It's law now, girlie," he said, and she heard *you lost* in the spaces between his words. "You think you know better than the Senate?"

Viv wanted to point out that he'd politically threatened any lawmaker who had tried to stand up to him on the issue. That argument wouldn't get her anywhere—he was clearly proud of his underhanded tactics.

"The language is too broad," she repeated, trying to remember the script she'd practiced so many times last night, terrified her tongue would tie in this moment. She waved to the books she'd brought. "Look me in the eye and tell me any of these actually constitute propaganda." When he didn't say anything, she pushed. "Under your policy, the army will have to ban its own instruction manual because it has a picture of President Roosevelt in it. How is that helping anyone?"

"The language has to be broad or people will find loopholes," Taft countered. "Some innocuous books might get caught up in the wider net, but that's the price we have to pay. If you knew anything about legislation or lawmaking you would know that. But you don't. Now, if you'll excuse me."

"It's not just these examples," Viv said, desperate. "It's most of our list."

"Well, then you see why my amendment was needed," Taft said, smiling so broadly that his eyes crinkled. She imagined him at a campaign stop and wondered if people actually bought this image. "Clearly your council required more guidance on which novels are appropriate for our soldiers to read."

Viv blinked at him. "The soldiers who are dying for us. They need to be told what to read?"

Seeming to sense he'd misstepped, Taft tried to buy himself time by picking up his napkin and dabbing at his chin. "Well, regardless, I'm protecting taxpayers who don't want to have their money spent on propaganda approved by a dictator looking to secure his fourth term."

That's where all of this had started, after all. Taft had a deep and abiding hatred of President Roosevelt, and it wasn't exactly secret. But Roosevelt was popular enough that Taft had to be crafty when he attacked the man. And Roosevelt was a vocal supporter of both the Council on Books in Wartime and its wildly successful initiative that every month shipped millions of paperback novels to the boys serving overseas. The ASE program had become so popular that Taft knew Roosevelt would use it as a campaign talking point come the fall. With his censorship policy essentially banning ninety percent of the books the council wanted to send to soldiers, Taft was handcuffing the initiative to the point of irrelevancy.

"Yes, I can tell you care about budgets," Viv said, her words dripping with ice as she glanced around at the remains of a meal that could have funded the council for a month.

Taft lashed out, his fingertips digging into the bones of her wrist. There would be bruises there tomorrow.

"I've been patient with your little tantrum here, young lady," Taft said, pressing her back into the booth with his bulk. "But I'll remind you, you are talking to a senator of the United States of America."

Viv refused to back down now. "Can you deny it? That this is nothing more than an attempt to destroy the council and hurt Roosevelt in the process?"

"I don't have to deny anything to you," Taft said, viciously spitting out the word *you*. She was less than a fly to be swatted away, she was nothing.

And maybe Viv—a woman who until six months ago had no more experience with life than throwing charity luncheons to help sell war bonds to her rich friends—was nothing in the grand scheme of things, in this war, in politics.

But in that moment, with Taft looming over her, believing without any doubt that he could intimidate her just like he intimidated everyone around him with bluster and violence, she decided this was her hill to die on.

It might be a small hill, but it was hers.

"The boys carry these books into battle," she said as softly as possible so that it would land that much harder. She didn't try to break away from his grasp. Maybe he would feel the steady thrum of her pulse, the surety of her conviction. "A man sent me a copy of *The Adventures of Tom Sawyer* last week that still had blood on it. He meant it as a thank-you. His buddy had a good laugh the night before he died because of that book."

She let that sit for a minute before continuing, "A book he wouldn't have had if your censorship policy had been in place just a few months earlier."

If she hadn't been watching closely, she wouldn't have noticed Taft's throat bob, a hard swallow, and for one achingly painful moment she thought she might have gotten through to him. Then he shifted back, reached into his coat pocket, and pulled out a few bills.

He tossed them on top of the ASEs she'd brought to throw in his face. "Go buy yourself something nice, sweetheart. And leave the important issues to the men."

Then he stood, signaled to his cronies, who had been hovering in the wings, and left without a single backward glance.

Chapter 2

Berlin
December 1932

The fairy lights stretching between booths at the winter market blurred into stars as the cold tickled Althea James's eyes. Laughter coiled around her, tugging her deeper into the noise and bustle that filled an otherwise quiet square a few blocks from the much busier Potsdamer Platz.

The market hummed with life and celebration, despite everything Althea had heard about the economic uncertainty that continued to plague Germany long after the Great War had ended. Hunchbacked grandmas haggled over trinkets and roasted nuts with the sellers, everyone tucking joy behind serious expressions so that they wouldn't be swindled. Children giggled and darted through the crowd, couples strolled arm in arm, somewhere in the near distance a band played rousing songs while the voices of a roving chorus weaved themselves into the air to make it pulse and sparkle.

Berlin was magical and Althea was charmed, wooed, nearly under a spell. She found herself—as she had so often in the week since she'd arrived in the city—with her notebook in hand, desperate to capture the scene that was so much bigger and overwhelming than anything she'd experienced in her sheltered life growing up in rural Maine.

Professor Diedrich Müller, her liaison from Humboldt University, watched her with enough affection in the slant of his smile that it had her ducking her head and tucking everything away in the pocket of her winter coat.

"No, don't stop on my account. I was enjoying watching a famous writer at work," Diedrich said, with the ease of someone apt at navigating socially awkward people.

The week before, when she'd stepped onto the docks at Rostock after her long trip from New York, she'd nearly tripped at the sight of him. She'd been informed that a literature professor would be waiting for her when she disembarked in Germany, but she'd pictured an older gentleman with a penchant for tweed jackets and esoteric poems. Not movie-star gorgeous Diedrich Müller, with his warmed-honey hair, snow-melt-blue eyes and effortless charm that poured off him in waves.

Even his voice was appealing, with an accent that conjured images of gothic castles rising against rich pine trees and stories of big, bad wolves who ate little girls in one bite.

If she ever added him into a novel, her editor would deem him too perfect, too unrealistic.

"It's not important," she demurred, still not used to being looked at as if she had something interesting to say. Before her debut novel had caught the world's attention so completely and unexpectedly, the only person she'd talked to with regularity had been her brother Joe. And he was family, so he didn't have a choice. "Just silly scribblings."

"Well, I hope you plan on including these 'silly scribblings' and other descriptions of our magnificent city in your next book."

"Of course." Althea supposed it was one of the reasons she'd been invited to Germany in the first place—to paint the country in a positive light.

She didn't mention that she seemed to have lost her ability to tell a story ever since she'd been plucked out of obscurity by a twist of fate. Every time she tried to start her next novel, the blank pages mocked her. How was she supposed to follow up lightning in a bottle?

Even the notebooks she'd filled since arriving in Berlin were full of hollow words that didn't quite live up to what she was seeing.

"There is nothing more beautiful than this city in winter," Diedrich continued, handing over a cup of steaming mulled wine he'd procured for her. "Except perhaps a lady who can appreciate its splendor."

Althea fought off a blush and wondered if she would ever get used to this man's flirtations. "Only perhaps?"

A flash of white teeth in genuine amusement. *What a big mouth you have.* Did that make her Little Red Riding Hood?

Diedrich bent close, his lips brushing the shell of her ear. "Depends on the lady."

Althea lost her battle with the flush that had been working its way up along her neck. He didn't mean her, he couldn't.

She had no delusions of her own beauty. It wasn't that she thought herself unappealing, but she was the type who was always lauded for her intellect over her looks. Everything about her was plain, from her pleasant, forgettable face and eyes to the spattering of freckles that had been deemed cute when she'd been younger but now got her unsolicited advice on face powder.

She *had* made an attempt tonight to match the image he must have of the sophisticated, world-renowned author she was on paper. There wasn't much she could do with the heavy curtain of hair that never seemed to want to stay where she put it, but she had visited a boutique the day before—one of those kinds of shops that made her fearful of touching anything—to purchase a dress that wasn't two decades out of style.

The way Diedrich's smile had turned sultry when he'd seen her in it confirmed that the risk had been worth the expense.

After Althea finished the wine, Diedrich handed her a sweet pastry. "You have to sample all that the culture has to offer, my dear."

"Do you include yourself on that list, Professor Müller?" Althea asked, knowing her cheeks must be impossibly pink. She hoped he'd blame it on the cold.

"Miss James," he murmured, a pleased chastisement lurking in his tone, one she recognized only secondhand from nights parked in the furthest corner of her brother's pub back home. This was how men who were interested in a particular woman talked.

As she often did when she was flustered, Althea tried to imagine she was writing instead of living this scene. What would she do if she were the main character instead of the dowdy friend there simply to add contrast, if she were Lizzy Bennet instead of Charlotte Collins?

Gathering all her bravery, Althea took a half step in front of Diedrich, enough to turn back with a saucy smile before taking off at something much faster than their meandering stroll, the dare implicit.

Catch me if you can.

In letting go of Diedrich, Althea had thought she might get disoriented, overwhelmed. Becoming untethered from a companion in the midst of a crowd could leave one dizzy and nauseous. Especially here in a city she didn't know, where she only passably spoke the language.

But there was something about the market—shoulders brushed against hers, faces turned with absent half smiles, children pulled at the hem of her coat. Rather than being caught in an avalanche, uncontrolled and terrifying, Althea was just a single snowflake in a storm that was so much larger than herself.

It was how she'd felt since she'd stepped off the train in Berlin.

Before this trip, she'd only ever left Owl's Head once in her life and that had been to meet her editor in New York on the publication day of her novel. The thought of going to a different country by herself had been terrifying. More than once, she'd unpacked her bags.

What is the worst that could happen? she'd asked herself.

You could die, the fear whispered back.

What is the best?

You could live.

Althea had repacked her bags and left her cottage by the cliffs.

She'd always been safe in the worlds she created for her characters, and always slightly out of place in the real one. But in Berlin she seemed to fit.

It took her a few seconds to realize she'd stopped in the middle of the crowd. Then she noticed what she'd been staring at.

Books.

They reeled her in, a hook caught in the softness of her belly, the line snapping taut, tugging until she found herself in front of the merchant, her fingers hovering over the leather-bound volumes on display.

"The lady has excellent taste," the man said in English, though there were enough pauses between the words to signal that he wasn't exactly comfortable with the language.

"Reinmar von Hagenau," Althea breathed out, snatching her hand back so as not to leave accidental fingerprints on the treasure. Von Hagenau was a beloved *Minnesänger*—the German equivalent of a troubadour. He hailed from the twelfth century and had been well respected by the peers of his day, all of whom wrote lyrical poems and songs featuring courtly love and honor.

The merchant's eyes lingered on the book in the same way parents gazed at precocious children. When he looked up, he seemed to read in her face that she might be a kindred soul. "Too expensive, yes?"

Althea smiled and shrugged and tried in German: "I'm sorry."

"No, no." The merchant waved away her apology and then squatted down behind his table. He pulled up a thick book that, while hardback and sturdy, was clearly less decadent than the one on display. He held it out with both hands. "For you."

She took it, rubbing a palm over the cover to brush away the few flakes that had landed, and nearly gasped in pleasure when she saw the title. It was a simpler volume of the von Hagenau collection.

"How much?" Althea asked, digging for her coin purse. It would be more affordable than the version meant for collectors, certainly, but she still didn't know if she had enough with her. The money her publisher had offered for another novel had been life changing, but she'd been cautious about spending any, worried that they might demand it all back when she failed to produce work of the quality they expected.

"A gift," the merchant said, bowing slightly. He tapped the spot over his heart once, and then pointed at her. "*Die Bücherfreundin.*"

"'A friend of books,'" Diedrich murmured from behind her,

his palm heavy on her waist, his chest close enough it brushed against her back when he inhaled.

"*Die Bücherfreundin,*" Althea repeated to herself. The polite part of her wanted to insist on paying for the collection, but the cost of the perceived rejection of his generosity would be far higher than that of the book.

Instead she held up a finger, then dug in her satchel so she could pull out a copy of *Alice in Wonderland,* one that she'd brought along as a safety blanket, the parallels between herself and a disoriented and dazzled Alice dropped into Wonderland too strong not to find comforting.

"A gift," she deliberately parroted, though she attempted it in German as he had in English.

He took it with the slightly shaking hands of the elderly, smiled once he realized what the book was, and then pressed it to himself in an approximation of a hug.

The man nodded once, an acknowledgment, a goodbye. And then turned his attention to another customer.

Althea wanted to linger, wanted to stay wrapped up in the experience, but Diedrich was already towing her along, and she trailed behind him toward the edges of the market, toward their dinner plans, and maybe toward their after-dinner plans if she continued to act as if she were the main character in the scene instead of the wallflower. If she continued to be Berlin's version of Althea James.

While she'd thought she'd been successful in the market with her clumsy flirtations, her few attempts on the stroll along the Spree to dinner fell flat. Diedrich had slipped into a thoughtful silence that was uncharacteristic to what she'd been learning was his natural affinity for bright conversation. Their dinner was a quiet affair, then, because she'd never mastered the art of small talk. She spent the time worrying, turning over everything she'd said, wondering if she'd done something wrong.

Despite the fact that the international literary community seemed to view her as someone important, she truly was just a simple, unsophisticated girl. Even now as she took part in a cultural program designed to bring "well-known and respected authors" of German origin back to their home country for six-month residencies, she couldn't help but feel like a fraud. Not only because she still hadn't come to terms with the idea of herself as a real writer, but because she'd never thought of herself as anything but American.

Her grandparents hailed from a village outside Cologne, but all she'd really ever known of them were the names scribbled in the family Bible. And her mother had never shown any interest in her heritage. They were Americans, and no one would tell Marta James otherwise.

After Marta had died young, Althea had been too busy raising her brother the rest of the way into adulthood to think much of anything beyond whether they had enough money to buy sugar that week.

Still, even if Althea didn't feel connected to her German ancestors, the offer to come to Berlin had been too tempting to pass up. If she agreed to participate, she'd get a round-trip ticket, a stipend, an apartment in a safe neighborhood, and a liaison from a local university to help show her around. In return, she'd be asked to attend a few political and social gatherings, as well as give a handful of talks about *The Unfractured Light,* the novel that had shifted Althea from a hobbyist into the category of "well-known and respected."

She chewed on her bottom lip now, studying Diedrich's face carefully. The lines between his brows weren't deep, nor was his frown. Not anger, then, but contemplation.

Althea was about to try to lighten the mood—how, she wasn't sure—when Diedrich seemed to shake off whatever strange emotion had settled around his shoulders.

"You enjoy German literature," he said, with that smile he'd bestowed on her back in the market.

She basked in the warmth of it, relieved that she hadn't somehow lost his affections. "Yes."

Diedrich beamed. "May I offer a suggestion?"

"Please."

"It's one of my favorites." Diedrich shifted to withdraw a book with a red cover from his inside jacket pocket.

The flickering candlelight on their table caught gold lettering as his fingers caressed the worn binding. Whatever this was, it was clearly treasured, so much so that he carried it around with him.

The cover was simple and straightforward, nothing too elaborate.

"I would very much enjoy hearing your thoughts on it."

"Of course." Althea gave him the best smile she could as she tapped the title. *Mein Kampf.* She could read German better than she could converse or write in it, so the translation came easily. "My Struggle."

Diedrich gave an approving nod. "I am positive you will find it quite fascinating."

Although she didn't tend to gravitate toward autobiographies, Althea was aware enough to recognize the name of the author as the head of the very party that was funding her trip to Berlin. To be polite, she murmured, "I'm sure I will."

Chapter 3

New York City
May 1944

Viv's femme fatale outfit had wilted right alongside her confidence, which had been thoroughly stamped out back in that steakhouse booth.

But she didn't have time to change into something less dramatic before she was due for drinks in the West Village. When she'd made the plans with Harrison Gardiner, one of William Morrow's rising editorial stars, she'd hoped they would be celebrating. Now she just wanted something strong to douse the strange blend of rage and sorrow and humiliation that tangled uncomfortably in her chest.

She walked because the tavern where they were meeting was only a handful of blocks from the restaurant, and she needed the air, afraid that if she sulked on the subway tears would ruin the mascara she'd swiped on that morning. And usually once she started crying she couldn't seem to stop. It was as if her grief was lurking, waiting for any hint of vulnerability. Mostly, she kept it at bay, but in moments like these when all she wanted to do was talk to Edward it tended to hit her the hardest that she would never be able to again.

Viv caught sight of Harrison through the grungy windows of the White Horse Tavern, chatting up a young woman who looked like she'd just stepped off the bus from Iowa.

Had there ever been a time when she'd been set to meet Harrison for cocktails where he hadn't immediately found the closest available woman to flirt with? She rolled her eyes, but for the first time since she'd sauntered into that restaurant an hour ago, she laughed.

She stepped into the tavern and earned herself a low whistle by the scruffy artist type who'd stationed himself by the door. The man was likely drunk enough he couldn't see straight, or else he wouldn't have blessed her with the so-called admiration.

It wasn't that Viv didn't know how to draw eyes to herself. She was sharper than the women gracing all the magazine pages, willowy in contrast to the Betty Boop ideal that men kept pinned to the control panels of their fighter planes. But she knew her long lines, combined with a pointy chin, high cheekbones, and strawberry-heavy blond hair held their own allure, made her interesting to look at. *Like a fox,* she'd been told more than once by men who had probably thought they were being creative. Still, she wasn't the type to earn wolf whistles from strangers. Not sober strangers, at least.

She ignored the man and crossed the room to shove herself into Harrison's side. The girl from Iowa startled, her big blue eyes snapping to Viv's, a blush on her milkmaid skin.

"I see what happens when I'm late," Viv teased, snatching the olive from Harrison's drink. "You find yourself another date. Did you even let the seat get cold?"

"No, I wasn't . . . ," the girl hurried to reassure, but Viv just winked at her. The girl flushed and then scrambled off the stool and out the door in a whirlwind of limbs and skirts.

Harrison watched her go and then swung his narrowed-eyed gaze back to Viv. "Mean."

Viv took the girl's vacated spot. "Please, it wasn't like that was love. You didn't even know her name."

"There are more important things in life than names, doll," Harrison said, but there was no heat in his voice and he was already signaling to the bartender hovering nearby for two fresh martinis.

"Right, like her measurements," Viv said, kicking his shin with the tip of her pumps. Harrison smirked and snatched the olive from her drink before she could protest.

The first time they'd met, Harrison had deployed his charm on her. He was dark haired and slim, almost handsome, though his face was a touch too long, his eyes too pinched together. But he'd made her laugh, and she thought that might be a large part of his appeal. When she hadn't flirted in return, he'd backed off immediately and they'd settled into friendship.

Sometimes on lonely nights she longed for the butterflies she'd felt only once in her life; in the darkest hours, she wished that when she met a witty, attractive man she could have that sense of *possibility* that made everyone else around her so giddy.

Then she remembered the pain that had come with the ghosts of those butterflies, thought of the warmth that bloomed in her with each friendship made. It had taken her a few years but she had realized love didn't have to be a white wedding; it could be sharing drinks and gossip on an otherwise terrible day.

"Congratulations on *Too Busy to Die,*" she said. Harrison might be a friend but he was also a bright young thing at a big publishing house, which meant she kept tabs on him because of her job with the council. It was within her scope of responsibilities to know what each house had on their list each season, what the next bestsellers would be, and what all the top editors were working on. These details helped her decide what books to include in each month's ASE shipment.

Too Busy was a delicious crime novel that included a public relations consultant as well as a spunky heroine who drank too much bourbon and excelled at craps. Not that she would admit it to Harrison, but Viv might have even channeled the character's gumption in crafting her desperate plan with Taft. "I read it in one sitting."

"You're buttering me up. What do you want?" He paused, eyeing her all-black getup. "And tell me, does it have anything to do with why you're dressed as a cat burglar?"

Viv struck a pose like she was one of the girls in those pulpy noirs. "Socialite turned jewelry thief with a heart of gold. I can see the cover already." Harrison laughed and she broke character with an impish smile.

The amusement left as soon as it came, and Viv tossed back her drink in two unladylike gulps. "Roosevelt let the Soldier Voting Act become law last week."

"Jesus wept," Harrison breathed out, because anyone who paid even a little attention knew what that meant.

Everyone and their mother had known the new Soldier Voting Act had to pass—after all, it had been shameful how few soldiers had been able to cast a ballot in the past election. The bill was technically supposed to solve for that. But Republicans knew more soldiers voting meant Roosevelt winning, and so they'd thrown as many wrenches as they could into the process. Once they realized the bill was going to get through Congress anyway, they started adding to it every single policy they'd ever wanted to see become law, no matter how useless, self-indulgent, or expensive.

Cue Taft's censorship amendment and his attack on Roosevelt's favorite pet project.

Harrison reached inside his jacket for his cigarettes. He held one out to her and then lit a match. She dipped the end in the flame as she thought of the way Edward had taught her how to smoke, back when she'd been eighteen and new to the world. He'd made shapes on his exhales, mirth held in the depths of his eyes.

An ache throbbed beneath her breastbone, and she locked the memory away once more.

"Where does that leave your little Armed Services Editions?" Harrison asked after taking his own drag.

Viv knew her smile flashed too much incisor. "I'm not certain 'little' is what I would call an initiative that ships millions of books to soldiers stationed abroad every month."

Then she sighed and nodded when the bartender gestured with a bottle of gin. Harrison wasn't her target, and it wasn't fair to take her frustration out on him. Viciously, she snuffed out the cigarette after only a few puffs.

"Functioning." Viv managed to provide the real answer to his question. Because that was the problem. The Armed Services Editions program could still function beneath Taft's policy. It would simply be gutted of everything that made it so effective.

"He's a right bastard, isn't he?"

"At the very least." Viv took a slower sip of her second martini. "It's frustrating to watch men like him win all the time."

"Politicians?" Harrison asked, one brow lifting.

"Bullies," Viv corrected. "He's no Hitler, of course. But I think he's just another flavor of bully and I'm so tired of them. Aren't you?"

"I was a scrawny book kid with glasses and bad lungs who went to public school in the Bronx," Harrison said, blowing a stream of smoke away from her. "What do you think?"

"I really thought I could stop him." She shook her head, laughed at herself. "Me."

"That sounds like you're giving up," Harrison said. "Come on, the Viv I know goes down swinging."

Viv chewed on her lower lip, shooting him a half-proud, half-embarrassed look. "I just ambushed him during his lunch in Midtown."

A surprised silence followed the confession before Harrison laughed, a rumbling sound that started in his chest and lasted long enough for Viv to smile wryly.

"He was only going to be in the city for two days, I had to do something," Viv said as Harrison swiped at the corner of his eye.

"Oh, to have been a fly on that wall," Harrison said, but then sobered. "I take it he didn't retract the blasted ban on the spot."

"I didn't even go big and ask for that. I just wanted him to rewrite the policy so it's not so broad."

"And now?"

Viv rubbed at her sore wrist, thought of Taft's stale, garlic-laced breath as he loomed over her. "Now? I want to destroy him."

She flushed a little at the tinge of evil mania she heard in her own voice, but Harrison let out something that came horribly close to a giggle. She'd chosen the right drinking partner for the afternoon, that was certain.

"What does destroying him look like?" he asked after a beat, having redonned his smooth modern man demeanor.

"I've already thrown everything I can think of at this and have gotten exactly diddly-squat for my efforts," Viv said.

"If this were a book, you know what point we'd be at right now?" Harrison asked.

"I have a feeling you're going to tell me."

"This right here?" Harrison jabbed his finger against the wood to make his point. "It's the all-is-lost moment."

"That sounds about right," Viv said dryly.

"But the all-is-lost moment isn't the conclusion, as you know very well." Harrison was picking up steam now. "No one ends the book with the all-is-lost moment. You have the rising action, the climax, the happy ending."

"How many of those drinks have you had, darling? We're not in a book," Viv pointed out.

"We're not?" Harrison asked with exaggerated shock, looking around all big eyed. Viv kicked at his shin again.

"Look," Harrison sighed, dropping the theatrics. "I know real life is a lot more dismal and hopeless than a well-structured novel. There aren't always happy endings, the villain is sometimes victorious, sure. But sometimes the good guys really *do* win. Why can't this be one of those times?"

"Because I can't pull a happy ending out of thin air just because I want it enough," Viv said. It almost hurt to talk about this, to hear him act like she had simply missed an obvious strategy. If she had only been better or smarter or craftier she could have gotten Taft's amendment killed the moment he'd introduced it.

"But what if you could create your own happy ending here?" Harrison asked. "You tell stories for your job as much as writers do, Viv."

"I can tell stories until I'm blue in the face," Viv said, a little waspishly. "That doesn't get rid of the fines and jail sentence attached to Taft's policy."

"I know, but—"

Viv cut him off with a raised hand. "What exactly are you suggesting I do?"

"I don't know," Harrison admitted, his shoulders slumping, and Viv laughed, the bitterness that had been brewing at his cavalier optimism dissolving. "I did believe my train of thought was going somewhere important, but the tracks ended abruptly at a cliff."

"Welcome to my past six months."

"Just think about it," Harrison said, ordering them both another round. "And we'll drink ourselves silly as you do."

"I like this idea very much." Viv clapped enthusiastically as she swiveled toward the bar and her empty glass.

They passed the rest of the afternoon crafting outrageous strategies to get from this all-is-lost moment to their big happy ending, some nonsensically involving farm animals, some more seriously involving Viv making an impassioned speech on the Senate floor to publicly shame Taft. How they would get her to the podium, they didn't bother figuring out. They both realized the conversation had taken a sharp left turn away from realistic hours earlier.

By the time the night started to creep in through the windows, Viv no longer felt like her chest had been hollowed out. But they were no closer to a good plan for overturning Taft's censorship policy, either.

"You know, I heard about a place the other day," Harrison said, his vowels all relaxed now with the liquor. "Maybe it would be worth a visit. Though it is quite the haul to Brooklyn."

He reached into his pocket for a pen and notepad and scribbled out an address.

"What's in Brooklyn?" Viv asked, trying to peer over his shoulder.

Harrison grinned as he slid her the paper. "Inspiration."

Weak tendrils of hope bloomed from the ash of her defeat as she ran a fingertip over the words.

The American Library of Nazi-Banned Books.

Chapter 4

Paris
October 1936

Hannah Brecht liked Paris best with winter on the horizon.

She knew that was an unpopular opinion, knew that many thought picnicking by the Eiffel Tower on a beautiful summer day the height of Parisian life, but just as she thought Paris was best with a broken heart, Hannah thought it was at its truest in the dreary cold.

Hannah bicycled through the streets on the outskirts of the fourteenth arrondissement, her wide-legged black trousers flirting precariously with the spokes of the tires; her soft, peach-colored wool hat threatening to fly off with the breeze; her dark curls teasing out from her tight chignon so that they brushed against cheeks she knew were wind-kissed pink.

The striped awning of her favorite patisserie beckoned ahead, the golden glow of the shop windows testing her ability to resist temptation. She had one more stop to make, but it could wait the five minutes.

She left her bike leaning against the wall of the building next door and stepped into the patisserie.

Notes of burnt sugar and yeast saturated the air, chocolate and espresso beans adding deeper layers beneath the lighter scents.

"Hannah," Marceline called from behind the glass case, her round face flushed with the warmth of the place. "Come in. A *café noisette*?"

"Please," Hannah said, not bothering to unwrap her scarf. She had only a short time to linger. "And a *canelé,* if you have any left."

Marceline grinned, pleased as always that Hannah could never pass up one of her signature caramel cakes. Hannah had found Marceline's patisserie on her first day in Paris nearly three years ago, and she tried to stop in at least once a week.

It helped that Marceline, with her German-born husband, spoke Hannah's native language. Since Hannah still struggled to get her practical Berlin tongue to curl around those lyrical French words, Marceline was one of the few Parisians Hannah knew she could talk to without getting a judgmental glare in return.

"Busy?" she asked as Marceline bustled around, putting the milk on to warm, plating the pastry. She slid it over the glass case, and Hannah, knowing that Marceline didn't stand on ceremony, picked up the fork right there. The outer crust put up a fight against the tines for a beat, perfectly, and then relented, letting her sink into the creamy vanilla center.

"Ehh." Marceline gave a Gallic shrug. "Sometimes yes, sometimes no. Xavier thinks he is too sophisticated now to work in his mother's patisserie. The young ones . . ."

Marceline clicked her tongue and shot Hannah a commiserating look despite the fact that Hannah hadn't yet reached thirty. Hannah wisely stuck some more cake in her mouth, nodding as if she understood. And maybe she did.

She thought about those Resistance meetings back in Berlin,

when they'd all been full of piss and vinegar and foolish ideals. How young they'd been to believe they could change the world.

"Well, maybe he's right," Marceline continued as she dressed the espresso with the milk. "Who knows how long our boys have left before they're pulled into another war."

And there was another reason why Marceline's had become one of Hannah's favorite spots in Paris. The woman's husband had enough friends left in Berlin that they knew as well as Hannah did what was headed their way.

"That's why I never pass up one of your *canelés,*" Hannah said with a grin, hoping to lighten the mood. She was usually the cynic in the room, but Marceline had three boys and two girls to get through the oncoming storm. Children made you vulnerable, your heart walking around outside your body. "Even though my skirts won't fit for much longer if I keep indulging."

Marceline tsked at Hannah, the distant look falling from her face. "As if you will ever be anything other than the most beautiful woman in Paris." She leaned in, wisps of gray hair plastered to her temples. "I include my own daughters in that, you know."

"Ah, but I pale in comparison to you," Hannah said, downing the *café noisette*.

"Compliments will get you free cake, don't let anyone tell you otherwise," Marceline said, waving off Hannah's offer of payment.

Hannah blew her a kiss, dropping some coins on the counter anyway before stepping out the door.

The sky had turned a gunmetal gray in the time she'd been in the store, and Hannah hurried to her bicycle, the threat of a downpour incentive enough to finish up her tasks for the afternoon. The pamphlets from the German Library of Burned Books fluttered in the front wicker basket as she headed toward her last stop of the day. They served as a reminder, as always, of how much her assignments for the library could differ from day to day.

The Deutsch Freiheitsbibliothek was part publisher, part lending library, part gathering place for the German émigré community that had made its home in the City of Lights after fleeing Nazi rule. Born from the scraps of another project—a research initiative that had collected hundreds of thousands of newspaper clippings, essays, and pamphlets on the dangers of totalitarianism—the library in Paris lived and breathed as a daily effort to counter the rising tide of fascism in France.

Because she was pretty and a woman, Hannah was often the one chosen to distribute the library's antifascist pamphlets to shops and organizations around Paris that were known to support its mission. At times, she wondered what would happen to her if she handed the little booklets over to a Nazi sympathizer. Hannah had already learned the painful lesson once that her own judgment wasn't reliable on that front.

She had to look no further than Adam for proof of that. Her brother was slowly dying in one of Hitler's horrific detention camps, most likely beaten and tortured daily, all because Hannah had trusted the wrong person.

Althea.

The name tangled itself into the wind that whipped at Hannah's jacket as she dismounted in front of the last address for the day. She tucked away the despair that came whenever she thought of Althea, of Adam, of that time in Berlin that remained as sharp as if it had happened yesterday, like how nightmares lingered while soft dreams dissolved into nothingness.

Her final stop was a Jewish-owned violin store, and she'd purposely left it for last. She adored both the man who ran it and his grandson, Lucien, but every time she came by with pamphlets, Lucien tried to convince her to attend the Resistance meetings he held every week in the back room of the store.

Hannah had too much experience with those kinds of gatherings, the ones that drew people who believed violence was the only way to disrupt the oncoming fascist tide that seemed set to sweep through Europe. It wasn't that Hannah disagreed, but she'd seen Adam's bruised and broken face after that first night he had been hauled off to jail by the Nazis. She'd seen friends whipped and beaten in the streets by brownshirts.

While violence might be the only answer here, it could never be the one Hannah turned to.

The golden bell above the door jangled as she entered.

Henri, the grandfather, was bent over a long counter that ran the length of the place, but he peered up at her through his spectacles, flashing a toothy grin.

"Bonjour, mademoiselle," he called, his gnarled hands continuing their swift, practiced movements along the neck of the violin he held.

"*Bonjour, Grand-père.*" He'd told her when they first met that everyone he liked was allowed to call him that and she'd been pleased to be included in that list. "Lucien?"

He jerked his head toward the hallway that led to the back. "*Dans le dos.*"

"*Merci,*" Hannah said, and he winced a little at her rough accent—a shared joke.

Hannah found Lucien setting up chairs in the small storage room. There must be a Resistance meeting that night. Without waiting to be asked, she helped him finish constructing the handful of rows facing a lectern in the corner.

When they were done, Lucien kissed both her cheeks before

taking the pamphlets. "That library of yours is printing these faster than we can even hand them out."

"They have many thoughts," Hannah drawled.

"As do we all, I suppose," Lucien said. "Tea?"

"Please." Hannah accepted gratefully. Although the coffee at Marceline's had warmed her, there was still a chill lingering in her core from riding around Paris all day. Her trousers were damp at the hem and her cardigan had valiantly tried to protect her from the wind, but both she and it were well aware of the fabric's limitations.

Lucien led the way to a tiny kitchen and put a kettle on. Hannah watched his graceful movements from her seat at the small table in the corner. He was pretty, with thick dark hair and a kind smile, built in the slim Parisian fashion that the girls here all seemed to swoon over. If she had been so inclined, she could see this being her life—the cozy violin shop, her providing a listening ear for a lover getting ready for a political gathering, music slipping in through the cracked-open door.

But she had never wanted to be a wife. Or she had never wanted to be a wife to a man, and that seemed to be the only option allowed.

"What do you do?" Hannah asked as she accepted her cup. "At the meetings, I mean."

Lucien, who had always been convinced Hannah was a Resistance fighter in librarian's clothing, got a gleam in his eyes that made her regret asking. "Come and see for yourself, darling."

Hannah stared down at her tea, her finger finding a chip in the rim of the cup. "I've been to enough meetings in my life."

"I knew it," Lucien said, leaning forward on his forearms, eager. "In Berlin? What were they like?"

"Useless," Hannah said, bitter and mean. But Lucien just smiled patiently, and she continued, more slowly. More thoughtfully. "It felt like we were playacting, perhaps? Hitler had just been named chancellor, and things went very bad, very quickly. But . . . it was still thirty-three, if you know what I mean."

"You never thought he'd last this long," Lucien said, following her thoughts.

"He lit a fire in so many, in his detractors and supporters alike," Hannah said. "But I thought that kind of flame burned bright and then burned out." She paused, trying to decide if she should actually answer his original question. "The meetings were silly. We talked about economic systems and political theories as if we were going to debate those monsters in the marketplace of ideas. We should have been talking about train tickets and overseas bank accounts and escape plans, instead."

Lucien plucked at his lower lip, watching her, contemplative. "In our last meeting, someone did a dramatic reading of *Das Kapital*."

He said it with enough self-deprecation that Hannah grinned.

"Yes, I've been to that meeting," she said, wanting to pat his cheek like he was a child. She restrained herself. "Maybe tonight, talk about whether anyone has family in the countryside who can provide hiding spots when the Germans inevitably cross the Maginot Line."

"You think it's inevitable," Lucien said, and she wondered at the doubt in his voice. It confirmed her belief that these Resistance meetings were nothing except for a place for men to talk about all the big thoughts they had. Not unlike the Library of Burned Books at its worst.

"Isn't war always inevitable," Hannah said lightly. And then she changed the topic with a brutal pivot. "So, tell me, my dear, have you broken any hearts lately?"

Lucien reared back, his hand over his chest. "You wound me."

Hannah rolled her eyes and he slid her a look, wearing an almost bashful expression, one she'd never seen on his face before.

"Who is she?" Hannah pressed, intrigued now.

"A university student," Lucien confessed and then winced. "American. Dreadful."

"At least she's not a Nazi."

"Mm. And you, Hannah?" He waggled his eyebrows. "Broken any hearts yourself?"

Hannah had certainly enjoyed a handful of lovers during her time in Paris. But . . . "Isn't it odd to fall in love right now?"

"Or perhaps that is the best time to fall in love?" Lucien, like the native Parisian he was, countered. He was the type to love Paris best on a summer evening with roses and chocolates. "What better thing to fight for than love?"

"Maybe for some." Hannah shrugged as carelessly as she could. "I might not make it through the coming storm. I would never want to leave someone who loved me behind like that."

"Hannah." Lucien reached across to grip her hand. "What are you talking about, silly girl? You will be fine."

"Will I?" Hannah asked, looking away, but not pulling away. It seemed like no matter how hard she tried, every conversation returned, like a magnet, to this subject. "Sometimes it seems like Paris wants to roll out the welcome mat for the Nazis."

Lucien didn't argue, just stroked her knuckles with his thumb. "You're leaving?"

"With which visa?"

"But if you could?" Lucien pressed.

"Paris isn't my homeland to defend," Hannah said. Harsh, maybe, but honest. "Mine was already taken. Which is why I refuse to fall in love."

"As if you could stop yourself if it was real," Lucien murmured.

That had been another lesson she'd learned already. "Tell me about the girl."

Lucien distracted her with a pleasant hour of chatter not only about the girl, but of salacious gossip about people they both knew, about any light topic they could find. It wasn't until he walked her back to the front of the shop that he nudged her. "You won't come tonight?"

"Fight the good fight for me, yes?" Hannah said and pretended not to notice the flash of disappointment as she kissed him goodbye. She paused on the threshold to wave to Henri, wondering for a brief, wild moment if she really should attend that evening's meeting.

But she shook off the thought and skirted around a man with a wheelbarrow full of cut flowers to get the bike she'd left leaning against the canal's railing.

She had just gripped the handlebars when she noticed a couple eyeing the front of the store and then her.

As the man passed, he spit, the glob of saliva landing on her cheek before trailing down to her jaw.

"*Juive,*" he muttered as the pair continued to stroll past as if nothing had happened. They didn't even walk fast to flee the scene.

Hannah didn't wipe the wetness away, she just stared at their retreating backs.

For every man like Lucien who existed, there were two more people like the ones who had spit on her in broad daylight in the middle of Paris.

Hannah knew the assault should strengthen her resolve, make her want to take up a sword. But every day that passed, she was less and less certain the world really was worth saving.

Chapter 5

New York City
May 1944

Viv checked the address on the paper Harrison had slipped her the day before, but it was hard to miss the imposing, block-long Brooklyn Jewish Center that apparently housed the American Library of Nazi-Banned Books.

"What are you doing here?" Viv asked herself beneath her breath, though she still spoke loudly enough to get a strange look from a passerby.

She wondered if she'd completely lost all of her senses. There was desperate-but-reasonable hope and then there were wild-goose chases, and the line between the two seemed pretty thin right now.

"You made the trip, you might as well go in," she told herself, and then made a note to learn how to keep her mouth shut when she was alone in public.

Then she walked into the lobby, where an elderly man blinked at her through Coke-bottle-thick glasses and had her repeat "Library of banned books?" three times before he seemed to catch on to what Viv was looking for.

"West wing." He pointed toward a long hallway before turning his attention back to the novel he'd been reading.

When Viv reached the correct door, she gently touched the gold lettering on the glass before stepping into the room.

It was surprisingly small but packed with towering shelves and tables crowded with sloppy stacks of books. Rays of light poured in from the windows, catching the dust in the air; an abandoned cup of tea sat on the sill; low music played from the wireless perched on the checkout desk, everything so cozy and lived in that Viv had to suppress the urge to pick a novel at random and curl up with it in one of the chairs.

"Welcome." A woman emerged from a broom-closet-sized office behind the checkout desk, reaching to turn down the volume on the radio as she gave Viv a restrained smile. "Can I help you?"

Viv pressed her lips together so she didn't spill out her whole sorry tale to this unsuspecting stranger. What had seemed like a sensible idea after a half bottle of gin now had her wondering if someone would question her sanity.

I'm searching for a happy ending to pull out of thin air.

"Erm . . ." Viv said, glancing around, inhaling the sour tang of old pages and glue, trying to find her balance.

The librarian studied her. "Forgive me for saying so, but you look like you could use a cup of tea."

"That obvious?" Viv asked with a laugh, fidgeting with her single-strand pearl necklace as if it were a talisman. It was the one piece of jewelry from her mother that she wore. She remembered toying with it in the same way when she'd sat on her mother's lap as a child, her fingers worrying the glossy beads. Some well-meaning nanny had looped it around Viv's neck on the morning of her parents' funeral and now she rarely took it off.

Whatever the librarian saw on Viv's face had her eyes narrowing. "Sit," she directed with a jerk of her head toward the table on the other side of the room.

"Thank you," Viv murmured to the woman's back before dropping into a chair near the window. A book across from her caught her attention, and she reached out so she could turn it around and read the title.

"Albert Einstein," the librarian said as she set a cup down at Viv's elbow a few minutes later. Viv had moved on to flipping through the book's pages, understanding about every tenth word. "He was the keynote speaker at our library's inauguration."

"Was he?" Viv asked, duly impressed.

The librarian hummed. "I heard it was quite a grand night, the invitations as coveted as sugar and coffee are now."

"You weren't here?"

"No." Something guarded slid into her expression.

Viv tried to tamp down her nosiness. "And that was when? Years ago now, correct?"

"The party was in December thirty-four," the librarian said, her shoulders relaxing. Viv wondered if it was because she was talking about the library instead of herself. "But the official opening didn't come until months later, to mark the second anniversary of the book burnings in Berlin."

Viv tried to recall the correct month. "So May? Thirty-five?"

"Yes." The woman gestured to the wall closest to them, where a propaganda poster hung. From Light to Darkness, the words blared over the images. Similar to others Viv had seen, this poster was a compilation of several events, the fire from the books licking up into the sky to burn what Viv recognized as the Reichstag building. The small, tightly wound figure of Joseph Goebbels oversaw it all.

Viv shifted her attention back to the librarian to find her

studying the poster, unshakeable despair written into every line on her face.

"You were there," Viv breathed out, unable to stop herself.

After a long moment in which Viv thought she might not answer at all, the librarian dipped her head. "Yes. I was in Berlin on the night of the burnings."

Viv swallowed the hundreds of follow-up questions that sat on the back of her tongue. There weren't many things Viv could confidently say she was expert at, but she knew how to read people. And there were thick walls here, ones that wouldn't be knocked down easily. She gestured to the stacks instead. "And these books, they were the ones that were burned that night?"

"Many, yes." The librarian looked around like she was seeing them for the first time. "It was difficult to compile a complete catalogue. There were some lists, of course." She shot Viv a wry look. "The Nazis love their lists."

"Indeed," Viv said, matching her tone.

"But the fires didn't simply last one night," the woman continued. "The night of May tenth was the grand demonstration, but Germans were encouraged to burn their own personal collections in the weeks after. Anything that was considered anti-German or that might undermine the Reich had to be purged."

Viv let that sit for a beat. "So anything written by Jewish authors."

"And communists and deviants and anyone not espousing the greatness of the master race," the librarian said. "I don't think we'll ever know the true number of how many books were lost in those weeks, and the years after."

"But you try," Viv said. "to keep track, to preserve them."

"We do. It's difficult work, but . . ." She trailed off, her eyes locked on the poster once more.

Viv didn't press and was rewarded for her patience when the woman continued. "Books are a way we leave a mark on the world, aren't they? They say we were here, we loved and we grieved and we laughed and we made mistakes and we *existed.* They can be burned halfway across the world, but the words cannot be unread, the stories cannot be untold. They do live on in this library, but more importantly they are immortalized in anyone who has read them."

Fire as fierce as the flames that destroyed these very books had crept into her voice, and an echoing warmth bloomed in Viv.

In that moment, Viv saw something enchanting behind the librarian's facade.

A guardian. It was a fanciful notion, perhaps, picturing this woman as a protector of books, but Viv liked the idea.

What will I find in Brooklyn?

Inspiration.

This was what Viv needed, this passion, this intensity. One of the more serious plans that had come from her gin-drenched afternoon with Harrison nudged at her: a speech to publicly shame Taft into retracting his amendment.

Obviously, Viv was never going to get herself—or this librarian—into the Senate chamber, but she didn't need to. She was the publicity director of an important war organization. Who needed a Senate chamber when you had the city's top reporters in your contact book?

Before Viv could firmly grab hold of that beautiful wisp of an idea, the librarian leaned forward. "Now, tell me, what has put that fervor in your eyes?"

Fervor in your eyes. Viv rolled the phrase around, found she liked it. "Well, I suppose I should introduce myself first. I'm Mrs. Edward Childs—but call me Viv, everyone does."

The silence that followed seemed to confirm Viv's suspicions that the librarian wasn't about to hand over her own name in return.

"I work at the Council on Books in Wartime," Viv rushed on over the awkward silence that fell whenever someone bucked social niceties.

"Council on Books in Wartime," the librarian repeated. "I'm afraid I haven't heard of the organization."

Viv laughed at that. "Yes, you and quite a few other people. I like to say we're small, but mighty."

She held her arm up like that of Rosie the Riveter on a We Can Do It poster. When the librarian simply stared, Viv cleared her throat and put on her more professional demeanor, the one she used when giving tours of the headquarters to visiting donors or doling out quotes to journalists writing about the council's initiatives.

"We're an organization made up of volunteers from all across the publishing world—from booksellers to authors to librarians to the big city houses and trade groups," Viv explained. "The council partners with the government on several big projects. But essentially what we do is try to use books in different ways to boost the morale of soldiers fighting abroad and to remind Americans at home why we're in this war in the first place."

"As they fight powerful men's wars for them," the librarian commented, flashing a hint of personality from beneath the cold marble.

"Well, yes." Viv couldn't help but agree with the sentiment despite the fact that it was usually frowned upon for her to admit as much, given that her job involved boosting morale.

"And how did all this bring you to our library?"

Viv sighed, wondering where to start. Then she decided just to spill out the whole sorry tale.

The librarian listened intently as Viv recounted her war with Taft, the devious way he'd gotten his petty revenge against the Democrats, the censorship policy that could easily grow legs into something even more dangerous if Taft ever got into the White House like he wanted.

"This all sounds like a vendetta," the librarian said after a thoughtful silence once Viv had finished.

Vendetta. Viv liked that word, the picture it painted. Again, she thought about the way to tell a story, the way to get people to care. People cared about vendettas. They found them interesting. One had to look no further than *Romeo and Juliet*'s lasting popularity to know that.

"I wish I had something helpful to offer," the librarian said. "I don't think that I do, though."

But Viv shook her head, still chasing that wisp of an idea.

She had never been able to craft the right narrative about this fight with Taft. The ASEs had simply gotten swept along in the bigger mess of the Soldier Voting Act—which had become so esoteric that eyes tended to glaze over when anyone tried to dive into the details.

Americans were exhausted from caring about too many things. The plight of a free book program could hardly make waves in an ocean of grief and loss and hardship that was this never-ending war. Especially when the bigger fight had always been about soldiers' voting rights.

But there was an important story here to tell, one that she knew the public would care about if everyone could be shown what the stakes were.

A *vendetta* against a program that was just trying to give soldiers a little entertainment? That would get people's attention.

"Actually," Viv said. "You might have been more help than you can know."

When the librarian huffed a little disbelieving laugh, Viv shook her head, stood, and grabbed her purse, her mind already three steps ahead, back out on the street and dashing for the subway, eager to put her new idea into motion. She paused, meeting the woman's eyes. "Believe me, you were." The librarian waited, as if she could sense another question was coming. "Can I come back?"

"Of course," the librarian said with that twitch of the lips that was almost a smile. "Our library is open to anyone who needs it. Always."

Chapter 6

Berlin
January 1933

Althea saw the torchlight first.

She froze, paralyzed, unsure if this was an unruly mob or an organized celebration.

A young man ran by, his jacket flapping open around his sides. If she hadn't caught the quick flash of his wide smile, Althea would have started running herself, away from an unknown threat. Instead, she pressed her back up against the stone wall of the bridge. To get out of the way, yes, but to watch, as well.

The man wasn't alone.

Behind him marched a group of young people, the flickering flames of their torches held high and proud against the darkness. Men wearing the brown and black shirts she'd come to associate with the National Socialist German Workers' Party flanked the crowd like guards.

Voices carried and blended, wrapping around Althea, and she realized the urge to flee had well and truly retreated, to be replaced with a desire to join their ranks, their joy, their clear triumph.

She decided to risk it, and reached out to the nearest passerby, grabbing hold of their wrist. "What happened?"

"Hitler is chancellor," the woman breathed out, glee and something close to mania in her face. "We will soon be free."

Althea gasped, though the woman was long gone by the time she did. Had this been what Diedrich had smiled about only a few days ago? Had he known this was coming?

It *had* been the first time in weeks that Diedrich had seemed optimistic about the state of his party. Before that he'd mostly sounded frustrated that the Nationalsozialistische Deutsche Arbeiterpartei, or NSDAP as the Germans called it, was still reeling from the blow that had come in the November elections, when they had lost seats despite revolutionary, and expensive, campaign efforts.

His enthusiasm for the cause certainly hadn't dimmed. For Althea, as someone who'd rarely, if ever, paid attention to politics before coming to Berlin, Diedrich's passion had been exhilarating.

"Chancellor?" Althea asked one of the revelers, this time in English, just in case she'd misunderstood.

"Chancellor," the young man agreed, tipping his head back to yell it to the night sky. The confirmation provoked a rolling cheer to ripple through the crowd, many of the men throwing up the salute that Hitler had made his own.

Flames burned bright above the marchers' heads as they made their way toward Alexanderplatz. Althea hesitated one moment, two, and then let herself be swept along into the flood of bodies, all of whom were busy chanting things she only half understood.

Once again, like in the marketplace, Althea expected to feel untethered, overwhelmed. Instead she became a part of the frenzied crowd, buoyed by their elation, their excitement.

"How did this happen?" she yelled to the young woman next to her but didn't get an answer. Althea had been foolish to expect one.

The crowd cut through the city, along the Spree, heading for the Reich Chancellery, the torches lighting their way. They sang in German, cried and laughed and danced, and Althea cried and laughed and danced alongside them, patriotism for her ancestors' country thrumming in her blood, heady and hot and irresistible despite the fact that the pride was so new to her.

In the month that she'd been in Berlin, Germany had started to seem more like hers than rural Maine ever had. She had expected to feel like Alice dumped in Wonderland, everything slightly skewed and upside down, wrong side out. Instead, Althea couldn't shake the idea that her old life had been the distorted one.

Althea had always been an odd child. The other girls at the small school in Owl's Head had certainly pointed out all the ways she was strange. She had been too small, too smart, too pale, too poor, had raised her hand when she knew the answer to any question, which everyone told her was too often.

It had been in stories that she had escaped from her peers' merciless taunts, and when the boring books on her mother's shelf hadn't been enough to keep her entertained, she'd started telling her own.

First they were about princesses and dragons and castles, fantasy acting as a refuge for her child's mind. But as she grew, they matured with her. They became the prism through which she viewed the world, the cruelty of it, the beauty of it. She had started using stories as a way of understanding all the reasons those other children, and then other adults, were both cruel and beautiful, as well. What she hadn't acknowledged was how much distance that let her put between herself and other people—she the viewer, the creator, the reader; they the characters, the subjects, the puppets.

As she sunk ever more in love with Berlin—the anonymity she had never before experienced, the bright lights, the laughter, the streets that never seemed to end but just turned into new places she'd never been before—she became aware of how stifling that desire to protect herself had become.

The habit was hard to break, especially when she became flustered, like with Diedrich's flirtations in the winter market. But Berlin was helping her realize she didn't need to hide in a story to escape life. Sometimes life was enough.

So how could she not be enchanted with the wave of German nationalism that was sweeping through the city?

Althea's fingers had gone numb from the cold by the time they reached the square in front of the Chancellery, but she couldn't be bothered by something as pedestrian as the weather in this moment.

"There." Someone beside her gasped and pointed. In the window was a simple black silhouette, the unimposing figure of a man who had inspired thousands to take to the streets that night.

By the time Herr Hitler opened the French windows to greet his adoring supporters, the square had filled to the point that Althea was pressed shoulder to shoulder with the students surrounding her. Tears streaked down the cheeks of the girl to Althea's left, while the boy to her right had his arm locked above his head, devotion clear in the way he tilted his face up to Hitler.

The new chancellor didn't speak, which was a disappointment. The man's oration skills were legendary.

Hitler watched them, though, seeming to bask in the cries of love and fealty. Althea was even close enough to the front of the crowd to imagine she could see the way his mouth ticked up in a self-satisfied smile.

The mob had well and truly settled in, content with their impromptu party, beer somehow materializing in the hands of the men nearby, songs swelling and cresting. A scuffle or two broke out, but the violence was nipped at the source by the blackshirts who were stationed sporadically throughout the crowd.

Althea caught sight of men congregating near the door of the building, recognizing Herr Joseph Goebbels from an introductory dinner when she'd first arrived in the city. She had made a special point of talking to him, as he had been the one to actually invite her to Berlin. Technically, her trip was funded through the Nazi Party, but Diedrich had informed her that it was Goebbels's pet project. Upon meeting him, Althea had been struck by his appreciation for how much books and art and even newer mediums like film could play a role in politics.

Diedrich told her that Goebbels was destined for a cultural cabinet position should Hitler ever became chancellor. That would certainly explain the smug expression Goebbels wore now.

Beside him, the light from the streetlamp glinted off blond hair, and Althea sucked in a breath.

Diedrich.

If she had been even slightly bigger, she didn't think she would have been able to maneuver her way toward the front, but her petite stature let her slip through the spaces until she broke free from the tangle of bodies.

She stumbled forward but only for a second, because in the next instant, Diedrich's arms were around her, warm and comforting and smelling faintly of tobacco as he always did. She buried her face in his chest as he swung her around, both of them laughing for absolutely no other reason than they were delighted.

"You'll see," Diedrich whispered into her temple when he set her on her feet once more. "You'll see how much better it will be now."

Althea didn't doubt it. She had heard enough from Diedrich's friends how dire it was to get Hitler into a position of power. He was seen as their only hope, their shining beacon, their savior from men who wanted to keep Germany locked in poverty simply to pad their own pockets. The men who wanted Germany to bow to the capricious, cruel whims of the rest of a world that had blamed the country for the entirety of the Great War, a world that wanted to salt the earth and let Germans die rather than offer compassion. The November Criminals who had gone along with the armistice and signed the country's death certificate.

"I know," Althea whispered, tipping her face up to smile at Diedrich. He hesitated a beat and then dropped his lips to hers. He tasted of whiskey and happiness and when she gasped in surprise his tongue slipped into her mouth.

A shiver of desire ran through her as she pressed into him, needy and confused and riding a rush of pleasure she'd never known before.

She was twenty-five, and this was her very first kiss.

He pulled back after pressing his lips chastely once more to the corner of her mouth. Something unbearably fond sparked behind his eyes, and he laughed once more. "Come, darling, let's find some champagne."

Althea let herself be tugged along.

After all, Adolf Hitler had come to power.

It was a night to celebrate.

Chapter 7

New York City
May 1944

Viv might have originally scoffed at Harrison's idea of mimicking the big final scene of a book in her fight with Taft, but as she rode the subway back from Brooklyn she couldn't remember why.

Americans who had been slogging through a seemingly never-ending war had been primed for years through films and propaganda to want a spectacular ending where the good guys triumphed, the handsome man got the girl, and the villain was served his just deserts.

Viv could give them two out of three of those at least.

If she played this right.

The train jolted to a shuddering stop, and Viv slipped through the subway doors just before they closed.

The stop was only a few blocks from the council's headquarters in the New York Times Hall, nestled as it was between the bold signs and bright facades of its Broadway neighbors.

"Viv, your letters," Miss Bernice Westwood called out when Viv stepped into the lobby of the renovated theater.

The greeting threw Viv off for a beat, her heels skittering on hardwood when she pivoted toward Bernice's desk.

"Thank you," she said, a bit breathless from the exertion. Viv took the bag she knew was filled with several bundles of envelopes tied together with twine.

They would all be from soldiers stationed abroad, writing to thank the council for the ASEs, asking for more books, wondering if they could have their messages sent directly to the authors. A few might even be from relatives of the boys, pleading for their loved ones to get any extra copies of the more popular novels. It was a large part of Viv's job to read them, reply when warranted, and pull out the notable ones for when journalists came calling, looking for quotes about the initiative.

"A light day?" Viv asked, looking behind Bernice for more. Sometimes there were too many sacks for her to carry in one trip.

"Mm-hmm," Bernice murmured absently before leaning forward, her mop of blond curls bouncing around her chin, eyes wide. "Rumor has it you ambushed Taft in a steakhouse yesterday. Is that why you ran in here just now like a chicken?"

She should have known better than to hope that her humiliating spectacle at the restaurant hadn't made its way through the council's headquarters. Especially since she'd seen the predicted mention of it in the *Post.* The write-up had been buried on the inside pages, but enough busybodies worked at the council and they read those anonymous gossip sheets religiously.

"No," Viv said, pursing her lips and deciding a distraction would be the best bet here. "But I do have a new idea on how to fight Taft."

"Do tell," Bernice demanded.

"I have to pitch it to Mr. Stern first." Viv reached out to give Bernice's hand an apologetic squeeze. "Wish me luck."

Bernice pouted her displeasure, but then smiled brightly. “You’re doing right by the boys, you know. By not giving up.”

Viv didn’t bother pointing out that she would likely crash and burn just like she had for the past six months. She’d learned a long time ago that if you faked confidence well enough, other people would start believing you knew what you were doing.

“Taft won’t know what hit him,” she said with a wink.

Mr. Philip Van Doren Stern, the head of the council, was a kind man, tall and thin with a long face. His wire-rimmed glasses and conservative suits gave him a serious look that Viv had realized quickly acted as camouflage to his understated humor and mischievous nature.

She tapped on his open door lightly, the letters still tucked beneath her arm.

The smile he’d been about to offer shifted into a contemplative frown when he caught sight of who was knocking. Viv should have known that if the rumors of her plan to confront Taft had reached Bernice, they certainly would have been brought to the attention of the president of the council. “Mrs. Childs.”

Viv cringed at the reprimand he delivered so easily with just her name, the full brunt of his disappointment landing on her shoulders. Mr. Stern had taken a chance on hiring her back in the fall, right after Edward had died, and she hated letting him down.

“I know, I shouldn’t have done it,” Viv said as she slunk into his office. “But I have a much better plan now. One that might actually work.”

“Oh, Vivian.” Mr. Stern sighed, and then got up to pour them both a glass of scotch. He tapped the rims together and handed over hers. “It may be time to throw in the towel.”

“But Congress changes laws every day,” Viv pointed out. It

was the most important part of her idea. The Soldier Voting Act had become law, but that didn't mean Taft's censorship amendment couldn't be excised from it.

"I suppose."

"And no one really liked Taft's ban in the first place," Viv soldiered on. "They just didn't want to endanger the voting act."

"They didn't want to go against Taft," Mr. Stern added gently. "Which they still won't want to do now."

"That's why we have to convince them it's more politically advantageous to side with us," Viv said, with more certainty than she felt. She'd learned firsthand how few of Taft's colleagues wanted to get on his bad side. "My mistake was focusing on Taft. We have to focus on everyone else and show them they're on the wrong side here."

"How do you propose we do that?" Mr. Stern asked, rubbing a thumb between his eyebrows as if he was staving off a headache. It wouldn't be the first time Viv had been likened to a brewing migraine.

"We convince their voters to make a fuss about it," Viv said, eager now. "And to do that, we put on a show."

Mr. Stern waved his hand to encourage her to elaborate.

"We hold an event, we invite the media, the publishing world, librarians, our best authors," Viv said, the words coming out in a rush. The concept was still half-formed, but the more she talked about it the more she was convinced it stood a chance of working. "I'll call all the big dailies to let them know it's happening. There are even a few people in radio I can tap." Viv paused and caught her breath. "Not enough people know what's at stake with this amendment. We need to show them why it's important."

"And the voting act won't muddy the waters this time," Mr. Stern said, nodding.

"If we get the public on our side, lawmakers won't be able to ignore the issue any longer," Viv said. "They only really care about something if it affects their chance at reelection, you know that. We need them to realize this could hurt their campaign war chests.

"Taft intimidated enough of his colleagues to get this amendment through," Viv continued. "But once we bring the full brunt of the public's outrage down on their heads, they'll switch their alliance like that." She snapped her fingers. "Every good story needs a villain, and lucky for us Taft has offered himself up on a silver platter."

She might feel guilty if she thought she was painting Taft as a ruthless, ambitious brute that he wasn't. But what lay beneath that folksy facade was exactly that, and she had no qualms about removing his mask.

"I can do this," Viv promised, mostly believing it. Or partly believing it, at least, which was good enough. "We lay the groundwork with articles and well-placed opinion pieces. We start getting attention from our usual supporters but then also from big political donors and the general public. Everything will build in momentum until the big day."

He was teetering, clearly, but not convinced yet. As the public face of the initiative, he had to play nice with lawmakers, even if they wanted to destroy the council. But as a man who believed in what they were doing, he wanted to see the amendment killed as much as she did.

"One event, held here, with speakers who will volunteer their time," she wheedled a bit. "All of this will be at minimal cost to the council."

On instinct, Viv reached into the bag that Bernice had handed her. She knew Mr. Stern appreciated how much the ASE program touched the soldiers. Still, there was a difference between knowing that in theory, and reading the letters every single day, as she did.

She plucked out a few, skimmed as fast as she could, and then held out the perfect one.

To Whom It May Concern—

My name is Sergeant Billie Flick. I'm with the 107th. I'm not a writer or nothing, don't have a good way with words, but I wanted to try to thank you all for the books you're sending. We lost a kid three days ago. He'd lied on his enlistment papers, said he was older than his sixteen years, we called him Cisco because he came from San Fran.

On his last few days, all he kept talking about was one of your books. Wind, Sand and Stars it was called, and I gotta tell you the boys laughed at that title. Told Cisco he should sign up for a literary salon. He said, no, you have to read it. It's about the "bonds of friendships forged in fire." Those were the words he used, can you imagine?

He got shot taking a piss outside the barracks by a bored Kraut sniper. Didn't see it coming, which is always a blessing.

Cisco won't be remembered by more than his mama and family, probably. He was brave in a quiet way, the kind that made him tell a lie to get sent over here in the first place. He didn't save no one, nor change the tides of the war. But he's worth someone other than us knowing about.

And I like to think he lives on by any man who carries a copy of that book in their pocket. So, thank you for that.

Respectfully,
Sergeant William Flick, 107

Viv wondered if Billie realized he'd never even included the kid's name. It probably didn't matter that he hadn't, anyway. To those men, that kid had been Cisco, and he'd likely be forgotten after the next dozen or so deaths they experienced.

That's how war was. Everyone had a touching story to tell, and yet because of that, it was almost like there were none.

"That book would have been banned from the series under Taft's amendment."

Mr. Stern didn't say anything, but he didn't hand the letter back, either. Instead, he folded it up and tucked it into the inside pocket of his jacket. "When would this big show be?"

Viv didn't waste time celebrating, instead doing quick math in her head.

She would need to organize it, get the word out, invite the press, invite lawmakers, invite all the council's volunteers. Create a killer lineup of guest speakers.

That last one was the hardest part, the thing her plan depended on the most. For a big finale, she needed people who could deliver speeches that would persuade even the most cynical or exhausted listener.

"End of July." A little less than three months.

"How much manpower do you need?" Mr. Stern asked.

"I'll do most of it on my own," Viv promised. "I'll need help on the day of, but a lot of this will be coordinating contacts I already have."

"I shouldn't," Mr. Stern said, staring into his empty glass. Then he tapped his jacket once, in the exact spot where the letter sat.

"All right, Vivian," Mr. Stern said, meeting her eyes. "But you're forgetting the biggest hurdle of them all."

Viv's mind stuttered, shifted, sorting through all the preparations. "What is that?"

"Getting Taft to show up," Mr. Stern said, his expression flicking between humor and pity. "And to not storm out once he realizes what's happening."

Something went tight in her chest as her fingers found the empty space where her wedding band once sat.

The answer to that problem was obvious, but that didn't make it easy.

She thought of butterflies and the silence that followed. Then she sighed, accepting what had to be done. "You leave that up to me."

Chapter 8

Paris
October 1936

Good morning," Hannah called in German as she pushed through the door of the Library of Burned Books at 65 boulevard Arago three days after the incident in front of the violin shop.

The library was nestled into a far corner of Montparnasse, an area on the left bank of the Seine, but despite the off-the-beaten-track location, it served a fair amount of people every day. Three different patrons glanced up to return her greeting.

Hannah warmed at the sight of them, their mere presence an antidote to the hatred she so often saw on display. Many of the philosophers, thinkers, students, and readers who were drawn to the library were Jewish exiles, and she felt a kinship with them now that had never been particularly strong back in Berlin.

Her parents had been fairly secular, leaning toward the Reform Judaism movement that had originated in their country. Her family had observed Shabbat, attended services at the temple, and upheld the ethical tenets of the faith, but they placed less emphasis on Jewish laws and personal rituals than did the more conservative strands of the faith.

That had always suited Hannah, who had never been able to completely reconcile who she was—who she *loved*—with any religion that condemned her lifestyle.

But her time in Paris and with the library was starting to shift her views. Just this past month, with many in her newfound community, she had celebrated Rosh Hashanah, had fasted on Yom Kippur, had been reminded during Sukkot of the long history that bound them all together—the story of a people forced into exile, persecuted, and still always able to find the light.

Some of the library's board were strictly practicing, some of the workers wore the Star of David on a necklace beneath their blouses, and while Hannah wasn't about to join them, she found it beautiful that her sense of belonging in the Jewish community had been strengthened rather than diminished in the face of so much hatred from the rest of the world.

As Hannah settled in behind the desk for the start of her shift, the bell above the door rang. Otto Koch stumbled in, newspaper clutched in his hands, and Hannah tried not to sigh at the boy.

Though *boy* was perhaps the wrong descriptor for Otto. Like her, he had reached his late twenties now, a man by most societies' definitions of one. But Hannah would always think of him as the sweet schoolmate who talked too fast, too earnestly, and skinned his knees every other step he took.

Even now he tripped twice more while crossing the small space to the counter. "Hannah."

It was just an exhale, his face flushed. He rested most of his weight on the solid wood as he panted.

"Do you need water?" she asked, eyeing the sweat beading at his hairline.

"No," he gasped out, more breath than sound.

"Let me guess," Hannah asked as she flipped open the cover

of Hermann Hesse's *Siddhartha*. Despite the fact that Hesse had been fairly apolitical at the time of the great exile of German writers, the Nazis had taken issue with Hesse's connection to those who had been outspoken. And so he'd earned his place in the library. "One of your beloved American authors is giving a talk in Paris."

"I wish," Otto said, his eyes big and round.

"One of these days, I'm going to get you to read some books by women, and you'll get over this infatuation," Hannah chided, but without any heat.

"My love burns eternal." Otto sighed dramatically, draping himself across the counter now, seemingly back in control of his lungs.

"What has you in this state?" Hannah asked, moving toward the shelves, knowing Otto would follow dutifully behind her. She slotted a pamphlet by a noted Nazi philosopher next to Hitler's *Mein Kampf*. When Hannah had first started working at the library, she'd recoiled at the sight of the red cover. But the library's founder, Alfred Kantorowicz, had insisted that any books and documents that helped inform their readers about Hitlerism and fascism were worth their place in the stacks. Knowledge was power. And if more people outside Germany read Hitler's manifesto, he'd said, they wouldn't be so eager to appease the madman.

"There's to be a book exposition," Otto said now, trailing in Hannah's wake, pulling novels slightly off the shelf as he went, a cat unable not to tug and shift and ruin if he could get his fingers on something. "It's to be held on the boulevard Saint-Germain and the Nazis are going to be there, showing off their best literature."

A memory of a sweet, round face, freckles, and a shy smile crept from behind Hannah's carefully constructed defenses. A pouty mouth and a quick wit. Impossibly thick hair that begged for fingers to be tangled in it.

Althea.

An ache settled in the soft spaces of her body, no longer unbearable, but quiet and insistent, a reminder that Hannah had been broken.

"There is no such thing as good Nazi literature," Hannah said, managing to keep her voice even and tart. She hated that she'd now thought of Althea twice in only a handful of days.

My love burns eternal, Otto had said. But Hannah was the practical one out of their little pair and she didn't work like that. The only thing that burned eternal for her were grudges and bridges.

"Doesn't matter, they're going to be showing off," Otto countered. "We need to fight back."

Hannah paused in front of the section for Ernest Hemingway, a man whom many in her Parisian literary circle had been close friends with. For the first time since Otto had burst through the door, she gave him her full attention. "What are you talking about?"

Otto slumped against the shelf, his eyes dark and baleful. "You never listen to me."

The sheer petulant disgruntlement of the statement made Hannah smirk. She and Otto had grown up together on the wealthy outskirts of Berlin. Their families had been close, which meant that they'd been pushed together since birth, first as playmates and then as potential *somethings.* As Hannah had never been able to look at Otto as anything other than a brother—with Otto returning the sentiment—they'd disappointed their parents dearly.

But they had become inseparable anyway, in defiance of every expectation that said two people of the opposite sex couldn't be friends. Hannah thought it might have to do with the fact that neither of them was particularly attracted to members of the opposite sex, but she didn't belabor the point.

Now, she ruffled the hair that she knew took him hours to fix just right. He tried to bat her hand away, but she'd already moved on.

When she rounded the corner with one of Helen Keller's books already in her hand, Otto stopped her, curling his fingers around her wrist. "I'm serious, Hannah."

Otto fell in and out of love with every cause out there. He was always *serious* about something. But his eyes were steady, his mouth set in a straight, thin line.

"All right," she said. "What exactly do you propose we do?"

"We come up with a brilliant plan to humiliate them while they're here," Otto said in a conspiratorial whisper, and Hannah tried not to roll her eyes again. "Over wine?"

Hannah checked the grandfather clock in the corner. "I'm done at five."

"Our café?" Otto asked, and kissed her cheek goodbye after she nodded.

She watched him leave and forced away thoughts of Althea, of soft skin beneath her fingers, a bed warmed by the early light of dawn creeping in the window. Forced away thoughts of the knock on the door that had followed.

When her shift was over at the library, Hannah stepped out into the crisp fall air, heading toward the café a few blocks over.

She was in no rush, and so she enjoyed the fading light along the Seine. Hannah didn't love Paris the way Otto did. She liked it well enough, but to her the Seine didn't compare to Berlin's Spree.

You're just being contrary, Otto had accused when she'd mentioned the comparison. And perhaps she was. Paris wasn't home, wouldn't ever be a home she chose. But it was a sanctuary, and for now, that was far more important.

Her only regret in leaving Berlin was that she wished she'd done so earlier, before she'd ever met Althea James. Wished she'd been able to convince Adam to pack his bags and flee the country, too. Maybe then she wouldn't see his cracked lip, his shattered nose, the bruises beneath haunted eyes every time she closed hers.

She spotted Otto up ahead, at a small table set out on the street.

Otto all but vibrated, waiting impatiently as she put in an order for her drink. He'd smoked his cigarette down to the nub, but it now sat forgotten between his fingers. She took it and stubbed it out completely.

"So, the Nazis are coming to Paris," she said, once the waiter had departed. He'd been dark and sultry and watched her through hooded eyes that she'd tried not to meet directly. She knew men found her attractive, had been told that enough in her life to believe it. With her dark brown hair and light-colored eyes; with the curves that had been put in all the right places; with the dimple that seemed to make men weak at the knees; and the smooth skin that was often compared to alabaster. Hannah knew and yet could not care less.

"Chilling, isn't it?" Otto leaned into the theatrics of it all, as he was wont to do.

Hannah dug out her own cigarette and spared a dim smile for the waiter, who set her wine down in front of her with a wink. "My skin is practically frozen."

"You're a riot."

"And you are losing my interest," she shot back, blowing the smoke away from him.

"All right, you pill," Otto said, toying with his own glass of some amber-colored liquid. She had been fairly certain he'd been favoring gin lately, but he did go through mercurial phases. "We can't let them get away with this."

"A book exposition?" she clarified, raising her brows.

"Don't give me that tone. Don't act like you don't understand the importance of this."

She looked away, unwilling to meet his eyes. "Fine."

Otto smirked in victory, splaying back in his seat and nearly knocking over their poor waiter. "Sorry, sorry," he murmured, watching the man from beneath his own lush lashes. Hannah nudged his knee with her own and he offered up a playful pout. "You always get the pretty ones."

"Only the pretty ones I don't want."

"And some that you do," Otto countered and, again, she looked away.

"The exposition," she prompted.

He didn't hesitate or protest the subject change. "November. On the boulevard Saint-Germain."

"Yes, we went over that part," Hannah drawled.

"But we didn't go over what we were going to do about it," Otto said, matching her tone.

"Shall we shoot them?" she asked, all innocence.

"Not a terrible suggestion," Otto said, with a lopsided grin.

"Otto," she murmured. He saw violence as the answer to the Nazis. He'd never thought that way when he'd been younger. He'd been so sweet, shy, and funny and kind. Otto was still all those things, but in the years since they'd left Berlin, he'd developed a hardness that scared Hannah.

He reminded her of Adam before her brother was dragged off by the blackshirts. He had always been fiercely committed to his beliefs but that spring when everything had gone to hell,

Adam had become a radical. Unpredictable, stubborn, and defiant when challenged.

She didn't want to watch that happen to Otto, too.

"What do you suggest instead?" Otto asked, downing the rest of his drink. She wondered how many he'd already had that day and then chastised herself for the thought. None of them were at their best at the moment.

Hannah considered his question, absently rubbing at the calluses on her fingers. She had found she liked them, a tangible marker of the work she was doing to fight the fascists. Even if she hadn't turned to bullets and bombs like the young radicals wanted to, her efforts were no less important in this battle.

The men who sought violence didn't understand that while swords could destroy bodies, a pen could destroy a nation.

If the Nazis were coming to Paris to show off their so-called literature, there was only one way to answer that particular war cry.

"What I always suggest," she said with quiet certainty. "A book."

Chapter 9

New York City
May 1944

Viv decided to cut her work day short after her meeting with Mr. Stern and return to the Upper West Side apartment she shared with her mother-in-law, Charlotte.

The rest of the afternoon would have been a wash, considering she couldn't think about anything beyond what she would have to do to ensure Taft's presence at her big event. When all of this had started, she'd been adamant about who she did—and more importantly *did not*—want to seek help from. But she knew better than most how best-laid plans could be derailed.

Her thumb worried the empty space on her ring finger as she rounded Columbus Circle. An old man sold books nearby on the corner of Sixtieth and Broadway, and Viv tried to pick up something anytime she passed by.

The man chewed on the end of his unlit pipe as he watched her fingers dance along the spines of his precious wares.

"In the mood for something?" His voice was rough and smoke-coated, with New York in its roots.

Any answer she'd been about to give died in her throat when she caught sight of a green volume, its title imposed in gold.

Oliver Twist.

She nearly laughed or cried or some mix of the two. She wasn't one to believe in fate where coincidence sufficed as an explanation. But she couldn't ignore this particular sign.

It makes me think of Hale, Edward had written. The two of them had so rarely talked about his brother, and sometimes she wondered if God had been laughing at her when he'd come up in Edward's last letter.

Viv plucked the novel from where it was nestled among its brethren and held it up to show the old man.

He grinned to reveal three missing teeth, and quoted, "'There are books of which the backs and covers are by far the best parts.'"

"But not this one," Viv said, and earned herself a nod.

"But not that one," the old man agreed and took her money, sliding it beneath the fisherman's cap he wore over his thick shock of white hair.

Tucking the book close to her chest, Viv once more started for home. She wondered what Edward would think if he could see her now, going toe-to-toe with a powerful senator.

You could accomplish anything you set your mind to, my dear, he'd told her after one of those high-society events that always left Viv feeling some strange mix of disdainful, angry, and ignorant.

She couldn't count how many evenings they'd ended sprawled in his study like that, long before they'd been married, him lounging in some state of dishabille on the leather couch he adored, her curled up in her favorite armchair. Both of them with their preferred liquors as they deconstructed any drama that had occurred at whatever party they'd attended.

That was her favorite way to picture Edward: there in the soft, vulnerable hours between midnight and dawn when they'd been at any given moment petty and kind and funny and despondent and every range of emotions a human could experience. The well of affection between them so deep, oftentimes they hadn't even needed to speak, able to sit comfortably in the other's silence.

Viv knew what the gossip pages had said about those nights she went home with Edward. Those same ladies had crowed at the wedding announcement, happy only to have been proven right, as if their prior innuendos hadn't been laced with cruelty.

At the time, Viv had been pleased that none of them actually knew what her and Edward's relationship was like. It had been a private thing, sacred and wonderful, and unimaginable to so many who thought only within the narrow boundaries of romantic love.

Now, she was lonely with the knowledge. No one prepared you for that, the way once-delicious secrets shared between you soured when they became yours alone to bear.

The night that Edward had told her she could accomplish anything, he had been coming up with increasingly humorous ways to inflict pain on the Vanderbilt heir who had humiliated Viv after she'd dared to voice some opinion on current affairs or politics or foreign investments. She couldn't even remember which it was anymore.

Come, Edward had said, beckoning her. She'd groaned, then stood, wobbling a little with the fizz of champagne in her blood. He'd taken her hand, crossed to the window overlooking Sixth Avenue, and pushed open the glass. *Roar.*

Viv had laughed, swaying into his body. *What? You're mad,* Viv had said. *And drunk.*

Roar, Edward demanded and then tipped his head back and bellowed into the night air.

Oh my goodness, Viv had murmured, but when he'd just stared at her with a cheeky smile and raised brows, she rolled her eyes and tried to mimic him.

You can do better than that, Edward had said. *You are fierce, you are clever, you are stubborn and brave and wonderful. Now roar.*

She had, screaming out every frustration and hurt from the evening, from a million similar evenings until her lungs throbbed and her throat ached.

Then a man on the street had yelled at them to *shut the hell up,* in true New York City fashion. They'd collapsed onto the rug beneath the window, giggling, their bodies slumping into each other's.

You could accomplish anything you set your mind to, Edward had repeated before his head tipped onto hers and his breathing evened out into sleep.

Viv had whispered, *What would I do without you?*

Viv traced the title of *Oliver Twist* as she rode the elevator up to the apartment, silently promising Edward that she would win against Taft.

Edward had never liked bullies, either.

"Is that you, Viv?" Charlotte called out when Viv stepped into the entryway. Instead of shouting an answer, Viv tracked Charlotte's voice to the kitchen.

Her mother-in-law stood covered in their flour ration for the week, a guilty, defiant expression on her sweet, round face. "Oops?"

Viv slid into one of the bright yellow chairs that flanked the island. The sunny color clashed horribly with the red countertops and turquoise touches Charlotte had added to the room, but Viv had always liked the comfort the chaos inspired. While Viv was growing up with her uncle Horace after both her parents had died, everything had been pristine, matching, and the height of fashion. Viv had been afraid of moving through the house at all, had been terrified of even breathing wrong. Here, with Charlotte, Viv finally felt at home.

"Cookies?" Viv asked. Eggs, butter, and sugar were hard to scrounge up, but Charlotte had her ways. And a deep pocketbook, which she opened without hesitation to keep the black market on Thirty-Second Street running.

"Cake," Charlotte proclaimed, gamely assessing the mess of white powder lining the rest of the baking instruments. She put her hands on her generous hips and looked up, hopeful. "Half a cake?" She shrugged and charged forward, cracking an egg into the bowl. "You bought another book?"

The question came tinged with slight exasperation and amusement. They were running out of shelf space for Viv's ever-expanding collection.

"*Oliver Twist,*" Viv murmured, holding out the novel.

Charlotte's face softened, her eyes going wet with tears Viv knew she wouldn't shed. "You can put it with your other copies."

Viv's laugh came out shaky. She couldn't deny she had picked up a bad habit of buying every volume she came across. "One of these days I'll have a whole row of them."

"And you'll be known as the mad lady who couldn't stop buying Dickens," Charlotte said, the grief gone, replaced by affectionate humor. Viv lived in awe of Charlotte's resilience and leaned on it more than she probably should considering the woman was mourning her only son as much as Viv was mourning her best friend. "And how was the library, dear?"

Viv wiped sweaty palms against the sunny yellow skirt of her dress and linked her ankles together to keep her feet from tapping out a nervous beat. "I think I need Hale's help."

"Hale," Charlotte repeated, her tone considering rather than suspicious. "Now why didn't I think of that in the first place?"

Viv had.

Emmett Hale, Edward's bastard brother, had grown up from the gangly shop boy he'd once been into Brooklyn's beloved representative in Congress. He was young and charismatic and passionate and there were plenty of rumors out there that his political career would lead him to the White House.

He was also someone Viv once upon a time had believed would be the love of her life.

Every time she'd been tempted to call upon him for help against Taft, something in her had balked. No matter how important the ASEs were, she couldn't forget the way he'd broken her heart. The way he'd treated her as if she were nothing but a summer plaything, to be discarded as soon as the shine wore off.

She touched her ring finger and pretended not to notice Charlotte's eyes tracking the gesture. "I'm getting desperate enough, I think."

"Do you want me to contact him for you, dear?"

Coming from anyone other than Charlotte Childs, the question might have seemed absurd.

Edward's father, Theodore Childs, had made his fortune in steel. He'd been part of the turn-of-the-century excess that the nouveau riche had worn as a badge of honor, whoring his way through opera singers and actresses before veering toward the alphabet streets where the girls didn't really have a choice.

One of those girls had been Mary Kathleen Sullivan. She had been left penniless and pregnant after Theodore grew bored with her.

Theodore had pretended Emmett hadn't existed, and the only reason any of them knew of the boy was because Mary Kathleen had confronted Charlotte right there on Fifth Avenue in front of Tiffany's.

If Charlotte could have, she would have given Mary Kathleen half of Theodore's vast fortune on the spot. But wives had limited resources. And so she'd handed over all the money she'd had on her person and then had set up a campaign against Theodore to make him support his child.

She had only ever had middling success on that front, but it hadn't mattered in the end. Mary Kathleen had met Mr. William Hale, a kind man who had married her, five months pregnant and all, given her son his name, and then moved them all across the river to Brooklyn.

Charlotte had never lost touch with the woman, though. Even now that Mary Kathleen had passed, Charlotte still met with Hale at least once a month for lunch.

"No. If I'm the one who needs the favor," Viv said, even though she actually wanted to say yes, "it should probably be me doing the asking."

"That's my girl." Charlotte gave her a sympathetic pat as she passed Viv on her way to the well-stocked liquor cart. "This calls for port."

Where other women put a kettle on, Charlotte splashed burnished-amber liquor into well-cut glasses.

Viv watched her now, a guilty knot pulling ever tighter in her chest. For a quick second, Viv resented Edward for putting her in this position.

Because Charlotte didn't realize that when she and Viv thought of the love of Viv's life they were thinking of different brothers. Charlotte believed Viv had lost a soul mate, believed Viv and Edward had a love story that rivaled the greats throughout history. Charlotte believed that the dizzying heights of their romance had been matched only—as it so often was in tales such as those—by the depths of their tragedy.

What Charlotte didn't know, what she could never know, was that it was a lie.

You can't tell her. Those had been the last words Edward had ever spoken to Viv, on the docks, just before he'd boarded his ship. Viv had repeated them to herself countless times in the months since he'd left. There had been moments where Viv had almost broken down and admitted to Charlotte that she and Edward hadn't been in love when they'd raced down the aisle only a week before he'd left for training. But she'd swallowed the confession every single time, knowing with some kind of certainty that Charlotte rested easier believing her son had found true love before he'd died in the war.

Viv took the glass of port with a shaky smile and wondered how much Charlotte knew or suspected about that first summer Viv had met both Hale and Edward. Wondered if she was really fooling her mother-in-law at all, or if the tale of Viv and Edward's romance was just a pretty story they both agreed to pretend was real.

Chapter 10

Berlin
February 1933

Helene Bechstein always smelled of mothballs and had a tendency to insinuate herself into any conversation Althea was having.

"You must tell me of the night at the Chancellery," Helene said, her long fingers gripping the soft flesh of Althea's arm. Althea gazed sadly at the retreating back of a young poet, who, although he spit when he became overexcited about a topic, had been one of the few interesting people Althea had encountered that night.

Out of all the events Althea was semirequired to attend as part of Goebbels's program, it was these parties she found the most tedious. Helene's were perhaps the worst, and she held quite a few of them.

Helene was married to Edwin Bechstein, the owner of one of the country's leading piano manufacturers. As a tall, stylish woman with dark eyebrows and a long face, she had probably sooner been called handsome than beautiful in her youth.

According to Diedrich, Helene adored Hitler ever since she'd met him over a decade prior and had been one of the leading ladies to shepherd the man through Berlin's high society in his early days in the city.

She calls him her little wolf.

Althea had tried not to roll her eyes at the moniker. She wasn't sure when some of the Nazi Party's sheen had started to wear off for her, but she thought it might have been around the time Diedrich had said *little wolf* with a straight face.

"It was a night I won't soon forget," Althea told Helene now, snagging a smoked salmon something or other. If Althea was going to have to simper along with society matrons all night, at least she was going to get some good food out of it.

"Oh, how I wish I could have been there," Helene said, her stern gaze still on the dance floor, where a dozen couples were locked in a strangely formal and outdated waltz.

Althea let her own attention wander around the beautiful room. The Bechsteins' mansion was located in the fashionable area just south of the Tiergarten on Leipziger Strasse, where many of Berlin's wealthy merchants lived. Helene had gone a little heavy on the gold for Althea's taste, but she couldn't deny the blatant opulence held an appeal. Especially decked out as it was for a party to celebrate Hitler's triumph the week earlier.

"Make sure Diedrich doesn't shirk his duties to you now that he'll likely be busy with Goebbels's ministry," Helene said. "He should still make plenty of time to show you around."

"That hasn't been a problem," Althea reassured her. In fact, Diedrich's constant presence, which had been so intoxicating in the early days of her residency, was starting to drift toward overbearing since Hitler had been named chancellor.

Whenever Althea had the thought, she chided herself. Diedrich and the NSDAP had been nothing but welcoming hosts. But Althea didn't like how it reminded her of Owl's Head, where she couldn't go anywhere without being watched, without being talked to, the suffocation of small-town life so familiar to Althea she hadn't even realized she couldn't breathe until coming to Berlin. Now the freedom she had so enjoyed in those first weeks was being stripped from her.

All Althea could think was that it had something to do with Hitler's new position of power. Maybe that was what had ultimately dulled some of her enthusiasm for his success.

"And I'm positive Diedrich is making sure you only partake in the right sort of culture?" Helene asked, raising her silly opera glasses to peer across the room to find said man.

The right sort of culture. Althea had heard the phrase bandied about a few times, at bookshops during readings, at the cafés where she and Diedrich met with his friends. But for the first time, it struck her as off.

"I'm sorry, I don't—"

"Well, hello," a new voice purred from behind Althea. "I don't believe we've been introduced."

Both Althea and Helene shifted to greet the newcomer. She was taller than Althea—but then most people were—with inky black hair cropped close to her face. Instead of the cut making her look boyish, it emphasized her delicate features, the big green eyes surrounded by thick lashes, the high cheekbones and plush mouth. Her skin was powdered to flawless perfection, a drawn-on mole above the corner of her mouth the only distraction.

Her silky, low-cut dress clung to her gentle curves, the color nearly matching her eyes exactly.

When Althea looked back up, amusement lurked in the corners of the woman's lips, though Althea got the impression she was used to the gobsmacked reaction of strangers.

That's what made Althea realize she recognized the woman, in that way of forgotten song lyrics that caught at the back of the throat.

"Deveraux Charles," the woman supplied, clearly seeing the hesitation in Althea's expression. "I'm sure you've seen some of my films, if you're trying to remember where you know me from."

Althea wanted to snap and point and say *ah, yes,* but she did have some manners.

"Miss Charles," Helene greeted her warmly, kissing both the woman's cheeks before turning back to Althea. "She's been in Munich filming a movie for Herr Goebbels, so you two have yet to meet."

"Chancellor Hitler despises Berlin, don't you know?" Miss Charles said. "He likes the Munich backdrop better for his propaganda pieces."

Helene tsked. "I hate when you call them that."

Miss Charles grinned and shrugged. "I call a pig a pig."

Althea looked between the two ladies, and then chose a neutral question. "You're American?"

It wasn't as if the woman was trying to hide her accent, the syrup-drenched lyrical drawl that conjured up images of Bayou nights. New Orleans or thereabouts, Althea guessed, though she'd never heard the accent in person before.

"Same as you," Miss Charles said. "And please, don't follow Helene's formality." She nudged Helene playfully. "Call me Dev."

"Deveraux is an interesting name," Althea said. It was a habit of hers, noticing names she could use for future characters.

"Blame my silly sixteen-year-old self for that one," Dev said, a laugh in her voice. "I thought it sounded tragically romantic and mysterious. I used it as my stage name once and there was no going back. But what can you do? Once something sticks, it's hard to wipe off."

"Miss Charles is a part of the same cultural program as you are, dear," Helene said as an aside to Althea. "It's a shame she's been out of the city."

"Munich is so dull," Dev bemoaned. "So much politics, so little playtime."

Her voice dipped low on the last bit and Althea blushed, though she was not even sure why she did.

"I thought the program was for writers," Althea asked carefully, not wanting to insult anyone but not sure what else to say. Tongue-tied and struck mute in the face of pretty people, that was Althea to a tee.

"She doesn't just star in the films," Helene rushed to say.

"I write them, too, though no one remembers that part," Dev said, sounding both bitter and resigned. "When you're the face in front of the camera, people tend to forget anything else."

Althea gasped. "How marvelous." Not that she'd met many sophisticated people of any kind, but a film writer seemed intriguing beyond her imagination. How it must differ from what she did. Novels had so much interiority to them, she spent most of the time living in her characters' heads, even their dialogue was heavily influenced by what she wanted them to share or hide or *be seen* sharing or hiding. "I can't fathom writing a screenplay."

Dev's eyes crinkled at the corners at Althea's obvious enthusiasm, not in a cruel or biting manner, just gently amused. "They're much easier than books, my dear, don't let anyone tell you differently. You'd do fine."

"Are you in Berlin for a while, Miss Charles?" Helene inquired, waving over a waiter with a tray of champagne coupes.

"Yes, Herr Goebbels has granted me at least a month to write the next film," Dev said, motioning the waiter to stay. She finished her bubbly wine in one long swallow, deposited the empty glass on the tray, took another, and then waved the man away. "I plan on taking advantage of my time here. I'm sure they'll ship me off to Bavaria or some such nonsense next."

"Bavaria is quite lovely in the spring, dear," Helene chastised.

"Tell that to my frozen tits," Dev said, downing half her champagne.

Althea inhaled into a cough, but Helene didn't look surprised at the language.

Dev winked at her. "I have to give Helene something to fret about."

"Shameless," Helene murmured, but she still sounded indulgent. Like Althea, Dev was a guest of the Third Reich, which Althea was realizing granted them almost unlimited impunity within social circles. "Miss Charles, you've been out of town, but tell me you've heard the threats."

Something flickered across Dev's face, before she nodded. "Who has not?"

"What threats?" Althea asked before she could think better of it.

Both women turned to her in surprise. Helene was the one who recovered first. "Hasn't Diedrich mentioned them? No? I shall have to take him to task."

Althea was only partly successful in fighting the urge to stutter some excuse. "We've been quite busy with other things."

Dev tossed back her head, laughing, the pale column of her throat on display. Althea looked away.

"I'm sure you have," Dev said, all innuendo, and Althea's mortification deepened. She and Diedrich had only kissed that once. Sometimes she thought, when his hand drifted low on her back or he linked his fingers through hers or he looked at her with fire burning behind his eyes . . . But, as a consummate gentleman, he hadn't pushed any further.

"No, I mean, well, you see—"

Helene patted Althea's forearm. "Pay Miss Charles no mind, dear. She likes to get a reaction. I'm sure Diedrich has kept you running around going to different readings."

Defending herself further would certainly end in disaster, so Althea just said, "The threats?"

"Ah, yes." Helene nodded. "From the communists. Now that our dear *Fürher* is chancellor, they've started stockpiling weapons and making plans to target upstanding German citizens."

"Have they?" Dev said blandly, not seeming too terrified with the prospect. Althea's fingers clutched at her glass. She could admit she'd led a sheltered life—the most dangerous thing she'd ever had to face was a particularly brutal snowstorm. And while she'd heard about an increase of violence in the streets between brownshirts and the hooligans, as Diedrich called them, she hadn't actually witnessed anything herself. The prospect of getting caught in a melee had her terrified.

Guilt crept in. Perhaps this was why Diedrich no longer liked when she wandered the city alone. He had just been trying to keep her safe. She should have given him more credit rather than chafing at the scrutiny.

"Our little wolf has issued decrees to shut down those filthy lie machines they call newspapers," Helene said, with a sniff. "Once their kind is dealt with, it makes me hopeful that he will be able to turn his attention to Aryanizing our shops and schools."

"'Aryanizing'?" The word tasted strange on Althea's tongue.

"Ensuring that good, hardworking Germans aren't being forced out by those people," Helene said with grim satisfaction.

"'Those people'?" Althea asked, doing quite the impression of a particularly slow parrot.

"The Jews, darling," Helene said as if it were obvious. "They just take and take and take, and nothing is left for our hardworking German merchants. We have to correct the balance."

"But . . ." Althea could feel her face doing something unpleasant. "What do you—"

Dev cut her off. "Darling, I think I've spotted Theo Carsters over there. He's an artist-in-residence as part of Goebbels's program, as well. Have you met him yet?"

Thrown, Althea craned to get a look, but the ballroom was too crowded. "No, I don't believe so."

"Let me, then," Dev said, before bestowing an apologetic smile on Helene. "You don't mind if I steal Althea, do you?"

"No, no, mingle, dears. Enjoy," Helene said with an absent, indulgent wave, her gaze already scanning the nearby groups, looking for the next important person to latch on to.

Once they were out of the woman's hearing, Dev leaned down, close enough that her breath was warm against Althea's neck. "The first rule of the Reich, darling, is don't question the Reich."

Althea lurched back a little, off-balance from the past few minutes. "What?"

Dev stopped, studied her. "How long have you been in Berlin, now?"

"Six weeks," Althea said, not liking the heat in her face. The warmth wasn't pleasant like it had been earlier when she'd been pinned in a very different way beneath this woman's gaze. Now, Althea crossed her arms, defensive.

"And you're still a good little foot soldier for the Reich, hmm?" Dev said, more to herself than Althea. "Tell me, do you hate Jews? Communists? Homosexuals?"

"What?" Althea was thrown enough to drop her stance. "Of course not."

"Do you know our hosts do?" Dev asked.

Althea shook her head, not sure what to say. That couldn't be right, there must be some nuance Dev was missing. She'd never heard Diedrich say anything so narrow minded.

Dev studied her for a long minute and then seemed to make a decision. "Shall we slip your handler tonight?"

Her eyes had found Diedrich where he stood with uniform-clad Nazi officials.

"My handler?" Althea tested out the label. She'd always thought of Diedrich as her liaison. But the idea of *handler* settled in her mind, feeling right.

Diedrich did tend to concern himself with the details of her comings and goings, where she went, who she went there with. She'd tolerated it, thinking he did it because he was concerned for her, a young, naive woman in a big unfamiliar city. But was that accurate?

"There we go," Dev murmured, watching Althea's face closely as she came to the realization. "Now." She clapped her hands. "Shall I show you the real Berlin?"

Chapter 11

New York City
May 1944

Viv took the train to Coney Island the day after she'd decided she would see Hale again, seeking solace in the memory of where she'd met both the man who would become her husband and the one who'd broken her heart.

She wasn't delaying her trip to talk to Hale through any excuse necessary. She wasn't.

The subway conductor announced the stop for Coney Island, and she stood, waiting for the doors to open. This far out from the city there were just a few other riders in the car and she was the only one getting off.

Brine, salt, and the unique fermented scent of garbage hit her nose first, and then her skin, the wind pulling at her loose curls until they blew around her face. She'd worn trousers today for that very reason, recalling a time or two that her skirt had flown up with a particularly cheeky breeze off the ocean and Viv had been left frantically trying to hold it down, mortified and laughing and carefree and young.

God, they'd all been so young.

The boardwalk was a ghost of what it had been in those days when Viv and the boys had roamed it like they'd owned the place.

She'd always adored the lights, the crowds, riding the Cyclone, and eating Nathan's hot dogs, sneaking away to kiss Hale under the pier while Edward snickered in the distance, humming the wedding march because he'd always been a troublemaker.

The summer Viv had turned sixteen she'd realized Uncle Horace didn't notice when she snuck out of the house at night. Usually he'd fall asleep no later than eight o'clock, a half-drunk snifter of brandy at his elbow.

The dance halls had always been a lark, but nothing beat Coney Island for Viv.

Somehow, she'd talked a friend into coming along on a steamy summer night in June, and that's where she'd first met Edward Childs and Emmett Hale. Hale had always gone by his surname, his way of honoring the man who'd claimed him as his own.

Viv and her friend Dot had been waiting in line to ride the Thunderbolt, when Edward had stumbled off the ride and promptly puked all over Viv's shoes. Dot had screamed, a birdlike shrill that had bothered Viv more than the sick cooling on her high heels.

The boys had offered to buy the girls cotton candy to apologize, and Viv had gladly stepped out of line, enthralled by the tall one with the dark curl twisting in devastating carelessness over his forehead. Captivated by the dimple that flashed in Hale's cheek, just on that one side and only when he smiled deeply enough so that it felt like a secret.

Edward, meanwhile, had charmed Dot. With his baby face and easy laugh and bronzed curls, he'd been a ladies' man from the start, never one to fall in love but quick to fall in lust.

Dark and mysterious and a bit dangerous, Hale, on the other hand, had always looked like a man who had a couple of girls on the line. But he'd never really had time for dating, Viv came to realize that summer. His adoptive father owned a store where Hale spent all of his time working, saving to get out of a life of living with day-to-day uncertainty.

While Edward had been busy talking his way up Dot's skirt, Hale and Viv had ducked under the pier, playing cat and mouse in between the wooden legs as he gave her an abbreviated version of his life story.

This is the first time I've had a Saturday evening free in I don't remember how long, Hale had said, but not like he was complaining. He smiled at the ground as if the statement was a private thing she could only peek at. Perhaps it was. She knew what it was like not to be wanted by family—how much different would her life be if some stranger had accepted her and then loved her unconditionally? Given her a name and a job and a life that maybe she didn't want but could appreciate at the very least?

You're spending it with Edward? she'd asked. Viv had been raised in wealth, and she could spot the difference in the boys' clothes, their manners, their speech. Edward Childs was clearly from her world, while Emmett Hale was not. And yet they had the same father, their fates only determined by a wedding ring. Wasn't that tailor-made for resentment?

We're brothers, Hale had said as if it were as simple as that. And maybe it was. Viv would have done anything for a sibling to have held her hand through the past few years. Hale slid her a look. *You're interested in him?*

Viv had blushed, not used to such bluntness. Uncle Horace rarely entertained, and Viv attended a girls' school on the Upper West Side. Even at the dance halls she snuck out to, she'd only encountered respectable boys who talked about the newest films and songs on the wireless.

No, she'd said, soft enough that the waves almost took it away. But he heard her, because he ducked his head once more to hide a grin and then brushed her knuckles with his. An invitation she took, slotting their fingers together, everything in her chest warm and tight and golden.

They had spent the rest of the summer at Coney Island, or at least it had seemed that way. Viv had also managed to make it to other parts of Brooklyn on a few of the weekends Uncle Horace had commitments elsewhere. Hale had dragged her into the street one unbearably hot August day and taught her how to play baseball with the neighborhood kids. They'd cheered for Viv when she'd made it to first base, and afterward, in the spray of a fire hydrant, Hale had kissed her, tasting of sweat and grape Popsicles.

They'd read to each other on fire escapes as the sun set in the distance, trading favorite lines; they'd spent hours drifting through the Met, lingering in front of paintings they liked, paintings they hated. Sometimes they rode the subway, intertwined more often than not, earning themselves glares from matrons and envious looks from girls just coming of age.

And then, at the tail end of the best summer of Viv's life, Uncle Horace had died.

At sixteen, Viv had pleaded with the government officials deciding her fate that she was old enough to be on her own. She had her parents' fortune, after all. The officials sent her to a boarding school in Connecticut instead.

She hadn't even had the chance to say goodbye to Hale before they had her on a train out of state.

Viv still cringed when she remembered the letters she'd sent him, all increasingly more desperate, then hurt. At sixteen, she hadn't known not to cut herself open for a boy. Hadn't understood that pretty words whispered like promises could be nothing but empty lies. Girls were taught how to catch boys, not how to protect themselves from them.

I miss you every day, every hour, every minute.

That's how she had always ended her letters. Even when she'd realized he was never going to write her back.

The last one she sent had been particularly mortifying. Had the letter been filled with righteous anger, she might have found some satisfaction in the memory of it. But she had just been sad and confused and still so in love anyway.

Was I wrong to believe we spoke the same language? That the words we used meant the same to each of us? That love is defined as sun-drenched days, baseball bats, your fingertips against my skin; that forever is defined as infinite?

You made me feel something I had never felt before and I put a name to it. I called it love.

I suppose that was my mistake.

I miss you every day, every hour, every minute, and I can't even hate you for that.

Because my definition is the right one.

When all she'd gotten back was dead silence, she'd truly realized she'd been a plaything, discarded at the first sign of inconvenience.

These violent delights have violent ends, she remembered thinking, sinking into the tragedy of *Romeo and Juliet* in a way she now found embarrassing for her younger self. But even then, she must have sensed that what Hale had sparked in her was unique.

She had never understood other girls' fascination with boys until Hale.

Edward, perhaps shockingly now that she thought about it, *had* written back. He'd always been there on the periphery that summer, but only when he'd sent his condolences did she realize they'd become something like friends even while both of them had been busy flirting with other people.

When Viv had thanked him for sending his sympathies, he'd replied, and then she'd replied to that reply, and so on until they were writing every week.

For the two years she'd been forced to stay at the school, Edward had become her best friend. He never mentioned Hale and ignored any of her subtle—and not so subtle—attempts to get information on the man, but everything else was fair game. They'd shared fears and dreams and embarrassing stories and everything in between. Somehow it was easier to put all that down on paper and it didn't matter that they'd only known each other in person for a handful of months before they'd started corresponding.

At eighteen, Viv had returned to the city and found that she and Edward were able to talk just as easily face-to-face. She'd found love there, in the way he'd offered his friendship without expecting anything in return. There were times she understood Charlotte's need for Edward to have been *in love* before he died. Viv had thought the same thing, more than once.

Sometimes, though, she wanted to shout that he had been loved. And she wondered why, for some people, that wasn't enough.

One time, about a year before Edward shipped out, he'd slid her a look so similar to how Hale had looked at her all those years prior that Viv had to hide a wince. "What ever happened between the two of you?"

The brothers still talked, Viv had known, and Charlotte had a relationship with Hale, as well. But Viv had gotten the message loud and clear back when she'd been sixteen.

"Summer fling," she'd answered with a dismissive shrug. Like it had been nothing, like it hadn't changed her and broken her, as, she supposed, first loves were designed to do.

Viv tried to picture what Hale would look like now. How had he aged? At twenty, he'd still had some baby-fat softness to his jaw, had a spot or two that had marred the perfection of his face. He'd be nearly thirty, and those faults would have disappeared. Perhaps a few lines would be in their place.

Gone would be young Emmett Hale, shopkeeper and bastard son.

In his place would be Representative Emmett Hale, beloved politician and ardent champion for New York's poorer citizens.

Would he even see her? Would he have an answer as to why he'd never replied to her letters, or would they pretend that part had never happened? Would they act like strangers even though she knew the shape of him beneath her hands, and he knew what her mouth tasted like?

She liked to think of herself as smooth, confident, and sophisticated. She worked for an important war organization, bantered with the smartest people in publishing on a daily basis, read all the classics and important literary novels, and yet just thinking of him returned her to a flustered sixteen-year-old who flushed because a boy wanted to hold her hand.

A cheerful wail interrupted her thoughts, and she turned to see two young girls celebrating near one of the games, the lights on top going wild.

She smiled at them, their joy nearly painful to watch, but in that way that muscles ached after a lovely walk in the city.

Then she shoved away her own memories, back into the well-locked box where she usually kept them. This was war, after all. There was no place for sentimentality.

Chapter 12

Paris
October 1936

No matter how tired she might be, Hannah made a point to always attend the weekly salon at Natalie Clifford Barney's mansion on the Left Bank across from the Louvre.

Hannah smoothed down her lavender cardigan—a nod to this particular crowd. *Not a single lesbian in Paris hasn't graced her doorway,* one of the attendees had informed Hannah on the first Friday night she'd been invited.

The sweater was serviceable, but Hannah grimaced down at the mud that flecked the hem of her wide-legged trousers. She'd decided to bicycle over from work at the library, and that had clearly been a mistake. Now there was nothing to be done about it.

Not that it mattered either way. Despite Natalie's fame and prestigious status on the Parisian literary scene, she wasn't one to quibble over sartorial choices. The playwright and poet did tend to dress every Friday—in heavy brocade ensembles that seemed better suited for the past century—but she'd yet to kick anyone out the door for not rising to her level.

"Hannah," someone called as she stepped into the hallway, the door always left unlocked on nights like these.

In the next moment, Hannah had a warm armful of a young artist who wore splatters of paint on her skin as a point of pride. Hannah caught the edge of a cerulean spot with her fingernail, as she kissed each of Patrice's cheeks. "I thought you were in Greece."

"It's so boring there," Patrice drawled out, pushing her long, wheat-blond hair off her face. In her black trousers and white blouse, she looked like Paris itself, far too fashionable and mysterious to associate with foreigners. "Sunshine all of the time, blue seas, magnificent food. Psh, how pedestrian. Give me miserable Paris any day. Here."

Hannah took the glass foisted into her hand without thought, eyeing the bubbles. "Are we celebrating?"

"I have a showing next week," Patrice said, slinging an arm around Hannah's waist, directing her further into the bowels of Natalie's house. "But, Hannah, Hannah, Hannah, you've been here long enough to know that we do not need to be celebrating to drink champagne."

Hannah downed half her glass in silent agreement, and Patrice winked at her before doing the same. She wasn't beautiful, but she had the kind of face that came alive beneath the distortion of a camera, exaggerated features that flattened into a striking kind of magnetism.

"How is Marie?" Hannah asked, scanning the room. On any given Friday, it wouldn't be unusual to see a famous writer or poet lurking in the shadows.

"Ah, Marie. She has taken a lover." Patrice slumped dramatically, letting Hannah hold her body weight.

"I'm sorry."

"Oh, don't be. The lover is quite pretty, in a provincial way," Patrice said. "And she's terribly good in bed, phenomenal at taking direction."

Hannah snagged two glasses of something pink from the side table as they started toward the main drawing room. "It sounds like all's well that ends well."

"We'll see." Patrice graciously took one of the drinks, handing off her empty glass to someone who Hannah thought was a rising poet that Otto always found himself in raptures over. Patrice didn't pay attention to the poet's disgruntled exclamation, but that was Patrice. She lived in a world of her own. "The girl is quite silly when we take her about. I'm not sure how long she'll last here. The city would be eating her alive if not for us."

Hannah swallowed the crass joke that was probably a result of too much wine too fast, and said instead, "Maybe she'll surprise you."

"But then I might fall in love with her, and wouldn't that be terrible." Patrice sighed, dragging Hannah down onto a tufted sofa.

"Would it be?" Hannah asked, thinking of her talk with Lucien. "So terrible?"

Natalie herself saved Patrice from answering when she dropped into the seat across from Hannah, the little black bulldog settling into her lap and watching them through beady eyes.

"You have a broken heart," Natalie said in lieu of a greeting. The expat had come to Paris by way of the United States and hadn't quite lost her blunt American accent—or her blunt American ways.

In a city of fluttering lashes and coyness, Hannah found Natalie refreshing. That didn't mean Hannah was ever the type to share her emotions easily, especially to someone who was all but a stranger to her. "It's the best way to be in Paris, no?"

Patrice laughed and stood. "I have not drunk enough wine for this conversation. Good luck."

Natalie squinted at Hannah, ignoring Patrice's exit. "You don't think it's best to be in love in the City of Lights?"

Hannah lifted one shoulder, wondering how she'd gotten herself into so many philosophical discussions about a topic she'd been steadfastly avoiding for the past three years. That was Paris for you, she supposed. "If you're a visitor, perhaps. Or a child."

"You've not been a child in a while, I take it."

"No," Hannah said softly. "You only fall in love like that once, and then forever you love with a fractured heart. Healed though it may be."

"Dire," Natalie proclaimed, her dog whining in her lap as she lifted her hand in a flourish. Natalie liked the dramatics as much as Otto did.

"Realistic," Hannah countered. "Do you not have a broken heart?"

"Perhaps," Natalie said, going back to stroking the dog's head and watching Hannah speculatively. "Have you heard of the art of *kintsugi*?"

Hannah shook her head.

"In Japan, when a piece of pottery breaks, the pieces are put back together using gold at the cracks," Natalie said. "That way the broken object is even more beautiful than the original."

"Poetic," Hannah drawled to hide the shake that would have been in her voice otherwise. There was something magical about the idea, yet it didn't match her reality. Any gold she used in the cracks of her heart would be false and fragile and chip at the slightest bit of trouble.

But Natalie didn't flinch. "You think poetry and life can't exist in harmony with each other?"

Hannah thought of Adam's bruised face as he sat across from her in the stark visitor room in the concentration camp, and then of Althea's tears and useless apology. "No."

"What a sad way to live, my dear," Natalie said, with that brutal honesty of hers. "Life is more than survival. I would have thought you knew that."

"Why?" Hannah asked, curious that this woman knew anything more than her name.

"Do you not work for that library in Montparnasse?" Natalie asked.

"I do," Hannah agreed hesitantly, already seeing the trap.

"Is it not poetic to exist solely to save a culture from burning to the ground?" Natalie asked. "Is your little library not a symbolic beacon to the world that words are more powerful than flames?"

"When you put it that way . . . ," Hannah said with a small smile, easing back from the argument. Natalie was right. Hannah knew she was only being contrary in the first place. But that's how she got when someone poked her sore spots. And what was her heart but one throbbing bruise?

"I am always right, my dear," Natalie agreed, with an imperious nod to show she didn't hold grudges. "Now tell me about this great love of yours, the one that put that wisdom in your eyes."

Hannah shook her head. "It wasn't a woman who did that," she said, only half lying. "It was a country."

Natalie lifted her sherry glass in a toast. "One and the same, my dear. One and the same."

HANNAH STAYED AT Natalie's too late and drank too much wine, so when she got home she was all but crawling up the stairs to her one-room flat—the little apartment she'd taken at the top of a house on a quiet street in the fifth arrondissement not far from the Luxembourg Gardens.

Her parents had settled out in the country, but Hannah had craved the freedom of city life and could afford it with the small stipend she was allowed each month from her father.

She needed that money, considering the library paid starvation wages. It was a good thing they all found satisfaction in the work, otherwise the place would be hard pressed to staff itself.

Mademoiselle Brigitte Blanchett stopped Hannah halfway up the stairs. Her landlady was a buxom woman with a dark mustache and the steely resolve of someone who'd seen quite a bit of outrageousness in her life. Hannah suspected that she'd made her living working in and then running a brothel from the few hints Brigitte had dropped.

"Mail," Brigitte barked in French. She seemed to assume, however correctly, that Hannah had little vocabulary in the language and so tended to hold conversations in one-word sentences.

"Merci." Hannah took the two envelopes, pretending not to notice Brigitte's nosy gaze. Her landlady wanted her to open the letters in front of her. Hannah on her own didn't provide nearly enough entertainment for Brigitte, which the woman had told her several times. "*Bonne nuit.*"

Brigitte glared, her large bosom heaving beneath her silk dressing gown, but Hannah ignored her, trudging the rest of the way up to her place.

She touched the mezuzah that hung beside her door, a recent addition. Despite their more secular bent, her parents had one also, the Hebrew verses from the Torah carefully tucked into the wooden casing. Her family had treated their mezuzah absently, almost as a habit that to them seemed more like a good-luck charm than a sacred blessing.

It's a statement, though, isn't it? one of her friends from the library had said when the absence of Hannah's came up in passing. *It says this is a Jewish household. And it's a symbol we get to decide to put on ourselves.*

That sentiment pulled at something in her chest. She had thought about all the ways Germany marked its Jewish citizens so that they would feel *less than*. The papers, the registries, the graffiti on shop windows marking them as Jewish-owned.

There was power in claiming—deliberately and with joy—a part of you that others wanted you to hate yourself for. Hannah feared a time would come when the mezuzah would be used against her and other Jews, but for now, it was one more way of owning her own humanity.

This was a Jewish household.

When she finally made it inside, Hannah collapsed onto her bed, into the soft embrace of her grandmother's sunny yellow quilt—the only bit of color in a somewhat drab apartment. She brought her knees up to her chest as she leaned back against the wall, holding the two envelopes.

She chewed on her lip as she touched the return address on the first one.

Owl's Head, Maine.

The writing was achingly familiar, and her eyes burned. Though she would not cry. Never that.

Hannah hated that she'd had to think of the woman so much in recent days. She'd been better in the past few months, her pain receding until it was small enough to carry around inside of her.

She couldn't exactly go weeks without remembering what had transpired before Hannah and her family had fled Germany, not when the consequences remained so painful. But more often now she could slide past the memory of Althea herself, pushing it away into a dark corner where she didn't have to look at it, didn't have to suffocate beneath the crushing weight of the betrayal.

Hannah tossed the letter aside without opening it. Later she would slot it into the box she kept in the loose floorboard in her closet, the one that held all the letters she'd received and never opened. The one that held that precious edition of *Alice in Wonderland* with the cat doodles drawn on the title page.

But for now, Hannah turned her attention to the second envelope. She recognized the writing just as easily, and she held the letter to her forehead for a long moment as she tried to get her breath back.

When she finally forced herself to open the damn thing, she realized her cheeks were damp.

"Silly girl," she murmured to herself, swiping at the tears.

The message was exactly what she'd expected and thankfully not what she had feared.

> *Heard news of Adam today, poorly but still alive. No progress on his trial.*
>
> *Will update if anything changes.*

She knew the swoopy, sloppy signature at the end to be Johann Bauer's. He tried to write to her and her parents at least once every few weeks to update them on Adam's case. Her brother had been a political prisoner at a concentration camp north of Berlin for the past three years, and every single day since his arrest, Hannah had been waiting for news that he'd been executed.

Their only chance was that Johann—one of the few friends who had remained loyal to their family after what had happened with Adam—could pull the limited strings he had left in the government. And he was the first to admit that as a lawyer who'd made most of his connections under the previous regime, he didn't have many allies left in the city.

Johann promised her that there was still hope. Hannah's parents believed the lie.

But in the dark of night, Hannah knew better.

Under the Third Reich, hope only existed as a weapon.

Chapter 13

Berlin
February 1933

Deveraux Charles had a private car waiting for her outside Helene Bechstein's house.

"When you're the favored pet, you get a gilded cage," Dev said at Althea's wide-eyed gaze.

"You don't like the Nazis," Althea remarked as they settled into the cushioned back seat.

Dev flicked her eyes toward their driver. "I just tease, darling."

Althea got the hint and kept her mouth closed for the rest of their ride.

She didn't know where they were headed, but she found she didn't care. Her body hummed with an excitement she hadn't felt since those first weeks with Diedrich, exploring the new city. Her resentment about being restricted took on a new layer.

Your handler.

Almost desperately, Althea tried to parse through what she knew of the NSDAP. Most people whom she encountered on university campuses spoke of the party with a feverish excitement that aligned with Diedrich's oft-cited statistics about young people's voting preferences. The communists Althea had met clearly did not like the party, but did she really care what they thought? When they were trying to incite a civil war in the country? When they clearly were prepared to resort to terroristic tactics?

Everyone had strong opinions about politics, it seemed. Althea sometimes wished she could just ignore it all, but that was proving nearly impossible. There were definite sides to be picked, and why wouldn't Althea support her hosts?

She liked Diedrich, liked especially when he held her hand and smiled at her like she was the most delightful person he'd ever met. Yes, sometimes he could be overbearing, almost militant, when it came to his party and beliefs, but so were the communists Althea had talked to.

She didn't know Deveraux, but for some reason she liked her, too. Dev hadn't said she was a communist, but Althea could tell almost immediately that the woman didn't trust the very political party that was hosting her.

Althea's head throbbed as she stared out the window at the blurred neon lights of the theater district. The problem wasn't going to be solved that night. For now, she would just enjoy whatever Dev had in store for her.

The car dropped them outside a club on Marburger Strasse.

Chez Ma Belle Soeur, the sign above the door read.

"'My beautiful sister,'" Dev translated, hooking her chin over Althea's shoulder.

"French?" Althea asked as she ran a nervous hand over her hair, such a mousey brown compared to Dev's sleek strands. At least she hadn't attempted anything too ambitious, simply pinning back the front and trying to tame the rest into soft waves.

Dev started inside, throwing a wink over her shoulder. "As all good cabaret is."

Decadence was all Althea could think when they stepped into the nightclub. The decorations leaned toward Grecian frescos, but it was the atmosphere rather than the paint on the walls that turned it otherworldly.

Althea had been struck dumb by Dev's beauty, but Dev was almost a dime a dozen among the women pressed up at the bar and seated at tables and booths throughout the room. The men were equally stunning, and Althea had never felt more drab.

Some in the crowd had their attention locked on the stage at the far side of the room—where women in skimpy lederhosen kicked like Rockettes—but just as many people chatted away, smoked, laughed, sang their own little versions of whatever the band was playing.

The noise, the music, the smoke, the beautiful women, the beautiful men—all pressed in on Althea until reality went a little blurry at the edges and she swayed into Dev.

Dev patted her cheek and righted her.

"The real Berlin," she whispered.

Dev proceeded to introduce her to group after group. It seemed like she knew everyone and everyone loved Dev. The brightest star in a constellation of bright stars.

But some were actually interested in Althea, a peculiarity she still wasn't used to.

"You're a writer," they gasped. "Tell us who you know."

"Well, you might have heard of her," Althea said to one particularly nosy woman. "Deveraux Charles, an up-and-coming playwright of monumental talent."

Everyone laughed, and Dev winked and Althea felt lightheaded and drunk from the attention.

"Did you hear about Eldorado?" one man asked Dev, whose lips parted in dismay.

"Don't tell me," she all but wailed.

"Ludwig handed it over to the SA brutes." The man—Althea thought his name might be Peter—shook his head sadly. "They're using it as a headquarters now."

"Sacrilege!" Dev cried. "Though poor Ludwig, he didn't have a choice."

"Not with the crackdown," Peter agreed. "He was bound to be arrested one of these days."

Dev turned to Althea. "Eldorado was *the* cabaret club for people who enjoy the company of . . ." Peter and Dev met each other's eyes as she paused, and then continued, "Well, it was the club to go to. Such a sad state of affairs."

"What crackdown?" Althea asked, as confused as if she were a small child begging for adult information.

"I'll explain it to you later," Dev said as an aside.

Then they were off to talk to another group, to lament curfews and club closings and the lack of coffee in stores. Althea let it all wash over her, and thought, *SA*.

The Sturmabteilung. The storm division, the storm troopers.

That was the more formal name for the brownshirts who were such a ubiquitous presence on the streets. There were also the SS, or the blackshirts, who acted more as bodyguards to Hitler and his top officials. But the SA were the ones who Althea saw the most.

Why would they be cracking down on cabaret clubs?

Deviants, Althea's mind supplied as she scanned the crowd around her. Men wearing makeup and women, with short, slicked hair, wearing suits. Women holding hands with other women, men doing the same with other men. She tried to imagine what

Diedrich would have to say about the affectionate displays. He didn't talk about it much, but she instinctively knew this was who he was referring to when he spit out that word like it was a foul thing on his tongue.

Your handler.

The first rule of the Reich is, don't question the Reich.

Deviants. Althea might not know much about the world, but she knew she would never call anyone such a hateful term.

Had she gotten this all wrong?

Althea lost track of time watching the dancers onstage. There seemed to be a master of ceremonies who would come out and tell jokes in between the little acts.

"*Heil*—damn it, now I've forgotten the name," the MC cried to riotous howls and jeers. At one point he brought out framed pictures of Hitler, Goebbels, and a few other men Althea didn't recognize.

"Now," he asked a rapt audience, who seemed desperate for whatever the punch line would be as he waved to the portraits, "shall I hang them or line them up against the wall?"

The approving bellow that followed rippled and rolled over even those who weren't paying attention.

"You've heard about what the new master race should look like, yes?" the MC asked the enthralled crowd. They hollered and he nodded like they'd actually said anything intelligible. "As thin as Göring, as blond as Hitler, and as tall as Goebbels."

The man talking to Dev shook his head. "He better be careful, he'll get a not-so-friendly visit from Göring at this rate."

"The Nazis love it, don't let them fool you," Dev said, and nodded at his skeptical look. "I think they think of it as a release valve? Toothless criticism that lets people blow off steam. For now, at least," she added with a shrug.

"You would know, I guess," the man said grimly. "But it won't be long that they tolerate it."

An hour in, Dev gave a little cry. "Oh."

In the next heartbeat, Dev had her hand wrapped around Althea's wrist, bringing her forward. She led Althea to a table somewhat off to the side, away from the main area of the floor.

"Darling, it's been too long," Dev said to the woman who stood up when she'd noticed Dev headed her way.

"That's what happens when they hide you away in Munich," the woman said, kissing Dev's cheeks.

Like the rest of the crowd, she was almost too attractive to look at. Her dark curls were pinned away from her face to reveal striking features—high, prominent cheekbones, wide-set eyes, and soft lips that were currently wrapped around a slim cigarette. She watched Althea watching her as she blew the smoke out the side.

Her neck hot, Althea glanced away, and then back, because she couldn't help herself. There was nothing provocative about the woman's dress, a black number with a tight waist and a sharp collar that highlighted well-defined collarbones. But the woman wore it like she wanted someone to take it off her.

Althea quickly shifted her attention to the woman's companion. He was just as pretty, though Althea hesitated to call a man that. There was no better word for him, though. He looked like what a Byron poem sounded like. Windswept and romantic even in the back of a smoky cabaret club in Berlin.

He smirked up at Dev. "Thank God you're back, Berlin was dreadfully boring without you."

"I'm sure you were able to entertain yourself," Dev said, with one of her sly winks. She turned to include Althea in the conversation. "My dears, this is Miss Althea James. She's an American writer who is too clever for her own good."

Althea blushed at the introduction but nodded a shy hello to the pair.

"That rascal who clearly doesn't have enough manners to stand to greet a lady—"

"Let me know when you see one, and I'll stand," the young man said with a cheeky smile.

"Is Otto Koch," Dev continued as if he hadn't said anything. "One of the best actors Germany has ever produced."

Otto finally leapt to his feet and took a dramatic bow. Then he brought Althea's hand to his mouth, his lips grazing over her knuckles. "A pleasure."

Dev shoved at his shoulder. "And this," she said, with a wave toward the woman, "is Hannah Brecht."

Chapter 14

New York City
May 1944

Even though Viv had gone straight from Coney Island to the ramshackle office of Brooklyn's beloved Representative Emmett Hale, she had now been pacing in front of it for so long she'd started drawing looks from the old men playing checkers at the end of the block.

People were protective of Hale around here, she knew. The quickest way to end up on the business side of a switchblade was to say something derogatory about the lawmaker. Viv tried to shoot the men a reassuring smile, which seemed to have the opposite effect. One stood, his eyes narrowed, and it was enough to get her up on the first step of the stoop of the building.

The door to Hale's office swung open even before Viv raised her hand to knock.

"Was wondering if you'd just stand there all day."

Her mouth went sawdust dry and her heart pounded at the sight of Hale. He leaned carelessly in the doorway, stripped down to his shirt and open vest, the charcoal color matching the trousers that stretched over well-muscled thighs. That one devastating, dark curl hung over his forehead, and he grinned down at her, a flash of white teeth and amusement at her expense.

"I was wondering if I would get tuberculosis just entering your office," Viv shot back, unsteady but unwilling to show even a hint of doubt. Fake it long enough . . .

Though she was a tall woman herself, Hale still managed to tower over her. Like he did now, straightening to his full height, those broad shoulders of his making her feel impossibly small.

His gaze flicked down to her bare hand before he met her eyes. His were some mix of green and gold and blue that never seemed to want to become fixed into one definable color. "Hello, sister."

Viv smiled so that she didn't grimace.

"Brother dearest," she said, just as sweetly. "You're looking very alive."

From a few veiled mentions from Charlotte, Viv knew it was a sore spot—that Edward had gone off and died tragically young and Hale hadn't.

Hale's smirk dimmed for a blink-and-miss-it second, but then grew wider than before. He waved toward the sky. "It's the lack of bombs that does it."

"Yes, I can imagine that's helpful."

"As entertaining as this is . . ."

Viv inhaled and exhaled, digging her fingernails into her palms. "I have a favor to ask."

"I figured as much. Contrary to what you may believe, I'm not an idiot," Hale said, though there was no anger in his voice. That had been one of her favorite things about him, how unflappable he was. Now, when she wanted to get under his skin, the trait was infuriating. "What else would bring Mrs. Childs slumming?" He held up a hand. "Don't tell me, let me guess."

Hale's head tipped as he studied her closely for an uncomfortably long minute and then he snapped his fingers. "I've got it." He gestured like he was some kind of cheap psychic on the Coney Island boardwalk. "The Soldier Voting Act and a certain senator who shall remain nameless."

Warmth crept into her chest at the thought of him keeping tabs on her, but Viv ignored it, annoyed. This used to be a game between them, a dance almost. Now the back-and-forth just grated on already raw skin.

"Stuff this," Viv said, turning on her heel.

There had to be a better way.

But warm fingers encircled her wrist, stopping her from walking away. "Ah, Viv, you used to be fun."

"You used to know when I was serious," Viv said, meeting his eyes, and finally—God, finally—the jagged amusement dropped away.

"Christ," he sighed and then pulled out the silver pocket watch she knew was the only thing he had from Theodore Childs. "I have ten minutes. But that's it."

"All I need," Viv promised, stepping around him. For all that she'd pinched Hale about the state of the place, the office was clean, neat and tidy, even if small. She could hardly fault him for that; he'd refused any money Edward had offered to help bankroll him years back when he'd first started running for Congress.

He sat behind a sturdy desk in an office that didn't have any frills. There was a childish sketch hung up on the wall behind him, one that looked like it came from a young constituent, and a few framed photographs of him with members of his community. But that was the extent of the bells and whistles.

Viv knew it was an image he cultivated—a man of the people.

She also knew it was real. Sometimes, maybe rarely, but sometimes, it could be both.

"You were right, of course, about why I'm here."

He didn't pounce on the opening as he would have even a few minutes earlier with a comeback something along the lines of *I'm always right.*

"The Armed Services Editions got caught up in the Soldier Voting Act," Hale said, serious and considering. "I tried to convince some of my colleagues to take the language out, but . . ."

She was so rarely surprised, but this news was enough to do it. "You fought for us?"

"For the project," Hale corrected, his eyes crinkling at the corners. "You aren't the only one who gets letters asking for more books."

"Well, then, you know how important this is," Viv said.

"I told you, I tried." Hale flicked his watch open in a distracted gesture, closing it again without even glancing at the time.

Viv chewed on her lip, trying to hold back words she knew would land heavy on his bruises. The most dangerous thing about knowing someone well was that you knew how to hurt them. And even after eight years of silence, she couldn't help but believe she still knew Hale well. "Then you didn't try hard enough."

A muscle in Hale's jaw flexed. "You don't get to tell me that. You don't know anything, Viv."

"I don't know anything?" she spat back at him, stung. "I know that you can't imagine what it's like to be over there with nothing but wet socks and the constant promise of death. You have no idea what it's like to be responsible for the lives of other men."

Hale took an audible breath at that, as if he knew one of them had to hold on to the reins of this conversation before it devolved into them both bloody and broken on the floor. She could almost hear the *and you do?* in the sudden silence that followed, but he managed to keep it to himself.

"What's the plan here?" His voice was even once more; he seemed to recognize they'd both needed to let a little venom out before they could settle into a reasonable conversation.

"I'm hosting a big event to try to get Taft to change his mind about the amendment," Viv said, throwing it out there between them with all the confidence she at least pretended she had.

"To publicly shame him, you mean."

"If that's what it takes," Viv said with a shrug.

"Viv, we debated this bill for nearly a year," he said. "Taft's not going to budge because a few librarians talk at him for an hour."

Her shoulders pulled back as she straightened her spine. She was slim and tall and had been raised to know how to deliver a cutting rebuke with just her posture alone. "I see."

She started to rise, but Hale made a frustrated sound and threw his hand out. "Viv, I didn't mean anything by that."

"Oh really?" Viv asked, her voice ice. "How else was I supposed to interpret *librarians talk at him for an hour* as anything other than dismissive?"

"I'm an ass, I'm sorry," he said, running a hand through his hair. "I was trying to be flippant to get my point across, but it was careless of me. I know this is important."

Viv sat back, surprised. She knew and worked with many men and she could name only a few who would apologize so easily and sincerely.

"All right," she said carefully.

"So, what exactly are you asking me to do?"

And here came the hard part. "I need there to be enough pressure on Taft from his colleagues that he attends the event in the first place. And doesn't leave once he realizes what's going on."

Hale whistled, long and low. "Taft isn't going to take kindly to being humiliated in public. Even if you do shame him into killing the policy, he'll retaliate in some other way."

Viv stared at her hands. She couldn't guarantee that Taft wouldn't take out his anger on anyone who supported her and this wild idea. They both knew that.

"What's your favorite book?" she asked instead of continuing to pound her head into brick. Viv had never asked him that—she'd wanted to, but stopped herself a thousand times. She hadn't wanted to be disappointed.

"Can you really pick one?" he shot back.

"Don't be a politician," Viv chastised, relaxing for the first time since she'd stepped onto the sidewalk outside of his office.

Hale laughed, leaning back in his chair and clasping his hands behind his neck as he studied her. "Should I tell you the one I tell everyone else is my favorite? Or my actual favorite?"

"I think you know the answer to that. But now I want both."

"What do I get in return?" Hale asked.

Her breath caught in her throat, and she was nervous all of a sudden. "What do you want?"

His full attention landed on her like a heavy quilt in summertime. Not unwanted but not exactly welcome, either. She struggled not to shift beneath his gaze.

"I want an answer," Hale finally said.

"To what question?"

"I haven't decided yet." His eyes were dark.

Why did you and Edward marry?

The words came as loud as if he'd actually put voice to them. She knew that's what he wanted to ask, even if he never would. Still, she could always lie if pressed. "All right."

He held a palm out to her. "Shake."

She scoffed but leaned forward enough to slot her own hand into his grip. They shook and there were no sparks, no electricity. Even the ghosts of those butterflies exorcised. Viv reclaimed her hand, not sure if she felt satisfied or disappointed and not willing to explore either.

"I tell most people it's *Of Mice and Men,*" Hale said as soon as they dropped their arms.

"Steinbeck," she said with a nod. "*Mice* hasn't been picked as an ASE but *Tortilla Flat* was one of our earlier books."

"Haven't read it," Hale said, not defensive as some were when she dropped names of novels.

"Camelot in California, replete with a merry band of knights," she said. "I enjoyed it enough."

"That describes what I felt about *Mice.*"

"It's not exactly the most uplifting of tales," Viv agreed. "What's your real favorite?"

"*Don Quixote,*" Hale admitted. "Or, more precisely, *The Ingenious Gentleman Don Quixote of La Mancha.*"

The answer surprised her enough that she almost grinned. "A romantic soul. I should have guessed that."

Hale hummed in agreement, a smile lurking beneath his open expression. Pleased that she'd remembered that about him, she supposed.

Instead of acknowledging their shared past, Viv saw an opportunity to press her argument. "Do you not agree with Cervantes, then?"

He paused, clearly thinking. And then quoted, "'When life itself seems lunatic, who knows where madness lies? . . . Too much sanity may be madness—and maddest of all: to see life as it is, and not as it should be!'?"

"Bravo."

"And that's why I don't tell people it's my favorite," Hale said, almost amused. "It'll be used against me, shamelessly." He paused, leaning forward once more to portray the earnest congressman he was. "I never said I don't respect your efforts, Viv. But I fear you will have about as much success fighting Taft as Quixote did tilting at windmills."

"Should we just give up, then?" Viv asked, the idea repellent. "Don't you want to see life as it should be rather than how it is?"

"I'm a politician, not a knight-errant."

"And I think our world would be a little better with more of the latter and fewer of the former," Viv shot back.

He watched her for a long moment. "You've gotten quite devious, haven't you?"

It was offered like a compliment. "Does that mean you'll do it?"

"I can't guarantee anything," Hale said. "I'm in the House, he's in the Senate."

"But you're extraordinarily popular," Viv pushed. "People want to support you, they know you're going places. I'm going to make sure there's public pressure on him, as well. I'm simply asking for you to nudge your colleagues so that Taft won't be able to just ignore this."

"The more lawmakers the better," Hale mused. "Like I said, I'll try."

Hale went to say something more, then shut his mouth, seeming to think better of it.

"What?" she pressed, because she could never leave well enough alone when it came to him.

"You know simply getting him to attend isn't enough," Hale said, almost cautiously.

"Yes, thank you, I'd realized that."

Hale held his hands up. "I'm simply saying that Taft's a stubborn ass. He won't go down easy."

"It's not about Taft," Viv said, each vulnerable word twisting her stomach. She didn't want Hale's thoughts or his judgment, and yet desperately she craved his approval for her plan. Not because she'd once cared about his opinion over all others', but because he had won his district with seventy percent of the vote. He knew politics, and this, if nothing else, was politics. "It's about his voters. All the voters, really. At the end of the day, I'm not really trying to get Taft to change his mind. I'm trying to make sure other lawmakers know how poisonous this issue is and do something to change it."

"And to get them to do that, you'll get their voters riled up," Hale said, with an approving nod. "I have to warn you, though, people are on their last leg in terms of caring about . . . well . . . anything beyond surviving."

"I know," Viv said, because she was exhausted, as well. It had been a dark few years, and the deaths and rationing and general despair that came with living during a war had taken a toll on all of them. "But you know better than anyone people love a good story. I just have to find the right one to tell."

Chapter 15

Berlin
February 1933

You're a writer."

Althea paused her pencil against the paper; she recognized the voice despite having heard it only once.

Hannah Brecht.

A week had passed since they'd met at that first cabaret, though it had been nothing more than a quick greeting before Dev had pulled Althea away to the next group. She had met so many people that night, most had blended together into a hazy memory.

For some reason Althea couldn't name, she had no trouble placing Hannah Brecht.

They were at another cabaret now, smaller but no less joyous. Dev had seemed to have made it her personal mission to drag Althea to every single nightclub that Berlin offered. This was the fourth they'd tried out, and while Althea was exhausted, she had never felt so free.

Diedrich had been asking increasingly pointed questions about where she was spending her free time, but his frustration was easy to ignore when she thought about the happiness the nights out had brought her.

Hannah Brecht took a seat across from Althea without waiting for a response, which was good because Althea was having trouble finding her tongue.

In the week since they'd met, Hannah had drifted in and out of her thoughts. Althea had convinced herself she had exaggerated the woman's beauty, that the atmosphere and excitement had led her to view everyone she'd met through a sheen of delight.

If anything, Hannah was even more arresting tonight, in a formfitting yellow dress, the fabric cut deep at the sides to reveal her rib cage, her back, the glimpse of skin all the more interesting because of the way the dress completely covered her chest, her legs. A study in subtle allure.

Something hot slipped into Althea's blood, and all she could think was that it must be jealousy. No other reason explained why she couldn't look away from how Hannah's body moved beneath the silk.

Their table was tiny and tucked into a dark corner of the room, and when Hannah's ankle brushed hers, Althea jolted back, trying to create more space. Her skittishness seemed to amuse Hannah.

"Or are you taking notes to report back to your Nazi masters?" Hannah asked, jerking her chin toward the notebook Althea had been scribbling in.

Althea flushed and fumbled, trying to stuff everything away into her small handbag, embarrassed about what, she didn't know. Being a writer? Acting like a writer in public?

"I'm not . . . They're not . . . ," she managed, before Dev's hand landed on her shoulder.

"Hannah, you're not scaring our little dove, are you?" Dev asked, and Althea both appreciated and resented the gesture.

"I don't think I'm scaring her, no. Not the way you mean," Hannah said after studying Althea's expression. Before Althea could ask what she was talking about, Hannah glanced up at Dev. "You're taking her on quite the whirlwind tour, aren't you?"

"We're making up for lost time," Dev said, petting Althea's hair.

Otto Koch appeared at Hannah's shoulder, flushed and happy and too pretty to look at. "I just got fleeced at the poker table. Come dance with me, Dev, please. Help me forget this injustice."

"How could I say no to that face," Dev asked, reaching out to squeeze his chin. Otto just laughed and snatched her hand, pulling her toward the small space that had been commandeered by dancing couples. Over her shoulder, Dev tossed out, "Be nice, Hannah."

"I'm always nice," Hannah said, though her eyes were on Althea's face and surely Dev wouldn't have been able to hear the reassurance. "You're a writer."

"I had a book published," Althea corrected.

The corner of Hannah's mouth ticked up, like she understood the difference. "Will your next one be about the Nazis, then? A love story, perhaps, between a young American and a burly German serving under Hitler?"

Althea flushed, thinking about that day in the winter market, when she had playacted a main character flirting with her blond and handsome liaison. Hannah's smile, smug with jagged amusement, spread.

"You hate them," Althea said, instead of defending herself. "Are they really so terrible?"

Everyone at the cabarets talked of the Nazis the same way

Diedrich and his friends did of the communists. It was . . . confusing, and made it hard to get an accurate picture of the state of political affairs in the country.

Hannah pursed her lips, and Althea couldn't help the way her gaze flicked down. She blinked, and refocused.

"If I told you yes, they are that terrible," Hannah said, "what would you think?"

"I . . . I don't know," Althea mumbled.

"You do," Hannah countered. "You would think we are two biased sides of the same coin."

She was right, of course. Althea had been thinking just that ever since she'd realized Dev didn't trust the very people who were hosting her.

Everyone had stories about how the other side was full of monsters, all the anecdotes equally atrocious. Yet neither had treated her terribly. It was a poor way to judge a person, Althea knew. People were nice to her back home in Owl's Head now that she was a famous writer—the same people who had forced her to find solace in books in the first place.

The way to judge people wasn't to look at how they acted toward people they wanted to impress; it was to look at the way they treated those who could do nothing for them.

Still, what examples of the latter did Althea have to go on? She had been shepherded to bookstores and readings and cabarets and coffeeshops and had only ever seen civilized behavior from both sides.

"Then why should I waste my breath?" Hannah asked, as if reading Althea's thoughts.

"Dev doesn't like them, either," Althea said, not sure why she was pressing when Hannah was giving her a way to end the thorny conversation. Maybe it was because the disappointed resignation on Hannah's face stung more than Althea could understand. Hannah was a stranger, and yet Althea wanted her approval. "But she still works for Goebbels."

And you're friends with her, Althea wanted to say but didn't. It would come out too needy, leave her raw and vulnerable, a callback to when she'd been young and didn't realize she shouldn't act as if she *wanted* to be liked.

Hannah seemed to hear the last part anyway. "Don't let the propaganda fool you, dove. The fervor for Hitler is not quite as ferocious as the Nazis would have you believe. There are plenty of people who hold their noses and work with him regardless."

For some reason that struck Althea as worse than picking a side.

"Life isn't a fairy tale," Hannah said, clearly reading Althea far better than she should be able to after two short encounters. "Good people do bad things, bad people do good things. And most people are just trying to survive." Hannah snuffed out her cigarette. "Now, tell me what you were writing."

"Just details," Althea admitted, her eyes skittering around the room. There were two men dressed in gowns, their hair slicked down like Dev's, their heels clicking against the tile as they swayed in each other's arms; there was a singer with a honey-coated voice and tears in her eyes whenever she reached an emotional chorus; there was a pair of French tourists, ladies in their sixties, who had clearly not known what they were in for but who had been smiling the entire time they'd been at their table.

"I . . . haven't traveled much," Althea confessed, trying not to stutter as Hannah shifted, the drape at the side of her dress hinting at the shadows near her hips. "Whenever I wrote before, I had to rely on magazines and books and, if I was lucky, photographs of the places I was describing."

"I never thought of that," Hannah said, the outside of her thigh pressing against Althea's knee. Althea pushed her drink away, the bubbles clearly having gone to her head. Or maybe it was just Hannah's attention on her, curious instead of disdainful now.

"There are universal details," Althea said. She turned her palm up on the table. "A wrist is always going to be a wrist. Veins under soft, paper-thin skin. If you touch—" She broke off as Hannah placed a fingertip against the blue lines, tracing them up and over the heel of her palm. Then back. Althea's mind emptied, her mouth dry, a buzzing in her ears.

"If you touch . . . ," Hannah prompted, her voice husky and slightly amused.

"You can feel a person's heart," Althea managed to get out.

Hannah held Althea's gaze. "There are things you can't imagine, though."

"No." Althea looked away first and then mourned the loss of Hannah's fingers when Hannah sat back.

Her eyes landed on two men lounging against a pillar next to their table and locked in a steamy kiss. The flash of tongue made Althea too aware of all the places Hannah's leg pressed against hers.

If you touch . . .

Sweat pooled in the dip of her spine as she went hot all over, a shiver chasing in the wake of the flames.

"A problem?" Hannah asked, her expression giving nothing away. But Althea could tell she cared about the answer.

"N-no." She cleared her throat, forced the hesitation out of her voice. "No, no problem."

"You were explaining to me about details," Hannah said, and Althea desperately tried to remember what she had already said.

"Um . . . some details you can extrapolate. A wrist is a wrist. It might have small differences, the color of the skin, the size of the bones, if it's fat or thin, but the basic characteristics are the same anywhere in the world," Althea said. "A car is a car, an icebox is an icebox.

"I can build a world that feels real to my readers," Althea continued. "Because of the way we all know that a wrist bends back only so far and an icebox makes things cold and a car gets you places fast. But there are limitations to that. I know what a restaurant looks like in Maine, but I don't know what a restaurant in India looks like. What makes it different than a restaurant in Australia and what makes that restaurant different than one in California?"

"What does a cabaret in Berlin look like?" Hannah said, following along.

Althea nodded. "So I research and I guess and I hope. But I can always tell when a writer has been somewhere other than the three square miles around where they were born because of the details." She looked around, cataloguing the scene as she had been doing before. "I never could have imagined this."

"You like it?" Hannah asked, her voice more gentle than it had been for the rest of the conversation. Althea guessed some of her awe most have shown.

"It's life itself, isn't it?" Althea asked, and blushed at her own earnestness. "It's as if the cabarets use different lights to make everything more vibrant, more intense. The anger, the joy, the . . . passion. Life. It's all *more* here."

Approval flickered into Hannah's expression and Althea wanted to bathe in it.

"So tell me, little dove, do you dance?"

Startled by the question, Althea could only blink as she pictured a tangle of limbs, thighs slotted together, bellies pressed tight to each other as brassy music played over the scene. As she pictured her fingers brushing over the silk of that dress, the silk of Hannah's skin.

If you touch . . .

"No, I've never . . . I don't." She untwisted her clumsy tongue. "No. I don't dance."

For a long moment, Hannah didn't react. Then she stood just as a petite brunette woman bumped into their table. The brunette smiled up at Hannah with an ease that caused the sparks beneath Althea's skin to snuff out.

"Pity," Hannah said, not taking her eyes off the other girl.

Althea could do nothing but watch as the two melted into the crowd.

Dev dropped into Hannah's empty seat, slung an arm around Althea, and planted a sloppy kiss right on her temple. "Chin up, darling. It's not a true night at the cabaret without a little heartache."

"You know you're not as reassuring as you think you are."

Dev just laughed, a bright wind-chime sound, and hauled Althea up out of her chair and onto the dance floor, ignoring Althea's protests. "And you're not as dull as you think you are."

"Not. Reassuring," Althea repeated, but she couldn't help giggling as Dev spun her into a twirl before pulling her back in again.

Not a single person in the nightclub took any special notice of them. Well, maybe a few did because of Dev, but not because two women were dancing together.

Althea ended up pressed against Dev, only for a moment, but far more intimately than how Hannah's leg had brushed hers. And yet, despite Dev's indisputable beauty, Althea's palms didn't sweat, her heart didn't race. She felt happy, but the kind of happy that came from laughing with a new friend.

She couldn't stop herself from finding Hannah and her partner, her eyes locking with Hannah's across the crowded space. The brunette girl had melted into Hannah's arms, the roll of their bodies sensuous and mesmerizing.

The singer crooned something with a fast beat that was also melancholic, the brash trumpets and bluesy strings layering into her voice. The dancers partnered off, the driving rhythm impossible to ignore. The crowd joined in on the chorus, tables and chairs screeching against the floor as more came to the dance floor.

And through it all, Hannah held on to Althea's gaze. Slowly, ever so slowly, Hannah lifted her partner's wrist to her mouth and pressed her lips against the thin skin there.

Althea nearly felt the whisper of heat against her own wrist.

If you touch . . . you can feel a person's heart.

Chapter 16

New York City
May 1944

It had been a week since Viv had first gone to visit the banned books library in Brooklyn, and for some strange reason, she was nervous to return.

Maybe because she knew the librarian would make the perfect addition to her showdown with Taft, maybe because Viv knew she'd likely say no if asked to speak.

There was plenty of work Viv should be doing instead of traipsing to Brooklyn. She had only a little over two months to single-handedly pull off a massive press event. But every time she'd doubted herself in the past few days she'd thought of this place, of the librarian with fire in her voice.

Getting another dose of that could only be a good thing.

This time the librarian wasn't lost among the shelves; instead, she was helping a young woman at the desk, both their heads bent close to the book they had open.

Viv didn't mean to interrupt them, but when her heel scuffed the wood floor, both women's eyes flew up to meet hers, one pair full of panic, the other full of ice.

"Um," Viv murmured, plagued by the uncomfortable sensation of being a copper who had just stepped into a speakeasy.

In the next second, the young woman rushed by Viv, knocking into her in clear desperation to escape.

Viv stared after her, dismayed. When she turned back to the librarian, the woman's face was stone. "I'm so sorry. I don't . . ."

The librarian sighed, and closed the book they'd been engrossed in. "What can I help you with, Mrs. Childs?"

"I came at a bad time, I'm sorry," Viv tried again, annoyed with the universe for sending her here at just the wrong moment.

The librarian's eyes flicked to the door where her visitor had fled. "It can't be helped."

Viv sidled closer, trying to get a glimpse of the cover, but the librarian pulled it to her chest. A protective gesture.

And once again, Viv had the image of her as more than a librarian.

A guardian.

There was something so compelling about that idea that Viv hadn't been able to let it go, despite the fact that she had no right to ask this woman for a favor.

"Perhaps I can help you, instead," Viv suggested, wiping her palms on her smart red skirt before gesturing to the cart that sat next to the librarian. It was stacked high with books. "And we can talk more about the library."

"All right," the librarian said, a warmth that hadn't been there before settling into the corners of her eyes and mouth. "You push. And follow me."

Viv jumped to it, eagerly gripping the handles of the tan metal cart and shoving.

The books jostled but didn't topple off.

"Did you know it was not only novels burned that night in

Berlin?" the librarian said, as they started toward the back shelves. "Not many people realize that only a few days before the burnings, the students raided the Institut für Sexualwissenschaft." At Viv's confused silence, the librarian looked back over her shoulder and then translated. "The Institute of Sexual Studies."

Viv blushed. "Oh."

"They destroyed the place, which was conducting groundbreaking research on women, homosexuals, and sexual intermediaries," the librarian said, without a single tremor in her voice. Viv wanted to be as blasé, wanted to be sophisticated, but in the circles she moved in she had not once heard two of those words spoken out loud.

"Interesting," she managed.

"The vandals stole the bust of the founder Magnus Hirschfeld from the lobby of the institute and days later carried it as a war trophy to the burnings in Opernplatz," the librarian continued, either unaware of or ignoring Viv's awkwardness. "They burned much of his research, along with the only copies that existed. It set the world back decades."

And finally, Viv got over her own discomfort. "That's terrible."

The librarian stopped in front of the sections of books and slid the one she still had clutched to her chest back into place. Viv caught the author's name.

Hirschfeld.

Oh.

Women, homosexuals, and sexual intermediaries.

Viv pictured the young woman who'd been so startled by Viv's presence, and she pressed her own hand to her heart. "Oh."

"But as I said, words cannot be unwritten simply because you burn them. Ideas cannot simply be erased. People cannot be erased." The librarian touched the spine of the book gently, reverently, before moving on. "Burning books about things you do not like or understand does not mean those things no longer exist."

"What was it like, that night?" Viv asked in hushed tones, almost wishing she could have stopped herself. The librarian's attention was heavy on Viv's face, and she wondered what the woman was searching for.

Tacky curiosity, maybe?

Viv couldn't call her motives completely pure—she was still desperately searching for a story, one that would move audiences beyond their general apathy toward anything political—but she also couldn't deny she simply wanted to get to know this woman, hear about her experiences.

"Wet," the librarian finally said wryly, as she held out her hand for the next book.

Viv's laugh filled the space between them. "Was it?"

"The Nazis had trouble keeping the fires lit, actually." The corners of her mouth twitched in that way of hers that betrayed at least some amusement, mixed as it might be with cynicism. "They had to keep pouring gasoline on the stacks of books."

"But they managed eventually."

"Sometimes it's the ones they didn't burn that bother me more," the librarian mused, shelving a volume of Freud's research.

"What do you mean by that?"

The librarian shot her a look, again assessing. She was wary, this one, though Viv guessed she'd earned it.

"What do you think happens to the books of the Jewish people who are shipped to the concentration camps?" the librarian asked.

"I guess . . . I didn't think about it."

The librarian tipped her head. "Few do. The Nazis started

raiding the private libraries of Germany's Jewish citizens around the same time they needed to collect enough books to burn to make a spectacle. They never stopped."

"Raiding. Like how they did with the"—Viv struggled with the German—"Institut für Sexualwissenschaft?"

That earned her an almost smile. "Close enough. And yes. The storm troopers confiscated 'un-German' books from communist bookshops, lending libraries, private homes. There was an apartment building in Berlin in those days that housed and protected writers who were actively fighting against censorship. All five hundred units were searched and vandalized before the burnings."

"Have they simply been incinerating books this whole time?" Viv asked, tracing a fingertip over one of the nicer volumes on the cart, an ache in her chest at the thought of them as nothing but ash.

"I don't believe they have," the librarian said. "I think they are hoarding them instead. The barbarian bastards study them."

"Know thy enemy?" Viv asked softly.

The librarian nodded. "Nazis are portrayed in propaganda as ignorant anti-intellectuals. But the leaders know just how powerful knowledge is. That's why they want to control it so strictly."

Viv couldn't help but think of Taft, but she didn't want to derail the librarian with her problems.

"They have a national book club, did you know?" the librarian asked, dark humor once again slipping into her voice.

"The Nazis?" Viv didn't know why she was aghast, but she was. It certainly wasn't the most atrocious thing Hitler had done, but for some reason it felt like a violation.

"They had hundreds of thousands of members reading Goethe and Schiller, and any pro-German literature they wanted to send out." The librarian shook her head. "I suppose it's like your ASEs."

"No," Viv gasped out. "We're nothing like that. We don't have a political agenda."

The librarian leveled her with a dubious stare. "Everyone has a political agenda. I do apologize, though; that wasn't fair of me."

But Viv was now morbidly curious. "Who runs the book club?"

"Oh, Goebbels's Propaganda Ministry has a National Chamber of Literature." All at once the librarian's amusement blinked out as a shadow flicked across her expression. The walls were back up and Viv was left reeling a bit at the abrupt change.

Blindly, she shelved the last book and then stared at the empty cart.

"Well, I did very little to help you, Mrs. Childs."

With every bit of the sincerity she felt, Viv said, "You've done more than you know."

"You've said that before and I still don't believe you," the librarian mused as she made her way back to the front desk.

"I think there's something about this place—" *And you,* though Viv wisely kept that part to herself. "The mission, the history. I know our battles are so different, but when I come here, it just reminds me of why I'm fighting as hard as I am."

"The madmen might be loud, but we can be, as well. In our own way."

Viv grappled for another question that didn't have to do with asking the librarian to lay bare all her secrets on a stage in front of lawmakers and New York City's press corps. "What's your favorite book?"

"Favorite book," the librarian repeated, as she situated herself on the stool. "I think that's like picking a favorite moment in your life. Perhaps you could name one but that doesn't mean there aren't a hundred others nearly as worthy."

She continued before Viv could completely retract the question.

"I do have a comfort book, something I turn to when I want the sensation of warm tea on a snowy day."

"What is it?" Viv asked, eager for the answer.

"Christopher Morley's *Parnassus on Wheels,*" the librarian said with a soft smile, her eyes going a bit dreamy, a bit distant. "'When you sell a man a book you don't sell him just twelve ounces of paper and ink and glue—you sell him a whole new life. Love and friendship and humor and ships at sea by night—there's all heaven and earth in a book.'"

It was as if someone had taken Viv's life and bottled it into a simple quote. "I'll have to read it."

"I think you would find it interesting," the librarian said.

There was something final in her tone, and Viv decided to take her leave so as not to overstay her welcome. But before she stepped away, she pressed her luck. "And can I know your name?"

A part of her almost didn't want to know, the mystery part of the allure.

So she wasn't upset when the librarian studied her for a long moment and then tilted her head in that way of hers. "Perhaps another day."

Chapter 17

Paris
November 1936

The Library of Burned Books had transformed into a workshop of sorts for the upcoming exhibition against the Nazis.

The library's board members had agreed with Hannah and decided to print their own novel that represented the émigré community's version of the German ideal. But the plan had evolved into something even larger over the past week.

The library didn't simply want to counter the Nazis, they wanted to reach the people of Paris, as well. Maybe not the ones who were already hoping Hitler's agenda would spread into France, but those who weren't sure, who didn't know what was truth and what was lies.

Students and volunteers had turned the center table into a pamphlet-making factory, the library's board members huddled in chairs in the back to select the best materials to display in their rented exhibition space, and the rest of the staff was running errands more than they were shelving books.

Hannah didn't mind; the thrill of doing *something* to counter the hateful rhetoric that was sure to be on display was exhilarating.

The last time she had felt hope this sharp and urgent had been in the spring before Adam had been arrested.

Mr. Heinrich Mann, the president of the library, had tasked Hannah with visiting local booksellers and asking for their help in showcasing the best of German literature. Hannah's assignment was to persuade the shops to provide some copies free of charge, so they'd be available for curious people to browse through without the pressure of having to buy them.

Just as Hannah was shrugging into her coat, the bell over the door dinged. Lucien, from the violin store, stood there, his hands shoved in his pockets.

"Did you come to see me?" Hannah asked, both surprised and pleased. She hadn't had time to keep up with her normal distribution schedule, and she missed some of the people she visited.

Lucien's eyes darted around, his shoulders rounding as if he didn't want to be there. Hannah's excitement faded. This didn't seem like a social call.

"Do you have a moment?" he asked, and she glanced at the clock. Shakespeare and Company would be closing soon and she'd wanted to speak with Sylvia Beach today.

"Can we walk?"

He didn't speak until they were blocks away from the library, and she didn't push him. But she could see the worry in the crease of his brows, in the slant of his mouth.

"You're friends with Otto Koch, yes?" he finally asked when they turned into the Luxembourg Gardens.

"Yes."

"He's not hurt," Lucien rushed to reassure her, probably noting how tight her voice had gone. "He's been coming to my meetings."

Hannah didn't know why that surprised her, except that she'd assumed Otto was as gun-shy as her when it came to Resistance gatherings. He had been close with Adam, as well.

"You wouldn't be telling me this if something hadn't happened," she said as evenly as possible.

Again, he went quiet. It was times like these that she felt the cultural differences most acutely. Another German wouldn't have worried about shocking her or hurting her feelings. "Tell me."

"You said you had a brother who was detained by the Nazis," Lucien said, and Hannah dug her fingernails into her own palms to stop from reaching out and shaking the information from him.

"Yes."

"Otto is . . . he's talking like he's going to get himself in trouble in the same way," Lucien finally got out. "At first when he came to the meetings, he sat in the back, kept to himself. He's been more vocal as of late. And then last night, he started a fight with one of the men there." He paused, looked at her. "It was a physical fight, Hannah."

She exhaled a shaky breath. It wasn't good, but it could have been worse.

"I had to throw him out," Lucien said. "I told him not to come back."

They both knew what that meant. Otto might seek out a more radical group that would welcome his fiery temper and praise his passion rather than stifle it.

"I have others to think about," Lucien said, like he was pleading at her not to be angry with him. She realized she hadn't said anything in several long minutes.

"Of course, darling," Hannah said, stopping them both to hug him. She brushed her lips against his cheek to show they were still friends. This was her problem, not his. He had done what he needed to protect his group. "I will talk to him."

"Thank you," Lucien said, as if he had shrugged off a weight. He turned to leave but then paused and looked back. "We need the kind of fire that lives in him. But if we burn the world down to destroy the Nazis . . ."

Hannah finished his thought. "There will be no world left to live in when they're gone."

HANNAH STRUGGLED AWAKE, not sure what had plucked her out of her nightmare of beaten bodies and broken bones, but grateful to whatever it had been.

That was until she realized it was a pounding on the door far below her small third-story apartment.

Something dark twisted in her belly in premonition, and she kicked at her thin blankets, stumbled out of bed, and crossed to the window.

"Hannah." It was said on a sob. "Hannah."

Heartbroken, devastated. Despairing. "Otto, stop."

She'd said it as quietly as possible, but he seemed to hear her, his face tilting up, his eyes searching.

In the next moment, the door of the house swung open and Brigitte grabbed Otto by the collar of his jacket and shook him. Hannah knew Brigitte didn't care about propriety, but she could not stand being woken up in the middle of the night. Otto would be lucky to escape without a bruised eye.

Hannah shrugged into a dressing grown and then flew out onto the landing and down the steps.

"*Mademoiselle, je suis désolé, désolé,*" Hannah babbled in her terrible French. "Please. Please."

Something in her voice caught Brigitte's attention, and the landlady stopped shaking Otto in order to glare at Hannah. Then she began what Hannah could only imagine was a cursing out of a lifetime while still holding the sobbing Otto. Finally, she pushed him in Hannah's direction and retreated back inside.

As long as nothing in that had been about eviction, Hannah decided to take the verbal slap as the best she could have asked for in this situation.

"Otto, darling, what am I to do with you?" she asked mostly to herself, because Otto was still caught up in his own emotional turmoil. She wrapped an arm around his waist and hauled him up the three flights of stairs, her arms aching by the time she reached her room.

Hannah maneuvered him so that when she let go he toppled onto her bed.

He stared up at her, his soulful eyes red-rimmed, his chin quivering as he tried to get control of himself. Hannah sat beside his shoulder and pet his hair. She tried not to remember Lucien's warning from earlier that day but couldn't help it.

Using the same voice as she would for a sick child, she asked, "What happened, darling?"

"I hate them." Here was that fire, so beautiful and yet so deadly.

"I know," Hannah said gently, as she tugged affectionately at one of his curls.

"They took everything from us," Otto said, not on a wail, but a whisper. It scared her more, that new determination in his voice. "Everything."

"Not our lives," Hannah reminded him.

"That's only because we are the lucky ones," Otto said on a sigh. "The lucky few."

Hannah nodded. Neither of them had to mention Adam.

"What happened, darling?" Hannah asked again. Because this was well-trodden ground. And despite Otto smelling like a distillery, it wasn't just the alcohol that had turned him newly maudlin.

He felt so much of the world sometimes. The joys of it, but also its cruelties. Still, in the past few months it seemed to have become worse, these wild emotions fueled by his drinking and what she suspected was occasional drug use, as well. She hadn't wanted to see it until Lucien forced her to, though.

She should have stepped in earlier, should have intervened. But she hadn't wanted the fight. Just getting through the day was exhausting enough, sometimes.

Now, Otto smiled, meeting her eyes. Then he pulled his shirt out of his trousers, lifting it enough to reveal slim hip bones. And the metal grip of a pistol.

Hannah's inhale caught, rough and painful, at the back of her throat. "Otto, no."

"I've made friends."

"Not the right ones if they're giving you weapons," Hannah said, hearing the crack in her voice that she hated. But all she could see was Adam's face when he spoke about his plans to destroy a Nazi building in Berlin. There had been a fervor, a light that she knew she wouldn't ever be able to dim with logic and careful warnings. She could see the same thing in Otto's eyes now, even as watery as they were.

"I told them about the exhibition," Otto continued as if she had said nothing. "They see it coming, too, Hannah. The war. They *know* like we do."

"Getting yourself shot by Nazis is going to do nothing to stop it," Hannah said, barely able to speak beyond the sharp, piercing wail in her head. She had to think, had to stop this.

"Maybe it will," Otto said. "Maybe it will make Paris wake up. And see them for the barbarians they are."

"No." Hannah gripped Otto's hands, her own clammy. "No, Otto. You know the Nazis, you know what they'll do if you kill one of them. They'll take it out on the Jews at home. You know they will. They'll make the victim a martyr of Jewish violence."

"We will never convince the Nazis of anything," Otto said, sounding far more lucid now. "It's not our job to convince them. We have to convince the world."

"Your friends are using you, Otto," Hannah said. "They want to cause trouble. This is anarchy, this won't convince anyone."

"Is anarchy so bad, then?" Otto asked. "When the other option is Hitler?"

Hannah pressed her lips together to stop herself from arguing. He wouldn't be convinced, not in this state. "Tell me about them. Your friends."

He squinted at her as if sensing a trap. But he was too practiced at sharing things with Hannah to stop himself now. "They're forming a Resistance group already. They want to have one established, have codes and safehouses already set up, before the Germans come."

"They are so certain of this?" Hannah asked despite being perhaps the loudest voice of those she knew about the inevitability of war. She was so used to being dismissed, though, that it felt suspicious for others to recognize what was going on.

"They are playwrights and theater actors, they have ties to people in Germany. They've seen what we've seen. They *know.*" He repeated that last bit several times until it slurred a little.

Hannah tried to keep her voice level when she asked, "And they want you to bring that pistol to the book exhibition?"

"I asked them for it," Otto said, again fierce and stubborn. "They didn't have to convince me, I asked them for it."

"All right, darling," Hannah cooed now, petting his hair once more. In the morning. She would talk to him in the morning. Make him see sense.

Otto's eyes slipped closed at her gentle ministrations, his breathing evening out.

The sky began to lighten by the time Hannah made up her mind, the rays creeping across her well-worn carpet. Slowly, just as slowly as Otto had done hours earlier, Hannah lifted up his shirt, her eyes locked on his face. When he didn't stir, she tugged at the grip of the pistol with two fingers, loath to actually touch the thing.

Once she got it free of his trousers, Hannah wrapped it in an old shawl. Then she kneeled by her closet, her hand searching for the notch she had to push to get the floorboard to lift up. She found it and as quietly as she could dropped the weapon into the darkness below.

Chapter 18

Berlin
February 1933

Dev urged Althea along faster, casting glances over her shoulder as the night settled around them. The caution struck Althea as strange since Dev never seemed aware that they were women alone in a city.

Tonight, though, she was clearly on edge.

"What's wrong?" Althea asked, skipping every few steps to keep up with Dev's long legs and her worried pace.

"I want to show you something," Dev said, a familiar reprise now. Althea had lost count of the number of times Dev had turned up at her door with that sentiment since they'd met three weeks ago.

I want to show you something could be anything from a bawdy act at a nightclub to a painting in one of the galleries on Museum Island to a particularly lively street band that had set up in the Tiergarten. Althea had seen more of the city on Dev's arm than she would have fit in during her entire residency had she relied on Diedrich only.

Althea had never really had a friend before. She loved her

brother, and he would drop anything the moment she needed something. But Althea's friends had always been found in the pages of books, or in her own work. A closeness she could only imagine and had clearly never gotten quite right.

Now that Dev had breezed into her life, making her presence known in every corner of it, Althea fully realized how much she'd been missing.

She bumped lightly into Dev when the other woman stopped. Without any further warning, Dev grabbed hold of Althea's wrist and yanked her into the closest alleyway. From there they walked at an even faster clip, dumping into the street and then ducking into the shadows again.

A breathless five minutes later, Dev pushed through the door of a nondescript café. There was no name on the sign or the door beyond a drawing of a cup of coffee. Yet Dev didn't even hesitate.

It was a quiet Monday night and most of the shop reflected that, a few solo patrons scattered at the small tables. But in the back was a group of men and women around Althea's age or younger. They had about four tables pushed together, with chairs shoved into every space, mugs and cups and even a few glasses of wine scattered all over. One of the young men was standing, clearly holding court, gesticulating with the air of a Shakespearean actor.

When he caught sight of Dev he cried out a greeting and quickly crossed the room to enfold her in a hug.

Dev was laughing by the time he let go and turned to Althea, who shifted back so as not to risk the same welcome. She was getting used to meeting new people all the time, but she did not have any interest in being scooped up by this strange man.

He took the hint easily, simply grinning at her. "Well, hello."

The man had the eyes of a puppy, liquid brown and big enough to be deployed to get what he wanted at all times. His flushed cheeks and tousled brown hair added to the sense of breathless excitement that poured off him in waves.

Althea found herself wanting to follow him wherever he would lead. She had read about characters who inspired that kind of immediate devotion but had never met one in real life.

"Althea, you know Hannah," Dev said, with perhaps more innuendo than Althea appreciated. "Well, this is Mr. Brecht."

For one gut-punched moment, Althea thought that meant he was Hannah's husband. Her eyes shifted to the group, searching to see if Hannah was among them. Althea caught sight of her, watching them. She quirked a brow at Althea's attention.

"Hannah's brother," the man clarified, and Althea could breathe again. Though, she noted, Dev looked too self-satisfied for that not to have been on purpose. "Please, though, I hear you are friends with Dev and Hannah, and I don't stand on formalities with friends. You must call me Adam."

The group shouted equally enthusiastic welcomes to Dev, as everyone shifted and budged and grabbed extra chairs. And somehow when all the bustle settled down, Althea found herself pressed up against Hannah once more.

She was dressed down today, which made sense considering the other times Althea had seen her had been at nightclubs. But she looked equally beautiful in her high-waisted trousers and plum-colored sweater, her hair tucked back in a rolled bun that emphasized her features as much as the touch of rouge did.

She smelled of oranges, fresh linen, and cigarette smoke, a scent Althea was beginning to learn was distinctly Hannah's.

"Welcome to our study group," Hannah murmured, as Adam commandeered his audience's attention once more.

"Study group?"

Hannah winked. "*Les Misérables* today."

Althea knew she was missing something, but just then Adam stomped one foot on the chair, his arms spread wide.

"'There are people who observe the rules of honor as we do the stars, from a very long way off,'" he projected, as if onstage. The girl at the counter of the shop rolled her eyes, but there was a smile at the edges of her mouth. The few other patrons in the café ignored the group, but no one seemed overly disturbed. "'It is nothing to die. It is frightful not to live.'"

"Is he just reciting random quotes?" Althea asked Hannah in a whisper. "Those do not go together."

Hannah's eyes widened and then her mouth pinched tight. Althea thought she might have offended her. But then she realized Hannah's shoulders were trembling, a smile trying to escape her tight control. In the end, Hannah lost her fight and laughed. It was a quiet, husky thing that suited her, and Althea immediately wanted to hear it again.

To be the one to make it happen.

"Oh my," Hannah said, dabbing her knuckle against the corner of her eye. "Please don't ever let Adam hear you, you'd crush his soul. He thinks his speeches are the height of inspiration."

"To be fair, his audience does seem inspired," Althea said. Everyone in the group was leaning forward as if to get closer to Adam, his enthusiasm, his magnetism, his youthful vigor. She was struck by the difference between the siblings, how bright Adam was in contrast to Hannah's coolness. The sun and the moon. "But it does make one curious if they actually read the book."

Hannah snorted out another quiet laugh, went to say something, and then touched Althea's thigh. "Wait, wait, this is the best part."

At this point, Adam was *on* the chair, his hands held out in front of him. "'Even the darkest night will end.'"

Althea knew the quote but was surprised when some of the others around the table rose, fists in the air, as they chanted back in unison, "'And the sun will rise.'"

A cheer went up as Adam jumped back down to the floor and began slapping those closest to him on their shoulders, accepting handshakes and hugs from others.

When Althea threw a startled look to Hannah, the woman had tears of mirth in her eyes. "They are very young and very earnest sometimes. It is sweet but also . . ."

She didn't finish, but she didn't need to, Althea was already nodding. Generally, she recoiled from anyone who took themselves too seriously. It was the first thing that had turned her off from some of the society ladies she'd met with Diedrich. She couldn't relate to someone who called Hitler their *little wolf* with no sense of irony.

But the atmosphere was different here, in this warm little café, where everyone seemed ready to march to the barricade to fight for liberty. It *was* sweet, but it also made Althea feel old and cynical.

She couldn't ignore the warmth that bloomed in her, though, that Hannah seemed to share the sentiment.

"Is this really a study group?" Althea asked, even though she was sure she sounded silly.

Hannah chewed on her lip, her eyes flicking between Althea, Dev, and Adam, then back to Althea.

"You're worried I'll tell my 'Nazi masters,'" Althea guessed. "I won't."

"Dev seems to trust you," Hannah said as an answer. "But how much does trust mean beneath the Nazis?"

Part of Althea wanted to leave merely to escape more political talk. It was all everyone wanted to discuss, and she didn't want to disappoint Hannah any further by spouting the wrong ideas. She just wished she knew what those were.

Althea looked away from Hannah, scanning the group once more, the happy faces, the comfortable press of bodies as if there was no need for personal space, the shared—*joy* wasn't quite the right word, but maybe *eagerness*. "I wouldn't want any of you to be hurt."

That, Hannah seemed to believe. She stubbed her cigarette out in the misshapen ashtray in front of them and sighed. "Nazis have taken to raiding political meetings held by anyone but them. They beat anyone there bloody and arrest at least half of them."

"What?" Althea breathed out.

"That's if the brutes don't murder them outright," Hannah said, her voice calm as if she were talking about the weather.

"They can't just murder . . ."

"Herr Göring has control of Prussia's law enforcement," Hannah said, again not like she was trying to convince Althea but like these were just the facts of life now. "Murders aren't even reported there. So now we don't know how many of the Nazis' political enemies have been killed, but we do know it's only going to get worse." Hannah waved at the crowd and then some of the copies of *Les Misérables* on the table. "So, we're a study group of local university students."

Althea glanced around at the others in the shop, and Hannah seemed to read the question in her suddenly tense shoulders.

"We're safe here." Hannah paused, and then added, "For now."

Before Althea could press any further, Adam good-naturedly shoved the man next to Hannah off his chair and took it himself.

With his sweat-damp hair and the fire in his eyes, he could have indeed stepped from the pages of Hugo's book.

"I read your novel," he said, leaning forward on the table so he could give Althea his full attention.

"Did you?" Hannah cut in, and then immediately pressed her lips together like she hadn't meant to show interest.

"I did." He shot his sister a lopsided grin. "You may borrow it if you ask very nicely."

"Scamp."

"I found it fascinating," Adam said, turning back to Althea, and all she heard in his voice was earnest truth. Some of Diedrich's friends had belittled her work, scoffed that she could write only in English, or made snide comments about her spending her time on something as *frivolous* as fiction. "And it was your first novel. How very impressive."

"It was my twenty-fifth novel," Althea admitted, with a sheepish smile. "It was the first to be published."

"Never say so," Dev said from behind her. Althea had almost forgotten the other woman was there, so caught up as she was in the Brecht siblings. "I thought you were plucked out of obscurity."

"That part's true, I suppose," Althea said, scooting back to include Dev in the conversation. Otto Koch, who was sprawled out in a chair on Dev's other side, also leaned in, and Althea tried not to get tongue-tied by the attention. "It was a fluke, really. My now editor's train broke down outside our tiny town and he stayed in the room above my brother's pub."

Althea knew it was a good story. Her publisher had used it to sell the book, her editor smug about finding a diamond covered in the sea guts of a tiny fishing town.

"I used to publish serialized mysteries in our local paper

because there really wasn't much else to fill up its pages. My brother kept copies of them in the room so the guests had something to read," Althea continued. "My editor read the whole series and then hunted down the previous ones. By the next day he was demanding to know who I was and if I had any unpublished work he could read."

"Next thing you know, you're a literary star," Dev announced the obvious conclusion.

"I haven't quite adjusted," Althea said, an understatement. They all laughed even though it hadn't been a joke. "I think my editor liked the idea of discovering me more than he liked the book itself, so he wanted the novel to be successful. That's really all it took."

"And it made it all the way to Goebbels's desk," Adam said, shaking his head, still wearing that easy smile. She saw the physical similarities with Hannah now, though Hannah's expression was hardly ever so friendly and open.

"I'm not quite sure how that happened," she admitted, and the others exchanged glances.

"The Nazis like their ancestry lists," Adam eventually said. "I hear you aren't sure about the current state of our politics."

The probing was gentler than Hannah's, but more straightforward than Dev's.

"I confess, I don't know if I have the mind for it," Althea said, staring at the table to avoid all their eyes. "I never paid much attention back home."

"Must be nice to be able to choose ignorance," a pocket-sized woman with a shaggy pixie cut said as she plopped herself in Adam's lap. He pressed a kiss into the corner of her mouth and then nuzzled against her cheek, and once again Althea was reminded of a puppy.

Hannah's expression had gone both fond and amused at the sight of them together.

"Hello, Cl—"

Hannah's greeting cut off abruptly when the woman kicked Hannah's thigh.

"Names are need-to-know only. Just because you all believe this little mouse isn't going to go squeaking back to the Schutzstaffel doesn't mean you have to get all of us killed."

"I wouldn't . . . ," Althea started, recognizing the name for the men in black shirts who acted as security for Hitler. It was then, though, that Althea realized the woman had ink smeared on her palms, her wrists, the men's trousers she wore, the open vest as well. "Are you printing something?"

The woman simply glared.

"Don't mind her," Adam said, and Althea noticed he didn't use the woman's name. He'd respected her wishes. "She gets cranky when we get close to deadline."

"Deadline?"

"The Nazis have shut down most opposition newspapers," Adam said, the woman's hand jerking toward his mouth like she wanted to physically stop him from answering. "If we want anyone to see the atrocities they're committing we have to print our own in secret."

"'Secret' being the operative word there," the pocket-sized woman huffed and then removed herself from Adam's lap. "I have to get back, I just wanted to say hello."

"Be safe," Adam said, taking her hand and pressing a kiss to the palm, regardless of the ink there.

Althea's stomach swooped as she remembered the cabaret, the way Hannah had brought a girl's wrist to her mouth in a similar gesture. All while watching Althea.

She chanced a quick look only to find Hannah staring at her, amused. Always amused by Althea, it seemed. Yet the laughter didn't feel jagged like she'd experienced when she was younger. Instead, it seemed to wrap around Althea, the edges soft and welcoming.

"I'm not the one who needs to be reminded to be safe," the woman said with one last pointed glare at Althea.

"I didn't ask to come," Althea muttered so that only Hannah could hear.

"That's Dev for you," Hannah said. "She likes you, and thinks she knows you better than you know yourself."

"That wouldn't be hard," Althea said, and Hannah's mouth twisted into a wry smile.

"She also thought Adam . . ."

Hannah trailed off, but Althea guessed at the rest of it. Adam had the personality to persuade someone sitting on the fence. It was partly the way he looked at you like you were the only person in the room. It was partly that he'd read her book to better connect with her. It was partly just an innate charm that few could ever hope to replicate.

"Tell me," Hannah said, this time at normal volume. "Do you still think we're just a different kind of monster than the Nazis?"

All of a sudden, Althea held the attention of everyone who had heard the question. And that turned out to be about half the crowd.

Obviously, if what they claimed was true, the Nazis were abhorrent barbarians who murdered their political opponents in order to seize total power for themselves. But the Nazis said the same thing about these people.

Not all information was equal, though, nor was its source. She thought about the Nazis she met, their supporters, the mean-spirited superiority that was laced into so many conversations. Thought about Helene talking about so-called real Germans, about Diedrich's dismissive comments anytime Althea mentioned particular authors.

Then she thought about the way she'd been embraced by this group, the open-minded curiosity in which they viewed the world, the kindness they showed toward people who were different and a little odd and had probably been excluded all their lives just like Althea had been.

The silence had dragged on too long, expressions wilting, closing off. Althea hated it. She didn't know why she was so resistant to think of her hosts as evil. A tiny part of her guessed it was because she didn't know what that would say about her. The Nazis had found her, after all, invited her here. Something about her appealed to them enough to pay for her to come all the way to Germany.

And she didn't want to acknowledge that.

She opened her mouth to say something, a denial, an explanation, a plea, she didn't know.

But it didn't matter.

The door of the shop slammed open. A young man stood there, panting, hands on his thighs, his face red.

The café went dead silent, and a shiver ran along Althea's skin.

When the man finally straightened, he delivered his news in a voice laced with fear. "The Reichstag is on fire."

Chapter 19

Paris

November 1936

Hannah shelved the last book on the return cart—Remarque's *All Quiet on the Western Front*—and stretched. It had been a long day at the Library of Burned Books, the exhibition on the boulevard Saint-Germain now a little more than a week away.

She returned to the desk she had been manning, instinctively glancing at the picture that hung across from it, a photograph of Goebbels presiding over the pyres in Berlin three years prior. Whenever she was in the building she made herself look at it. Once, Hannah had asked why they kept that evil man on their walls—just like she'd asked why they kept those evil men on the shelves—and had been told it had been a decision made by founder Alfred Kantorowicz himself.

So that no one ever forgot the library's purpose.

The time and distance that came with history had a way of letting people forget.

"You should get some rest, Miss Brecht," Mr. Mann said from behind her.

She turned to study his own exhausted face. As the library's president, he was working even more than the rest of them. She couldn't help the question that slipped out. "Do you think we'll make a difference?"

His silence was thoughtful rather than offended.

"I suppose it's like the library itself, isn't it? It matters that the Nazis see the whole world isn't standing beside them," he finally said. "It matters that there are Resistance efforts and that they see those. Even if they're small. Even if they don't accomplish anything other than showing those people they are not the only voice in the world."

"In Germany they're the only voice that can be heard," she said, bitter with the knowledge.

"But not in Paris," Mr. Mann said with a decisive nod, and she clung to his optimism all the way home.

Brigitte stopped Hannah before she got to the stairs of her apartment with a barked out "Mail."

The landlady had been even more terse than usual since Otto's scene, but she hadn't booted Hannah out, and for that Hannah was grateful.

She took the envelope with a tentative smile. Then she saw the priority stamp.

Her knees buckled and Brigitte's shout of concern registered only dimly over the pounding in her ears.

She ripped at the paper, terrified she would shred it but unable to wait the second longer it would take to be careful.

The letters blurred, but she saw Johann's signature at the bottom and she knew.

Hannah pressed the heels of her hands into her eyes before trying once more to make the words make sense.

Adam's trial was a sham. They held it on Nov. 2, 1936, and he was executed the next day. I am sorry, Hannah. My thoughts are with you and your family.

A low, keening cry filled the vestibule and only when Brigitte lightly slapped Hannah's face did she realize it was coming from her.

"*Je suis désolé,*" Hannah managed, swiping at her eyes with her fingertips. "*Je suis—*"

Her words cut off with a sob so unlike her that Hannah scared herself. Brigitte tsked, and then hauled Hannah up beneath her armpits, hustling her into the small apartment on the main floor.

Brigitte wrapped a blanket around her shoulders and then shoved a cup of whiskey-laced tea in her hands. It burned going down, the world regaining its sharp edges when the drink hit her stomach.

Her pulse still pounded in her ears, but the nausea had receded to a bearable amount.

"Your lover?" Brigitte asked.

Pressing the letter into herself as if she could feel Adam's heartbeat in the dead wood and glue, Hannah shook her head. "Brother."

"Ah." Brigitte forwent the pretense of tea and poured more liquor straight from her flask. "May his memory be a blessing," she said, in near-perfect English. She tapped the edge of her cup against Hannah's.

At Hannah's questioning look, Brigitte shrugged. "I have Jewish lovers. I have English lovers."

They sat in a silence that was comforting. Hannah didn't feel rushed to make her legs move.

She had known Adam's fate the moment he had been arrested,

and she'd mourned for the past three years. It had almost felt cruel that they kept him alive, torturing him. More often than not when she thought of him, she pictured how he'd been that day in the detention center's visiting room, with the Nazi guards looming over all of them.

Hannah and her parents had brought him his favorite cake, a pair of socks, a deck of cards, which had probably all been confiscated, but what else could they have done?

Even bruised, with a split lip and newly gaunt cheeks, Adam had tried to smile. Had tried to *comfort* them. In the years before his arrest, Hannah had teased him mercilessly—as siblings did—about his optimism. And yet she'd never told him how much he inspired her.

She was a woman with many regrets in her life, but that was one of the biggest. He should have known—known how hard it was to look around a cold and barren world and see not hate and death and destruction but possibility.

For once, Hannah pictured him not in that room, but before, on that very first night some fire had lit behind his eyes. It had been in the summer of 1930, after the chancellor at the time had enacted emergency decrees that let him pass laws without the approval of the Reichstag. Adam had always been passionate, a natural leader, inquisitive, and clever if not book smart. But he hadn't found the right outlet for it until then.

What can we do? Hannah had asked him, sure the answer would be *Nothing.*

Something, anything, he'd said. *It is not failure we should fear but inaction.*

She decided that was how she would picture him from now on, convinced that if he wanted to live in a better world he had to help it become what he believed it could be.

"I knew it was coming," Hannah told Brigitte. "His execution."

"Doesn't mean it doesn't hurt," Brigitte said, sipping straight from the flask. "We know too much death already. And the sad thing? It's only the beginning, I believe."

"An intermission," Hannah offered. That's where they were living. The Great War may have completed its first act, but it wasn't over. And she knew it would continue to claim the lives of its audience for years to come.

"Let's pray there's no encore," Brigitte muttered.

Eventually Hannah was able to gather the strength to make it up the stairs. She lingered by the mezuzah longer than normal, and when she kissed her fingertips she thought of Adam. *May his memory be a blessing,* Brigitte had said. In Jewish tradition, that meant it was the responsibility of those who remembered the deceased to carry on his goodness.

Hannah had been viewing her work with the library as the antithesis of what Adam had done, but maybe his work had never been far from her own.

It mattered that the Nazis saw the whole world wasn't standing with them.

Tomorrow, she would distribute flyers for the book exhibition, shelve the novels the Nazis didn't want read, toil alongside the people so many were being taught to hate.

Tonight may be for grief.

But tomorrow, tomorrow and every day after that, she would carry on Adam's goodness.

Chapter 20

New York City
May 1944

Viv glanced up from her position on the floor when Edith Stone, a librarian who worked with the council on ASE book selections, popped her head into Viv's office.

"*Strange Fruit* was approved for one of next year's series. As long as you win against Taft," Edith said. "Which you will."

Viv looked up and pumped her fist in the air. "You're a gift from heaven. You knew I needed a victory, didn't you?"

Strange Fruit, a novel about an interracial romance in the South, had been published back in February and had since then been banned in Boston and Detroit. Earlier in May, the United States Postal Office had tried to join that bandwagon. The decision had been reversed after Eleanor Roosevelt herself had intervened, but the book remained a controversial topic.

Edith had made the novel her pet project, arguing that the boys overseas would love it. Besides stories that reminded them strongly of home—like *A Tree Grows in Brooklyn* and *Chicken Every Sunday*—their next favorites tended to be about, well, sex. Sex and scandal and anything that combined the two.

"Fill me in on the Taft brouhaha," Edith directed as she took a seat across from Viv.

"Well, I've made a very extensive to-do list," Viv said, half-joking, half-serious, "and get very overwhelmed every time I look at it."

"Let me help," Edith said, leaning forward as if she were going to start grabbing papers at random.

"You're overworked as it is," Viv protested. All of their volunteers were, but the librarians like Edith who had other jobs, as well, were stretched particularly thin. "I'll get it all done, I just . . ."

"What's your goal?" Edith asked when Viv trailed off. She waved a hand as Viv stared at her, confused. "I know your ultimate goal. But with the actual day itself. What's your goal?"

"To make people care," Viv said without missing a beat.

"So how are you going to do that?" Edith pressed.

"Well, first they need to hear about it," Viv said. She tapped the papers on her desk. "I'm going to contact the big daily newspapers across the country, especially ones that have written articles about our program before. Then I also have a list of papers in districts of lawmakers who Taft finds influential." Another favor owed to Hale. "I've written up a letter explaining the situation to each and inviting them to cover the event."

"That sounds like a good start. What else?"

"I have a friend at the *New York Times* who may be able to help get better placement for any articles there," Viv said.

"So your press coverage is sorted," Edith said. "What else do you need to do?"

"Set the guest list and arrange the speaker lineup." And that's where things started getting tricky. Calling reporters and securing articles and opinion pieces was second nature to her now, having always been part of her main responsibilities as the council's publicity director. Crafting the day of the event was different. Important.

"I could help with the invitations to the volunteers," Edith nudged, and Viv shot her a grateful smile.

"That would be lovely," Viv said, trying to ignore the guilty pinch in her chest. This was her crusade, and she hated dragging others into it knowing how unlikely they were to win this fight. "I want to make a splash with the guest list. Big names, political donors, the like. I want every single congressman to realize that this issue will affect their campaign funds."

"Sure, and I want a million dollars," Edith joked. "How exactly are you going to get Millionaire's Row to turn out to an event about a free book program?"

"Charlotte," Viv said with a wicked grin. "She's my secret weapon."

"Ah, the mother-in-law." Edith nodded knowingly. "The rare but mighty ally."

"Charlotte has pull with anyone in the city who has deep enough pockets to spend on political campaigns." Viv grabbed a pen and scrawled a note on her to-do list. "That reminds me, I should send the gossip columnists an invitation as well. It's going to be *the* event of the summer."

"Who would have thought an event about censorship would be something to draw out the gossipmongers," Edith said. She had no patience for such frivolous things, but they both knew that those society ladies were powerful.

"Well, that brings me to my biggest problem," Viv admitted.

"Which is?"

"I don't have my hook yet," Viv said. "Something that makes people care about our cause. Having the same old supporters preach to the choir isn't going to make waves. I could invite Roosevelt himself to the event, but if I don't bring out some kind of big gun, everyone will forget about the whole thing the next day."

"There have been plenty of complimentary articles and editorials written about our program already and it has yet to be enough to get Taft to budge."

"Precisely," Viv said. "I need something shocking and interesting, something people won't be able to look away from."

"What speakers can you count on?" Edith asked, pursing her lips, her eyes a bit distant. "Will any of them be a particular draw?"

"Betty Smith said she'd be happy to come," Viv said.

"A coup." Edith knew as well as Viv that *A Tree Grows in Brooklyn* was such a popular novel that they were going to send it out a second time as an ASE. "But she's been outspoken from the start."

"Right. And a few others, not as big," Viv said. "Some army officials are going to talk as well, and maybe a few soldiers."

"But . . . ," Edith prompted.

"The people who will show up for Betty Smith and some injured men are already the type to write their congressman in support of the ASEs," Viv said. "I just don't think they'll cut through all the noise of the rest of the news out there."

She thought about the librarian, the way she'd said, *I was in Berlin on the night of the burnings.* Maybe that would be enough. People were fascinated with what life was like as the Nazis rose to power. If the librarian would speak about her time in Germany it *could* warrant the coverage Viv was lining up.

Edith interrupted that thought. "Do you know of Althea James?"

"Who doesn't?" The woman was legendary for her solitude. She'd written two of the bestselling novels of the past two decades but had not given a single interview about either of them. The fact that she was a hermit made her all the more appealing to her audience. Everyone wanted to know exactly who Althea James was. And no one was ever granted access. Viv didn't even know what the woman looked like, and she doubted she was alone in that.

"Have you read her books?" Edith asked.

"Not yet," Viv said, a little ashamed. "But we're offering the second one as part of the ASE list in the fall. That is if I get Taft to rescind his amendment."

"*An Inconceivable Dark,*" Edith supplied the title absently. "It's all about censorship."

"Is it really?" Viv asked, swiveling on her chair as if a copy would miraculously appear in her office.

"Yes, and it made her more famous than her first one—"

"*The Unfractured Light,*" Viv said.

"Yes, I think you'd like that one." Edith was Viv's most trusted person for recommendations, so Viv made an immediate note to read the book. "It's about the Civil War. One family with sons and daughters on different sides of the Mason-Dixon line. It's quite . . ."

"Bleak?" Viv guessed.

Edith shook her head as she searched for the right word. "Naive. But hopeful."

"And you think I would like it?" Viv asked, trying not to be insulted.

"Don't pretend you're not a marshmallow on the inside."

"Slander," Viv accused. "And the second book?"

"Darker. I remember many of the reviewers commented on the tone change," Edith said. "It's quite striking."

"This was before the war?" Viv asked and Edith nodded. "Then it wouldn't have been what influenced her new tone."

"Maybe something personal." Edith shrugged. "But the book itself is set as a trial. A local school board is being sued to have a certain scandalous book removed from the curriculum because it was written by a former slave."

"A real book?"

"No." Edith shook her head. "But the whole thing was rather grim. No fairy-tale ending, no knight coming in to save the day. It was . . ." She paused. "Brutal. Aching, even. A lesson about good fights and the ways that they are often lost anyway."

"Well, that sounds familiar," Viv muttered, then realized what she'd just said. She perked up. "And perfect."

"She would certainly be a big draw if you could get her to agree to attend," Edith said. "People would be elbowing their way to the front of the line if they could say they'd seen *the* Althea James in person."

Viv's pulse ticked up, a buzz settling in beneath her skin. This was it. She could feel it. A famous recluse who'd written about the very topic Viv was championing.

"She wouldn't ever say yes, though, would she?" Viv asked, meeting Edith's steady gaze, knowing her own was wide-eyed and dazed with possibilities.

"I don't know. But you know what, Viv?" Edith tapped a nail against her chin, thoughtful. "I'm starting to learn not to bet against you when you want something. Her publisher is Harper & Brothers, by the way."

Viv stood, rounded the desk, and placed a loud, noisy kiss on Edith's cheek. "You are a queen."

"And don't you forget it."

Althea James. It might be a long shot, but so was this whole fight. And if they were going to lose, this was one way to at least go down swinging.

Chapter 21

Berlin
March 1933

Althea had never before heard the distinct sound of a whip flaying layers of flesh from bone.

The leather cracked in the air, cutting through the wails and the thunk of knuckles against bone.

At first, she didn't understand what she was seeing.

Flying fists and blurs of motion for a brief moment reminded Althea of the marchers on their way to the Chancellery. But there were no wide smiles here in this small square in an unremarkable neighborhood in the middle of Berlin.

Her vision blurred with tears even before she was able to fully grasp the horror of the scene in front of her. She swiped at them ruthlessly and tried to catch her breath.

Too many bodies to count lay unconscious on the ground, blood smeared on their faces, limbs twisted in strange angles, whimpers that sounded closer to those of wounded animals than humans slipping beneath the vicious curses.

A handful of men were still engaged in the brawl, hurling obscenities at each other. Though there was a mix of brownshirts and civilians involved, none of the men on the ground wore a uniform.

Althea's hand pressed down a sob, forcing it back so she didn't draw any attention to herself.

A Saint Andrew's cross had been placed in the center of the square, the man tied to it slumped so that his wrists bore his weight. His back, which faced the crowd, was so torn that there seemed to be no skin left to protect him from the barbaric weapon.

A woman on her knees by his feet sobbed. "Please, no more," she said. "No more. No more."

Not a single trace of mercy could be found in the expression of the brownshirt standing over both of them. Without hesitating, the man brought the stinging end of his whip down on exposed muscle and blood.

The spatter flecked the officer's boots, the woman's face. The man on the cross didn't cry, didn't yell. He was unconscious.

Or dead.

"They're Bolsheviks, dear," a middle-aged woman next to Althea whispered. "You're wasting your tears on them."

The nonchalance with which the words were said sent Althea rocking back on her heels. She took one, two steps away from the woman. Then her elbow connected with someone behind her.

She whirled and met the stony stare of a brownshirt, whose thin lips pursed, his eyes assessing. Hastily, she dropped her gaze, her arms numb with the idea of being dragged out into that violence.

The man didn't waste time on Althea, though. His attention shifted past her shoulder and then returned to the person he'd been hauling behind him. The woman's head was shaved, and around her neck hung a sign: RACE BETRAYER.

The sunlight caught the gold of the woman's wedding band as she passed, her eyes sliding over Althea with pure hatred, pure contempt. It burned in every newly hollowed-out part of Althea's body.

Then the brownshirt dragged her along, and Althea became just one more face in a crowd of bystanders who weren't doing a single thing to stop this.

The woman was thrown to the ground, but she didn't sprawl out, didn't end up in an undignified heap. Instead, she was all contained fury, her body tight, nearly vibrating with rage. Her chin tipped up in defiance as a glob of saliva landed just short of the brownshirt's boots.

Althea feared her and loved her and couldn't even look at her in that moment, so deep was her own shame. Had this been a book she was writing, Althea would have charged into the square, stood in front of the woman, and faced down her abuser, no matter the consequences. In real life, Althea stood in shadows and watched.

Within the next heartbeat, the brownshirt backhanded the woman.

"What did she do?" Althea breathed out and the older woman from earlier leaned in, seemingly not put off by Althea's disgust.

"She married a Jew," came the simple answer.

Althea nearly retched into the street.

The woman with the shaved head had pushed herself back onto her knees, graceful beyond measure, a thin line of blood trickling from the corner of her mouth.

In the end, it wasn't the blood or the bruises, the destroyed flesh or the broken bones that had Althea turning away. It was the look on that woman's face.

Her hands shaking, tears sliding hot down her cheeks, Althea stumbled toward the alley, her legs nearly giving out, nearly taking her into the sewage where she thought she might belong.

Dirty. That's how she felt. Like she could scrub and scrub and scrub with scalding hot water and not ever be clean again.

Her heart beat so hard against her ribs she thought the bones might shatter, and she couldn't quite catch her breath. Someone stopped her, asked how she was, in German first and then English. She shook her head.

And then more hands, gripping her arms.

Dragging her back into the square.

Where the flesh would be torn from her back with that evil whip.

No. *No.* The person let her go, stepped away.

She had to find Diedrich, had to get him to explain, to make sense of what she'd just witnessed.

Althea stopped, leaned against the wall.

A thin trickle of blood down a chin lifted in defiance.

Diedrich. He'd be at the café, the one he spent most of his afternoons in. His friends would hold court in the back of the shop, eventually drifting out into the night, finding a bar and a few pints.

She caught sight of blond hair as she stumbled over the threshold.

He was by her side in an instant.

"Althea, darling," he murmured, his warm hands on her back, rubbing slow, comforting circles into her skin. She cringed away from him, on instinct.

"Why?" she managed to get out.

He blinked those snow-melt eyes she'd found so enchanting in those first days in Berlin. Now they just looked cold. Calculating.

"They beat a woman," Althea said, not sure where she found

the strength to even describe what she'd seen. "For marrying a Jew."

Diedrich went completely still. "Ah."

"Why?" she asked again.

"It's a civil war out there," Diedrich said, low and urgent, shielding their conversation from the rest of the café with his body. "After the attack on the Reichstag, you know it's not safe on the streets."

Althea nodded, because she did know. Adam's group from that night had scattered nearly before the breathless man had finished his announcement. Still, it had taken a few days to realize how dangerous that moment had been for them.

Thousands of communists had been arrested since the fire. Dev had informed her that one of them had been the girl who'd sat in Adam's lap, and Althea had nearly wept at the news despite the fact that she'd only been a nameless stranger.

Diedrich and the Nazi newspapers justified the arrests, of course. They warned of roving bands of communists who would murder innocent children as soon as look at them. They were monsters who wanted to burn Germany to the ground just because they could. And look, the Nazis said, they had started with the seat of power.

All the Nazis were doing was trying to protect Germany's law-abiding citizens.

"But . . . why?" she asked Diedrich again, knowing she wasn't quite making sense. That woman in the square had been so thin, her cheekbone already bruised long before she'd been forced to kneel before her prosecutor.

"Althea, you just don't understand," Diedrich said, and she could tell he was trying to be soothing. His thumb tucked in under her jaw, tipped her face up to his. "You're scared, I know. But it will all get better soon. I promise. It's war, darling. It isn't pretty, but it's necessary. To keep us all safe."

She wanted to lean into him. It would be so much easier just to believe what he was saying rather than face her own shame.

She stepped back. Stepped out of his arms. Turned. Walked out of the café, into the streets.

No one tried to stop her this time.

In the café with Adam's group, Althea had been unable to denounce the Nazis because she had been worried that if she admitted they were monsters that meant she was one, too. No one wrote themselves as the bad person in their own story.

Althea might not have studied literature at a fancy college, but she was skilled enough to know how to craft a compelling villain. No character was ever completely good or evil, but rather they were made up of a number of traits. Those traits plus the choices they made defined what role they played in the story.

A hero could be stubborn and use that to defend his homeland. A villain could be stubborn and because of that refuse to see that his views were immoral. Only few traits were inherently bad.

Cowardice had to be one of them.

Looking around now, Althea burned with remorse as she finally saw what she hadn't wanted to see before, when she catalogued everything that she should have been horrified at all along. What so many people had *told* her to be horrified at all along.

Storefront windows were smashed in, the word *Juden* painted in bright yellow on the remaining panes. No one greeted each other on the street, everyone walked with their faces down, their steps hurried and purposeful. Posters plastered every inch of public space, yelling in big, bold letters about the atrocities endured by Aryans at the hands of the reds, of the Jews, of anyone else but themselves.

By the time she made it back to her place, her soul felt wrapped in barbed wire that had been pulled taut and left her bleeding all over the floor.

She fell to her knees next to the bookshelf where she'd stashed the copy of *Mein Kampf* Diedrich had given her to read months ago. She'd never managed to get past the first chapter but now she forced herself to sit and read.

The light was dying by the time she finished it.

Althea wasn't simple no matter what anyone in Berlin might think. She just preferred the safety of books to reality. For better or worse, the fictional stories allowed her to wear blinders, allowed her to grow close to people, made-up though they might be, without the vulnerability that came with actually being known. When she'd been six and nine and thirteen, books had offered a refuge, a comforting hug, a best friend who had never existed in real life, even sometimes a vindictive plan that Althea herself would never carry out on her enemies but that felt good to think about anyway.

When Goebbels had written her, Althea had gone to the library and had old Mrs. Malikowski help her look up articles mentioning the NSDAP. None of them had scared her off coming to Germany.

When Diedrich had met her at the port and talked to her of literature and themes and style choices, nothing had made Althea look at him and think, *He's evil.*

Althea had been raised to trust her government, trust the people who had done right by her.

She had never learned to view the world through a suspicious lens.

But after reading *Mein Kampf*, any innocence she'd had left following that afternoon was well and truly lost.

It was the rare book that offered her no safety, just an ugly, terrible reality.

Chapter 22

New York City
May 1944

Grease coated the air in the Midtown pizzeria, the chatter of workers and families filling the space. The ovens at the back pushed the already hot shop toward sweltering as the lunch hour crowd strained its capacity.

It was the day after Viv had decided Althea James might be her best shot at beating Taft, but as she'd started drawing up her plan of attack, Charlotte had intervened.

"It's Saturday, Viv, and you've been working yourself to death," she'd said. "You're taking a break, so help me God."

When Viv had simply stared at her, not sure what she would even do with free time, Charlotte had rolled her eyes.

"You are twenty-four years old and you don't know how to have a good day in one of the best cities on earth? That's shameful."

Viv hadn't been able to deny the truth of that comment, so she'd let herself be goaded into taking the day off.

She'd walked around the city blindly for a while, and swore she used to know how to fill her time.

Eventually, she'd stumbled into a pizzeria that sold slices as large as her head and now she laughed as cheese dripped onto her plate while she tried to maneuver the thing into her mouth.

"You gotta fold it," the kid next to her said, and she turned to look at him.

He wasn't a kid, not really, though she doubted he was much older than the eighteen he'd needed to be to enlist. The pretty blue of the navy uniform brought out the green in his big eyes. He had spots on his chin and thick lashes and the buzz cut that Viv wished she would never see again once this goddamn war was over.

"Like this," he said, his words molasses. Georgia, she guessed, and decided to call him that.

He laughed and didn't correct her. She thought about Cisco, that sixteen-year-old boy who'd gotten shot by a bored Kraut sniper and who had loved *Wind, Sand and Stars.*

Then she didn't think about anything but the burst of oregano on her tongue.

"I ship out tomorrow," Georgia said, staring at a cigarette burn on the table they'd decided to share.

"I bet you say that to all the girls," Viv teased past her newly tight throat.

Georgia's eyes snapped to hers. Earnest. Young.

"No, ma'am, I don't," he said.

"Well, then, let's show you around the Big Apple."

She took him to all the sights she could think of. They stood at the base of the Empire State Building and debated the merits of *King Kong.* Viv didn't mention how much Hitler loved the movie and Georgia made only one sly comment about Fay Wray's hips.

Viv dragged him into the Met and then dragged him right back out again when she noticed his eyes glazing over. His last day in the States should be fun, not torture. Near the museum's steps, she bought him a hot dog and showed him how to smear it with mustard and eat it while waiting at the crosswalk. They strolled through Central Park, and Viv let him link their fingers together.

"Don't you have something you want to do?" Viv asked as she watched a little girl's balloon drift out of a careless grip, up and over the trees. It was late afternoon and the fabric of her sweat-damp light blue dress stuck to the small of her back. She plucked at it with her free hand, making sure not to let go of his. "I think I've picked everything so far."

Georgia slid her a glance from beneath his eyelashes, and she jabbed him with her elbow.

"Cheeky," she chastised.

He giggled, and she was once again reminded of how young he must be. "I was thinking about chocolate cake."

"Of course you were," Viv drawled. But one of her favorite bakeries was only a ten-minute walk away, near the west side of the park.

They got a tiny table by the window, their knees bumping together as they sat. One of the shop girls was sweeping up—they'd come just at closing—but the proprietress had looked at Georgia with tear-drenched eyes and cut him an extra big slice, adding ice cream and all.

Viv spared a moment to wonder if it had been a son or husband the woman had lost, and then shoved the question away. Today was for not thinking.

"What's your favorite book?" Viv asked, despite knowing the question hedged a little too close to the list of off-limits topics Charlotte had read her before pushing her out the door that morning.

Georgia got that mischievous look on his face, the one she was already starting to recognize after only a few hours. The thing that saved him was that he never seemed to take any of his innuendos—or himself—seriously. He teased her how he might tease a schoolmate.

"Do the bluesies count?" he asked, leaning in and wiggling his brows.

She indulged him with a reaction, not having the heart to mention that she was friends with enough men not to blush at the mention of dirty comic strips. She had even seen a few herself, though she hadn't understood the appeal. "Scoundrel."

When he just smirked and took another forkful of his cake, she nudged his knee, purposefully this time. "Tell me your real answer."

The amusement dropped out of Georgia's expression and it was only when his face went blank that she realized how much that lighthearted humor had been a part of him. "Um. Never been much for reading."

It wasn't that she hadn't heard that answer plenty of times. But Viv got the sense that his aversion had to do with something other than disinterest. Gently, she prodded. "Why is that?"

"The letters never stay still for me."

"Oh," Viv murmured, a twinge of guilt curling in her chest. This was clearly a sore subject. "That's all right."

"I guess," Georgia said, his throat bobbing. "I guess I'm just slow. It never bothered me before but I'm worried I won't be able to read any letters from my mama." He chewed on his lower lip and then added unnecessarily, but in a rush, "When I'm over there."

Viv wanted to hug him but thought any show of sympathy might be read as pity. "You're not slow." She set down her fork and decided this was worth breaking Charlotte's rules. "Someone will read it for you."

His eyes finally lifted to hers. "What?"

"I get letters from soldiers every day. It's part of my role as—"

She waved her hand. "That doesn't matter. What does is that there are plenty of men over there who don't have the easiest time reading. The others will help you. Just don't be afraid to ask."

"You don't think they'll laugh?"

"They might," Viv admitted, going with honesty because these were GIs they were talking about here. "But just to rib you a bit. Then they'll read the letters for you. And write a reply, I'm sure of it."

Georgia pursed his lips, nodded once, and then redonned his mischievous persona. "Will they read me the bluesies, too?"

"As if you look at those for the words," Viv said with an eye roll and Georgia barked out a surprised, pleased laugh. Viv wanted to freeze him in that moment, like a snapshot. As if she could keep him safe inside a picture, free him once the war was over. To go back to Georgia, back to his mama and his life.

She forced a smile in return and let him change the topic.

After the bakery came dinner and then they were in a cab on their way to a place where Georgia said they could find good jazz music.

They met up with a friend of his in a club on 115th Street, and a few minutes later Viv found herself squeezed into a booth along with three men in uniforms and two ladies draped in silk and sequins. The girls were gorgeous in a way Viv would never be, and she fought the self-conscious urge to fidget beneath their stares.

"I think you're real pretty," Georgia drawled in her ear, his voice even looser with the vats of alcohol they'd managed to consume since they'd arrived in the club. He was sweet, she'd realized over the course of the afternoon, his humor dirty, and his curiosity compelling. In another life he'd have made some Georgia peach a fine husband.

In this life, he'd probably end up as cannon fodder.

Viv pretended her breath hadn't hitched at that and nudged his hip with hers. "Let's dance."

Georgia didn't hesitate, just pulled her close, the brassy wail of the trumpets, the twang of the cello leading them into something far more intimate than Viv would have allowed in any other situation.

"I'm shipping out tomorrow," Georgia said again, his mouth against the line of her jaw. No desire pooled in the cradle of her hips. Instead she felt the sorrow of millions of women who could do nothing but watch their men walk away from them.

"I bet you say that to all the girls," she repeated back. And then—because he was shipping out tomorrow—she shifted, letting him catch her lips with his own.

And she didn't think about anything.

Chapter 23

Berlin
March 1933

You're quiet," Diedrich commented, his voice thick with concern.

It had been two days since Althea had seen the brownshirts take the skin off a man's back and hit a woman in the face, and if the worst Diedrich could say about her appearance was that she was quiet, she would count her blessings.

Quiet was better than terrified, confused, enraged.

She'd been operating as normal ever since, not sure what else she could do. When she remembered she had to attend this party, this celebration for the elections, she'd simply pulled on her dress, slipped into her shoes, and slid into the sleek black car Diedrich had sent for her.

Doing anything else felt too overwhelming at the moment.

Diedrich brought her hand to his mouth now so that his lips brushed her knuckles. He stared into her eyes, making the moment as intimate as their kiss in front of the Chancellery back in January.

She watched it all play out as if she were separate from herself, and at a distance, she saw the ploy for what it was. Whenever Althea had doubts, whenever she began questioning the Nazis, Diedrich shifted them into romance. A kiss, a hand on her lower back, a whisper, a tease. He was charming, naturally, but he acted like a lover only when he wanted to control her.

Acid burned in her throat as she swallowed convulsively, trying not to cry. She hadn't been silly enough to think him in love with her, but she hadn't realized how dispassionate Diedrich must be to make this charade work.

"You look as if you've seen a ghost, darling," Lina Fischer said as she sidled up to them. Lina was a young graduate student studying literature and history and Althea had never been so intimidated by another person in her life. They'd met for the first time at one of Althea's readings, and when Diedrich had tried to force a copy of Althea's book into Lina's hands he'd been answered with an amused *I don't have time to read such frivolous stories.*

She and Diedrich had been lovers at one point, maybe still were. The way they oftentimes forgot about the space in between them made Althea think it was the latter and that they were being discreet because of her.

Whenever Lina spoke to Althea, her voice carried a thick layer of condescension in it, but it was particularly heavy tonight, here among people who wanted to talk to Althea because of who she was.

They were supposed to be celebrating tonight. The Nazis hadn't picked up enough seats in the elections the week before to gain a majority in the Reichstag, but Hitler had officially banned the eighty-one elected communists the following day. It was the communists, after all, who had plotted to burn down the Reichstag, Diedrich had said. If you acted like a traitor you couldn't cry about being treated like one.

It made her wonder about the timing of the fire—right before the election, when the Nazis needed the electorate on their side the most. How perfect would it be to label one madman a representative of an entire party and create mass panic of an impending civil war?

The family hosting the party was fabulously wealthy even by the standards of those who supported the Nazis. Champagne flowed freely, as did the food. There were no signs of economic hardship in sight.

The guests sang the Nazi battle song "Kampflied der Nationalsozialisten" as well as the "Horst Wessel Song" and danced and grinned and hugged like they were all on the right side of things.

"A ghost," Lina repeated when Althea didn't reply. "That is the correct expression, yes?"

"It is," Diedrich reassured her, Althea's hand still caught in his. He squeezed it and Althea realized she would have once read his attention as affectionate concern.

She met his eyes and remembered that moment when he'd handed her *Mein Kampf.* The copy she had was his and it was well used. Read often. The soft pages and creases in the binding told her that.

"Excuse me" was all she could manage, as she wrenched herself out of his grasp. She made herself walk instead of run like she wanted to. Calm, without any urgency. The jubilant crowd swallowed her after only a few steps, bodies pressing in, wine splashing onto her shoes, and all the while Althea fought the tears that had pressed against her eyelids for the past two days.

Since Althea had arrived in Berlin, she had been in bed with monsters. She had been used by them, put on display as an example of the accomplishments of the master race.

And she had gone along willingly, with a smile on her face and stars in her eyes for a man who had finally given her attention. For a girl who had never had so much as a single boy ask her on a date, that had been heady, overwhelming, dizzying. He had not been picked by the Nazis to be her liaison because he was a top literature professor with the university. He had been picked because he had pretty eyes and pretty hair and a pretty smile that he could deploy at will.

Again, Althea stumbled through the streets, not sure where she was headed until she looked around and recognized the neighborhood.

Darkness had well and truly fallen by the time Althea reached Dev's place.

A small part of her whispered how dangerous it was to be out that night with all the violence that crackled through the city.

A small part of her whispered back that she might deserve whatever violence she encountered.

She rang the bell and waited.

When Dev opened the door, her face brightened and then fell.

"Oh, darling." She pulled Althea into an embrace, smelling of roses and cigar smoke and something purely spicy that Althea couldn't place. Of comfort in an unimaginable way. "Come, we're getting properly sloshed."

Althea didn't bother to ask who, just trailed after Dev obediently up the stairs to a flat that was luxurious compared to her own humble place. Hannah Brecht sprawled on the velvet sofa in an emerald silk dress that hugged every curve she had like a lover's caress. Otto was artfully sprawled on the floor next to her.

"Look what the cat dragged in." Hannah's eyes were heavy and assessing. The last time they had seen each other had been at that café, the night of the fire. When she had asked if Althea still thought the communist group was the same as the Nazis.

The night Althea had hesitated too long in giving her answer.

Dev shoved a glass of something strong in Althea's hands and said to Hannah, "She's having a come-to-Jesus moment—as we call it in the States."

Hannah laughed, throaty and appealing and a touch disdainful. "A little late for that."

"Never too late," Dev said, uncharacteristically serious. Althea blinked away tears as she swallowed the liquor.

She coughed while it burned a path down her throat to settle, warm and sinful, in her belly. "I didn't know," Althea managed, her voice breaking.

"You didn't want to know," Hannah corrected, though she pursed her plush lips as she studied Althea.

"You could have asked," Otto said, presenting a united front with Hannah. Althea wondered about them; it seemed rare for one to be found without the other nearby. They were clearly close, but they acted more like siblings than lovers.

"No one wants to be the villain of the book," Althea said as she sunk onto the settee across from Hannah. Dev settled into a beautiful wingback near the window, cradling a tumbler of something amber. She didn't seem inclined to smooth the waters between Hannah and Althea.

"A villain. Is that what you are?" Hannah asked.

Althea searched every part of herself for the right answer. "What else would you call a person who willfully buries their head in the sand when evil is taking place all around them?"

The corners of Hannah's eyes crinkled. "A German."

The punch line hung between them for a fraught second and then Althea pressed her hand over her mouth to stop the giggles that arose out of her dying panic. "Oh, you should be one of those masters of ceremony at the cabarets."

"They do seem to get away with a shameful amount, don't they?" Hannah remarked. "I think I would not be so lucky."

Althea's humor died. "You must hate me."

"Please, you are no worse than every country in the world, no different than every leader who sees Hitler as a fringe lunatic who lucked into power," Hannah said, and Otto hoisted his glass in what looked like agreement. "The evil should be all the more apparent to them, yet they refuse to look at it and see it for what it is. I don't blame you."

"You should," Althea whispered, the words cutting up the soft tissue of her throat as they came out. "How is Adam?"

Hannah's eyes narrowed in suspicion. "Why do you care?"

Althea thought about his puppy dog eyes, the warm *I read your novel.* "How is he?"

"Distraught," Hannah said, and Otto made an agreeing sound in the back of his throat. "The woman, the one with the ink stains? She was arrested that night."

Althea licked her lips and flicked a glance toward Dev. "I know."

"They won't kill her, probably," Hannah said in an offhand manner. "But I worry what Adam will do. In his anger."

"Hannah," Otto murmured, his eyes on Althea. Everyone had to be careful. Althea understood. She just wondered how many times she would have to say she wouldn't betray them before they believed her.

"They're not who I thought they were," she admitted.

"This is so serious," Hannah complained, sinking back into the corner of the sofa. She tapped her nail against her glass, her gaze flicking to Dev before flitting back to Althea's face. "What I say will be hard to swallow."

Althea braced herself. There were no more excuses she could offer, no protestations.

Hannah inhaled then leaned forward, like she was about to tell a secret. "Right now? You're making this all about you. It's not about you. It's about a dictator who wants to kill every non-Aryan in the world. And please believe me, if he somehow accomplishes that horrific feat, he will move on to killing Aryans with brown eyes, and then ones with too-long fingers or crooked teeth." She paused, exhaled. "This is not about you."

"But if I—"

"If you spoke up, if you disobeyed a boycott, if you slapped that handler of yours across the face, do you know what would happen?" Hannah asked, clear-eyed and serious, yet still not malicious. These were harsh words, but not ones meant to eviscerate Althea. "Hitler would still be rounding up communists to put into his little jails. He would still be launching his war against the Jews, he would still be murdering his political opponents by the handful. This is not about you."

She said that last bit with enough weight for it to settle into Althea, uncomfortable and unwieldy. But still Althea couldn't help but ask, "You don't think one person can make a difference?"

"I think one person can," Hannah said, without blinking. "I don't think that person is you."

Althea was too used to thinking in terms of protagonists and main characters. They were the reason for the world they existed in—they saved the day, or saved the princess, or saved humanity. They were the reason for everything.

But she wasn't living in a book any longer.

Hannah sighed, the silk of her dress sliding down her creamy shoulders as she did. "I wouldn't be defending you to yourself had you explicitly known what they were doing and agreed with them. But it seems you've learned and you don't, and so you need to move on."

"Then what do I do? Leave?"

She had plenty of money to buy her own ticket back to the States. If what Hannah was saying was true, then Althea had no power here to stop this madness. Wouldn't it be better if she just fled the country?

Dev made a sound, a dissent, half-formed. Like she could see the logic but didn't want to agree with it.

It was Hannah, however, who answered. "You could run. Or . . ."

"Or?" Althea pressed.

Hannah glanced at Dev, who gave a jerky little nod, the two locked in some silent conversation. "You want to do something?"

"Yes," Althea gasped out, terrified but certain of that.

"Stay, then," Hannah said. "See the real Berlin for the next three months. Our Berlin. And then when you go back home, make sure the people there know exactly what's happening in Germany. Not just the headline version, but what's really happening. You can correct assumptions you hear, you can tell one person and they can tell one person and so on. Push back on bigotry even if you want to smooth it over. Eventually it will add up to something more than nothing, even if it isn't the grand gesture your current emotions want you to make."

Althea shook her head. "That won't . . . I'm not as important as everyone here thinks."

Heat raced into her cheeks at the admission, which she'd been keeping as her deepest secret ever since she'd stepped onto German soil.

"I don't know," Hannah said, watching her so closely, just as she had since Althea had walked in. "Maybe you'll be the hero of the story yet."

Chapter 24

New York City
May 1944

Viv couldn't deny Charlotte had been right. The Saturday off, Georgia's embarrassed confession, the break from thinking only about Taft and the ASEs had reinvigorated her. By Monday, she was ready to launch her campaign to get Althea James on board with her event.

The first step was research, and research meant one place.

She stopped to adjust her heel strap before climbing the steps of the New York Public Library, affectionately saluting one of the lions as she passed.

While the library certainly was impressive, Viv found herself comparing the high, ostentatious ceilings and marble floors to the coziness of the banned books library in Brooklyn, with the latter coming out ahead in her own personal preference.

A young woman sat at the desk near the lobby, her dark hair cut into stylish waves, her crisp blouse and dove-gray skirt the height of fashion. "Can I help you?"

"I'm looking for old newspapers, from about a decade ago," Viv told her.

"Of course," the woman said, standing and directing Viv to follow. "I'm Missy."

Viv nearly smiled at how easily the name was offered. "Viv."

Missy helped her locate the newspapers around the release dates of both of Althea's books and settled Viv into a table toward the back of the main reading room.

The sun crept along the room, sliding over Viv's hands, her arms, her shoulders. She had to shift once when her eyes began to water, but for the most part the passing of time seemed to exist as something outside of that particular room.

Edith had been right about the reviews. The first mentions of Althea had come a couple of days before the release of *The Unfractured Light*. Critics heaped praise on Althea's style, her themes, her expert use of stream of consciousness when inside the head of the main character's daughter. Viv could find only one review that was anything but glowing, mentioning a pat ending that felt too easy.

Viv did pick up on a slight condescending tone throughout all of the reviews. They made sure to mention in the same tone that Althea had no formal education, as if she were some special dog who could ride a bicycle, and there were several velvet-covered barbs about her ability *despite* the fact that she was a woman. Her editor, a man who had discovered her through a quirk of fate, also featured heavily, something Viv doubted would have happened had Althea also been a man.

Viv flipped through the years to find the reaction to *An Inconceivable Dark*. And if she'd thought the earlier ones were kind, these were rapturous. They talked about the new depth to Althea's writing; the way her characters were all morally gray rather than having the stark ethics that were at play in *The Light*.

And the rejection of the fairy-tale structure had clearly won over even the most pretentious readers.

The *New York Post*'s book editor mused that the change might have been down to the fact that Althea had spent six months in 1932 and 1933 as a guest of Joseph Goebbels and his initiative to bring authors to Germany for residencies to show off the successes of the master race.

The sentence was a throwaway at the bottom of the article but Viv's eyes snagged on it. She had to read it three times before she could truly understand, her mind whirling through every possibility before landing on what seemed like an inevitable truth.

Althea James was a Nazi supporter.

Viv absorbed that gut punch for a moment before shaking her head.

No. That wasn't necessarily true. While there had been a flourishing fascist movement in the States in the thirties, it was believable that a small-town girl from rural Maine would not have known what she was signing up for when she agreed to participate in such a cultural program.

Viv couldn't ignore the fact now that she'd learned it, though. She spared a quick minute to be thankful both that she lived in New York and that this library was incredibly well funded. Then she went looking.

She found editions of the *Portland Daily News* from November and December 1932, turned to go back to her table, and then paused. *Six months.*

The June editions joined her stacks.

It took another hour to find a mention of prominent local writer Althea James being invited to Berlin and then another forty minutes to find the article about her return.

Neither of them had accompanying photos with the mentions. The reviews hadn't, either. If Viv hadn't realized it before, it was obvious now. This was an intensely private woman. It didn't bode well for Viv's chances in convincing her to speak at the Taft event.

She pushed the thought aside. Something for future Viv to deal with.

What these articles did have were the first quotes she'd ever seen from Althea. Viv wondered if they were the only ones to exist.

> "I'm terribly excited to expand my literary horizons with this trip," Miss James, 25, says. "Perhaps it will be the start of a wonderful exchange program between Germany and the United States."

She shifted her attention to the article of Althea coming home. Most of it was just a light biography and a summarization of Althea's literary success to date. But at the end, Althea was asked if she enjoyed her time in Berlin.

> "As much as one can enjoy living among monsters," Miss James, 26, said, before demurring further.

Viv snatched up both papers and placed them side by side, her fingertip touching each quote, lingering, thinking.

Though the quotes were short, the marked change in tone was a clear echo of what reviewers—and Edith—had said about Althea's books, as well.

Naive, hopeful. And then brutal and dark.

Monsters. Had Althea been talking about the Nazis? Or was that the story Viv wanted to tell herself? Time certainly had a way of obscuring reality, of putting a rose-colored tinge on troubling behavior.

At the end of the day, though, the fact remained—Althea James would be a showstopper. And Viv needed guests in the seats and attention for her cause. If it turned out Althea was a Nazi sympathizer, Viv would have to adjust her plans. But, as of now, there wasn't enough to definitively say either way and Viv had always been an optimist.

When she left the library, she had to admit to a confidence she'd been faking up until then.

She couldn't deny that despite all the ways she'd been barreling forward, some nights she locked herself in her tiny turquoise bathroom and drank a half a bottle of wine in the tub, staring at the tiles and wondering if this was all going to blow up in her face.

To calm herself down, Viv had taken to reading the *Oliver Twist* she'd gotten from her street bookseller and thinking about Edward doing the same all those months ago in Italy somewhere.

When her parents had died, when she'd been sent to live with Uncle Horace, her whole world had shrunk down to his town house, to her school, and to church. Those were the only places she'd been allowed to go those first years with him. Her life had been so small.

The books were what gave her a big life; they let her into a thousand different worlds where she could be a thousand different people. For the longest time she walked around like she had a secret no one else knew.

She had been thinking about it all wrong, she now realized. The success of the ASEs proved that sharing the secret was so much more powerful than hoarding it close to her chest. In doing so, the thread of humanity that ran between all of them tightened, strengthened, became all the more vibrant for the worlds and emotions and journeys that every reader experienced together.

It didn't take knowing a soldier personally for Viv to reach out into the night and know someone else in the world was finding solace in the very words she was reading at that very moment. It was like looking up at the moon and feeling a connection to anyone who was touched by its light.

Everyone slogging through this endless war—even those on the home front—had to find their own reason to keep going.

Making sure that connection wasn't taken away from the soldiers was Viv's.

VIV DECIDED TO proceed as if success was inevitable—not only would Althea James show up at the Taft event, she would deliver a fiery speech putting to rest any worries that she was a Nazi sympathizer.

While the blind optimism may have been a tiny bit foolhardy on her part, it did allow her to move forward with the rest of her plans after she'd finished up at the library.

Off the record, she rang up a journalist at the *Columbus Dispatch* in Ohio who'd reached out to her a few months back about a puff piece on the ASEs.

"An exclusive?" Marion Samuel pressed when Viv pitched her a profile on Althea James. Marion sounded interested if hesitant. Althea James had become something of a national celebrity, and the fact that she never gave interviews or talked to anyone at all really made her that much more intriguing to most people.

Viv hedged. "If I get her to agree to it."

"Well, I won't hold my breath," Marion said. "But for an exclusive interview with Althea James? I'd guess you'd make front page with that."

The next call was to Leonard Aston, a veteran of the Great War who had come home with demons in his eyes and a permanent limp that had kept him out of the current mess.

He had also been one of Charlotte's longer-term paramours, once Theodore Childs had moved into his own, separate residence. Sometimes Viv dreamed Leonard might think of her like a daughter, but she guessed they weren't actually close enough for that. Still, he answered her calls, and that's what mattered.

And that worked out in her favor because he was currently the Life & Style editor at *Time* magazine.

"You gave the exclusive away?" he shouted over the phone, but Leonard's bark was notoriously worse than his bite.

"How many of Taft's voters are subscribers, Leo?" Viv asked patiently.

"Tons, hundreds, thousands even, I'm sure of it." But she heard the humor this time. "All right, all right. I get my own interview, though, yeah?"

"If I can get her to say yes," Viv hedged once more.

"Would never bet against you, kid," Leonard said, and she would have found it sweet had he not hung up without waiting for a response.

With those boxes checked, Viv contacted Harper & Brothers, where a friendly but firm assistant informed her that the house wouldn't give out any information on its writers. When she asked for the name of the editor, at least, the woman had hung up on her.

She didn't have any close contacts at that particular publisher, but she knew someone who might.

Viv tempted Harrison Gardiner out of his office the next day with an offer to stroll Booksellers' Row on Fourth Avenue. As one of publishing's bright young things, Harrison liked to stay well-informed about what the big shops were keeping stocked and he rarely said no to leaving the office early.

While waiting for Harrison outside Biblo & Tannen, Viv ran her fingers over the spines of the books stacked high on one of the tables.

There had been an added benefit in keeping herself busy this afternoon—Memorial Day had never been a holiday she'd thought too much about before, but now she couldn't avoid it. Not when every store in the city wanted to do its part in honoring their fallen boys.

She didn't want to think about Edward as a fallen boy. She wanted to think about him as the man who'd loved spending lazy afternoons on this very street, browsing through the wares.

Edward hadn't been a book lover. Like many men she knew, he'd forced himself to read for school and had never learned to do so for pleasure.

But Edward had always enjoyed watching the shoppers on Booksellers' Row, endlessly delighted by each person's choice, especially if it offered a contradiction to who the world probably thought they were. Like a tiny Italian grandmother buying a book with the raciest cover on the table.

Viv blinked back the swell of emotion, annoyed with herself for remembering Edward in public. She rarely thought about him outside the privacy of her own home, not wanting to be caught sobbing in the middle of a sidewalk. Part of the reason she was so focused on Taft and the ASEs was because it didn't leave much room for the grief to run rampant and swallow her whole.

At some point she had to believe it would become bearable. She would be able to walk down this avenue and remember the way he created stories for the strangers, making them more and more outrageous the harder Viv laughed. Or how he would pluck her new purchases out of her hand to theatrically recite embarrassing sections right there on the street.

She knew one of these days she'd stop turning to the space beside her, ready to point out the mysterious widow draped in furs and jewels, only to find nothing but air. But today was not that day.

"You look far too sad for someone who is taking on Capitol Hill and winning," Harrison said from behind her.

Viv forced a smile until it became natural, the memory of Edward tucked back in that locked box of hers.

"'Winning' might be a generous description," Viv said as they fell into step, arm in arm.

"Considering you had given up a few weeks ago, I think this counts as winning," he argued, looking very pleased with himself.

"You want me to say thank you, don't you?" Viv said, pretending to be put out.

"A little appreciation goes a long way to getting any favors you want," Harrison teased. "And I assume that's why I'm really here, as much as you clearly enjoy my company."

"Ulterior motives? Who, me?" Viv asked, all innocence, to make him laugh. But then she broke and updated him on all the ducks she was lining up for the Taft conference, including her long-shot hope of getting Althea James to show up.

"I have a college buddy at Harper," Harrison mused, as they stopped at one of the book racks. It was what she'd been counting on—publishing was small, the inner circle of stars even smaller. But she did have to stamp down on a flicker of irritation that it was so easy for him. "I can't promise anything. But I'll make the case."

"That's all I ask," Viv said, grateful despite the quick second of resentment. "Thank you."

As they shifted toward the next sidewalk table, a man in a bright-white ten-gallon Stetson stepped out from the shop, white pistols tucked into jewel-covered holsters, his handlebar mustache nearly touching his collar.

Viv turned to her left, where Edward so often stood, some silly comment sitting on her tongue.

The space was empty, though. Just as it always would be.

Chapter 25

Paris
November 1936

The news that Hannah's parents had received visas to England came on the first day of the book exhibition.

Hannah stared at the letter, stunned as she realized her parents were already aboard a ship headed toward Southampton without saying goodbye. If she were a different person, she might have cried. But Hannah had always known that in her parents' rank of priorities she came as an afterthought.

They'd told her time and again that they didn't blame her for what happened to Adam, even though she'd confessed the truth to them not long after he'd been dragged off to that concentration camp. But Hannah knew she'd been blinded by a pretty face, and they'd all paid the price for it.

The note informed Hannah that a hefty sum had been deposited in her bank account, enough to get her through several years. The only nod to the familial duty they still felt toward her.

Hannah read the entire message one more time, and then she breathed deep and said goodbye. Goodbye to parents who had never loved her the way parents should love a child, the way they had loved Adam.

Goodbye to the innocence of believing love could be unconditional.

Crossing the room to the fireplace in three quick strides, Hannah tossed the envelope into the flames. The ink and paper hissed their protest as they were devoured by the fire, as they devolved to ash.

Otto was her family now. She clung to that thought as she dressed, pinched color into her cheeks, slipped on her shoes, and waved adieu to Brigitte, who had warmed to her in recent days. She didn't think about how she'd felt Otto drifting away from her since they'd moved to Paris.

Otto greeted her on the street with a happy, carefree smile that she hoped to mimic. As they walked toward the boulevard Saint-Germain and the exhibition, she steered the conversation toward silly, lighthearted gossip, trying to wash away the darkness of the morning. The darkness of what was going to come.

But at the first sight of the swastika, Hannah could no longer participate in idle chatter.

This was Paris.

This was free land.

This was not Nazi Germany.

Hannah repeated those facts over and over and over as she walked toward the banners that carried that sign of pure hate.

The Library of Burned Books had set up shop in the Société de Géographie two doors down from where Nazis in German military uniforms lingered outside a storefront. Mister Heinrich Mann and his equally famous brother, Thomas Mann, were both present, overseeing the library's display, along with a handful of other big names, authors Hannah recognized from shelving their books time and again. Everyone was kind, everyone was cheerful, and every smile was brittle at the edges as eyes continued to wander toward the banners, toward the uniforms, toward the Parisians who were being enticed by the Nazi exhibit.

The library had put out apple cider for the occasion as well as pastries to lure in the casual passersby. Hannah made a concerted effort to talk to anyone who left the Nazis' storefront with a brown bag tucked under their arm.

If this was a fight they were going to win, they couldn't hold grudges against the people they wanted to persuade.

Otto lounged in a corner chair, offering amusing commentary as the day went on, and then bitter asides as they all realized this endeavor wouldn't be as successful as they'd hoped. People stopped, they browsed, they even engaged sometimes. But Hannah didn't get the sense the library was changing anyone's minds.

"The Nazis can't really be so bad" she heard.

"They're shaking things up" she heard

". . . but the Jews do seem to have a lot of power."

The last one was whispered just loudly enough for everyone to hear.

Hannah turned away from the man, forced a smile, and ushered an older woman closer to the display of Jewish-authored books that Hannah had so carefully curated.

She knew, though, that they all heard the comment. If this had been a battle for the soul of Paris, the Library of Burned Books had lost.

When her shift was over for the day, she collected Otto and stepped out onto the boulevard.

Wolf whistles greeted them, despite the fact that Otto was there as a deterrent.

His arm tensed beneath her hand, but Hannah kept walking,

pulling him along, silently begging him not to engage even as she knew this could be the excuse he'd been waiting for all day. The urge had itched beneath both their skins; the difference was Hannah could ignore it in favor of heading home for a cup of tea.

Otto didn't have that much self-control.

Hannah closed her eyes briefly when she realized two of the Nazis had broken off to follow them. *Please, please.* Her fingernails dug into the fabric of Otto's coat.

"Fräulein," one called, his voice arrogant and amused. Hannah kept walking.

His friend drew the word out. "Fräulein."

"Don't ignore our poor, lonely souls," they called in German, earning themselves a few looks from people passing on the street.

Otto stilled beside her, and she hurried to whisper beneath her breath, "Ignore them, ignore them."

But of course the men were uncouth. They were Nazis in Paris—they were born to offend in this very moment. Like so many of Hitler's brownshirts, they were clearly battle-worn, had been stripped bare and then rebuilt in the name of violence during the Great War.

"Look at her walking away," the first one crooned.

"I am." The second took the baton and ran with it. "And that's one fine ass."

Before Hannah could realize what was happening, Otto turned and landed his fist on the jaw of the bigger Nazi.

Everything froze for one heartbeat, two, time stretching then collapsing on itself.

And then the man howled, more out of surprise than pain. Otto wasn't strong enough to cause a bruise, but that didn't matter. When men like these tasted violence, they swarmed.

Knuckles connected with Otto's face, and his head snapped back with a crack as if his spine had broken.

He's dead.

Hannah's vision went white at the thought.

But Otto didn't collapse, simply stumbled, his arms and legs still working.

Otto steadied himself, his hands clenched and up in front of him, a boxer preparing for a match.

Move.

Hannah couldn't, though. Her legs wouldn't listen. They wouldn't *listen.*

They'll hit you, too.

But it wasn't fear that held her rooted to the spot. It was shock.

This was *Paris.*

If she could think . . . if she could . . . think . . .

The commotion had drawn a crowd, and her eyes flew from one face to the next, desperate, searching.

No one stepped forward.

The Nazi Otto had hit was on the balls of his feet, taking quick little jabs at Otto's jaw. Mocking taunts, almost, more than anything.

Otto stumbled but managed to land a few punches himself.

Could she stop this now? Before it went further? The Nazis were circling, but they hadn't descended.

Just move.

But before she could step in front of Otto, blocking him with her body, the Nazi grew tired of playing with his food. And he lashed out fully. Between blinks, Otto crumpled to the ground, a puppet whose strings had been snipped.

Blood flecked one of the man's knuckles.

Blood flecked the pavement.

Blood roared in her ears.

Help.

They needed help.

And then both of the Nazis were on the ground, on top of Otto.

No one else had moved. Hannah hadn't moved. She hadn't stepped in front of Otto. She hadn't protected him.

A whimper cut through the noise, so quiet she probably shouldn't have heard it. But she had. It was a low, broken sound that shattered a heart she'd thought was already in as many pieces as it could be.

Hannah heard every moment of her life in that whimper, every moment of Otto's.

Do something.

Now.

Hannah ducked under a swinging arm, throwing herself onto the pile of bodies, going for anything she could reach on Otto—a leg, his coat, a hand. Anything.

Pain bloomed in her cheekbone, sharp and staticky, racing along her spine.

A boot, she realized as the ache settled into a throb of misery.

As she held her face with a shaky hand, she met the Nazi's eyes, the one who had kicked her. In that one moment, remorse flickered into his expression. And then an errant elbow caught his jaw, and everything about him hardened.

He drew his fist back and then his knuckles connected with her already bruised cheek.

A tinny sound rang in her ears as she lay on the sidewalk, her teeth too loose in her mouth, her body heavy and unwieldy. Nausea threatened and if she could only close her eyes, just for a second, just for a . . .

Otto cried out.

Hannah gasped as she pressed herself up, her elbow sending out dull ripples of pain as she did.

But that didn't matter right now. Without hesitating, Hannah threw herself back into the pile, reaching, reaching, reaching until finally her fingers tangled in Otto's shirt.

"Stop," she cried in German.

"Please help." This time she managed it in French, calling to the crowd. And she thought of the pistol, thought of pressing the barrel to one of the men's foreheads and pulling the trigger. It was the first time in her life she'd imagined killing someone. But in that moment, she knew if she'd had the weapon she would have at least tried. "Please help."

No one came to help them. The tides pulled her down, pulled her beneath the waves of pounding hands and evil men.

Otto, she thought as she tried to wrap herself around his broken and battered body.

Hannah breathed out. Thought *No.*

And then she kicked. Her foot landed. A crack broke the strange stillness of the night.

She kicked again. Howled. Scratched. Flailed until arms connected with vulnerable faces, until hands struck lucky blows.

The police arrived.

But their help came too little, too late.

Chapter 26

New York City
May 1944

Viv paced in front of Hale's campaign office, restless following her afternoon with Harrison on Booksellers' Row. She hadn't wanted to go home to an empty apartment—it was Charlotte's bridge night with her two oldest, dearest friends. So Viv had found herself in Brooklyn and marveled how familiar she was becoming with this side of the river.

Hale caught her midstride as he stepped out onto his stoop, shrugging into his jacket despite the heat of the day.

"Manhattan's that way," he called, pointing west.

Viv swiveled theatrically. "You mean I'm not on Broadway? I could have sworn I took the correct left at Times Square."

Hale's lips tipped up in a gentle smile. "Hiya, Childs."

"Hiya, Hale," she called back, just as irreverently, her hands on her hips, the wind catching at her skirt.

"What's that look for?" Hale asked after he'd skipped down the three steps.

She held a hand to her forehead to block the setting sun as she squinted up at him. "Just thinking about life, I guess."

"Makes sense, thinking about life in a war," he said, shifting so that she could look up into his face without her eyes tearing. "Here for another favor?"

Shaking her head, she nudged his elbow with her own. "A distraction."

He sent her a knowing look. Viv was sure he'd had at least a few appearances to honor Memorial Day, had probably accepted more condolences than he could count from well-meaning folks.

"Walk with me?" she asked.

Surprise came and went in a blink-and-miss-it heartbeat. His smile was cautious but he nodded once. "It's a nice enough evening. Where to?"

"Where our feet take us," she suggested.

He hesitated, clearly unsure of her mood. She didn't blame him. The last time they'd spoken she'd come wrapped in protective barbed wire.

But today she'd found herself wanting to talk to someone who'd known Edward. Not because the two of them were alike in any way—in terms of personality they were polar opposites. Just . . . it was easier. Knowing someone shared her specific grief. Not the larger feeling of mourning for all the soldiers who had died.

For Edward.

Viv's knees went wobbly, her thighs weak, her breathing ragged. Her fingertips found the solid brick of a rowhouse, and she leaned back against it, let the wall hold her up.

Ignoring Hale's concerned expression as he came back to stand in front of her, Viv closed her eyes and focused on the next inhale, the next exhale.

Edward was dead.

Never again would she see the sly humor slip into his eyes right before he told a joke, never again would she seek comfort in the warmth of his hug, never again would she tease secrets from him and let her own be teased out in return.

Fingers encircled her wrist, not chaining her, but grounding her.

Hale stood shielding her from the street—and any nosy passerby's hungry gaze—his thumb rubbing out a small circle on the skin that stretched over her rabbiting pulse. Neither of them said anything as her heart slowed, but neither of them looked away either.

"Most of the time I'm all right," Viv managed to rasp out. Hale's thumb paused for just a second before continuing its soothing rhythm. "Most of the time I can just not think about it."

In the fading light of early evening, Hale's eyes had gone a stormy green, the gold flecks little bursts of lightning among the clouds.

"Does that make me terrible?" she asked in a rush. "That I don't always think about it?"

Hale huffed out a breath, his body swaying toward hers. With anyone else it would have made her feel cornered, but instead she sunk into the protectiveness of the gesture.

"If you made yourself think about it all the time you'd spend your life on your knees, unable to do anything but cry," Hale said softly. "I can get up every day only because I don't let myself think about him."

Viv sniffed and studied his face. Maybe Hale and Edward should never have been as close as they were, but they had been. Two men who had decided to be brothers instead of enemies.

In that moment, she loved them both fiercely, without restraint or condition or scars. Loved Hale for loving Edward, for giving him family where he so easily could have withheld his affection.

She pressed a hand to Hale's chest, over his heart. He dropped his forehead to hers, and they stood like that even as the street bustled around them, workers heading home from jobs, mothers pushing prams, girls giggling as they tried not to stare.

They only broke apart when something bumped gently against Viv's foot.

Startled, she looked down to see a baseball. It wasn't the pristine white you'd see at a Dodgers game, but rather the dirty and frayed kind that was so familiar to that summer Hale had first taught her how to play. Her body ached with the memory.

When she looked up, Hale grinned at her, mischievous, the despair of the last few minutes forgotten, a practice they were all good at now.

Viv bent down, picked up the baseball, and looked around for the owners. The boy stood on the curb a few feet away, a battered mitt dangling from one hand, his eyes big and awed as he stared at Hale, clearly recognizing him as the beloved neighborhood institution that he was.

Viv met Hale's eyes one more time and quirked her lips into a questioning smile.

Hale's shoulders lifted in an amused inhale as he took the ball from her and turned to the boy. "You have room for two more?"

"But what if you muss up your suit, Congressman Hale?" Viv teased quietly as the boy simply continued to gape.

Hale's eyes traced over her flirty dress, her heels, the little hat that perched atop her hair. "I don't think *my suit* is going to be the problem."

She was spared having to come up with a response—which was good because his slow, assessing gaze had her tongue-tied—when the boy with the mitt whooped and hollered and called back to his friends.

Viv and Hale followed, Hale shrugging out of his well-tailored jacket and draping it over a fire hydrant while Viv chewed on her lip. There was no fixing the dress but the heels would have to go.

The street was mostly smooth and she thankfully wasn't wearing her stockings, so she didn't have to worry about rips. She stepped out of her shoes, earning a smirk from Hale. The boys took it as invitation to crowd around both of them, talking all at once.

They were about ten years old if Viv had to guess. Too often, when Viv saw girls and boys their age, they wore the serious faces of children forced to grow old too soon. But these boys were alight with the simple summer pleasure of baseball in the street, their smiles almost too big to bear.

"Missus," one of them said to Viv, nudging her shin with the bat. "Mr. Hale says you're up first."

"Oh he did, did he?" Viv slid a look to Hale, who was watching her with an emotion she couldn't identify. Whatever it was made some dormant part of her crack open, tendrils of spring-green hope seeking the warmth she saw in his eyes.

"Move in," one of the older boys called to the haphazard outfield. "A dime says she can't even swing the bat."

Viv's eyes narrowed.

By this point, girls had started congregating on the sidewalk to watch also, the spectacle of two respectable adults joining in the children's game too interesting to pass by.

"I'll take that bet," one of the taller girls yelled. She was slim with long dark hair and a set jaw that carried a stubbornness Viv recognized from her own youth. Viv pointed the bat at the girl, in a universal gesture of appreciation and earned herself a toothy grin in response.

Behind her Hale clapped and hollered along, the tough talk almost as familiar as the dirty baseball had been.

Viv stepped up to the busted street sign that was acting as home plate, gripped the bat, stuck her behind out in a way that earned her a few wolf whistles by a passing pair of young men, and glared at the pitcher. He, with the cockiness that came from being ten years old and the center of attention, cackled and carelessly tossed the ball in the air.

“Bring it on,” she called out.

“You want a girl’s pitch?” he asked, and once again the girls on the sidewalk shouted him down.

“You can’t even hit a girl’s pitch yourself, Bobby.”

“When was the last time you got to first?”

“You want me to tell your momma you’re talking like that?”

Viv didn’t smile, though she wanted to. Instead, drawing her brows down even further, she said, “I’m starting to think you’re all talk. Can’t even throw the ball, I’d bet.”

The gentle gibe had the intended effect. It wiped the amusement from his face and got him to pitch to the best of his abilities—which meant the ball was easier to hit than if he’d been messing around, trying to throw underhand.

Viv swung to miss, because she liked drama. But she also swung to miss because the joy that radiated from every person on this small block in Brooklyn was unmistakable. Women were leaning in doorways now, their eyes always tracking back to Hale, but some of them paid enough attention to Viv to call out encouragement. A couple of sailors lounged against the wall of a grocery, the owner coming to watch in the window.

With the simple addition of two adults joining the game, the entire atmosphere had become that of a party, a treat, a celebration of summer and life and happiness.

And Viv wanted to draw it out as long as possible.

"Told ya," the same boy who'd called out earlier said from his spot on third base. The lanky girl on the sidewalk rolled her eyes.

"I know you ain't so smart, Jimmy, but in baseball you get three strikes before you're out," the girl said, and Viv tossed her a wink.

Viv let the second pitch slide by her, and Hale, who seemed to have taken on the role of umpire, hollered out, "Strike," as if he were at Ebbets Field.

"This one's for all the marbles," some voice called from the audience now gathered. The boys were practically thrumming with excitement from the attention.

Viv regripped the bat. Drama was only fun if she could pull off the grand finale.

It made her think of her fight with Senator Taft. But in the next moment she pushed the thought aside. There was no space for that tonight; she had to be here, present, ready to swing.

The ball left the boy's fingertips and she lifted her elbow, shifted her weight. Exhaled, just like Hale had taught her.

The bat connected with a satisfying crack that reverberated through the crowd. For one eternal heartbeat, everyone seemed to hold their breath as the ball sailed up and over the heads of the furthest line of boys. Then Viv dropped the bat and took off, the roar that followed pushing her on, even as her skirt flew up around her legs.

Rocks cut into the soles of her feet, sweat gathered beneath her arms, pins fell out of her hair and tumbled to the ground, and she ignored all of it as she rounded second and headed toward third. The boys were scrambling, after having sent two outfielders sprinting after the ball that had seemed to lodge itself under some distant car. Shouts of encouragement and disbelief greeted her at third, and the lanky girl from the sidewalk was there, grinning so hard it took over her entire face, her arm wheeling in the signal to haul off toward home base. The other girls had gathered behind the tall one, their bodies all but vibrating as they hollered out their encouragement.

Out of the corner of Viv's eye, a flurry of movement nearly distracted her. They'd found the ball and had started up a chain to get it back to the boy who now guarded home. Viv ducked her chin, reached down for every bit of energy she had left, pumped her arms, and lengthened her stride.

The pitcher had the ball.

She was two, maybe three steps away.

The ball sailed toward her—toward the glove the catcher held outstretched.

It landed in the mitt, only one heartbeat after her foot touched metal. She skidded a little at the change of surface, but managed to stay upright as everyone, en masse, shifted toward Hale.

He let the suspense hang, build, and nearly crescendo as the audience leaned toward him, ready to accept his judgment.

Finally, with all the grandiosity of deciding a World Series game, he yelled out, "Safe!"

The girls whooped with a victory they'd taken on as their own, the boys poor-sport arguing in the way that seemed necessary for a losing team. The women who'd taken a break from their days smiled indulgently, the grocer laughed, and the sailors winked at Viv before continuing on to wherever they were headed.

And Viv stood panting, her hands on her hips, smiling so that she didn't cry. Not from grief, but from some overwhelming tidal wave of joy that pressed at every frayed and vulnerable seam of her body.

It had been such a long war, so many years of hardship, of sacrifice, of fear and loss and pain and the dull monotony of helplessness. But none of that had crushed them completely. Even in the darkest days, in their deepest grief, at their most exhausted, humans found a way to create moments that were so fundamentally hopeful that they couldn't help but inspire you to take one more step forward. And then one more.

Hale swooped in behind her, slinging an arm over her shoulder. "I knew you had it in you, Childs."

Feeling magnanimous, Viv shot him a look. "Learned from the best."

His fingers tightened on her arm and a panic-laced thrill raced through her at the thought of him pulling her into a kiss. But Hale just stepped away, clapping his hands to get the boys' attention.

He, like Viv, knew the power of a good ending and didn't bother taking his turn at the plate. Instead, he congratulated the boys on a good game, led them all to the grocer who had watched Viv's triumph, and bought out his entire icebox of Popsicles.

Viv took grape and tried not to think about the way the flavor tasted on Hale's tongue.

Hale was swamped with adoring constituents after that, but every so often his eyes would drift back to where Viv had situated herself on a stoop, talking to a pregnant young woman who had brought her sewing out to work on so she could enjoy the fun.

In another time, Viv would have asked about the woman's husband, but she kept quiet. There were so few nights like this, ones that weren't tainted by the war. The evening was tinged gold and pink, and Viv had no desire to bring any darkness into it.

Instead, they talked about the baseball games of their youths, of the woman's son, who had been playing first base, of Hale, even.

Tomorrow would come, it always did. And with it, the sorrow they'd so carefully pushed away tonight.

Maybe the reprieve felt small given the enormity of what they were all coping with. But it felt similar to how Viv viewed the reprieve the ASEs must give the soldiers. A small reminder that life wasn't just blood and bombs and fear.

And if they could all hold on to those reminders, if they could help each other create them, maybe together they would be able to make it through this godforsaken war. Not necessarily whole, but human.

Chapter 27

Paris
November 1936

The bitter smell of carbonic soap sat in the back of Hannah's nostrils as she watched Otto's chest rise and fall in the hospital bed.

He would live, the doctors had promised.

She didn't need to hear the hesitation in their voices to know it had been a near thing.

Hannah's fingers found the butt of the pistol she now carried with her anywhere she went.

It had been three days since the attack on the boulevard Saint-Germain and she'd only been home once to change and to fish the weapon out of the dark space beneath her floorboards. Never again would she be as defenseless as she had been on the street, desperate and pleading for help that just wouldn't come.

The fight itself had been a blur, snatches of memories elusive and yet viscerally horrifying. But she wasn't sure she would ever forget locking eyes with her colleagues. All of the other library volunteers must have rushed out on the street, because they'd all been there. Standing, watching, doing nothing.

Her eyes drifted toward the window, to the sun creeping above the Parisian skyline.

For perhaps the thousandth time, she told herself her friends from the library were intellectuals, thinkers. They probably had never thrown a punch in their lives, let alone fought the kind of brutes whose bodies had been crafted for violence. It would have been a death sentence for them.

Otto moaned, twisted beneath the sheets, then settled.

The doctors said he would live. But what would become of him? What would become of Hannah?

The way she knew the coming war would change her—had already changed her—was terrifying. Once upon a time, she had been happy and lighthearted. She had always been the cynic to Adam's idealist, but she had never had ice around her heart.

There had been so many nights in Berlin that she had danced, and laughed and loved, where she'd drunk too much champagne and worn expensive silk dresses and went on bicycle rides on the first day of spring simply to collect tulips in her basket. She had believed in the basic goodness of people, that most were just trying to do their best in a world that could sometimes be hard. She had been open and kind and sarcastic, a good friend and a good sister. Not necessarily a good daughter, but she didn't blame herself for that. She had loved bread and orange marmalade and a night at the theater, and she had quiet dreams that had seemed like they might be possible.

War—and she had decided they *were* at war—had a way of stripping away all those small things and then amplifying what was left. There were no tiny irritations or minor celebrations. It was all love and hate, fear and courage, poetry and destruction, everything more intense because of the contrast, the middle ground no longer there.

But the small things were what made a person. Hannah already felt gutted from grief, from betrayal, from a slow erosion of her faith in mankind.

What would she look like next year, and the next? Who would she be? Because the woman she had been in Berlin would never have dreamed she could pull a trigger.

Now, Hannah palmed the pistol, wincing when the metal nudged against her fingers. One of the Nazis had broken three of them. She hadn't even noticed at the time.

The green-purple-yellow bruises that had bloomed along Hannah's cheekbone were still the worst of her injuries, though. At the very edge of them she swore she could make out the shape of a boot.

IT TOOK TWO more days before Otto's lashes fluttered against his pale skin, once, twice. Then he opened his eyes.

Tears spilled down Hannah's cheeks, trickling onto the split lip that had barely been worth mentioning.

She wasn't sure what she would have done if she'd lost Otto so close to the news of Adam's death. Hannah had always considered herself strong. She'd survived Berlin in Hitler's rising days, she'd survived Althea's betrayal, she'd survived every day knowing she'd played a part in her brother's capture.

But she was certain that if Otto had died, she would have finally—finally—broken.

"He'll need someone to watch him for a few days," the doctor said as if it was even a question of who that would be.

They made it back to Otto's apartment after only having to stop the driver once to pull over so Otto could retch into the gutter. Hannah stroked the hair back from his forehead and made soothing sounds until it was over.

When they arrived at Otto's, Hannah tucked him beneath a warm blanket and crossed the room to put the kettle on. She touched the copy of *Macbeth* that sat next to the stove and wondered if his injuries meant Otto would lose the role he'd just been cast in the week before.

"You're hurt," Otto murmured when she turned back to him. He reached one gentle, shaky finger up to trace the outside line of her bruises.

"Hardly," she scoffed. "You should see the other guys."

Otto laughed so hard he ended up bent over, coughing up blood, the pristine white handkerchief flecked in the same way the Nazi's knuckles had been. Hannah swallowed the bile that rose in her throat.

"Rest, darling," she said, pressing a warm cloth to his forehead.

He didn't argue, a clear sign of his exhaustion.

In the following days, he slept more than he was awake, and through it all, Hannah sat in the rocking chair next to his bed. At some point, she helped him into a bath, scrubbing the dried sweat and blood from his precious skin. He winced and then sighed and then nearly dozed off as she dragged the soap along his shoulders, his thighs, his groin, his stomach. The intimacy of it should have been heavier than it was. But Hannah could barely think straight let alone be squeamish about such things as a body that she knew nearly better than her own.

She wrapped him in a towel and dried him with careful hands. He slept then, and she refilled the tub, stepping in herself.

As she soaped herself clean, she tried to grasp onto the resentment that had burned bright in her while she'd stood helpless over the fight.

They had been on a main street in Paris. She could almost forgive the strangers, the ones who had no reason to involve themselves in a brawl that vicious. But so many in the crowd that had surrounded them had been friends, people who thought of themselves as soldiers in the war against fascism.

Hannah sincerely believed in the power of words to fight this battle, so much so that it had become her life's work. The library was important. It had started as a symbol, a beacon, a bulwark. From there it had grown into a practical resource. The people who worked there *had* won people over with the information they offered.

But if one side of this war was made up of men wild with bloodlust, and the other was made up of men who froze at the sight of violence, Hannah wasn't sure the latter stood a chance.

The pen might be able to destroy a nation eventually, but by the time it did, how many bodies would the sword have claimed?

What would happen when the Nazis marched into Paris, when they occupied it, as she was certain would happen? Would anyone fight back?

Did bravery actually exist in real life, or was it just for fairy tales?

Chapter 28

Berlin
March 1933

Two days after that night at Dev's place when Althea had her come-to-Jesus moment, Hannah showed up with two bicycles.

"Let's go," Hannah said, straddling the saddle of the sunny yellow one and holding on to the bars of the other. It was sky blue with little roses painted along the metal. A wicker basket sat at the front, and Althea imagined procuring books or flowers to fill it with.

"I'm not very agile," Althea warned as she swung herself into the seat.

"Babies can ride bicycles," Hannah called over. "I think you'll manage."

"You have far too much faith in my athletic abilities," Althea cried over her shoulder as her front tire headed straight for a tree.

Despite a few clumps of dirty snow left over from a late-spring storm, the day was beautiful, the sun warm on Althea's face as they pedaled through the streets.

Hannah kept them to the quiet ones, avoiding the boulevards and thoroughfares that surely would have thrown Althea into a panic.

Instead it was all quaint storefronts, strolling couples, and giggling children. They worked their way along the Spree and stopped when they felt like it, rested and walked and shared silly anecdotes about similar days when they'd been young.

At a small park, Althea hopped off her bicycle, letting it drop on the grass so she could explore the garden of tulips that were just starting to bloom. Hannah trailed behind her, a small smile the only indication that she didn't mind Althea's chattering.

They sprawled in a sunny patch of grass and Hannah positioned herself so she was providing shade for Althea's face.

"You love Berlin," Althea commented idly, smoothing her blouse down over her stomach.

"I've always been able to be myself here," Hannah said, and Althea wondered at the depth of emotion in her voice. "You can't see it with the Nazis, but before they took over, you could be anyone you wanted in this city and you would find people who loved you for it."

Althea tried to parse through that. "Like at the cabarets?"

"Precisely," Hannah said with a smile. "There, it doesn't matter what you dress like, or who you dance with, or what you do for a living. It doesn't matter who your parents are or what neighborhood you live in or what God you pray to. All you have to do is appreciate and respect the people around you and you'll have a home with them."

Hannah's gaze shifted toward two Nazis strolling by on the sidewalk, and then to the swastikas hanging from the streetlamps nearby. "Plus, Hitler hates it here, you know."

"I'd heard that."

"Anywhere Hitler hates is a good place in my book," Hannah said, grinning down at Althea.

Althea flushed then looked away. "I wish . . ."

She trailed off because she didn't truly know how to finish the thought. Althea couldn't say *I wish I'd never come here.* That would be a lie.

But Hannah just kicked Althea's ankle lightly with the toe of her boot. "I wish I had a day where I could pretend all this wasn't happening."

Althea studied Hannah's face, but her expression was hidden in shadows. "What would you do with that day?"

"Go on a bicycle ride," Hannah said, with a wicked curve to her mouth. "Read a book, drink a glass of wine. Kiss a pretty . . ."

This time it was Hannah who didn't finish her thought. But Althea saw the words lingering on her lips.

Fumbling for her bag gave Althea an excuse to tuck her face down and hide whatever emotions played across her expression. "Well, I have a book."

It was a copy of *Alice in Wonderland,* one she'd picked up only a few days after she'd gifted her other one to the bookseller at the winter market. It had been only a few months since that night and yet it felt like years.

"Are we checking things off my list, then?" Hannah asked, with a wink in her voice. Maybe this was just how she talked, and Althea was reading too much in between the lines. But the sweat on her lower back and the slight tremble of her hands suggested she might not be.

She turned to one of her favorite passages and began reading, just loud enough for Hannah to hear, so they could get lost in their own little world.

> "Who are you?" said the Caterpillar.
>
> This was not an encouraging opening for a conversation. Alice replied, rather shyly, "I—I hardly know, Sir, just at present—at least I know who I was when I got up this morning, but I think I must have been changed several times since then."

After Althea finished the chapter, she let the open book fall to her chest, let her eyes slip closed as she relished the sensation of just lying in the sun with a heartbeat next to her own. Hannah's knee nudged hers after a few long minutes.

"We have a list, don't we?" Hannah whispered, as if it were their secret. She stood and held her hand out to Althea.

Warm palm met warm palm, and Hannah easily pulled Althea to her feet. Althea stumbled on the way up, her body tipping into Hannah's. Her skin tingled and went hot at the places where they touched and she looked away and then stepped away.

As they climbed back onto their bikes, Althea couldn't help that her eyes slid to Hannah, couldn't help that they lingered on her profile, on the curve of her neck and the slope of her shoulders, on her calves as they flexed against the pedals.

A few blocks later, Hannah signaled for Althea to dismount in front of a small café.

Drink a glass of wine.

They took a table outside, cramming into the small bit of shade offered up by the striped awning. The waiter brought them goblets filled with pale pink wine that must match the blush on Althea's face as she refused to think of the next item on Hannah's list.

"When did you know you wanted to be a writer?" Hannah asked, lightly skimming Althea's knuckles with the tips of her fingers before sitting back with her glass. It could have been an absent touch, but something about the knowing smile Hannah now wore made Althea think otherwise.

"Always, I think," she said, fighting shyness. "My brother was a fussy child, and my father died when we were young, so it was just my mother and us. I wanted to help, and that's what came out."

"Stories," Hannah said.

"Stories," Althea agreed. "And then when he got older . . ." She paused and chewed on her lip.

Hannah nudged Althea's ankle with her own and then left it there, caught, her calf pressed against Althea's, a warm point of connection.

"My town was so small," she said, with just a slight tremor in her voice. "It was a habit, I guess. To tell stories. But when he no longer needed them, I started telling them to myself." She stared down at her drink.

"Of course." Not mocking but fond. Almost. Maybe.

"It started out because there was nothing else to do," Althea said. "A way to pass the time, telling stories in my head. But then . . ." She huffed, frustrated. She'd always had a harder time talking, saying anything, than she did writing it. "I never really fit in. I was quiet and shy, I liked reading as much as I liked telling myself stories. And I never really cared about the things that I should have cared about.

"And when you write a story, you get to decide exactly how it goes," Althea continued. "It doesn't have to hurt like real life does."

"But it also can't bring the joy real life does," Hannah countered, and Althea tipped her head in acknowledgment. The highs had never been worth the lows before.

Before Berlin.

"The world scared me before I came here," Althea admitted. "I was sensitive as a child, so even the smallest cut felt like it would bleed forever. Emotionally speaking."

"Of course."

"So, I wrapped myself in pretend so that nothing could reach me," Althea said. "But then I came to Berlin." She shook her head and met Hannah's eyes. "What did I have to be scared of? Some cruel taunts? That's it. Nothing compared to—"

Hannah reached out to squeeze Althea's hand. "Not today." Her thumb brushed against the inside of Althea's wrist. "Please."

"Well, so I told myself stories about a world where I wasn't different," Althea said, but then shook her head. That wasn't quite right. She hurried to correct herself. "I mean a world where being different was all right. It was good to be different."

"That sounds nice," Hannah said, something encouraging layered beneath the neutral words.

"Then I realized I could tell other stories, too," Althea rushed on before she opened up her chest any further. "And that became a habit, as well."

Hannah smiled over the rim of her glass. "Will you tell me a story now?"

Althea blushed, but scrambled to find words, because Hannah asked for so little. And so as they finished their drinks and moved on to a second glass, Althea did what she'd always done for her brother and made Hannah the protagonist of her tale. "Once upon a time, there was a young girl who was very brave . . ."

She sent young Hannah on an adventure to fight a dragon who was terrorizing a village. But the Hannah in her story realized that the elders in the village wanted her to kill the dragon so they could steal its gold. They'd slaughtered their own cattle and burned their own neighbors' houses to the ground to make their lies about the imaginary dragon believable.

"How does it end?" Hannah asked, eyes wide.

Althea chewed on her lip before asking, "Do you want a happy ending or a complicated one?"

Hannah thought about it for long enough that Althea could tell she had taken the question seriously. "The latter."

"Hannah exposes the elders' treachery to the village. It is decided that for their evil deeds, the men should be sacrificed to the dragon."

"The dragon would never eat them, though," Hannah decided, and Althea smiled at that.

"No, the dragon intervened and had the men banished instead," Althea continued.

"That's not the end?" Hannah asked.

"It would be, if you liked happy endings," Althea said. "But no. For a while, the village thrived beneath the protection of both Hannah and the dragon. Then a new leader was chosen to fill the void the elders left. The man viewed Hannah as a rival. He knew she was very brave, though, so instead of threatening *her* life, he threatened the dragon's. Hannah was forced to flee the village, forced to leave behind her family in order to protect her beloved friend."

"Did the dragon go with her?"

"Of course," Althea said, dipping her head. "They walked for days and days until they found a new cave, one that fit both of them."

"They found a home, together," Hannah said, in a tone weightier than a silly tale about a dragon and an adventurer should merit.

"They started their own village," Althea continued. "And the word spread far and wide that anyone who didn't belong anywhere, who didn't feel like they had a home, could find refuge with them."

The corners of Hannah's mouth tipped up as she studied Althea's face. "I was right."

"About what?" Althea asked, warm and a bit dizzy from the careful attention.

"The complicated ending was better."

Chapter 29

New York City
May 1944

"You have to get Althea's ASE pushed up," Viv said without preamble as she slid into the seat across from Mr. Stern the day after her impromptu baseball game with Hale.

He looked up from whatever he'd been working on and blinked at her from behind his glasses. "What?"

"Althea James," Viv said, as if it were obvious even though this request could be the definition of *long shot*. "*An Inconceivable Dark* is slated for the August series of the Armed Services Editions. We need to get her moved up to June."

"Which is tomorrow," Mr. Stern said, stating the obvious.

The logistics of changing up the ASE schedule were daunting at best. The system had been built with speed and efficiency in mind, but each step of the process took time that Viv didn't have. The only reason she could even ask for this favor was because the print run for Althea's book should be wrapping up any day now.

"Is there any way to do a special shipment?" Viv asked. "To a limited number of bases, possibly. I know there's some wiggle room in the budget for distribution."

Mail was always uncertain these days, but Viv would hand-deliver the soldiers' letters to Miss James if she had to.

"What do you hope to accomplish?" Mr. Stern asked, which wasn't a no.

"Well, the book is political enough that I think it would get caught up in the restrictions from the Taft amendment if we wait until August," Viv said. "If we get it out in the next couple of weeks we can say the bill was signed too late to alter the series."

"That is true," Mr. Stern said.

"And I just spoke with Althea's editor from Harper & Brothers," Viv said. As she'd predicted, Harrison had easily been able to arrange a phone call. "He won't 'betray her trust'—his exact words—by setting up a meeting between us. But he did promise to make my case to her and let her decide what she wants after that. We know that every time we send out a book the author gets flooded with letters from soldiers. Even if the distribution is limited, we would still likely receive a bagful, at least. It might help persuade her."

"There's no guarantee she'd receive the letters in time, even if we sent her book to the men today," Mr. Stern pointed out. "Why not choose someone else? She hasn't made a public appearance in a decade. I worry you're putting too many eggs in one basket here."

"You know how much press and attention we would get if she spoke at the event," Viv said. "It's just . . . her editor says she gets a bit odd when the subject of politics is raised. I think she's wary of the legislation side of this because of whatever happened to her with the Nazis."

"A guest of the Reich may not play as well as you think it will." Mr. Stern held up a hand to cut off her protests. "All right, let's set aside the fact that she may be a Nazi sympathizer. Do you honestly believe a few more letters from soldiers will be enough to convince her to show? If she despises politics—and the spotlight—as much as you think she does."

Viv searched for a good argument but couldn't quite find one. She threw up her hands. "Well, maybe not. But will it hurt to try?"

Mr. Stern removed his glasses and squeezed the bridge of his nose, and Viv didn't push. She knew when to shut up—another one of her skills.

"Christ," Mr. Stern said.

The way he all but sighed out the word caught her attention. The weariness in it had to have come from something other than her somewhat simple request.

"What?" Viv asked.

His eyes flicked behind her and he took a breath. But instead of saying anything, he stood up, closed the door, returned to his seat, and continued not to say anything.

"Is this confidential?" Viv asked, leaning forward and keeping her voice low.

He sighed and then seemed to nod to himself. "There is something happening."

"All right," she said.

"I can say almost nothing about it . . ."

She waved her hand in the universal *go on* gesture.

"Roosevelt has been particularly interested—and by that I mean *personally* interested—in the June series of ASEs," Mr. Stern said, each word loaded with a significance she didn't quite understand yet.

Viv shook her head. "Why would . . ."

He just stared at her, and she desperately willed her mind to keep up.

Roosevelt had championed the ASE program since the beginning, saying it did wonders for the morale of the troops, for the soldiers who were risking their lives on the daily—

Viv inhaled sharply. She tried to swallow but her mouth had gone dry. This was too big for her to know. As softly as she could, she managed, "They're planning an invasion."

Mr. Stern made a sound like he wanted to stop the words even as they tumbled out of her mouth. "I didn't say that."

"No, but why else would he personally intervene?" Viv asked, her eyes dropping to the floor as her mind finally caught up now that the panic-induced crashing cymbals had stopped echoing against the walls of her skull. "He wants the boys to have the books when they go to slaughter. Christ."

"Stop, Vivian, I'm serious, none of that leaves this room," he said. "You have to act like you don't know anything."

"Why did you . . ." She couldn't even finish the sentence. *Why did you tell me? Why did you burden me with this?*

"Because General Eisenhower requested that each and every man participating in the invasion have a book. Which means I already changed the publishing schedule three weeks ago," Mr. Stern said, and Viv's eyes snapped to his. "We needed to add several more selections to June's series."

"One of which was Althea's?" Viv asked, barely daring to hope. But something about the mischievous tilt of Mr. Stern's smile told her the answer anyway. "You let me make my case knowing full well—"

Mr. Stern cut off her tirade before it could gain speed. "As you can imagine, it's been handled as need-to-know information. Only the board and the army liaisons were kept up to date."

Viv wasn't about to look a gift horse in the mouth. If Althea

James's book had gone out with the last shipment, that meant soldiers would potentially be reading it within the next week. The timing would still be tight for the letters, but she could always reliably count on a couple dozen coming in within a month of the books being distributed.

Mr. Stern cleared his throat. "There's something else you should know. As I've said before, I believe I have to comply with Taft's amendment now that it's law. But the council's executive board met yesterday and the members have voiced their own concerns." He paused, tapping his desk with absent fingers. He wouldn't meet her eyes. "They specifically mentioned the *Strange Fruit* brouhaha in Boston, as well. They said between that and Taft, the censorship movement is starting to gain some traction. They're worried about where it's headed."

"That's why I'm putting on this event," Viv said, feeling slow for pointing out the obvious.

"The board has asked Mr. Marshal Best of Viking Books and Mr. Curtis Hitchcock of Reynal & Hitchcock to draw up an official resolution against the amendment."

Viv blinked at him, and could only manage to get out a breathy "What?"

"The executive board of course appreciates your efforts," Mr. Stern said stiffly, in that overly formal way he used when delivering bad news. "But they see an official resolution as a more concrete step to getting Taft to rescind the amendment."

Viv knew some members of the board viewed her as a bit of fluff with a meaningless title granted to a woman with a deep wallet. They thought she read the newspapers for mentions of the ASEs, clipped them, and sent them up the chain of command. They thought she parroted to journalists pat quotes that had been approved by more important men. They thought she gave tours to prominent librarians while reading from a script someone else wrote.

She supposed looking from the outside in those things probably seemed true. But Mr. Stern had never made her feel like he agreed with them. Until now.

"Do they want me to cancel my event, then?" Viv asked.

Mr. Stern's eyes widened. "No, no. No. They, of course, hope that the event will no longer be necessary. But they see it as an excellent backup plan."

Viv took a breath as she imagined all her work becoming redundant. And then exhaled. This could only be a good thing. The public weight of the council coming out against Taft was no small matter. "How can I help?"

The tense lines of Mr. Stern's mouth relaxed. "I thought you would be angry."

"I am," she admitted with a shrug that was far more careless than she felt. "But stomping out of here would be chopping off my nose to spite my face."

He smiled, almost sadly. "The resolution will carry little political weight. Since it's more of a statement than anything. But we want to get it out to newspapers across the country, run it as a full-page ad in as many magazines as you see fit. Use the discretionary funds."

She stood up, then hesitated. "Why did you choose Althea's book? That was before I even knew I wanted her to speak at the event."

"It was one of the books that was ready to ship," Mr. Stern said. When she lifted her brows at the silent *and* she could hear, he sighed and sat back in his chair. "As you know the book is about censorship efforts. I . . . may have wanted to stack the deck in our favor." He laughed. "Don't look so surprised. I don't want Taft's amendment to succeed any more than you do. I might not have envisioned a public shaming to get him to change his mind, but you're not the only one who reads the soldiers' letters. I know how persuasive they can be."

Viv pressed her lips together to hide a pleased smile. "We're not being selfish, are we? Would a different book have been better for the troops?"

"It's a good book, I didn't pick it just because of this fight with Taft," he said. "Maybe when Miss James gets the letters that will inevitably pour in, she'll start to think of herself as something other than a political pawn."

"She still would be one, of course. But"—Viv shook her head—"maybe she would realize that's not all she is."

Chapter 30

Berlin
April 1933

The Resistance meetings terrified Althea, and yet she was proud of herself for going.

Adam Brecht hugged her at the first one she'd gone to after her day with Hannah.

"Why does he care?" Althea asked Hannah after Adam drifted away again. "Like you said, I'm just one person. I can't mean all that much."

They took a seat in the back, and Hannah was quiet so long Althea thought she might not answer at all.

"He doesn't necessarily care about you personally changing your mind about the Nazis," Hannah said. "It's that you were able to once you learned more about them."

"I represent hope." Althea had represented many things to many people, but she thought this might be the best she'd heard.

"It's good for him to see," Hannah said. There was something in her voice that had Althea shifting toward her.

"You're worried about him."

"He's been different since the fire, since Clara was arrested," Hannah said. "I don't blame him, but, yes, I worry."

"What do you think he'll do?" Althea asked, hating that the fear she was so familiar with was suffocating her newfound courage.

Hannah narrowed her eyes on Althea's face, but she didn't hesitate as long as she would have before. "Something to get everyone's attention."

"Something like what?" Althea's voice rose enough that a few people around them glanced over in concern. She leaned forward to whisper, "Like an assassination?"

"I don't know," Hannah said, but she sounded like she did. "But he's being reckless. He won't do anyone any good sitting in a detention center beside Clara."

Neither of them mentioned that Adam, as a man, would be far more likely to be executed if he were caught plotting against the Nazis. Hannah didn't need to hear that from Althea.

"Will he listen to you?" Althea asked. "If you try to tell him not to."

"He won't listen to any of us," Hannah said. "I've had Dev talk to him, too. And Otto. But Adam keeps saying that we can't think small any longer."

Althea's eyes found Adam. He was at the front, speaking with a woman a head taller than him, his expression one of intense concentration. Always looking at someone he was with as if they were the only other person in the world.

She tried not to picture him in the square, strapped to a Saint Andrew's cross with a woman on her knees in front of him. But he was a young Jewish man, a communist with a rebellious spirit and a soul that was built for revolution. Althea could tell that after only meeting him twice.

Even if Hannah managed to derail whatever revenge he was plotting, what was his future in a country full of men like Diedrich and Goebbels and Hitler?

What was Hannah's?

A warm hand settled against her arm. Hannah's hand. Her thumb stroked the soft skin of Althea's wrist, a comforting gesture that had become a secret message between them.

If you touch . . . you can feel a person's heart.

The meeting went long into the night. Some participants talked strategy—slashing the tires on Nazi officers' cars and sabotaging train lines. Others focused on propaganda, still believing they could win over the general public with mailers and clever graffiti. Still others talked about patrolling the streets to help anyone targeted by the brownshirts.

Adam gave a speech at the end that Althea's writer's mind couldn't help critiquing as too fiery, with no chance to build.

Still, when he ended it once more with his quote from *Les Misérables* neither Hannah nor Althea laughed.

Attending the meetings became a routine, as much as going to the cabarets in February had. Diedrich was growing more and more frustrated that she wouldn't keep him apprised of what she was doing at night, but he was so busy working for Goebbels now that she was able to get away with it.

Adam's group met often, especially in the days following the Nazis' first official Jewish boycott. The boycott itself hadn't been very successful for the Nazis—who'd deliberately held it on Shabbat when many Jewish businesses were closed anyway. But it signaled the start of what everyone could tell was coming. Only a week later, Hitler passed a law that excluded Jews from working in civil service positions. It would only get worse from there.

Hannah was clearly growing increasingly worried for Adam. She still hadn't managed to figure out what exactly he had planned, but the way she described how he talked about it had Althea just as concerned. She couldn't imagine it was anything but a suicide mission.

When she carefully mentioned that possibility, Hannah's mouth went tight, but she didn't disagree.

"We'll tie him to a chair if we have to," Dev said. There were shadows beneath her eyes as well when she talked of Adam these days.

It wasn't all terrible, though.

Most of the nights, Hannah walked Althea home when the group disbanded. They talked of literature just like Althea and Diedrich had, but Hannah actually listened instead of waiting for her turn to make her own opinion known.

"I'm worried everyone will be disappointed," Althea confessed one night as they strolled along the river. "With my second novel. What if my first was just a fluke? What if people bought it because they liked the story of an uneducated girl and the American Dream, or something like that?"

"You can't control other people's reactions to your art. You can only control what you produce." Hannah glanced at her. "Do you know what you'll write about?"

"Fear," Althea said with a certainty she hadn't realized she had until the word tumbled from her mouth. She didn't know in what context she'd place the novel, but she knew that would be its central tenet. "So much of this is because of fear, isn't it? All Hitler had to do was make people afraid: There is a monster out there who will attack you if you don't let me protect you."

"And if that requires sacrificing a few freedoms, then that's the price for law and order, isn't it?" Hannah finished the thought.

"I know it's more complicated," Althea admitted. "But it's one of the roots, and it's a deep one." She didn't mention that she worried it was one of *her* roots, as well, one that was curled around the fabric of her soul. She changed the subject before Hannah could share that realization. "What will you do?"

"After university?" Hannah asked. When Althea nodded, Hannah tipped her head. "I think I've stopped considering I have a future."

Althea inhaled, harshly and overloud in the quiet night. "Don't say that."

"It's true," Hannah said, her mouth set in a grim line. "My future is trying to survive, if anything."

As much as Althea wanted to argue with that, she couldn't. "What would you do, if you could do anything?"

Hannah shook her head. "Pretty fantasies hurt more."

"You'd work with books," Althea pressed, an itch at the base of her spine making her do it. She needed to picture Hannah happy, free, doing what she loved. Even if it was impossible and they both knew it.

"There's a song," Hannah said. Then she sang, in her low husky voice. "'We are children of a different world, we only love the lavender night that is sultry . . .'"

Althea recognized the melody, had caught snippets of it at cabarets. It was one of those songs that everyone stopped, sang, and swayed along with. She didn't really understand it, though Hannah sang it as if it meant something more to her than just words and notes.

"It's for people like . . . ," Hannah said after finishing. "People like me."

"Jews?" Althea asked.

"No," Hannah said, but then didn't expand further. "I've always loved the line about wandering through a thousand wonders."

Althea tried to call up the exact verse.

We are just different from the others,
who curiously wander at first through a thousand wonders,
and yet only see the banal in the end.

"I think, if I could, I would have a bookshop," Hannah said, before Althea could really think through the lyrics. "And I would call it that."

"A thousand wonders." Althea liked the way that sentiment tasted on her tongue. What were books, what were stories, if not just that?

"Where would you want it to be?" Althea asked.

Hannah simply smiled sadly. "Here."

No conversation topic was too private, too much, too sensitive, and oftentimes they took the long way home, their knuckles brushing, their shoulders pressed together.

One night, Hannah lingered in front of Althea's door, leaning in close as pedestrians passed on the sidewalk behind her.

Althea's breath hitched, her body going too hot and then cold. But Hannah just swiped her thumb against the inside of Althea's wrist.

Hannah watched her for a minute longer, and then whispered, "Good night," before turning and heading off down the street.

Somehow Althea made it inside the apartment before her knees gave out and she sunk to the floor, dizzy and confused and a little excited all at once.

She wasn't some silly schoolgirl who didn't know what this

was. The same flutter had lived in her chest, the same heat had pooled between her legs in those early days in Germany when she'd thought Diedrich the most beautiful man she'd ever met.

This was stronger, though, more terrifying because of how it had settled into her bones like it was a part of her now.

Althea was a coward, and the idea of this, of *them* together, made her want to hide beneath her bed and never come out.

But she was now Berlin's version of Althea James. Berlin's version of Althea James flirted, and laughed, and went to cabarets with beautiful women who smiled like they were giving something of themselves over to you.

So maybe she could be brave. Just this once.

Chapter 31

New York City
June 1944

The invasion came on a warm summer day in New York City.

Charlotte woke Viv only a few minutes past six A.M., the day's *New York Times* in her hands.

"Special early edition," Charlotte explained in a tight voice as she handed it over.

Viv blinked the sleep out of her eyes as she took it. The headline dominated much of the top of the page.

ALLIED ARMIES LAND IN FRANCE IN THE HAVRE-CHERBOURG AREA; GREAT INVASION IS UNDER WAY

Underneath was a map of the English Channel and northern France. Viv devoured the accompanying article.

> In the gray light of a summer dawn Gen. Dwight D. Eisenhower threw his great Anglo-American force into action. . . . Eisenhower's first communique was terse and calculated to give little information to the enemy. . . . German broadcasts

> gave first word of the assault. . . . Eisenhower told his forces they were about to embark on a "great crusade." The eyes of the world are upon you, he said, and the "hopes and prayers of liberty-loving people everywhere march with you."

By the time Viv finished reading, her hand had flown to her mouth. She met Charlotte's grim eyes. "It's begun."

Those were the only two words they spoke to each other as they headed toward the kitchen, flipped on the wireless, and sat on the stools for the next three hours listening to every report they could find.

Eventually, though, Viv's skin went tight and itchy, her legs restless. "We can't sit here all day."

Charlotte nodded once. "You're right. Church first, though."

Again in silence, they parted ways to dress. Viv didn't take any extra time, simply pinned her hair back from her face, shrugged into a simple white shirt and gray skirt, and smudged on lipstick, smearing some of the color into her cheeks so she didn't appear deathly pale.

She paused only when she went to step into her shoes, eyeing her dresser drawers. If today wasn't a special occasion, what was?

In two strides she crossed the room and found her precious silk stockings. She dug out her garters, and then methodically went through the familiar motions of putting them on. The swish of nylon against skin not only soothed her but hinted at a future she hadn't dared think about since the moment she'd read that headline.

When she and Charlotte stepped out into the street, at first it seemed like any other day.

Then Viv looked closer.

The same strange tangle of grief and elation that Viv had

been grappling with all morning was reflected in the face of every passerby; people were gathering in groups in front of stores as men stood on soapboxes reading the news straight from the paper; stories-high American flags flapped against building fronts; men, women, and children wandered the streets, aimless, but, like Viv and Charlotte, too antsy to stay inside.

When they reached the church, a new sign beckoned them inside: INVASION DAY: Come In and Pray for Allied Victory.

There was only enough space to stand, and Viv found herself pressed tight to strangers who didn't feel like strangers at the moment. She wrapped an arm around the woman next to her, whose mascara had smeared down her cheeks, held Charlotte's hand with her own free one, and closed her eyes.

The priest wasn't giving mass, but simply leading the congregation in prayer, the words a balm against the sour wound that had opened with the knowledge that thousands of men would be slaughtered today. Had been slaughtered already. Even if the Allies emerged victorious, there could be no celebrating that kind of death. There could only be celebrating the possible end to such violence.

Bodies continued to pour into the church and Viv squeezed Charlotte's hand. They had been there long enough that Viv thought they should make room for others. Charlotte nodded once.

"Times Square," Charlotte muttered after they stumbled outside. It was getting hard to maneuver on the sidewalk outside St. Vincente's.

A few blocks later, they passed a synagogue offering twenty-four-hour service, and Viv thought of the librarian in Brooklyn. Wondered how she'd woken up to the news. Wondered if she had someone to hold her today, to offer her comfort.

Viv hoped she did.

It wouldn't be fair to say Times Square had come to a standstill, but it almost seemed that way. Everyone was turned in one direction, their faces tilted up toward the *New York Times* ticker that read simply: ALLIED ARMIES INVADE EUROPE. Taxis blared their horns to get people to move, but they were all caught in some sort of stasis.

"Viv," someone cried from the crowd, and Viv turned to see Bernice Westwood from the council weaving her way toward her and Charlotte.

When Bernice caught up to them, Viv hugged her tight. "Are you alone?"

"No," Bernice sighed out, pulling back just enough to talk. "My boy's home on leave for a broken arm, if you can imagine."

Her laugh came out watery, and Viv knew she must be guilt-ridden at the relief she felt over her lover's luck.

Squeezing the girl's arms fiercely, Viv said, "I'm so glad."

"The mayor is holding an event in Madison Square if you'd like to join."

Viv silently checked in with Charlotte, who had torn her eyes from the ticker to watch the exchange. They had been walking for a long time now, and Viv could barely feel her own feet. She couldn't imagine how exhausted Charlotte must be.

But Charlotte simply nodded, and who was Viv to doubt her resilience?

"We'll come, of course," Viv said.

Signs urging victory and American flags flapped above the heads of the crowd. A man bearing a tuba and playing "The Star-Spangled Banner" barreled past Viv, the metal of his horn knocking into her elbow. Toddlers dressed in garb designed to mimic American uniforms sat on fathers' shoulders, squealing in delight, their enthusiasm undampened by the tension that kept the adults restrained.

"Good news for the ASEs," Bernice managed to yell into Viv's ear as they neared Madison Square. It was getting tough to move as those behind them pressed ever forward into a space that could hold only so many people.

Viv fought the urge to slap back at Bernice for thinking of such petty things right now, knowing she didn't actually deserve it. Viv's own mind had tracked a similar path back in Mr. Stern's office when she first realized what an invasion would mean for her own plans. "Yes, I think it might be."

Charlotte seemed to sense her distress, though, and gave her a discreet tug. It was enough to separate her from Bernice, and quickly three women rushed into the opening they'd created.

A makeshift stage had been set up at one end of the square, with a band flanked by American flags. A man with a film-reel camera stood perched on the hood of a car a few feet over from Viv, capturing the scene.

Only a few minutes later, Mayor Fiorello La Guardia took the stage in front of a bank of microphones rigged to speakers so that even the furthest person back could hear his nasally voice. After a squeal of audio had the crowd flinching in unison, La Guardia led those gathered in prayer and urged them to hold tight to their faith.

"We, the people of the City of New York, humbly petition Him to bring total victory to your arms in the great and valiant struggle for the liberation of the world from tyranny," he cried out, the tubas breaking into song at his feet.

Viv and Charlotte lost themselves in the momentum of the day. Singers came onstage following La Guardia's address, as did more speakers. The crowd ebbed and flowed, a man started selling bottles of Coke on the corner nearest them, another began handing out signs proclaiming support for Roosevelt and the troops, music erupted from various points in the audience, men saluted, and over it all American flags presided.

Eventually, Charlotte slipped an arm around Viv's waist. "I think it's time to go home."

The streets became more subdued as they made their way north. Charlotte was limping after only a few blocks, so Viv directed her toward the subway, which she wasn't sure Charlotte had ever ridden in her life. Taxis were jamming the streets, though, unable to maneuver around the crowds spilling off the sidewalks.

In the subway car they chose, three men played fiddles for a sad Irish song that a woman seated next to them crooned out in Gaelic. Beside Viv, Charlotte wept silently.

"Seven months," she managed, and Viv knew she was talking about Edward, knew she was wondering why God couldn't have spared him just to make it to the end of the war.

Viv had no platitudes to offer. They'd both heard them all.

When they got home, Viv realized neither of them had eaten since a quick breakfast that morning. She nudged Charlotte onto a kitchen stool and then plucked the apron off the pantry hook and tied it around her own waist.

"Pancakes," Viv decided.

"For dinner?" Charlotte asked, her eyes still red but the tears dried up.

Viv didn't mention how they were Edward's favorite. Instead, she winked. "We're adventurous women. Why not?"

"This adventurous woman needs some port to go along with those," Charlotte said, groaning as she climbed to her feet once more. She managed to hobble to the drink cart to pour them both a generous dose, sliding Viv's glass across the counter as she climbed back onto the stool with a moan. "I won't be able to walk for a week, I don't think."

Cracking a precious egg into a bowl, Viv smiled. "We'll hire men to carry you like Cleopatra."

"I like how you think, my dear." Charlotte raised her glass to Viv.

They talked as Viv worked, but not about the invasion, not about the day. There was too much to worry about, so, in silent agreement, they both pretended it was a normal evening.

They got away with it, too, until Charlotte turned the wireless on just in time to catch the introduction for the president. Viv could all but hear the hum of a thousand radios tuned in to one message.

Roosevelt's voice rang clear and true in the kitchen. "Almighty God: Our sons, pride of our Nation, this day have set upon a mighty endeavor, a struggle to preserve our Republic, our religion, and our civilization, and to set free a suffering humanity.

"Lead them straight and true; give strength to their arms, stoutness to their hearts, steadfastness in their faith."

Viv tossed back the remainder of her port.

It was going to be a long, dark few months ahead.

Chapter 32

Paris
December 1936

Althea's last letter arrived on the first day of winter.

At the time, Hannah didn't realize it would be the last, though as the weeks passed without any more, she thought of it, hidden away beneath the *Alice in Wonderland* just like the rest of the mail Althea had sent.

On the back of the envelope was a message in delicate cursive: *Important! Don't be stubborn.*

Hannah actually considered opening it. It was bulkier than most of the previous ones. She also considered tossing it in the fire out of spite. This was the first one that had arrived after Hannah had learned about Adam's death, and somehow that made it harder to keep.

But a little voice niggled at her, the curious and practical part of her outweighing the stubborn one that Althea had warned her about.

So Hannah got out her box, slid the letter in place with the rest of them, and then took out the battered copy of *Alice*.

Althea had published another novel, Hannah knew. It was

hard to avoid, considering Hannah ran in literary circles and the book had been praised to high heavens by the international press. Althea was the apple of America's eye at the moment, and Hannah wondered if the Nazis had forced shops to stock the book.

Reading the thing had never crossed Hannah's mind. Or it had, for a heartbeat, but the immediate headache that had followed the thought dissuaded her from the foolish idea.

Hannah wondered why Althea still wrote to her, if it was guilt or some other misplaced emotion. They had known each other only a few months, even before it had all ended in disaster. She was neither blind nor oblivious and knew Althea had been interested enough in her that the woman's eyes tended to linger in soft, intimate places. Hannah's lips, her breasts, her hips.

That didn't mean Althea had even realized what was brewing between them up until that night, that one night, which must have sent her into a panic.

In the deepest, darkest part of her, Hannah could sometimes admit that she might have been able to fall in love with Althea. Her earnest eyes, her optimism, the humor that peeked out at the oddest moments. The way she blushed and the way she walked through tulip gardens, how she touched books with reverent fingertips and spoke of language like it was a good friend of hers.

They were different from each other in all the right ways, and the same in the places that mattered.

Or so Hannah had thought.

If Hannah had had to guess, she would have predicted that she would never hear from Althea James once the woman had fled Berlin like a coward after everything had come crashing down.

When Althea's first letter had arrived at Hannah's Paris apartment, her initial reaction had been paranoia. She'd wondered if she should pack up and move that very night, wondered if Nazis would be waiting at the foot of her stairs. But then she realized Althea must still talk with Deveraux Charles, one of the limited handful of people who knew Hannah's exact address.

After that, the messages had come once every few weeks or so.

Hannah had never opened a single one, let alone replied to any. Yet Althea kept writing.

Maybe one day soon, Hannah's curiosity would get the better of her.

That day was not today, though.

She stashed the box back beneath the floorboard in the closet and got ready for work.

There was nothing to be gained from living in the past and wishing for a different future. Her present was what she had, and, for now, it was enough. It had to be.

Chapter 33

New York City
June 1944

The invasion had the effect of a dam rupturing. Where for weeks, months, years, Americans had buckled down and put their best faces forward, now Viv found girls crying in the hallways at all times of day, strangers on the subway ended up in brawls, men poured out of the bars in the wee hours of the morning sobbing and singing in equal measures.

The war might be over soon. But it was going to be a brutal trudge to get there, full of unimaginable loss and sorrow.

Eleanor Roosevelt's daily column in the newspaper addressed the invasion the day after it happened, and Viv couldn't get the First Lady's words out of her head.

"Curiously enough, I have no sense of excitement whatsoever," Mrs. Roosevelt wrote. "It seems as though we have been waiting for this day for weeks, and dreading it, and now all emotion is drained away."

Now all emotion is drained away. In the weeks following the fateful day, Viv woke up, made her commute, answered letters from soldiers, worked on planning her event for Taft, went home, slept, and did it all over again. There was a fog through which she moved, though. It dragged at her limbs, clouded her thinking, made her lethargic yet too anxious to sleep.

Eleven days into the invasion, more than three thousand Americans had died, another nearly thirteen thousand were reported wounded.

It was too much for a nation to bear, let alone a single person.

So Viv focused on what she could control: the Armed Services Editions.

As reports started to trickle in about D-Day itself, everything Viv heard only solidified her belief that although this personal fight of hers might look small from the outside, what she was doing was important. War correspondents wrote to her that the soldiers had been allowed to bring only the most essential items onto the beaches—and for many that included their lightweight paperbacks.

On July 9, a little over a month since the invasion, Betty Smith, one of the most popular authors in the Armed Services Editions project, published an essay. In it she spoke of boys they all knew, the ones who went door to door asking to mow neighbors' lawns to earn some money to spend on candy; of boys who rode bikes and delivered newspapers; of boys whose mothers loved them more than anything in the world. Betty ended with a call to the nation for every person not on those beaches to do their part, whatever that part may be.

Viv found the essay in a newspaper, clipped it out, and sent it to Senator Taft, along with letters diligently copied from originals pouring in from servicemen stationed around the globe. Men who were watching the invasion from afar, aghast and disheartened that they weren't fighting alongside their brothers.

The ASEs provided them an escape from the feelings that they, just like the rest of the world, didn't know what to do with. Books gave them an excuse to cry, a reason to laugh, a place to put their relief that they weren't the ones being slaughtered, a place to put the guilt that they weren't the ones being slaughtered.

She also had her hands full keeping track of the letters to the editor, opinion pieces, and articles flooding newspapers across the country. The council's formal resolution against the Taft amendment meant Viv was no longer waging a personal crusade against the senator, that she no longer had to scrape together foot soldiers from nervous publishing houses or overtaxed libraries. An army had risen up, incensed by the far-reaching amendment.

Several papers had obtained—from Viv, but that was no one's business—a list of titles that had been affected by the policy. Journalists had painstakingly gone through each book, searching for anything that might be political, and reported that they'd found nothing.

Undoubtedly, the public was on the council's side. Yet Taft still refused to budge.

A gentle rap on Viv's office door startled her out of her thoughts. Edith stood there, her bag in hand.

"Don't forget to sleep, doll," Edith said, with a jerk of her chin toward the clock. Viv blinked at it until the numbers came into focus. It was nearly eight at night.

She ran a tired hand over her face. "Just one or two things to wrap up."

"You want me to wait?" Edith asked, her brows drawn in concern. "You'll have to walk to the subway in the dark."

Viv waved her away. "It's only a few blocks. Thank you, though."

"If you're sure," Edith said, hesitant. But Edith wasn't one to baby her friends. "Good night, then. Don't stay too late."

"I'm right on your heels," Viv promised. She finished snipping out two articles from local papers in Texas of all places, and then slipped them into the envelope she was planning to send to Taft in the morning. It wouldn't do any good, but she had to keep the pressure on him.

The one thing she could hold on to, though, was that Hale seemed to think Taft would indeed show his face at the event, if only to appear magnanimous.

While that outcome was one Viv had been counting on, she still wished she had Althea James in the bag. Instead, it was looking more and more likely that Viv would have to find someone else to close out the event.

Her thoughts shifted toward her Brooklyn librarian. Viv was convinced that the woman was only slightly less private than Althea James, but at least she could make her case in person.

Times Hall was mostly dark when Viv finally left her office, but the shadows weren't menacing. Viv now knew each nook and cranny of this place, like a second home to her.

It wasn't until she stepped onto the street that her defenses came up. She'd grown up in the city, walked by herself most of the time without a thought. But many of Broadway's bright lights had been dimmed either through closures or temporary brownouts. Out here, the shadows crept along in her wake, menacing rather than friendly.

Her fingers clenched against the coins she already had out for her subway ticket, a precaution she'd learned long ago. Part of not being scared to navigate the city alone came with being smart about the real dangers.

When she was only a few steps away from the subway entrance, a man crept out of one of the darkened doorways.

Viv squeaked, the noise embarrassing and high and hopeless, and her heart raced as she fumbled for the hat pin she kept at the bottom of her purse.

But the man held his hands up and stepped back so that the streetlamp caught his features, throwing his cheekbones, his nose, his chin into relief. He was short and well-dressed and his brown hair was just starting to gray and go thin at the edges. His three-piece suit was expertly tailored and clearly expensive, his shoes shiny and slick, and his watch Cartier. None of that meant he didn't pose a danger, but Viv adjusted her thinking about what he might want from her.

She managed to curl her hand around the hat pin. She wanted to scan the street for help, but she couldn't risk taking her eyes off the potential predator.

"Mrs. Childs, I promise you there's no need for all that," the man said in a molasses-tinged Southern drawl.

Viv didn't believe him for a second. "Who are you? What do you want? How do you know my name?"

His pencil-thin eyebrows rose. "Which question do you want answered?"

This was no time for games. Viv yanked the hat pin out of her purse and jabbed the air between them. "All of them," she said from behind bared teeth. "And quickly."

"All right, all right, calm down," the man said. "I guess I should have expected theatrics given where we are."

He smirked at his own joke, but then sobered as Viv lunged closer.

"You have ten seconds," Viv threatened.

"Kitten's got claws," he said. "I've come to talk, that's it."

"Talk about what?"

The man's already raised brows lifted as if it were a silly question. "The thing that's got you all hot and bothered, Mrs. Childs."

Viv was so surprised, she nearly fumbled the hat pin. "The Taft amendment? This cloak-and-dagger routine is because of my event?"

"You're the one who brought a dagger into this," the man said, and then coughed into his hand, the lines at the corners of his eyes revealing that amusement she found so off-putting. "I mean a hat pin. I was simply waiting for you to come out; it's not my fault you're walking the streets alone at night. Who knows what could happen to you?"

"What do you want?" Viv asked, her fingers retightening on her weapon. For all that he mocked it, she had seen what kind of damage the metal could do.

"I've been so inconsiderate," the man said, swiping both hands down the front of his suit. "I haven't even introduced myself yet. Mr. Howard Danes at your service."

"What do you want?" Viv repeated, each word landing hard and heavy between them.

Howard sighed, like he was the long-suffering patient man in their little tableau and she the hysterical woman. "Just to talk. I think maybe we could come to an agreement, you and me."

"Unless you're here to tell me Taft is going to remove the fines from the amendment—or better yet get rid of it altogether—we have nothing to talk about," Viv said. She truly doubted this man brought good news, considering he had decided to approach her and not Mr. Stern. Considering he'd chosen to do so at night, when she was alone and vulnerable. This was not Taft waving a white flag.

"You're a smart girl," Howard said in that elongated drawl. "You know you're not going to accomplish anything with this stunt of yours."

And at that Viv finally relaxed. "Really? You don't think so?"

"It's admirable what you're trying to do, but you're in over your head, girl," Howard continued, as if he sensed weakness. "I think we could come to some sort of arrangement."

"An arrangement?"

"Now I know your husband died for this great country of ours," Howard said, putting a hand over his heart and bowing his head. In doing so, he missed the way she tensed again. "Senator Taft would be honored to put forth Mr. Childs's name for official recognition for his bravery in serving."

She itched to slap Edward's name out of this despicable man's mouth.

"You're saying you'll give my husband a Medal of Honor for the cheap, cheap price of both his and my souls?" Viv said, as syrupy as his voice was. "I'm not for sale. And neither was Edward."

"Mrs. Childs, be reasonable—" Howard said, ingratiating once again.

"No," Viv cut him off. "You think I can't accomplish anything with my little . . . stunt, did you call it? Well, I've already accomplished more in the past four weeks than I had in the six months prior to that. And you want to know how I know that?"

His eyes narrowed as if sensing a trap. And she nearly smiled when out of the corner of her eye she saw a flash of movement.

"Because of you," Viv said, with careful enunciation. "You see, you wouldn't be here if we weren't making progress. So thank you for the update." She shifted and then waved down the night patrolman she'd seen rounding the corner. "Please, sir, help."

And with one final smirk, she tucked the hat pin in her purse, turned, and walked into the subway station as Mr. Howard Danes stuttered excuses to the patrolman. She was tired, she was shaky from the encounter, she was sad that anyone thought that kind of trade would actually work. But more than anything, for the first time in ages, she was confident she was doing something right.

Chapter 34

Berlin
May 1933

I brought a present," Dev said as she stepped into Althea's room one day in early May holding a garment bag.

Althea clapped her hands in overdramatic excitement. "Is it a poodle?"

Dev eyed her and then grinned. "You have a better sense of humor than you let people believe."

Flushing at the compliment—backhanded though it might be—Althea shifted her attention to the dress Dev now held out. The fabric was a dark blue that edged toward velvety black. A thin silver webbing added depth to the color, creating the effect of looking at the night sky.

Althea gasped, her eyes flying to Dev's. "I can't wear that."

"Because it's actually fashionable?" Dev asked with the practiced lift of a brow. Then she held out a pair of heels to go with the dress and nudged Althea toward the privacy screen in one corner of the apartment. "I won't take no for an answer, darling."

"Where are we going?" Althea said, without taking the dress.

"Moka Efti, it's a nightclub I haven't taken you to yet," Dev said, shoving over the bundle of fabric into Althea's arms. "I'm tired of all these Resistance meetings. It's time for some fun. Now get changed, Hannah awaits."

Hannah. Clearly Dev knew that was the magic word to get Althea to agree. Still, Althea hesitated for one heartbeat longer, picturing what she would look like in this dress. She knew enough about style to recognize that the depth of the blue would shift her skin from ghostly pale to polished porcelain; the shimmer of the webbing would lighten up her face; the cut would highlight her slim calves and delicate collarbone while hiding a lack of curves.

"What shall I do with my hair?" Althea asked a bit desperately, a bit hopelessly. The heavy curtain of it was always her burden to bear.

Dev eyed her for a long moment and then she crossed the room in three decisive strides. "Pins."

Althea scrambled for a handful and then stood still as Dev divided her hair into three sections. With the meticulousness of an army general, Dev rolled Althea's hair into a low chignon, tugging pieces loose so that it wouldn't be too severe. When Althea looked in the mirror, she nearly gaped at what she saw. The softness of the style didn't add roundness to her face like it did when she attempted such a thing. Rather, it highlighted the line of her jaw, the fullness of her lips. Even the dash of freckles across her nose contributed to the dreamy, Monet-like picture Dev had created out of her.

Dev patted Althea's shoulder as she looked on with satisfaction. "Now the dress."

As Althea changed, careful not to disrupt her hair, Dev poked around in her apartment as she was wont to do. "I forgot, have you heard about the book burnings?"

"The what?" Althea called, certain she hadn't heard right.

"It's shameful, darling," Dev said. "A group of students have been organizing it for tomorrow night. Hannah wants to go to protest."

"That's terrible," Althea said as she stepped back around the privacy screen. "What books are they burning?"

"Anything with anti-German sentiment," Dev said, with an eye roll. "Which can pretty much mean any book they want. You look stunning. Hannah is going to swoon."

Althea's eyes dropped to the floor at the knowing affection in Dev's smile. But she couldn't help the small, answering grin at the thought.

The atmosphere in the new nightclub was more like a party than a show, and when they arrived Dev ordered Althea a drink that tasted of sugar and fire, and was far too good to be drunk slowly.

They found Hannah and Otto dancing in a dark corner, the two of them spinning in happy circles. Hannah wore a dress in that plum color Althea was learning she favored. It was cut low in the back, revealing creamy skin and the slight knobs of her spine. The skirt was shorter than Hannah usually wore, the hint of a garter peeking out as Hannah twirled away from Otto.

"Oh, Hannah imbibed," Dev crowed in delight. "She is her most fun when she indulges, but it is a rare treat, let me tell you."

"Friends," Hannah cried out when she saw them, detangling herself from Otto to press wet kisses on their cheeks. "Dance with me."

Dev nudged Althea into Hannah's arms, taking the glass from her hands before it spilled everywhere.

The band struck up something fast and brassy, and Hannah's hand settled into the small of Althea's back, pressing her in close, so their bodies were flush against each other.

The room spun and not because of how they moved to the music.

"You look pretty tonight." Hannah's mouth brushed against the hinge of Althea's jaw, her fingers dangerously low on Althea's back. "You always look so pretty."

This was what Althea had wanted, it was why she'd slipped the dress on in the first place. Heat gathered at her center as her legs brushed against Hannah's, the tips of her breasts tightening as she became aware of the soft swell of Hannah's beneath the silken fabric of her own gown.

Althea tipped her face up and she realized how close they were. They were breathing the same air, the act so intimate Althea's throat went dry with expectation. It would be so easy just to let gravity pull her into Hannah, to erase that final centimeter.

Her life would change forever then. No more ignoring, no more pleading ignorance.

Hannah's fingers flexed against her back, her pinkie dragging against the subtle curve of Althea's derriere.

And then all of a sudden, it was too much.

She wanted to be brave, but she wasn't. She wanted to be Berlin's Althea James, but she knew better.

She was just a silly, stupid girl from Owl's Head, Maine, and she'd never be anything but that.

Althea wrenched herself away, gasping, near tears, and stumbled through the crowd. Bodies crashed into her, the laughter too loud, the smoke too thick to breathe properly, the lights popping in her eyes.

Air came, blessed and a little too warm to help completely calm her scattered nerves. She found herself leaning against the brick wall of the cabaret's alley, taking gulping breaths that made her light-headed. That was still better than the roaring panic from inside.

Suddenly there was a hand on the back of her neck. She flinched away, her eyes widening, her arms coming up to protect herself. But it was just Dev, watching her with a gentle expression that shredded all of Althea's defenses.

She blinked up at her friend, unwelcome tears spilling from the corners of her eyes.

"Oh, little dove," Dev sighed, throwing an arm around her shoulder, directing her back to the street. As Dev nudged her into a waiting car, Althea thought she heard Dev say, "Alas, too much, too fast."

The ride passed in a blur of colors as Althea carefully kept her mind blank. She would not think of that moment in the dark corner, surrounded by sweaty, pulsing bodies, her own responding in kind. She would not think of the sweet smell of Hannah's skin or the soft press of her hands.

She would not think of the devastated look Hannah had shot her in the moment she'd wrenched herself out of Hannah's arms.

Althea crawled into bed, vaguely aware of Dev tucking her in. Afraid, of everything that would change after tonight—because they couldn't just laugh off what happened as inconsequential—Althea stared out the window until dawn crept in. Only then did she allow herself to sleep.

One of Althea's biggest fears was that Hannah would stop talking to her. Instead, when Hannah and Dev stopped by Althea's apartment the next day to collect her to protest the book burnings, Althea realized she should have been worried about something else.

Hannah was acting like nothing had happened at all.

Meanwhile, Althea had trouble looking directly at her.

Dev decided to counter the strained awkwardness with chatter.

"Goebbels is calling for Germans all over the country to burn their own private collections," Dev said. "And they're going to broadcast the burnings from Berlin tonight, as well. They expect quite the crowd, apparently."

"Will it be dangerous?" Althea asked, her mind reeling at the idea of a mass bonfire. Surely, it would be just a few radical students, and not the large event Dev seemed to believe was planned.

"You should be safe enough," Dev said, and Hannah held up her hands.

"I'm going, you can't convince me otherwise," Hannah said with a stubborn slant to her jaw.

"Why they think this is a good strategy, I have no idea." Dev grabbed Althea's bag for her and started nudging them toward the door. "It's not like books can be unread."

Althea's stomach heaved at the image of ink and paper disintegrating into ash.

She couldn't help but think of Heinrich Heine's prediction. *Where they burn books, they will also ultimately burn people.*

Only when Dev and Hannah turned to Althea with wide eyes did she realize she'd said that part out loud.

Dev grimaced. "Well, poets are dramatic, aren't they?" She said it flippantly, but none of them, including her, laughed.

The evening drew them forward, all of them walking in a silence heavy with terrible thoughts. As they neared Opernplatz, in front of the state opera building, the torchlight illuminated the crowd.

"Here's where I leave you." Dev kissed them goodbye before disappearing.

"She's working tonight, isn't she?" Althea asked.

"The Nazis will want footage of this," Hannah said. "They'll want a pretty face to narrate."

Despite the fact that Althea was a guest of the same program Dev was, she didn't understand how Hannah could be so calm about it.

"Don't you care?"

"I wish the world was different," Hannah said, a bit of a slap in her voice, and Althea realized she was close to crossing some line. Hannah didn't want—or deserve—Althea's judgment about her friends.

Althea remembered the night Hitler had been named chancellor, how she'd joined in the marchers, joyous and giddy to be a part of something so much bigger than herself. She had no right to say anything about Dev.

The thought was consumed by the flames that licked up toward the stars of the darkening sky and the happy, startled cries of those watching as hundreds of stories burned to nothingness.

Althea nearly dropped to her knees at the sight of the pyre. It roared into the night sky, an angry lion consuming everything it was fed.

And it was fed well.

Piles of books were stacked in what seemed like every inch of the square. Students rolled in wheelbarrows full, young people came bearing sacks that strained at the seams, cars' trunks stood open as volumes spilled out onto the pavement.

It was not just a few books, not just a symbolic fire.

There were thousands upon thousands upon thousands of books being tossed into the flames.

Thousands upon thousands upon thousands of people cheered

and howled and threw up the Nazi salute. They chanted, "We are the fire, we are the flame; we burn before Germany's altars."

The flames were feeding the feverish excitement of the crowd just as the crowd fed the flames. Enormous Nazi banners hung from every building in the square, spectators leaning out of the windows, calling down their support. A band played, the music adding an eerie soundtrack to the delirious revelers.

Hannah gripped Althea's arms and it was only then that Althea realized she'd been crying. Not dignified tears, but noisy, messy sobs.

"It's sacrilege," Althea whispered. If Althea had a church, it was within the covers of books; if she had a religion, it was in the words written there. Hannah just nodded.

"I know."

And Hannah did know. Of that, Althea was certain.

A light rain had started to fall as if God himself was crying over the atrocity.

Goebbels took the stage then, the flames turning his face sunken and skeletal. Althea remembered when she'd first met him at a party, and it had been soft candlelight flickering against his skin. He'd been awkward, a touch strange, but mostly pleasant, interested in intellectual conversation, curious and thoughtful.

Now he was a ghost from her own personal nightmare.

"No to decadence and moral corruption," Goebbels yelled from the podium. He spoke of the death to Jewish intellectualism, to the smut and trash of the old era of Germany. Toward the end of the speech he gestured to the students pressed up against the stage, hanging on his every word. "This is a strong, great, and symbolic deed—a deed which should document the following for the world to know: Here the intellectual foundation of the November Republic is sinking to the ground, but from this wreckage the phoenix of a new spirit will triumphantly rise."

The audience went wild at that, dancing in the rain, as the pyre's flames threw them into silhouettes.

"I can't breathe," Althea gasped.

Hannah tried to rub her back, whispering soothing words. But they were lost beneath the voices rising in unison all around them.

This wasn't just some pointless rally, this wasn't just people whipped up into a frothing roar because of mostly empty words spoken by a strong orator. This was the gleeful destruction of knowledge, of science, of poetry, of love. The students who should have cherished such things were giddy as they watched all of it burn.

And Althea broke.

She took off, pushing through the crowd, knowing Diedrich would be near the front of this spectacle with his Nazi friends.

Hannah called her name, but Althea didn't stop. Couldn't.

She did catch sight of one of the covers of the books waiting to go into the pyre, let out a little wounded sound, and saved it without thought. She held it close to her as she would a child, as she continued to weave through the mass of bodies.

Then there was Diedrich. Where she'd thought he'd be.

Laughing.

Althea's vision darkened at the edges. Before she knew it, she was in front of him. She placed her free hand dead center on his chest and pushed with all the rage and pain that had fueled her since she'd seen the first book tossed into the flames.

"You brute," she all but sobbed. He stumbled back, but she guessed that was from sheer shock rather than the force of her shove.

"Althea." His voice came like a slap. "Get ahold of yourself."

"You think this is noble? Just?" Althea waved back to the spectacle. "You think this is anything but small-minded men doing their best impression of tyrants? You are nothing but incurious bullies and history will judge you as bigoted, intolerant barbarians."

Diedrich surged forward and gripped her chin hard enough that she knew there would be bruises. Although the noise of the crowd hadn't dimmed, the men behind Diedrich had gone deathly silent.

"You forget your place," he growled in her face.

And she . . . laughed. Derisively. Putting every ounce of disdain into it that she held for this man, this party, these weak-willed politicians who couldn't win fairly and so tried to burn any idea that would undermine their house of cards.

The slap didn't come as a surprise. The strength of it did, though.

Diedrich's hand sent her sprawling, leaving a stinging heat in its wake.

Her lip bleeding, her elbow throbbing, her body scraped and bruised, Althea finally realized that there were bigger things in the world than fear.

Chapter 35

New York City
June 1944

It had been weeks since Viv had had enough time to attend one of Charlotte's parties. The events were designed to sell war bonds, which was of course important, but they included a lot of high-society small talk and posturing. Viv had lost whatever tolerance she used to have for that kind of evening since she'd started spending most of hers on the ASEs.

Charlotte promised this one would be of particular interest to Viv. "We're holding it at the Morgan Library, dear. It will be the perfect place for you to drum up interest in your grand finale."

Viv had stared for a few stunned seconds before rushing in to hug Charlotte. "You are a treasure."

Now, Viv wandered through the rooms of the Morgan Library, a glass of champagne in one hand, her eyes on the gilded ceilings, the rich tapestries, the volumes and volumes of priceless books behind delicate gold cages.

She had talked to three high-profile city officials, editors from the *New Yorker* and the *Saturday Evening Post*—vastly different audiences that would both be important—the chief of staff to the New York City mayor, and four separate society matrons who were well known for donating generously to politicians they favored.

All but glowing from the buzz of a successful evening so far, Viv had given herself ten minutes off to enjoy the space before she started hunting down other potentially influential guests.

It had now been two weeks since Viv had let go of the notion that Althea James's presence would make or break the event, and since then she'd gotten more accomplished than she had in the three weeks before that. Maybe her speakers wouldn't create quite the stir Althea would, but so far no one had turned down an invitation, and Viv had even had dozens of letters from out-of-town reporters asking for passes.

On top of all that, Taft was nervous enough to have sent a goon after her.

The event was to be held in a little over a month, and Viv still had plenty left to do to secure the grand finale she wanted. But the buzzing beneath her skin had calmed a bit as everything began to take shape.

"Of all the libraries in all the world," a voice came from behind her in a decent impression of Bogie. Viv spun to find Hale there, holding out a fresh glass of wine to her. She traded her empty flute for the new one and he effortlessly passed it off to a roving waiter. As he did, his eyes dragged down her body, admiring.

Viv flushed, pleased that she'd chosen one of her favorite dresses for the occasion. The style was from the thirties, but she found it flattering enough not to care. The silky pearl-white fabric clung to the juts of her hips, the gentle swell of her bottom. The neckline cut high in the front before dipping into a vee in the back, and a row of small buttons sat like little soldiers against her spine. The skirt caressed her thighs suggestively, the candlelight revealing almost more than it hid.

The atmosphere equally suited Hale, who was wearing a blue suit and crisp white shirt. He had enough years in politics now to look as comfortable in the rarified air of a charity gala as he did in rolled-up shirtsleeves playing baseball in the streets.

"Hi," she said, inanely. The energy she'd once had for flirtations and banter had been drained out of her and now she struggled to make basic conversation some days.

"Hi," he said, gently. This time when he eyed her it wasn't with appreciation, but concern, clearly reading the exhaustion she couldn't hide. She realized she wasn't even trying. Not with him. He was now allowed in behind her walls. That was a startling enough realization that she tucked it away to think about at some later time.

"Can I help?" he asked.

Viv huffed out a breath. "Stop being so charming."

"You have low expectations for charm," Hale teased, that dimple popping out.

Everything in her swayed toward him. When she'd first seen him in Brooklyn, she'd been almost relieved not to feel that magnetic pull any longer. Anger, humiliation, and pain had snuffed out the connection between them. But as she'd gotten to know him as an adult in the past few weeks, it was getting harder and harder to pretend the spark of *something* wasn't still there between them, waiting to reignite.

It wasn't the right time to ask, she knew she should just keep quiet. But she was exhausted, tired of tiptoeing around the shared history they could never quite look directly at. It still existed on the periphery of every conversation anyway, just waiting for their words to turn antagonistic.

"Why didn't you write back?" she asked.

She had caught him off guard. He was a politician and so an expert at hiding his reactions, but he stiffened, his fingers flexing against his glass. "Not here."

Viv was about to protest, but when he guided her out of the crowded reading room, she realized *not here* didn't mean *not now*.

He found an alcove that afforded them privacy, and she leaned back against the marble wall, waiting.

"I thought it would be easier for you," Hale finally said. "If I didn't write back."

"Easier for what?"

"Your life." He sounded so matter-of-fact. "I was a bastard boy from Brooklyn, Viv. It was never going to be more than a few stolen kisses between us. Not with the future I had back then."

"You couldn't have known that. I lo—"

"No," he cut her off. "We were just kids, Viv."

That wasn't fair. She knew what she'd felt, had been even more certain as time had passed because it had been so rare for her. She had loved him, fully, desperately. Stupidly.

"We weren't kids. You were twenty."

"Old enough to know better," he said, with a little shake of his head. "You would have figured it out eventually. I just made it so you didn't have to."

Viv blinked at him, struggling to understand. That summer was tinted rose in her memory, but it hadn't been all shallow happiness. They'd scraped at each other, they'd made up. They'd seen each other's petty sides, their jealous sides. They might have known each other for only a short time, but the foundation had felt like it could last.

She played his words over again in her head. *You would have figured it out eventually.*

"You were scared," Viv said on a nod, everything making sense all of a sudden. He had been so afraid of being hurt, so afraid she was going to reject him, that he had done it first. Hale had been used to those of her station and wealth telling him he didn't matter, shunning him, walking away from him. Why would she be any different?

"I was a realist," he corrected, not sounding defensive about it. He still thought he'd made the right choice. "You thought you were in love with me. You would have married me. And then later, maybe a year, maybe five, you would have looked around your life and realized you could have been so much more."

Viv stared at his profile, dismayed. "I thought you knew me better."

"People who come from money always tell themselves they could do without," Hale said, his voice bitter and knowing. "But real life isn't a fairy tale."

Before she could argue that point further, Hale added, "Anyway, then you started writing to Edward."

Viv nearly cracked her head against the wall in surprise. She hadn't been sure what Edward had insinuated to Hale about his relationship with Viv, but she had assumed that for most of the time Edward had called her exactly what she'd been—a dear friend. Looking at the set of Hale's jaw, though, she revised that opinion.

"You think I replaced one brother with the other," Viv realized.

His eyes flicked down to her hand.

"Didn't Edward . . ." Her shock must have shown on her face, because the certainty in his expression flickered.

For one moment, Viv wanted Edward to be here to explain it all as he absolutely should have done when he was alive. The image of the three of them all crammed into the alcove, discussing

Viv and Edward's marriage, was so utterly ridiculous she couldn't stop the stray giggle that escaped.

"Care to share what's so amusing?" Hale asked, stiff with some kind of emotion that toed the line between anger and pain.

Viv couldn't stop once she started. She rounded her shoulders, ducking her head to try to muffle her laughter. Her ribs ached and her thighs trembled and she couldn't remember the last time she'd laughed with her whole body.

Probably it had been with Edward.

She felt the tug of real tears, ones brought on from grief rather than humor, but she pushed them back, leaning against the wall once more, panting a little.

"I was thinking about my husband threatening his brother to treat me right," Viv finally admitted, because why dance around it now? The tight line of Hale's mouth twitched into an almost smile. "I thought he would have talked to you about it. Maybe not the reason we got married, but the fact that we weren't in love when we did."

"I knew he was worried about something before he left, but everything happened quickly," Hale said. "He wouldn't let me ask about you."

"Nor me you," Viv said, with a rush of affection for Edward. He hadn't wanted to get in the middle, to accidentally hurt either one of the two people he loved. "You can't tell Charlotte."

"Of course."

"Your father's will," Viv said, cautiously. Hale had never acted like the wealth he had missed out on was important, but it still had to be a sensitive topic.

"Theodore Childs," Hale corrected. "My father was William Hale."

She dipped her head in acknowledgment. "Theodore left the

bulk of his fortune to Edward, of course; however, there was a provision in the will that if Edward died before marrying, the estate would pass into the hands of various charities. Leaving Charlotte with nothing."

"Theodore Childs was not a man who would give a penny to charity."

"He knew it would never come to that," Viv said. "He had just grown tired of Edward's carousing. Edward risked bachelorhood for as long as possible . . ."

"But with the war . . ." Hale finished the thought for Viv, who nodded.

"He didn't even have to ask me to do it," Viv said. "We could never take the chance that Charlotte would be left destitute. And she's too proud to take money from me."

"You love her, too," Hale said after a minute of studying her face. "I assumed, but I thought you loved him, as well. So, I couldn't be sure what I was right about."

"I did love him," Viv said, reaching out to squeeze Hale's forearm. "Just as a dear friend."

"I wanted to punch him when he'd mention his conquests. I thought . . . well, I thought wrong, clearly."

"If only there had been some way to ask me about it. Some easy method of communication that would have cleared everything up," Viv teased, the years-old wound healing over a smidge. There were moments like these in life, presenting themselves sometimes rarely, where you could hold on to grudges, burn relationships to the ground, salt the earth, and only look back to seethe in anger. Or you could acknowledge that people made mistakes, were flawed, and deserved second chances. Especially when those choices had been made when they were young and hurting from their own deep-seated pain.

Hale dropped his head, but there was that private smile on his face. Like he heard the forgiveness in her voice. "I missed you, every day, every hour, every minute."

"Oh," Viv breathed as she actually felt the last of her resentment burn away. It wasn't the confession itself that did it, but the implicit acknowledgment that Hale had not only read all the letters she'd written him but memorized them well enough to quote them all these years later. She imagined a twenty-year-old Hale steeling himself against her confessions, convinced the world was going to hurt him once again if he let it.

Viv was too close to tears to do anything but try to make a joke. "Yes, well. It prepared me for my current disappointment."

Hale seemed just as eager to navigate away from the emotional topic. "Althea James still ignoring you?" When she nodded he shrugged. "Then you have to go to her."

"What?"

"You have to talk to her in person," Hale said with a nod. "You have to explain why you're doing this."

Viv shook her head. "I should leave her alone."

Hale watched her through hooded eyes. "I've read the same reports you have from Normandy. These books aren't a trivial thing."

"It's like the tables have turned." Viv met his eyes through her lashes. "You convincing me to go forward with this."

"You know I like hopeless causes," Hale said, with a small genuine smile Viv thought he saved just for her. "I'm a romantic soul, after all."

"In the suit of a heartless politician," Viv teased, and then sobered once more. "Thank you for caring."

"Shouldn't be thanking me for caring about our boys," Hale said.

"Then thank you for the advice," Viv said, instead of arguing that it meant more to her that Hale, bone-tired himself, was still trying to help her with her cause.

"Maybe it will all be pointless. Even if Althea says yes, Taft might not change his mind."

"But?" she prompted.

"But the only way you'll sleep at night is if you throw everything you have at this," Hale said, looking up once more, his eyes dark. "The good fight isn't always about winning. Sometimes it's a reminder to the world that there are people out there who are willing to try."

Chapter 36

Paris
February 1937

An itch settled beneath Hannah's skin when she started to suspect that Althea's December letter had been her last.

Work at the library had slowed down now that they weren't preparing for the exhibition, so Hannah could no longer distract herself with that. She thought briefly of dropping by Lucien's to see if he was holding a Resistance meeting, but despite her newfound appreciation for fists and bullets, she was still wary.

She had too much anger in her. If she poured gasoline on the flames they might consume her entirely.

So instead she went to Natalie Clifford Barney's salon. Patrice was there again, paint-speckled and newly single. They shared a bottle of wine near the fire, pausing in their conversation to listen to the newest poet on the scene recite a few verses and a pretty writer stutter through a chapter of her work.

"Will you stay in France?" Hannah asked Patrice during a break in the action.

"Do I look meant for war?"

She had a point. Patrice was flimsy, delicate. Hannah forgave herself for the cruelness of thinking the woman would die during an occupation, since Patrice was the one who had said it first.

"You're meant for war," Patrice continued, drawing her brows down to make a comically serious face. "Always somber, always ready for battle."

"I am not," Hannah protested. She was meant for words, not wars. But . . . hadn't she jumped into the fray to save Otto?

"Kill some Nazis for me, yes?" Patrice said, patting her hand. "I'm going to California. Hollywood, to be famous."

Hannah giggled and then caught Natalie Clifford Barney's eye as she passed, her little bulldog tucked beneath her arm.

"Oh, Hannah," Natalie called out, making her way over to them. "I forgot, I ran into a friend of yours."

Hannah glanced up. "And who would that be?"

"Deveraux Charles."

"Dev?" Hannah asked. The last she'd seen Deveraux had been one final night on the town in Berlin years ago before Hannah left for Paris.

"The very one," Natalie said. "She says the Nazis are filming some terrible movie here, wanted to use the Eiffel Tower and Notre Dame as backdrops. She'll be in the city for the rest of the week."

"She must be terribly busy," Hannah said, though she wondered why Dev hadn't sought her out. "When was this?"

"Mm, maybe three days or so ago," Natalie said. "She was eager to hear how you were, though, once we realized we both knew you."

"Maybe she'll stop by the library," Hannah said with a vague smile. Dev had always been flighty, but she knew where Hannah was working, had been the one who'd given her address to Althea. She would come by when she had time.

"A former lover?" Patrice asked.

"No. A friend. From a different life it seems."

"To old friends," Patrice said, raising her glass. When they finished the bottle, they opened another, the wine and flirtation finally scratching the itch beneath Hannah's skin.

She had never expected Althea to write to her in the first place. She wasn't sure why she cared that the letters had now stopped.

When Patrice suggested going to Le Monocle—the best lesbian bar in Paris—Hannah didn't hesitate. They danced together and drank something sweet and bubbly, and laughed at nothing as they stumbled back to Hannah's apartment.

They ended up sweaty, panting, and tangled in the sheets. When Patrice asked if she should leave, Hannah pressed a thumb to her lower lip in a gentle caress and told her to sleep.

Hannah didn't cuddle up behind her, didn't follow her into the sweet relief of dreams. Instead she stood by the window, wrapped only in a sheet, watching the sun creep over the buildings.

And she wondered what Deveraux Charles was really doing in Paris.

HANNAH TRIED NOT to let Deveraux's presence in Paris eat at her.

Dev was a world-famous actress by now, it wasn't surprising that she would show up in the city. They had written each other after Hannah had first moved here, but with Dev's lifestyle, steady correspondence hadn't exactly been feasible. They had drifted as two friends living a country apart often did.

Maybe it had been more than that. Dev was still working for the Nazis, making her films, penning scripts that the Dev from nights at the cabaret would mock relentlessly. In that spring of 1933 it had been different, though.

Don't you care? Althea had asked once. And Hannah knew that if she had spun on Althea, said *yes,* and blamed her for being just as much a part of the program as Dev was, Althea would have taken the slap and slunk off into the night.

And the truth was, Hannah *had* cared that two of her closest friends in those months were technically guests of the Reich.

The Hannah of now would never have allowed that to come to pass. But it hadn't felt completely real at the time. Hitler had been installed as chancellor because the moderates had thought they could control him. Most people who paid attention to politics in those days expected him to fade into obscurity, his madness burning bright but then snuffing out quickly.

Also, there had been something deliciously subversive about converting the very Americans whom the Nazis hoped would go home and spread their message of hate and bigotry.

And Althea had stopped willingly spending time with any Nazis not long after the Reichstag fire. It hadn't been hard to forget about the reason she was there.

Dev, though . . .

She hadn't stopped. Despite having the money and fame that would have easily let her escape the clutches of the Nazis, she hadn't stopped.

Hannah didn't mention Dev's presence to Otto. He was worrying her as of late, drinking too much, partaking at opium dens, searching out fights, and coming to the library with fading bruises on his jaw.

When she asked him about it, he told her not to baby him, and then skillfully avoided her for days after. She stopped asking him.

But she hadn't stopped being concerned.

It was sheer coincidence, a joke by fate maybe, that the two of them ran into Dev a week later.

Hannah and Otto were taking an easy afternoon stroll around the Left Bank, stopping into shops when the mood struck. The sun was starting to go a bit too warm, and Hannah was just about to suggest a café, when Otto stopped abruptly, his eyes on something across the street.

"Is that . . . ," Otto started. "My God, it is."

Hannah followed his gaze, and there, of course, was Deveraux Charles in all her glory. She was nearly impossible to miss, riveting in her chic trousers and black top that draped suggestively over her shoulders. The color should have made her sallow, but instead highlighted the pure paleness of her skin. She wore big black sunglasses and her short hair was slicked down close to her head in her signature style.

Otto was already running across the road, checking only briefly for cars, before he swooped Dev up in an exuberant hug.

Dev cried out in surprise and then let Otto swing her around before slapping his shoulder to get him to put her down.

Hannah followed at a more sedate pace.

"And Hannah." Dev smiled when she saw Hannah and pushed her glasses onto her head. "I should have expected it. Where Otto goes, there's Hannah and vice versa."

In the olden days, Hannah would have laughed at the light teasing. But there was something stark and barbed beneath Dev's words now.

"Deveraux," Hannah greeted her. "What brings you to Paris?"

"So formal," Dev joked, nudging Hannah's shoulder. "What brings anyone to Paris? Paris itself, darling."

Dev's eyes flicked over Hannah's shoulder, though, and Hannah realized the woman was tense, her body turned half away from them like she was ready to flee.

"How long are you here for?" Otto asked.

"We are leaving tonight, unfortunately," Dev said with a little pout of her red-stained lips. "Next time you'll have to take me to dinner and dancing, like the old days."

"We?" Hannah asked.

Dev flinched. It was barely perceptible, but Hannah was watching her closely.

"Sorry, must run, dears," Dev said, kissing them both goodbye, hurried and sloppy.

Hannah reached up to rub the lipstick from her cheek as she watched a man dressed in a Nazi officer's uniform step out of a store a few doors down.

Dev looped her arm through his, her head thrown back in amusement at something he said.

She didn't look back at them once.

Chapter 37

New York City
July 1944

It took until a month after the invasion for Viv to gather her courage to return to the banned books library in Brooklyn.

Viv's upcoming trip to Maine to find Althea James was what nudged her along. She wanted to talk to the author knowing that she had a solid backup plan already in place with the librarian.

Which meant it was time to beg.

Despite the late hour, the sun was still bright when Viv stepped out of the subway station closest to the Brooklyn Jewish Center. This was about the time her librarian left for the evening. Viv wanted to catch her, of course, but a small part of her hoped she wouldn't.

Fate was either with or against her—she couldn't decide—because the librarian was coming down the steps just as Viv crossed the street.

The woman paused when she saw Viv, but then continued so that they greeted each other on the sidewalk.

"Will this be a common occurrence, then?" the librarian asked.

"Me showing up at your work completely uninvited?" Viv asked, keeping it light. "Tell me not to and I won't."

"I didn't say that." But the librarian's voice was cautious. "I'm curious about your continued curiosity, I suppose."

Viv lifted a shoulder. "Seems like you could use a friend?"

"Try again," the librarian directed. But she sounded amused.

"That's not a lie," Viv said. "But you're right, it's not the full truth."

"I know." It was said with such wise certainty that Viv almost gave up then and there for no other reason than that she was intimidated by this woman. "So I ask, what's the full truth?"

"Tea first?" Viv suggested. The sooner the librarian heard her request, the sooner the woman would walk away. And Viv hadn't been lying—she liked the librarian's company.

"I'd like you to speak at my event with Senator Taft," Viv said, once they took their seats in a nearby café.

The librarian blinked at her. "Pardon?"

"I know this is a big favor to ask," Viv said, rushing on. "I know that. But I think you would be a compelling addition to the program."

"You say things like that but I still don't see the connection you see," the librarian said. Not like she was trying to be hurtful, but like she was trying not to be. "Between what I do and your ASEs."

Viv licked her lips, the weight of her entire event on her shoulders.

"When I first visited your library, I couldn't see a way forward with this fight," Viv admitted. "But then you put into words *why* all of this is so important. We . . . we humans, we love telling each other stories, don't we? We've done just that in caves and in amphitheaters and in the Globe and in kitchens and around campfires and in the trenches. Every culture, every country, every type of person in the world tells stories. They've been whispered and sung and written down on scraps of paper and they have always, always been an indelible part of our very humanity." Viv blushed and stared very hard at her tea, aware that she had spent too many nights crafting exactly what her *own* speech would be in front of Taft. "And when I walked into the library and you stood there like a guardian of those stories, I just . . ." Viv swallowed hard. "My fight with Taft might seem petty and political, but why I care, why I've always cared, is that I want to protect that idea. That stories can help us understand each other and ourselves and our world. That even our darkest days can be about more than simply survival. The way you talk about the library and the books, that's the message you send. Every time."

The librarian waited a beat, seeming to check if Viv was done. "You should just say that instead of bringing me into all this."

Viv sputtered a little. "I'm the author of all this, not a character." Then she shot the librarian a self-deprecating grin. "Plus, I've been saying all that for months and have gotten nowhere. I'm not the story to tell."

"But you think I am," the librarian said.

It was strange how obvious that answer was to Viv. "What was it like that night?" she asked again, wanting to provoke the same reply as she had on her last visit. "At the burnings."

The librarian tilted her head, curious but willing to play along. "Wet."

The corner of Viv's mouth twitched up. "How many people would give me that answer?"

"About ten thousand?" the librarian suggested.

Viv shook her head. "No, they wouldn't. Goebbels would say 'successful' or 'patriotic.' A Resistance fighter might say 'tragic.'

A German student would say 'rousing.' It matters who is talking, who is telling the story."

"And 'wet' is a more accurate story?"

"No," Viv said, frustrated. "But it *is* what makes it *your* story. And people recognize authenticity when they see it."

The librarian stared at a spot beyond Viv's shoulder for a long moment and then sighed, shifting to meet Viv's gaze once more.

"What would this require?" the librarian asked, hesitant but . . . her response wasn't a no. Viv could work with that.

"A speech at this event I'm holding at the end of July, a few interviews if you're willing," Viv said, eager to make everything seem simple and grand at the same time. "I tried to craft the speakers into a semblance of a narrative, as well. Starting with librarians who will talk about the program, and then wounded soldiers and then authors, and then you. And . . ."

When she trailed off, the librarian raised her brows. "And?"

"Well, ideally, I want to end with you and then one of our ASE writers who was also in Germany during the book burnings."

Everything about the woman sharpened, including her voice, when she asked, "And who would that be?"

"Althea James."

The librarian sat back against her chair, her eyes wide. "Come again?"

"Althea James," Viv repeated, though she knew the librarian had heard her the first time. "She's an American author of some prominence. But she's never given any public interviews or done any events here in America, so it would be quite remarkable if she did."

Viv couldn't read the complicated flutter of emotions that answer provoked, but then the librarian's face crumpled. At first, Viv thought she was sobbing, and she started to reach for a handkerchief in a panic. Soon, though, she realized it was laughter that spilled from the woman, not tears. Uncontrolled, uninhibited laughter. It transformed her from coldly beautiful to enchanting.

Several moments passed before the woman was able to rein in her amusement. And even then, she erupted in what seemed to be out-of-character giggles a few times as she wiped the tears from the corners of her eyes.

"Are you . . ." Viv didn't know how to finish that question. Clearly, she was fine, but also maybe she wasn't?

"I apologize," the woman said, and then promptly dissolved once more. When that wave passed, she cleared her throat and visibly collected herself. "The world is extraordinarily and exquisitely small."

"You know Althea James?" Viv guessed, tentative because the reaction still didn't match if that were the case.

"You could say that," the librarian murmured. She sipped from her tea and then seemed to make some decision. "All right, Mrs. Childs. I shall be your story."

Victory burst pure and bright in Viv, even as her curiosity about what had just occurred went mostly unstated. "Wonderful."

"I guess it is finally time to introduce myself," the librarian said, and Viv almost mourned the mystery of not knowing. It was outweighed, of course, by everything else, but it was still there as a twinge. The librarian held out her hand, making the introduction quite formal. Viv took it as the woman said, "It's a pleasure to meet you. My name is Hannah Brecht."

Chapter 38

Berlin
May 1933

Diedrich lifted his boot—perhaps to press against Althea's neck as she lay on the ground. But then Hannah was there, hauling her back to her feet and hustling her into the protection and anonymity of the crowd.

"You silly little fool," Hannah muttered, sounding both exasperated and fond. "Come on."

They were both drenched. The mist had turned to a full-on rain, protecting the books that had yet to make it to the fire. Both of them took off running, through the revelers, who hadn't let the weather dampen their enthusiasm at all, through the streets, giggling for no reason other than being punch-drunk on the experience.

Althea unlocked her door and pulled Hannah inside quickly. They stared at each other hopelessly, then Althea laughed again. This time bright and free and easy.

"Did I really just do that?" she asked, dazed. Only then did she realize she was still clutching the novel she'd grabbed.

Alice in Wonderland.

"You really did," Hannah said, sounding just as stunned.

Althea set the book down. "Let me get you a towel." She pursed her mouth as she took in the state of Hannah's dress. "And clothes, perhaps?"

"I'm not sure they'll fit," Hannah teased.

"You may be right," Althea said on a sigh, looking down at her own short legs. "Well, I guess we should start a fire, at least."

"Yes, but will it be the kind to burn the ashes of the old republic and birth a phoenix of the Third Reich?" Hannah asked, dry as dust.

Grinning, Althea shook her head. "God, they're pompous, aren't they?"

"It is their worst trait," Hannah agreed solemnly as she went about lighting the fire.

Althea watched her, the way she moved, how the wet dress hugged the curve of her hips, how her dark hair framed her pale face.

Then she turned and went in search of towels and linens.

They sat on the floor, their thighs and shoulders touching, watching the flames, drinking the last bit of vodka Althea had stashed in a back corner of a cabinet in the kitchen. It loosened both of their tongues.

"You humiliated him," Hannah said. "He won't forget that."

"I'm leaving," Althea reminded her, and it almost hurt to say. Not because she wasn't anxious to flee these people, this country. But she didn't want to leave . . .

"Not soon enough," Hannah said. "You'll have to be careful."

"I will." She licked her lips. "I'm . . . more worried about you."

"Because of Adam," Hannah said, following Althea's train of thought easily.

"It makes me nervous how he talks." That wasn't anything

new. She and Hannah discussed it frequently, tried to come up with ways to dampen his anger. But Althea had never confessed that she was terrified for Hannah, too. "I'm worried he'll pull you into whatever he has planned. That you'll be destroyed beside him."

Hannah just stared into the fire.

Althea went on alert. By now, Althea could read her far better than Hannah probably realized. "Hannah."

Her lips parted, then closed.

"Hannah." Althea gathered Hannah's hands in hers. "No. You have to stay far away from it. Convincing him not to get himself killed is one thing, getting involved . . . No, you can't."

"He's my brother." Hannah said it so simply Althea wanted to shake her.

"And he's not thinking right," Althea said. "You know that."

Hannah shot her a guilty look.

"What did you do?" Althea asked, her chest tight, the air in the room gone.

"I followed him."

Althea looked down at her own hands, realized she was clutching on to Hannah, and tried to relax her grip. Her fingers didn't listen. "Oh God. Followed him where?"

"The Adlon, near the Brandenburg Gate," Hannah said, her voice distant like she didn't actually realize she'd answered.

Althea had heard of the hotel, which was often referred to as Little Switzerland because it played host to diplomatic events. She cursed softly.

"I don't know what he's going to do," Hannah admitted. "But the location scares me."

It scared Althea, too. World leaders met there. Nazi leaders met there.

But as much as Althea liked Adam, he wasn't her priority. "You have to stay away from there."

"I can't just let him die," Hannah said, unshed tears in her eyes. "I don't know what else to do, though."

"He knows that you care if he lives," Althea said. It was all she could offer at the moment. Hannah and her friends and the rest of the Resistance group had all tried to reason with Adam, apparently to no avail. At some point, they had to trust that he would make the right decision. "It's good for him to know, that someone cares about him. It might stop him from doing something stupid."

Hannah didn't say anything, but she didn't pull away, either, both of them watching the fire for a long time.

Finally, Althea cleared her throat, debating if she should say what she wanted to. But the world was going up in flames anyway. "You should know, too. That someone cares. That *I* . . . that I care. I would care if something happened to you."

Hannah's breath caught, audibly, and she seemed to come back to herself. Then she lifted Althea's hand, bringing Althea's wrist to her mouth. She pressed a kiss there, her eyes locked on Althea's. "I'll be safe. I promise."

Something loosened in Althea's chest, for reasons she couldn't explain. She remembered the terror she'd felt back at the cabaret, searched for it now, and found nothing but a pleasant, buzzing excitement.

Althea had spent her whole life afraid. Now that she had marched up to a bully and said no, had pushed him, had been pushed *by* him and survived, nothing seemed as terrifying anymore.

When she had come to the city, she had tried to be a version of herself that hadn't existed. She had wanted to be Berlin's Althea James. But now she knew. She didn't have to be anyone but herself.

She stood, holding out her hand.

Hannah inhaled, her beautiful golden eyes big and round.

Surprised.

Althea's heart thudded in her ears, and for a moment, she wondered if she had misunderstood.

But then Hannah slid her palm into Althea's and let herself be tugged to her feet, let herself be led to the bed.

Althea sat, her knees bracketing Hannah's thighs. Hannah bent down, cupping the jaw that was bruised from Diedrich's violence, her thumb brushing along Althea's cheekbone, waiting, questioning.

"Yes," Althea breathed out, and Hannah's mouth met hers, swallowing the word before it even landed in between them.

The kiss was slow and so different than Althea had imagined. At first, it was just a gentle press of lips, a hello, and then it deepened, Hannah's tongue slipping inside, tracing the ridge of Althea's palate, everything hot and slick. Hannah surrounded her, the subtle, sweet smell of rain and oranges wrapping around Althea as Hannah nudged her up the bed without relinquishing her mouth.

Althea went, gloried in the weight of Hannah's hips pushing her own into the mattress. Her calves came up, wrapped around Hannah's thighs, bringing her even closer still, chasing the pleasure that was building between her legs.

Hannah softened the kiss, nipped at Althea's lower lip. The tiny pinprick of pain had Althea arching her back, baring her throat. "Please."

She didn't even know what she was asking for, but Hannah seemed to understand, trailing her lips down along Althea's neck, pressing an open-mouthed kiss against a delicate collarbone, one hand tracing up Althea's body to cup her breast.

Everything in Althea throbbed at the contact, and she whimpered.

"Shhh, sweetheart," Hannah murmured, and Althea sunk into the warmth that the endearment offered. She wanted this woman to take her apart, because she trusted Hannah to put her back together again.

The sensations blurred after that, became almost too much and then not enough. Hannah was at times gentle, soothing, and at others demanding, challenging, like a dance that Althea was learning as she went.

When everything quieted, they lay in Althea's narrow bed, facing each other like a pair of commas, their knees brushing, their hands petting affectionately.

Hannah was part of Althea's story now, woven tightly into the tapestry of her. Even when Althea left, Hannah would remain.

Althea traced Hannah's lower lip. "Do people like us get happy endings?"

It wasn't what she'd meant to say. She hadn't even been trying to tell herself that she and Hannah could have a happily ever after. They lived worlds apart, and that wasn't likely to change anytime soon.

But this was all new to Althea, the fact that *this* even existed. And so she'd blurted it out without thinking.

"Yes," Hannah whispered and the answer wrapped around Althea just as surely as Hannah's scent had earlier. "They may be complicated, but that doesn't make them any less happy. In fact, I think they're all the better for it."

"Promise?" Althea demanded.

"Promise."

They drifted like that until the sun had well and truly risen. Althea was just finally starting to sleep when the pounding came.

She sat up, staring at the door before glancing back at Hannah. The woman was shrugging into a button-up shirt Althea had left hanging over the chair near the bed.

Her mouth was set in a grim line. “You’ll have to answer it, or they’ll come in.”

Althea dressed as quickly as possible, making sure Hannah was decent before she crossed the room.

When she opened the door, Diedrich stood there, his fist raised. His eyes flew over her shoulder to where Hannah must be standing, his expression going furious in the blink of an eye.

Only after she flinched back did Althea notice the brownshirts standing behind him.

Chapter 39

Paris
March 1937

Paris might not have been home for Hannah, but she wasn't without resources.

She started to ask around about Deveraux Charles. The consensus seemed to be that the pretty actress had been won over by the Nazis.

Hannah tried to recall those months at the end of thirty-two, the beginning of thirty-three, the memories syrupy and fetid all at once. There had been nights at the cabarets but then also nights at Resistance meetings. There had been the thrill of university but then there had also been the disappearing student body, friends being expelled simply for being Jewish. There had been a hint of economic recovery in the air, but also clashes in the street where death had been an acceptable outcome of any skirmish.

Now, Hannah couldn't even remember how she'd met Deveraux. A friend of a friend of a friend, perhaps. The woman had seemed so glamorous, so cynical, so worldly. Her insults directed toward the Nazis were neither veiled nor subtle. She had been up-front about the fact that she was going to use them to fund her visit to Germany, but she wasn't on their side.

In 1933, that had seemed like an understandable bargain.

All Hannah could think now was that it was people like that who had let Hitler rise to power. The terrible men Hitler had surrounded himself with were absolutely complicit in what was happening, but so were the otherwise decent people who thought that Hitler's success could ultimately benefit them if they simply held their noses over the parts of him they didn't like.

"The only thing I know is that she's staying at the Hotel Majestic," Natalie said, when Hannah questioned her about the run-in she'd had with Dev. "In the sixteenth arrondissement. She had told me she was leaving, but someone said she was spotted at Le Chat last night."

"Have you ever heard anything about her?" Hannah asked, aiming for mildly curious. She couldn't even explain to herself why there was an itch at the back of her skull making her pursue this line of questioning.

"Nazi *putain,*" Natalie said, without hesitation. Hannah didn't yet speak French fluently, but *whore* was one of those words you learned when you first got to the country. "She makes their films, sleeps with the highest official she can nab. Bounces around between them. Gets glowing press articles written about her."

"Makes the Nazis more palatable to the Americans." Hannah finished that train of thought, and Natalie tipped her head in agreement.

"Not that many of them need much encouragement."

"Not that many people anywhere do," Hannah countered, and again Natalie nodded.

"I was surprised you knew her."

"In another life, it seems," Hannah said, her attention slipping into the past.

And she realized what had been lurking there, that image of Althea crumpled on a sidewalk, tears in her eyes as she whispered *I didn't.*

On Sunday morning, Hannah found herself in front of the Hotel Majestic, loitering on the corner outside the massive building, the weight of Otto's pistol heavy against her side, tucked into her jacket pocket.

The hotel looked like the rest of Parisian architecture, ostentatious in design but built with bland white marble that had the city all blending together into one unforgettable blur.

After Hannah had waited for an hour or so, a sleek black Mercedes slid to the curb, and Deveraux spilled out onto the sidewalk, her silky, slinky dress clearly from the night before riding high on her thigh.

A man dressed in a Nazi uniform followed, just as unsteady. Both were still drunk, it seemed.

They laughed, loud and obnoxious, drawing scandalized scowls and impressed smirks from those passing in and out of the hotel lobby.

Hannah closed her eyes, called herself foolish, erratic, even. But then with a single nod, she decided.

She followed behind them, using two older men with briefcases as cover.

By luck, she was close enough to hear Deveraux slur out a room number to the elevator operator. Fourth floor.

Hannah detoured toward the back hallway to find the stairs, sparing a moment to be thankful she had worn trousers and sensible shoes.

A woman passed her on the way down but didn't spare her a second glance.

Still, Hannah wondered what she was doing, wondered what her plan was. Knowing Dev's room number changed nothing, not if she didn't want to burst in on the woman and her Nazi lover, perhaps midcoitus.

The thought did nothing to deter Hannah, though. She continued on, only pausing at the door to the fourth floor, listening for the *ding* that signaled the arrival of the elevator.

Hannah palmed the grip of the pistol.

Was she really this person? What was she planning on doing with the weapon? What did she even suspect? She didn't quite know. She just knew that the power that came with wrapping her fingers around the metal centered her in a way nothing had since 1933 Berlin, when her world had been pulled apart.

Hannah stepped out into the hallway.

The pair had disappeared from sight, but Dev's wind-chime laughter trailed behind her like a bad perfume. All Hannah had to do was follow it.

When she turned the corner, she saw them.

Dev pressed up against the wall beside a hotel room door, her Nazi lover's face buried in her neck, her thigh hooked up around his waist, her hand threaded through his hair, her head angled back to give him more access.

Hannah knew she hadn't made a sound herself, but Dev's eyes snapped to her. They weren't clouded with alcohol, like Hannah had expected, but rather were clear and sharp. Her gaze dropped to the pistol, and then came back to Hannah's face with some kind of grim understanding.

Dev gripped the man's hair, and somehow directed him inside

the room without letting him turn to potentially spot Hannah. And more importantly the pistol she had gripped tight and pointed at the pair of them.

Once the man had stumbled inside, Dev closed the door and leaned back against it. She regarded Hannah through hooded eyes. "You figured it out."

Hannah hadn't, not really. But she didn't want to give away her cards. "Why did you do it?"

Dev breathed in, breathed out, stared down the hallway, and then looked back at Hannah. "Not here."

"Where?"

"The roof," Dev said, looking toward the ceiling.

"Why would I go anywhere with you?"

Dev sailed past her with a sure and steady stride. She paused when she reached Hannah's side and leaned down to whisper in her ear. "Just think how much easier it will be to kill me up there."

Hannah followed her to the elevator.

Chapter 40

Owl's Head, Maine
July 1944

The problem was that the train sign had lied to Viv.

It had said Owl's Head, identifying the stop as clear as day. Apparently, though, its definition of *stop* varied wildly from her own.

Viv had now been walking for near on an hour down a dirt road to nowhere and she was about to scream. Blisters had formed not only on her heels, but also on her hand where she was lugging a bag that would have been packed far more carefully had Viv known she would need to be carrying it for miles on end.

On the verge of tears, Viv finally decided it was time to rest. She set her valise down and then sat on top of it, ignoring the cloud of dust that rippled up at the disturbance.

She would not cry.

That's what she kept telling herself, at least.

Just when Viv was contemplating heading back to the station, catching a train to New York, and pretending this whole thing hadn't happened, she heard the purr of an engine.

Viv clasped her hands together, sent up a prayer of gratitude, and stood, ready to wave down whoever was in the little red truck headed her way.

They had to be better than death by lack of water and too much walking.

She didn't even need to flash any leg. The Ford stopped right next to her, the driver reaching across the bench to roll down the window.

"Help you?" he called.

He was exactly what she would have guessed Maine looked like. Big and burly with an overgrown beard and bear-paw hands.

Viv tried to speak, but her throat was coated with dirt. She coughed, realizing how unattractive that was, and then dipped her head down to look in the window, hoping her batting eyelashes covered up for the sputtering.

"Owl's Head?" she managed.

He looked amused at her plight. "Another two miles down the road."

"Christ," Viv cursed without thinking, but he just popped the door open.

"Get in," he said with a little wave.

Unbelievably grateful, Viv slid onto the cracked-leather bench and hauled her bag in behind her. "You, my good sir, are my savior."

"You would have made it."

"Maybe so," she said, "but my feet certainly thank you."

"It's further from the station than it looks." He slid her a look. "You're from New York."

"Is it that obvious?" Viv asked, though she knew it was. For all that she'd dressed for travel, she'd still *dressed*. Her clothes were fine and stylish, her hair and makeup more so.

"Joe," the man said, without answering. He held out his calloused hand, and she slotted her own into his palm.

"Vivian," she returned, since he'd kept it informal.

"What's your purpose in Owl's Head?" Joe asked. He drove with an enviable confidence despite the rutted road.

"I'm looking for Althea James."

"Oh ho." Joe hooted a little. "One of those."

"No," Viv retorted, peeved that he might think her a lookie-loo of some sort. "I have actual business with her."

"'Actual business,'" Joe repeated, mockingly, in an accent that sounded nothing like her. She wrinkled her nose at him, despite the fact that he wasn't looking at her to notice. "What *actual* business do you have with her, then?"

"As if it's any of *your* concern," Viv shot back.

"As both her brother and her manager, I would say it is," Joe said, shooting her a smug smile. "Or I could turn around and take you to the train station."

Viv dropped her head back against the seat. "Small towns."

"They'll get you every time," Joe agreed.

"Can I at least get lunch somewhere before you give me the boot?" Viv asked.

Joe drove her into the quaint town that had one main street and a few side ones with residential houses and nothing else. Viv could actually hear the roar of the sea when she stepped out of the truck, and she had to admit she was charmed.

"My place," Joe said, with a nod toward the pub they'd parked in front of.

It was all dark leather and rich mahogany, a beautiful bar running the length of the joint, deep booths, and well-cared-for tables decorating the rest of it.

"Fish and chips?" he offered and she agreed, both knowing she didn't have a choice and wanting the meal anyway.

She was glad to take it when it came—the chips were perfect and greasy, the fish fresh and delicate despite the oil.

Only when she was licking her fingers did she acknowledge how ravenous she'd been.

"All right." Joe leaned on the bar, a rag tossed over one shoulder. "I've given you long enough. What do you want with my sister?"

And so Viv explained. About the Armed Services Editions, the Taft amendment, the attempted censorship, even D-Day, and everything she'd heard since.

"I sincerely think she could make a difference," Viv finished, lamely after the grandiosity of the rest of her story.

Joe eyed her, then walked away. He grabbed a thick pint glass from the hooks and filled it to the brim with frothy beer. He downed half of it in one go and then crossed back over to her.

"You know what my sister has been through?"

It seemed like a genuine question so Viv tried to answer honestly. "Only a guess."

"I can't fight."

Viv didn't question that admission. People said strange things these days, out of nowhere. Instead, she nodded. "That's all right."

"I wanted to," Joe continued. "But I've got asthma of all things."

"That must be difficult." She wasn't placating him. She'd seen what being left behind did to the boys back home. Those overseas, of course, had it much worse. But she would never write off the pain of being the one who couldn't go over. The one who was stared at by old men and young women who had lost too much. Viv had seen a boy slapped for not being over there, despite the fact that Viv knew he was blind in one eye. Some people wanted them as cannon fodder anyway, some just didn't know what to do with the sight of a seemingly healthy boy who had it better than someone in their own family.

"Althea hates the Nazis," he said, in what she was beginning to realize was his way of speaking. Disjointed thought followed by disjointed thought.

"Don't we all?" Viv asked.

"No," Joe said, brutal and honest, and Viv couldn't argue. She was fairly certain that at least some number of Americans secretly agreed with the hateful speech the Nazis spewed.

"Well, I do," Viv said, watching him. "What do you need me to do to show you I'm earnest?"

"You don't need to do anything," he said. "You came all this way. I'll let you take your shot."

Viv slumped on her barstool in relief. "Thank you."

"Don't thank me 'til you meet her." Joe signaled to a pimply boy working the taps at the end of the bar. "Let's go."

"Now?" Viv asked but she was already scrambling off the seat, grabbing her bag.

Joe called down to the boy to have him watch the bar, and then they headed back outside. He gestured to the truck and she climbed in once more. The drive was quiet but not tense, both of their windows down. Viv had never smelled the sea before, except when she went to Coney Island, and it wasn't pure there.

Here she could all but taste the salt in the air, the waves a siren's call. The road followed the black cliffs, and she could stare out into forever. She wasn't sure she'd ever felt so small as this.

A cottage stood on what seemed like the end of the earth. Pink, purple, yellow, white flowers surrounded it, looking for all the world like a painting come to life.

"Either have her ring me, or take the bicycle and ride back,"

Joe directed with a jerk of his head to the fence where a bike rested. Viv thought about the drive and hoped Althea would at least grant her the use of the phone before kicking her out, if that's what she was going to do.

"Thank you," Viv said, before gathering her courage in both hands to get herself to climb out of the truck.

Joe honked once as he reversed, and Viv winced. There was no hiding that she was here now, no hesitating to prepare what she would say. Even as she had the thought the curtain behind the window twitched.

Now or never. Viv walked up to the door, raised her fist, and knocked.

It opened almost immediately.

Standing there was a petite woman with thick hair she wore down around her shoulders. She had a sweet, round face with a smattering of freckles, both of which made her seem much younger than what Viv knew was her thirty-six years of age.

"Whatever you want," Althea James said, her voice raspy like this was the first time in a long time that she'd used it. "The answer is no."

And then the door promptly slammed in Viv's face.

Chapter 41

Berlin
May 1933

The room Althea was taken to was small and windowless, the smell of rot almost unbearable. At the sight of the stark, bare walls, her breath came in shallow gasps, until the world started to narrow into a pinprick.

The men who'd dragged her from her apartment threw her into the single chair, and her body went with the force of their movement, like she was a rag doll unable to resist.

Desperate to ground herself to reality, Althea counted her fingers where they clenched against her thighs. One, two, three . . . This was real. Not a horrific nightmare.

All at once, she saw that man tied to a Saint Andrew's cross in the middle of the square, unconscious as the woman wept at his feet, his blood spattered across her face.

There had been no mercy in the Nazi's expression.

Althea's forehead pressed against the cool metal of the table, everything in her aching.

Diedrich prowled into the room, a vicious smile twisting his features and making him ugly in a way she could never have predicted.

"You think you can humiliate me?" he asked, his voice pitched low and even, all the more frightening because of its control. "You. A plain, ignorant American woman."

Althea tried not to flinch. She'd known he'd never really been interested in her romantically; that had all been a lie to keep her compliant. Still, the ghost of those butterflies from those first days acted as a harsh reminder of her own foolishness. She looked away and gritted her teeth.

"I was so kind to you," Diedrich continued, pacing the space, his hands locked behind his back. It took him only a stride or two before he had to turn, which would have been comical had Althea not been trying to hold herself together at her rapidly fraying seams. "I showed you everything you could want in life, things you could only dream of attaining." He paused then gestured to himself. "People you could only dream of having."

"I would never want you," Althea managed, proud of herself for being able to form words, let alone spit the insult at him. Her hands trembled, but still, she'd done it.

He was on her in a blink, his thumb and forefinger pinching her chin, forcing her to meet his eyes. "Oh, pet," he all but purred. "We both know that's not true."

Maybe yesterday, she would have cowered. But something had bloomed within her last night. A power she had never known she had caught fire, and the flames burned away the fear that she had been coming to believe was one of her foundation stones.

"My head might have been turned by the pretty mask," Althea said, trying to lace as much acid as possible into the words. "But we both know the monster beneath is hideous."

Diedrich laughed as if she were a child lashing out with ineffective fists. He continued as if she hadn't said anything. "And how did you repay me? By cavorting with that Jewess whore."

Althea sucked in a breath. "She's a hundred times the person you are."

Diedrich gripped her face harder, and she saw the rage simmering beneath the surface. But to her surprise, he let her go and stepped back enough so that he was leaning against the wall.

After an unbearable silence, Althea glanced at the door. Was this when he called in those thugs of his to beat her senseless? Her stomach rolled as she imagined her body bruised and bloody on the ground. Or worse. They could do something much worse to her. "What are you going to do to me?"

That question seemed to be what Diedrich had been waiting for. A slow, disturbing smile spread over his face that looked skeletal now, his evilness shaping his features into a macabre facsimile of amusement. "Absolutely nothing."

His reply should have been a relief. But Althea's entire body tightened, as if waiting for a blow he was promising wouldn't come. "What do you mean?"

"We would never hurt one of our friends from America," Diedrich drawled. "You will leave here without a single scratch on your person. And you can tell your embassy that when they ask."

Althea shook her head, the lurking sense of danger refusing to fade. "I don't understand. Why bring me here, then?"

She recognized the look in Diedrich's eyes when he'd seen Hannah standing behind her in the apartment. That anger had gone beyond politics. Men like Diedrich did not take kindly to being humiliated. He wouldn't let her just walk away now.

This wasn't a social call. This wasn't just a slap on the wrists. But the fear had muddled her mind. Althea couldn't see what Diedrich had planned.

"I thought about throwing you to the men," Diedrich said, casual contempt in every word. "But I have to admit, this will be more fun."

"What do you mean?" Althea called as Diedrich tossed her one last grin and then headed toward the door. She tried again, though she knew he wouldn't hear her. "What do you mean?"

Only the echo of her own voice ricocheting off the tiled walls of the tiny room answered her.

THEY KEPT ALTHEA for eleven hours.

She was given a piece of bread and a glass of water and was escorted to the toilet twice.

None of the lower-ranking men answered her questions, her pleas, her hysterical begging.

The walls pulsed around her, closing in until they all but brushed her shoulders, the sour mildew choking her lungs. In those moments, she closed her eyes, thought of Hannah when they'd danced at the cabaret, thought of her fingers tracing soothing patterns on Althea's naked back, her eyes quiet and serious.

Althea held those moments tight to her chest, tried to breathe them in, breathe them out.

After what seemed like days, two brownshirts opened the room to her makeshift cell and pulled her out into the hallway.

The darkness threatened at the edges of her vision as her heart tripped dangerously in her chest. A high-pitched siren wailed against the inside of her skull, spots popped into starbursts in her eyes, and she couldn't feel her feet or hands.

They were going to kill her. She was sure of it.

Flashes of her life played against her eyelids. Her brother. Her cliffs. Those fairy lights at the winter market, the books. That day in the early spring when Hannah had sat shading Althea's face. Last night, the fire warm against her skin.

She didn't want to die.

Althea let them take all her weight, making them drag her as she screamed at the ceiling, her throat raw by the time they reached the lobby of the building. And then, they let her go so that she crumpled to the floor from her unexpected freedom, and they turned and walked away without once uttering a word.

She scrambled to stand, her legs wobbly, her head too light, her stomach heaving. Althea stumbled to the door, managed to grasp the handle with unreliable fingers, somehow, somehow, somehow *pushed,* and she was outside.

Breathing in air not tainted with the rancid traces of fear and torture.

Suddenly there were hands on her, and Althea cowered away.

But the hands were soft, gentle, careful. Blinking, Althea tried to focus on the face in front of her.

All she could see were warm, golden eyes.

Everything in her relaxed, and she exhaled, letting her body sag into Hannah's sure grip.

"Althea, tell me you're unhurt, please, tell me," Hannah said, desperate and urgent, yet still somehow soothing. "What did they do to you?"

Shaking her head, Althea tried to get her numb lips to move, to do something other than mouth useless words. "Nothing," she finally managed.

"What?" Hannah asked, her hands still exploring, looking for broken bones, bruised flesh, torn skin.

Althea licked her suddenly dry lips, not sure why she was nervous when she answered, "Nothing."

"That doesn't . . ." Hannah trailed off like she didn't believe Althea, wouldn't take her word for it.

"I don't know why," Althea confessed on a whisper, wishing the fog that had settled over her mind would clear. There was something *wrong* and she couldn't figure out what it was. Not when Hannah was looking at her like that, with such heartbreaking concern. "You were waiting for me."

"Of course." Hannah finally pulled Althea in tight, her steady arms providing the solace Althea had been desperately craving without her having to ask for it. "Once they took you . . . You don't know how frightened I was."

Althea buried her face in the warm, soft space of Hannah's neck, wanting to live there forever, to never have to remember this day, that horrible, overwhelming terror, the nothingness that had followed. "You warned me he would get his revenge."

"And he didn't hurt you?" Hannah asked again, a rumble emitting from her chest. She didn't let Althea go, just let her nestle there, up against her body, Hannah's palms rubbing slow circles on Althea's back.

"No," Althea said slowly. "He said this was more fun."

"What was more—"

A shout interrupted them. Otto, calling Hannah's name.

He was still a half block away, but he'd yelled loud enough to get their attention. Althea reluctantly stepped out of Hannah's embrace as they turned to greet him.

A flush rode high on Otto's neck and cheeks. His always artfully disheveled hair stood up as if he'd been yanking at the strands. When he reached them, he panted, half bent over.

"Otto?" Hannah asked, a quiet alertness about her. Althea couldn't help but match her rigid posture. Something was clearly wrong.

"They have Adam."

"But how?" Hannah breathed out.

"I don't know, I don't know," Otto said, straightening, his eyes wide, unfocused.

"No one knew where he was," Hannah said, the words rushing out, as if stating these facts would somehow change the reality. "Did he leave the Adlon?"

"No, he made a scene in the lobby of the hotel," Otto said, shaking his head. "It's how I heard about it. They dragged him out of his room."

"But nobody knew where—"

Hannah cut herself off, shifting her attention to Althea.

Her gaze locked on Althea's face and then slipped to the building behind them, where Althea had just been held by the Nazis. Then her eyes darted back to Althea, likely noticing once again that Althea was whole, in one piece, without any new bruises or marks.

Althea tripped behind Hannah's thought process, desperate and anxious, her mind not moving quickly enough for this conversation. "No."

"You knew where he was," Hannah said. "I told you."

Otto's ragged inhale sliced into the air between them, but he didn't interrupt.

"No, no." Althea reached out shaking hands to Hannah, who flinched and stepped away. Althea curled her fists up into her chest, worried her knees might buckle, might take her down to the sidewalk. "Diedrich already knew, he must have known."

"How?" The question didn't come like Hannah was giving her the benefit of the doubt. It came like a slap, a judgment already rendered.

Even as Althea's throat spasmed dangerously, she tried to think. "He said . . ." Her eyes flew to Hannah's. "He said this was more fun than hurting me himself. He planned this, Hannah."

But Hannah had been lost to her. Althea could tell from how her words slammed up against a concrete facade. There was no give, no softness, none of the affection that Althea only now realized had been granted to her since the moment she'd met Hannah.

"Please." Althea stumbled forward, not sure what she was even doing. But again, Hannah retreated, contempt in every line of her face.

"Don't touch me," she all but spat at Althea, and Althea thought she might have preferred that. Instead the words landed, cut into her skin, created the very scars she was missing to prove her innocence.

"I didn't." It was all she could manage, her arms wrapped protectively around her waist, her vision blurred with the tears she was refusing to let fall. If they slipped out, Hannah might read them as guilt.

Otto finally stepped forward, putting an arm around Hannah's shoulder, pulling her closer, offering her the comfort Althea wished she could. He pointed a long finger at Althea. "You stay away from us." And then he called her a name that she didn't know but which seared itself onto her bones.

Whore, traitor, bitch. A combination of the three? It didn't matter. Disgust was easily conveyed across languages.

"Come on, darling," Otto murmured to Hannah, who by now had paled and was leaning against Otto like he was the only thing keeping her upright.

"They have him," Hannah said so quietly that it was almost

just as if her lips moved and nothing came out. But Althea heard her anyway. "I told her."

Althea took a wavering breath, wanting, God, *wanting,* to do something other than stand there and watch her world fall apart.

And then she heard Hannah's voice in her head. *This isn't about you.*

Every part of her longed to reach out, to grasp Hannah's arms, *make* Hannah believe her, talk and talk and talk at Hannah until she gave in and admitted there had to be another way that the Nazis had found her brother.

But this wasn't about Althea right now.

So she stepped back, her body collapsing in on itself. "I'm sorry."

They would both take the apology as an admission, but she didn't care. She was sorry, sorry about all of this, sorry she'd ever met Diedrich, sorry that she'd ever believed the Nazis' lies, that she'd accepted Nazi money to come to the city in the first place. Maybe she hadn't revealed Adam's location under torture, but wasn't she complicit in his capture?

Because Diedrich had orchestrated this as punishment, there was no doubt about that. And that started and ended with Althea.

The only thing she wasn't sorry about was meeting Hannah. Maybe the world was ending, but for once Althea had been able to understand something everyone else seemed to grasp intrinsically. Love didn't have to be hard. It could be the quiet moments while drinking wine on a café's patio; the gentle touch of fingers against sweat-glistening skin; the laughter of dancing through the shelves of a bookstore; a shared look of understanding that didn't need any words to accompany it.

Hannah stared at her with a wounded expression that sliced

into Althea deep and permanent. She could live to a hundred and never forget the way Hannah looked at her in that moment.

The weight of Hannah's betrayal leaned so heavily on her shoulders that Althea's legs finally gave out. It happened so quickly that Althea wasn't even aware she was falling until her knees hit pavement. There would be bruises, and she wished they were visible now.

"I didn't," she whispered one more time, not able to look up to where they stood over her, Otto an avenging angel, Hannah a destroyed one.

"Save your lies for someone who will believe them," Otto said, and then he tugged at Hannah. "Come on, she's not worth it."

"No," Hannah agreed softly. "She isn't."

Chapter 42

Owl's Head, Maine
July 1944

Viv did end up riding the bicycle back to the village. When Joe saw her coming, he laughed so hard he had to rest one hand on the hood of this truck.

She imagined she looked a sight and must be covered in yet another layer of dust.

He gave her a room above the pub, and she used the bicycle the next morning to ride out to Althea's little cottage. And then the next morning and the next morning.

Viv figured she had a little less than two weeks before she had to be back in New York City to prepare for the event with Taft. She was going to use all the time she had.

On the fifth day Althea brought her a cup of coffee. She then proceeded to shut the door in Viv's face once more, but Viv took the victory anyway.

She gloated that night at the pub, and Joe just shook his head at her. But he smiled a little, too, and she took that as another good sign.

On the eighth day, Althea stepped outside as the afternoon was properly setting in. When Viv stood up from where she'd been reading on the little garden bench, Althea jerked her head toward the cliffs. "Walk with me."

Viv managed to contain her grin, but only just.

They strolled along the cliffs in silence, Viv somehow knowing not to push it.

After twenty minutes, Althea nodded to the paperback Viv had forgotten about under her arm. "What are you reading?"

"*Vanity Fair,*" Viv rushed to answer, thrilled that Althea had initiated conversation. "It was in our June series for the ASEs."

"Along with mine," Althea mused. "Is it any good? I haven't read it."

Viv considered that. "I think so. The subtitle for it is *A Novel Without a Hero,* which feels like an apt warning."

"A cast of unlikable characters?" Althea asked.

"Or at least flawed," Viv said after a moment of consideration. "I find flawed characters so much more interesting, though. I imagine you do, as well."

"You've read my books."

It wasn't a question. "I have."

"Well, where's the endless flattery, then?" Althea prodded, her expression twisting into something unpleasant.

"I think you've probably had enough of that to last a lifetime," Viv guessed, and Althea's brows rose.

"When you're asking for a favor, it's good advice to butter up the person first," Althea said, and despite the words, it felt like agreement.

"Flattery won't work for you."

Curiosity would, though. And Viv was proven right when Althea asked, "And what, pray tell, do you think you know about me?"

Viv's heart beat fast. If she got this wrong, it would be her one shot, lost. "You write not for flattery, but as a penance."

Althea stopped short, her arms wrapping around herself, her eyes big and nearly wounded as she studied Viv's face.

When she didn't say anything, Viv continued. "People don't want praise for penance. They want to be forgiven."

Althea's mouth opened once, shut, pressed into a thin line. And then she whirled, leaving Viv standing on the cliffs, a metaphorical door slamming.

When Viv recounted the conversation to Joe that night, asking if she should give up, he watched her, thoughtful. "Try one more day."

"Are you sure?" Viv asked, going for light and not certain she hit the right tone. "I don't want to end up on the wrong side of a shotgun."

"She finds you interesting," Joe said, shaking his head. "It's been a long time since she's found anything interesting. Try one more day."

The next morning, Althea was waiting by the gate for her. Without saying anything, she jerked her chin toward the path, and Viv nearly wept with relief.

"You want me to come to New York," Althea said, a half hour into the otherwise silent walk. Viv had been enjoying the salt-laden breeze and was startled from the trance she'd half dozed into.

"Yes, I'll pay, if that's an issue," Viv said, then winced. Althea James did not need anyone to pay for anything.

Althea looked like she wanted to laugh, but didn't. "What do you want me to say? To this senator."

"Whatever you want," Viv said. "Perhaps something about the dangers of government censorship?"

"Why do you suppose I know enough to talk about that?" Althea asked.

Viv wondered if this was a test. "Because of *An Inconceivable Dark*."

"And not because I was in Berlin for the book burnings?"

"Well, that, too," Viv admitted.

"I thought so."

"It's not just on you," Viv said. "I want you there, because I think Americans will connect with your story. But if you say no, I'll leave."

"A door in the face wasn't direct enough?" Althea asked, though there was something teasing in her voice.

"I've been told I'm . . . persistent," Viv admitted. "I wanted you to know what you were saying no to."

Althea eyed Viv and she felt a test coming. "What's your favorite book?"

"That's my line," Viv said, more to herself, but Althea hummed a curious little sound. "I always ask people that. It's my barometer."

"What do you consider a bad answer?" Althea asked, for the first time sounding truly engaged.

"That they don't like to read," Viv said, with a small smile.

"Ah, but it's not their fault. Some people simply haven't found their books." Althea nodded to a stone bench overlooking the waves and Viv took a seat quickly before the woman could rescind the invitation.

"I think the ASEs help soldiers find theirs," Viv said.

Althea's mouth pursed in humor. "Quite on message."

"A dog with a bone." Viv shrugged. "But truly, that's partly how we got the publishers on board. We're creating a generation of men who understand what it is to read for pleasure. Whereas before they might never have been exposed to books that they could actually like and not just be forced to read for school."

"You're trying to convince me your cause is just. But I don't worry that you're like the Nazis," Althea said, a finger tapping on her leg. "I worry that others will be."

"And once you've been featured in newspapers across the country, people won't stop hounding you," Viv said, getting it now.

"I like my hermit life on the cliffs," Althea said, and she almost sounded apologetic. "It keeps me out of trouble."

"But it keeps you away from the good things, too, doesn't it?" Viv asked.

"There might have been a time where I cared about that," Althea said, staring out to sea. "Now I think sometimes the best we can do is protect the world from ourselves."

Viv studied her, wondering how she would take what Viv was about to say. "I think you give yourself too much credit."

Althea's eyes snapped to Viv's face and for one horrible second Viv thought she'd lost Althea completely. And then the woman threw her head back, her laughter cutting through the rhythmic slap of waves from below. After a few moments she swiped at the corner of her eye with her thumb. "I'm sorry. You reminded me of someone just then."

"Who?" Viv asked.

Althea's smile slipped, though it didn't disappear. "Someone who never pulled her punches. She said that the Nazis taking power wasn't about *me*. And that thinking it so made me incredibly self-centered."

"Oh, I didn't—"

"You did, it's all right," Althea interrupted gently. "I think I've once again made myself the protagonist of a story that isn't really mine to star in. You'll have to forgive me, I do live quite an isolated life." She paused. "But it's always been my greatest flaw, I suppose."

"Isn't it all of ours?" Viv asked, with a little huff. "I'm sitting here on a grand quest thinking I'm going to make all the difference in the world if I can just convince you to come to New York."

Althea tipped her head in acknowledgment and then pierced her with a look. "You didn't say. What is your favorite book?"

"I've always answered *Frankenstein* to that," Viv said, weighing the words. "And I adore Mary Shelley. She was so ahead of her time and surrounded by all these men who the world deemed brilliant, and yet, I'm sure her legacy will outlast all of theirs."

Althea cocked her head. "Is that not your real answer?"

"I would be a terrible critic," Viv said, shrugging one shoulder. "I always feel like the book I'm reading is my favorite, even if it's not technically better than others that I adore." Viv smirked. "But I like the question anyway."

"So, you can instantly tell if you won't like someone?" Althea asked, sliding her a look. "You do know Hitler's favorites include Dante and Jonathan Swift. Liking reading isn't synonymous with being a good person."

"You're right," Viv said, with a little bow. She hadn't expected that argument from a world-famous author, but Viv liked Althea better for it. Too often there was a snobbery in the literary world that kept people from finding what they enjoyed reading. Viv didn't care if that was comic books, or murder mysteries, or happily-ever-after romances. There was no real right answer to her question, because they were all the right answer. "What's your favorite?"

"Book?" Althea asked, though it seemed rhetorical, so Viv just waited. "I have different ones for different stages in my life.

My mother had a beautiful version of *Grimms' Fairy Tales* that I loved when I was younger. Then it was *Ivanhoe,* and then *Alice in Wonderland.*" She grimaced at that. "Now? *Tender Is the Night.*"

"F. Scott Fitzgerald," Viv noted absently. "Not his most popular."

"Fitzgerald always looks better a few years out. It's a bit dark," Althea said dryly. She turned back to the sea. "He talks about loving a person in one particular moment in their lives. Not about loving them forever, but remembering that there was and will always be something once upon a time that made the person love the other."

"That's romantic," Viv said, as neutrally as possible, sensing somehow that the ice beneath her feet was paper thin.

"He wrote it when Zelda was in the hospital for her madness," Althea said, again with that same almost sarcastic tone. "But, yes, it is."

They both watched the waves for a long time after that, long enough for the sun to slip low in the sky behind them.

Finally, Althea slapped both hands to her legs and stood. "All right, I'll be your dancing monkey."

"Surely, you at least rank as a lion jumping through flaming hoops," Viv said lightly, though a tangle of emotion fluttered like a bird's wings against her rib cage at the agreement.

Althea laughed, looking alive and bright and beautiful for the first time. "I'll settle for roller-skating hippopotamus."

They started back toward the cottage, and Viv knew, she *knew,* she shouldn't push it. But if Althea had a fatal flaw, then so did Viv. "What made you decide?"

"I may not have it in me to be the hero of anyone's story," Althea said, wrapping her arms around herself. "But this time, it's within my power not to be the villain."

Chapter 43

Paris
March 1937

The air on the roof of the Hotel Majestic was crisp enough for Hannah to shiver as she held the pistol on Deveraux.

It wasn't nerves, she told herself. It was the cold.

Dev reached into her evening bag and withdrew a slim cigarette case, all while leaning indolently against the balustrade. Her eyes didn't once flick down to the weapon.

"Of all the luck in the world," Dev mused as she watched her own smoke dissolve into nothing. "You had to end up in Paris. *I* had to end up in Paris."

Hannah didn't say anything. Dev had known she was here. It wasn't like she was the one who was the surprise.

"True, I knew where you were," Dev agreed, as if Hannah had spoken out loud. "But Paris is such a big city."

"Not in our circles," Hannah managed, her tongue thick and clumsy. But she thought she might have come off as unruffled.

"The Nazis and those fleeing from them."

"And which are you?" Hannah asked.

"You haven't already made up your mind on that?" Dev shot

back, and for the first time since they'd stepped onto the roof she gestured toward the pistol. "About what side I'm on."

Hannah had stopped trusting people a long time ago, right around the moment Althea had emerged from that Nazi building, tearful and unharmed. But she also knew sometimes answers were more complicated than they looked. "You tell me."

Dev was a consummate actress, but even she couldn't hide the surprise on her face. It came and went, a lightning flash that Hannah might have missed had she blinked. The woman stubbed her cigarette out in what looked like a careless gesture, but one that also allowed her to turn away from Hannah, allowed her to hide.

When she looked back, the mask was firmly back in place. "I told them where Adam was."

It shouldn't have felt like a punch, but the force of the admission almost knocked Hannah back a step. Until this very moment, Hannah hadn't been convinced, had thought herself crazy for even suspecting Dev had been involved. "Why?"

"Being a Nazi whore isn't enough?" Dev asked, throwing the truth between them like a grenade. And Hannah might have believed her, had she not heard that exact tone so many times years ago. Dev had hated the Nazis nearly as much as Hannah had, back then.

Could it really have all been an act?

While Hannah knew plenty of people who despised the Nazis and then joined their cause—because of fear, because of exhaustion, because if they didn't their own lives would fall apart—the fact remained that Dev had never needed to.

She could have gone home.

"No," Hannah said, as steady as she could.

Once again, that shock, come and gone. Dev took out another cigarette, didn't answer.

"He died, you know," Hannah said. "In November."

A muscle in Dev's jaw ticked. Still she didn't say anything.

"They must have tortured him first, though," Hannah continued, feeling detached, as if she were watching the scene instead of participating in it. "Johann said he was so small by the end."

Dev wouldn't look at Hannah.

"That was your fault," Hannah said, twisting the knife. "Do you even care?"

"Of course I care," Dev gritted out, then exhaled heavily like she hadn't meant to admit that. "You think he wouldn't have been caught without me?"

Hannah laughed, though it was bitter, disbelieving. "You turned him in."

"On a suicide mission. You know that better than I do. He wouldn't be talked out of it, wouldn't listen to reason," Dev said, her composure cracking. "He would have been killed on the spot."

"Please don't tell me you gave him up to the Nazis to save his life," Hannah said. "Even you couldn't be that stupid."

Again, Dev crushed out her cigarette, and this time Hannah noticed her hands shook.

"Why?" Hannah repeated softly, not with sympathy but with a gentleness that the moment called for if Hannah wanted answers.

The question hung between them, a heavy thing that dragged both of them toward it. The world held its breath.

"I had to give them something," Dev finally said, the words wavering. "I'd given them too much wrong information."

And the world inhaled, Hannah along with it. The noise rushed back in, the birds, the chatter on the streets below them, a far-off engine sputtering. Hannah's arm dropped, the pistol pointing to the ground, her limbs no longer obeying her commands.

"You're a spy," Hannah whispered.

"An amateur," Dev corrected, with a crooked, self-deprecating smile. Hannah recognized the loathing there. "At least back then. Now I'm better." But then she looked at the ground, shook her head before her eyes flicked to the pistol. "I thought I was."

"I knew you when," Hannah muttered, then lifted the weapon once more. "Tell me."

Dev didn't flinch. "I didn't go to Berlin expecting anything. I was an actress, a screenwriter, a director. That was it."

"You saw an opportunity," Hannah guessed.

"Almost immediately," Dev agreed. "Not many in our government saw a problem with the Nazis back then, but a few did. I asked around, offered myself in case it might be useful."

"Even if they didn't care about the Nazis, I'm guessing they cared about inside information on competing nations," Hannah said.

"Right on the money," Dev agreed. "But my handler was persuadable. His bosses might not have recognized the threat, but he did once I started detailing what was happening behind the pretty walls the Nazis put up for the rest of the world."

"So Adam was what?" Hannah asked. "An unfortunate casualty to your need to stay informed?"

"This is war, darling," Dev said, but again, her expression was so tight Hannah thought it might shatter. "Even if it hasn't been declared yet, you know as well as I do what's coming. There are no easy answers in war."

"No, but there are wrong ones," Hannah countered. "Adam wasn't just a pawn in your game. He was a person."

"He was a person who'd made the decision already that his life meant more if it was used in taking out the Nazis," Dev countered, no longer shaken, no longer upset. Here was a quiet resolve like Hannah had never seen before. "Handing over Adam before he could hand over himself meant that I was trusted again. Do you know how many people I've saved because of that trust?"

"So we're just trading lives now?" Hannah asked. "No better than Nazis. How many lives is one Jew worth?"

At that, Dev recoiled as if slapped. "That was ugly."

"So are your choices," Hannah shot back.

"I've used my position with the Nazis to help smuggle hundreds of Jewish Germans out of the country," Dev said. "Not that I need to justify myself to you."

Hannah waved her pistol a little bit. "Actually, you do need to."

"Shoot me or don't," Dev said, her chin tilted up in defiance. "I live with the weight of my decisions every day, but that's my reality now. I can't be sorry for it."

"You won't even apologize?" Hannah asked. "With your life in my hands."

"You want my empty words?" Dev asked. "You can have them. But they don't mean anything. Adam was going to get caught and killed if he went through with his plan. You know that as well as I do."

And Hannah did. She'd spent countless nights trying to convince Adam of the futility of his idea. But he'd never not succeeded at something—all that charm, all that intelligence. He'd lived a life that had convinced him he was right all the time. And the world had always seemed to confirm it. The plan had been haphazard, poorly thought out, doomed to fail.

Yet he'd been certain it would make a difference.

Hannah would never forgive Dev's decision—and she herself would have died before making a similar choice—but in her heart she would admit that perhaps, just perhaps, she understood it.

Still . . . "You didn't know where Adam was. I know he didn't tell you."

Dev watched her steadily.

Hannah shook her head, something twisting in her gut, though she didn't know why it hurt so much yet. "Only three people knew. Adam, Althea, and me."

"Oh, darling," Dev said, more of an exhale than anything.

"No." Hannah's fingers scrambled for cold stone as her body went numb. "No."

"It wasn't just Althea you told," Dev said, gently. So gently it hurt.

Hannah stepped back as if she could escape the truth of it. But Dev was right. Of course she was. "He wouldn't. He—"

The world compressed into a pinprick, everything going dark, except Dev's expression. Regret, understanding. Pity.

"You know about the drinking," Dev said. "But he never told you about the gambling because he was too ashamed. He had debts to pay off and information I needed."

Hannah blinked hard, the tears spilling out freely now as she acknowledged the truth of that. Her body ached, her skin sliced open. If she had been given the choice, she would have taken a knife wound instead of this pain.

When she breathed out, it was just a name. "Otto."

Chapter 44

New York City
July 1944

Everything moved quickly after Althea agreed to speak at the Taft event.

Viv set up an interview between Althea and Marion Samuel of the *Columbus Dispatch,* as well as with Leo Aston of *Time*. The magazine piece wouldn't come out until August, a few weeks after the Taft event, but Viv thought the timing perfect. If Taft was wavering, unsteady on his feet, both articles about reclusive, bestselling author Althea James would come as the knockout blow.

The invasion of Western Europe continued to slog on, but the number of letters the council received only kept increasing. Roosevelt's insistence that the boys have reading material during the mission had cemented the ASEs' importance in the morale efforts once more. Viv had more letters to deliver to Althea than bags to hold them all.

They'd set the woman up at the Plaza. Or rather, Viv had used her personal money to get Althea a room.

"It's a small price to pay to be on the right side of history," Viv told Hale the day she got back to New York City.

Hale had just smiled and nudged her with his elbow. "I'm proud of you."

Weeks ago, Viv might have bristled at the words and hunted for sarcasm in his voice. Now she blushed a little, unused to sincerity, shy with it almost. She bumped her forehead against his shoulder in acknowledgment and then peeled away from him to address the fourteen urgent things that had come up ahead of Taft's visit.

Eventually, she would have to do something about her messy revelations when it came to Hale, but a few days before the event she'd been planning for so long was not that time. For his part, Hale seemed endlessly patient and slightly amused, following her lead just like he had since she'd walked back into his life.

That night, when she took the letters to Althea, the woman stared at them half-fascinated, half-terrified.

They sat on the floor of Althea's sumptuous hotel room, drinking the champagne the Plaza had supplied, opening the messages, sharing them, crying as stoically as possible.

"'I had long forgotten what I was fighting for,'" Viv read. "'Whenever I closed my eyes at night, all I could think about was the feeling of the bodies beneath the water, the ones I'd walked over as I made my way to shore. Those first days, I hated everyone. I punched my way through several black eyes, officers and enlisted be damned. I did more damage than the Krauts, but I couldn't stop myself.'"

Althea hummed low in her throat to show she was listening, but she didn't interrupt. So Viv continued.

"'Then one night a buddy of mine he pulled out your book. He read the first chapter, then the second. Then he said, he'd read more the next night, if we all survived. And for the first time since I got off the boats, I actually wanted to survive."

"'I liked the book well enough'"—Althea snorted at that faint praise—"'but more than anything, I woke up this morning hoping the bullets would miss me rather than wanting them to hit me right in the heart. And if you take something away from this, Miss James, it's that you helped at least one miserable soldier get up and fight another day. May God bless you. Sergeant Tommy D'Annunzio, Second Infantry Division.'"

"Well," Althea said, reaching for the half-empty bottle of champagne, while Viv considered ordering yet another. Althea raised her glass. "To small victories."

The night went on like that until the sunrise crept into the room, startling them both.

Viv stood, stretched, groaned. "Bagels?"

Althea's face lit up, almost comically, confirming that she was more in touch with the Jewish community than she let on. Most people in New York City didn't even know what a bagel was. In February, when a truckload of fifteen hundred of them had been stolen by the Mob, the police had been confused about what had even been taken.

"You can get them?" Althea asked.

Viv winked. "Only a select few of us are in the know."

The closest bakery that had bagels was four blocks away. It wasn't a trek, by any means, but it gave them room to breathe after being cooped up all night.

"What happened over there?" Viv asked, too tired to guard her questions.

Althea yawned and tipped her face up to the sun. "Nothing special."

Viv thought she was lying, but Viv also thought her own question impertinent, so she went ahead and shut her mouth.

They stood on a corner eating bagels and lox, at a loss as to what else to do. Viv couldn't speak for Althea but the way her body felt drained was reminiscent of the morning after a night on the town. Going to sleep didn't seem to be an option, but neither did going to work. Staring at a blank wall for nine hours might do the trick, but that didn't seem ideal considering the event with Taft was in two days.

Viv took one more stab at starting a conversation with Althea. "Are you working on another book?"

"Always," Althea said with a little smirk that Viv didn't fully understand. "In theory. In practice? I don't know if I have anything else to say."

"Is it your job to always say something?" Viv asked, without intending to poke at bruises. She was genuinely curious.

"As opposed to?"

"I don't know, that letter," Viv said, jerking her head toward the hotel as if it would mean something. "He didn't really care about the message. I mean not enough to write about it. He did care about the story."

"You see those as different things?" Althea asked, though not in an aggressive way.

"Your message is perfectly tailored to inspire men to go to war for this country's values," Viv said, trying to think through something with a foggy mind and not insult the world-renowned author at her side at the same time. "He even started the letter saying he didn't know what he was fighting for. Yet . . ."

"He was more interested in what happened next," Althea said, catching on. "It was about engaging his attention rather than spilling some kind of truth."

"Don't get me wrong," Viv hastened to add. "Your themes are important. But . . ."

"But?"

"I think sometimes people get so caught up in the literary

prestige of a novel," Viv said, with a little shrug, "the idea that reading should be fun is lost."

"*One Thousand and One Nights,*" Althea said, and Viv bowed her head in agreement.

"I don't think an author's job is always to change the world," Viv said. "I think sometimes it's to make it more enjoyable. Even for a brief amount of time."

"Your ASE project," Althea said. "Always on message."

Viv laughed, caught out. "My ASE project."

"I hope this war doesn't last long enough that another one of my books would help some hapless soldier," Althea said, and Viv had to squeeze her arm to show her agreement. "But you're not backing down against Taft? Even though it might all be moot in a few months."

Viv shook her head. "I don't think the need is going to disappear, even should the war end tomorrow. These boys are going to be haunted by what they saw over there. If we take away books, what are they left with? Nightmares, and that's it."

"They'll still have nightmares," Althea said in that way that made it clear she had her own.

"Yes," Viv agreed. "But at least that's not all they'll have."

Chapter 45

Berlin
May 1933

Somehow Althea scraped herself up off the sidewalk.

Her legs didn't want to cooperate, but neither did her arms, so it all evened out. She walked toward her apartment, not sure she was headed in the right direction. Not caring if she was.

Hannah's expression haunted her. With each step she saw the wounded eyes, the bruised lips, the shuttered face. For one glorious night, Althea had been let in behind those walls. Now she was blocked forever.

The stairs to her place presented a challenge, but Althea forced her feet to climb them, her arms still wrapped around her center, as if she could really protect herself from the blow.

By the time she got back inside, every part of her trembled beneath the weight of all that had happened.

Not just the news about Adam, not just the detainment by the Nazis, not just Diedrich's cruel amusement as he'd enacted his revenge. But the soft moments of the night before. When Hannah had been there, cupping her jaw, pressing her lips to Althea's, her hands exploring Althea's body like they'd already staked a claim.

Back at the cabaret, Althea had been terrified of what she'd felt when Hannah's mouth had grazed her jaw. But here, in this sanctuary, she'd been set on fire. Consumed, burned down to ash. Then she had risen from the remains, a new person.

Althea had never known, had never imagined, that it could be like that. A conversation between two bodies without a single word being uttered. She'd always thought herself deficient in some way when she tried to flirt with someone. Too flustered, or too uninterested, or too self-conscious. And then Hannah had come along, her eyes so golden and warm, her touch so gentle but firm.

Althea realized once again that she was on the floor only when the ache in her knees became too much to bear. She shifted her weight so that she was sitting instead of kneeling and took stock of the apartment, the still-rumpled sheets, the mug of tea from two nights earlier, the book she'd placed on the table.

Her fingers groped for it, without thought. *Alice in Wonderland.*

It didn't make sense that the Nazis had been burning a copy of the book; the story didn't contradict any of their beliefs. Althea wondered if it had been placed on a stack by mistake. But had she had to watch it burn, she thought she would have lost part of herself that she would never have been able to get back.

She thought of that winter night, when she'd been young and naive. The bookseller had given her a gift and she'd handed over her copy of *Alice* in return.

Die Bücherfreundin.

Friend of books.

The label felt dirty now, tainted.

Althea had three more weeks in the country before she could leave. Diedrich wouldn't come stalk her, he'd enacted his punishment already. She'd humiliated him and so he'd destroyed her. How he'd known about Adam Brecht, she didn't know. But that no longer mattered.

Hannah hadn't even considered any other possibility. And that hurt the most, Althea realized.

Tears soaked into the collar of Althea's shirt, and she wanted to burrow into it. She remembered just that morning shrugging it on, Hannah watching her with affection. Or at least what Althea had thought was affection.

Althea shook her head. Maybe she didn't know a lot about this world, but she knew that what they'd had was real. Just as she'd always known Diedrich's affections weren't.

If nothing else, Hannah had given her that.

Althea swiped at her cheeks and then pressed up to her feet. There had to be a way to get on an earlier ship home; she couldn't imagine the Nazis would try to stop her from leaving. They were done with her, well and truly.

She crossed the room to the closet, dug out her bag, tossed it on the bed. It was only then she realized she was still holding *Alice*.

It was a thin volume, light in her hands. She stared down at it for a long moment, debating. Then she set it aside, and began, with more speed than grace, packing up the tiny apartment she'd called home for the past few months.

ON THE WAY to the train station that would take her to the port in Rostock, Althea made a detour toward Hannah's apartment.

She didn't dare ring the bell. She knew she wouldn't be welcome there.

Instead, she left the copy of *Alice* that she'd wrapped and addressed to Hannah on the little table in the entryway. Perhaps Hannah would get it, perhaps she wouldn't.

On the title page, Althea had left one last message, in Alice's own words.

I know who I was when I got up this morning, but I think I must have been changed several times since then.

Beneath the quote, Althea had scrawled *Thank you,* and hoped Hannah would understand.

Chapter 46

New York City
July 1944

Viv woke the morning of the Taft event with a steel stomach and steady hands. She had been plotting and planning and crafting this day for so long it almost felt like it wasn't really happening at all.

But it was. She was Wellington and this—finally—was her Waterloo.

She dressed carefully in an impeccable dove-gray suit with a pencil skirt and a crisp white blouse beneath the jacket. Viv rolled on the stockings she'd paid an obscene twenty-two dollars for because she'd ripped her last precious pair, and then slicked on a nice red lip that she could only think of as armor.

She was about to walk out of her bedroom when she stopped, her hand still on the knob. Turning around, she stared at the window overlooking the avenue below.

In a handful of quick strides, she crossed the room and threw open the glass.

Roar, Edward had said.

With everything that she had inside of her, Viv tipped back her head and bellowed into the morning sky.

Every doubt, every fear, every ache and bit of joy from the past three months layered into her voice, into her primal scream.

She roared for Edward reading *Oliver Twist,* Althea on the cliffs, Hannah Brecht lost among her bookshelves. For Charlotte wielding her spatula and then for Charlotte crying on the subway. She roared for Georgia in that club in Harlem and Bernice on D-Day and those kids in Brooklyn who had just wanted to play baseball.

And then she roared for herself from six months ago, a year ago, with nothing on her schedule beyond selling war bonds to her rich friends.

As her voice trailed off, a man on the street yelled "Shut the hell up," because in New York City that was as inevitable as breathing.

She laughed, flipped him the bird, and then closed the window.

Viv could accomplish anything she set her mind to. That had to be true, because her dearest friend in the world had told her so.

Charlotte sent her off with a hug after a hearty pancake breakfast and effusive praise that made pinching color into her cheeks unnecessary.

Viv didn't bother pulling out an ASE for the subway ride. She couldn't be distracted today. Instead, she ran through her to-do list, making sure she hadn't overlooked a single thing.

Bernice and Edith greeted her in the lobby of Times Hall, both wearing the determined smiles of foot soldiers ready to take orders. Viv pulled each of them into an embrace, because she couldn't deny the swell of emotion that came with their obvious show of support. And then she gave them tasks, because she would be foolish to turn down help today.

The reporters would start filing in within the hour, but she had a feeling Senator Robert Taft had already arrived.

That suspicion was confirmed when she caught sight of Mr. Howard Danes leaning on the wall outside of Mr. Stern's office.

When he noticed her, he held his hands up in exaggerated innocence. "Don't sic the coppers on me, missus. I was invited, I swear."

In his voice was the same irreverent humor from that night, and now it grated against Viv's skin just like it had on the darkened street. "Don't make me get my hat pin," she threatened, sailing by him without waiting for an answer. His laugh followed her into Mr. Stern's office.

Taft stood by the desk, his thick fingers curled tightly around Mr. Stern's shoulder. Viv could tell she was interrupting some rant about the propaganda poster that hung on the wall. The one proclaiming books as weapons in this war.

Both men glanced up when she cleared her throat. Taft's eyes traveled along her body, sending an unpleasant shiver along her spine.

"I take my coffee with milk," Taft said, with that folksy drawl she knew disappeared when he became enraged.

Viv's mouth pinched in so her rejoinder didn't fall out and ruin the day before it had even started. With all the patience she could muster, she said calmly, "We have a coffee bar set up in the lobby. I'm sure someone can point you in the right direction."

Mr. Stern disguised a snort of amusement with a cough, and he moved to reintroduce them. "Senator, I'm sure you remember Mrs. Childs, our publicity director."

None of them mentioned the ambush at the restaurant.

"She's been instrumental in organizing the event for today," Mr. Stern continued.

"Mrs. Childs." Taft sounded out her name with the same amount of disdain as he would have had he been saying *Hitler.*

"Senator Taft. I hope this program will be . . . educational . . . for you," Viv said, letting her voice go syrupy sweet. "We're so grateful you came so that you can truly see how much the ASEs mean to the boys overseas." Viv paused. "That's what you're most concerned about, of course."

"There are plenty of ways to help the boys," Taft said, yanking at his lapels. "Perhaps you've heard of the G.I. Bill I sponsored, meant to help them continue their education after we bring them home."

"I have," Viv gritted out. "Isn't it lovely how well the initiatives work in tandem?"

Taft's eyes narrowed as if he were about to truly settle into this debate, but Mr. Stern coughed again to break the tension. "Wins all around."

"Indeed," Viv managed. And she knew Mr. Stern wanted to give the senator a way to exit this gracefully. Her better angels had her agreeing with him. The devil on her shoulder wanted her to verbally stomp all over this man who'd become her nemesis.

Without bothering to agree as well, Taft shifted to call out through the open doorway. "Danes. Coffee."

Viv nearly smiled at the image of the sarcastic little man having to run the menial errand. When she caught Mr. Stern's eye, he nodded once and she got the message that he was letting her escape. Since she had no interest in wasting any more of her own time with the smug, supercilious senator, she took the opening and slipped back out into the hallway.

She pushed the hateful man out of her thoughts, for now, as she made her way down to one side of the main theater, where the press had started to gather.

Among the nearly matching suits and heads of hair, she spotted Leo Aston. She wove her way through the little crowd, greeting the other reporters she knew and thanking the ones she didn't for coming.

"Taft's a sleazy, self-serving politician and he'll show his hand today," Leo promised her when she came close. "Too many people are watching for him not to slip up. And if we get one killer quote, you'll have your public backing in no time."

"He's smart, though," Viv said, playing with the pearl necklace she'd wound so carefully around her neck that morning.

"Eh." Leo scrunched his nose. "He's arrogant and not well-liked when you get outside the Capitol Hill gang. People are going to be looking for a reason to distance themselves from him as long as they have political cover to do so. This"—he gestured to the slowly filling seats, populated with lawmakers and literati, with notable public figures, and, most importantly, the wealthiest political donors in the city—"this is political cover. Well done, kiddo."

Smoothing out her already smooth skirt with a shaking hand, Viv nodded. "Ears to the ground, yeah?"

"Always," Leo promised, squeezing her shoulder once before melting back into the crowd of other journalists.

Viv moved through the aisles, surveying the attendees, pride and affection in equal measures blanketing her nerves. Leo hadn't been exaggerating when he'd made note of the crowd. It hadn't just been the media that had shown up in spades. There were a dozen women throughout the audience that Viv recognized as librarian volunteers; there was Harrison Gardiner and a cadre of other bright young things from the publishing houses along with their older, stodgier bosses; there was the elderly man from the Jewish Center where Hannah Brecht worked and several others whom Viv guessed were Hannah's colleagues; there was Hale, and at least two dozen men Viv knew to be politicians. She sent Hale a grateful smile that he returned easily.

Betty Smith held court near the stage, her dark hair pinned back in a serious manner. Viv had met her a handful of times, and had been startled anew by her magnetism on each encounter. Her fame from *A Tree Grows in Brooklyn* would have guaranteed her attention today, but it was her thoughtful demeanor that would keep it.

Betty nodded once when she caught Viv's eyes, and the approval in the other woman's expression made something warm bloom in Viv's chest.

Viv thought about that drunken afternoon back in May when Harrison had jabbed a finger against the bar.

If this were a book, you know what point we'd be at right now? . . . It's the all-is-lost moment.

Now, they had their spectacle. They had their army.

Viv just had to trust that it was enough to pull a happy ending out of thin air.

Chapter 47

Paris
March 1937

Hannah's lungs collapsed on themselves, the air gone in one shaky exhale. "Otto."

Dev watched Hannah, her hands lifted as if she was ready to catch Hannah should she fall. As if she hadn't been the one doing the pushing.

For one startling moment Hannah saw herself using the pistol. Saw the blood that would spread from a gaping wound in Dev's chest, the way her fingers would touch the torn flesh as if they could sear the pieces back together. That final realization that would flash across Dev's face before she collapsed, lifeless, to the ground.

Hannah let the weapon drop. It clattered against the concrete, loud and jarring so that Dev flinched from the sound.

"Would you have done it again?" Hannah asked, hearing the question through an endless tunnel, her words soft and slurred. "Knowing how it turned out."

"In a heartbeat," Dev answered.

The answer didn't surprise Hannah—she wasn't sure she could be surprised any longer—but she'd needed to hear it.

Nodding, she turned, forced her legs to listen, and stumbled to the door that had led out to the hotel's rooftop.

"Hannah," Dev called from behind her, her voice laced with pity. "It wasn't Otto's fault. If you must blame someone, let it be me."

Hannah didn't stop, didn't hesitate, didn't beg for more details about how her dearest friend for all her life had betrayed her.

Years before, on that sidewalk in Berlin when Althea had looked at her with watery, guilty eyes, Hannah had thought she'd lost every part of her innocence.

But like Dev had said, with Otto the trust was so innate, so much a part of Hannah, that she didn't even think about it. It would be like wondering if her own hand could stab a knife into her heart.

Paris pressed in around her, suffocating and loud even on a quiet Sunday morning. Hannah knew she was walking, making the right turns, avoiding the cars and the bicycles as she went, but she didn't feel anchored to her body.

She didn't know how long it took, but she ended up at Otto's door. The wood mocked her inability to raise her hand and knock. The sun baked the back of her neck so that sweat slipped down her spine, pooling in the small of her back. Her legs trembled with the weight of holding still for so long.

Finally, the knob turned, the door opened. Otto stood there, the bruises under his eyes, the thinness of his face, the frown lines cutting deep at the sides of his mouth making all the more sense now.

Otto hadn't ever been the same after they'd left Germany. The drinking, the distance, the crying, the brawl with the Nazis, the goddamn gun. How had she not seen it?

Did he have debts even now that he couldn't repay? He must. That kind of behavior didn't disappear overnight.

He stared at her now, his gaze intent. Then he nodded once. "You know."

Without waiting for an answer, he turned, leaving the door open. Stumbling, he worked his way through the dark hallway back toward the kitchen of his little flat. There was a window seat there that she'd always adored curling up in so she could drink tea and watch the birds flit in and out of the lush little garden behind his place.

There was a mostly empty decanter of liquor sitting on the table in front of that window seat now. Otto threw himself down on the cushions, his body a lazy sprawl. But the casual splay of his legs belied a tension she could read so clearly in his face.

On his way down, he'd managed to snag the alcohol. Taking a swig directly from the bottle, he watched her with the indolent nonchalance of a young man tired of the world.

It was a facade, of course, but it made her want to slap him all the more. When she couldn't take looking at him for a second longer, she shifted, walking toward the sink that had a window above it overlooking the roses that were not yet in bloom.

Hannah let the silence expand between them as she thought about every memory she had with him. Running through fields of flowers as young children, fishing in the stream behind his parents' country home, practicing kissing and then realizing neither was very interested in the act, sneaking out on warm summer days to read books under trees, sharing secrets, sharing their biggest ones. Then had come university in Berlin and nightclubs and a freedom they'd only dreamed of having when they were growing up. Hannah attending Otto's plays, and Otto keeping Hannah company at readings in bookshops. Drunken nights and then the aching heads that came with the mornings that followed.

Then Adam and Althea, the Nazis, and life falling apart around them. Building a new one in a foreign city that only ever felt like home when Otto was with her.

Hannah wanted to ask why, but she couldn't get her lips to move.

And anyway, Otto broke first. He always did.

"Will you say something?" he finally yelled, flinging himself to his feet with the drama that was bred into his very bones. His eyes were wild, his knuckles white around the now-empty decanter. She wondered if he wanted to hurl it at the wall just to see something besides himself shatter.

"How much?" Hannah asked, knowing the very softness of her words would make them cut all the deeper. "What was the cost of my brother's life?"

A gutted, brutal sound punched its way out of Otto's chest. "Does it matter?"

Hannah closed her eyes against the unending waves of pain. "Yes."

"Ten thousand," Otto confessed on a whisper.

"Oh, Otto." Hannah couldn't keep the empathy from creeping in. Her beloved, her everything. He must have been so scared, so desperate.

But Adam had been scared, too. And desperate. Sitting across from her in that Nazi prison, his face broken and swollen and nearly unrecognizable.

"Why didn't you"—Hannah forced the question out from a throat gone tight with grief—"say something."

"What would it have changed?" he asked, the mania in his expression sliding into his voice. He was on the edge, tight as a drawn bow, all but shaking with it, drunk and guilt-ridden and trying to pretend he was neither.

"Maybe nothing," Hannah agreed. She turned so she was leaning against the sink, arms crossed.

Otto looked away, his jaw tense. "What do you want me to say?"

Hannah huffed out a laugh. What did she want him to say? *Sorry* would be a start, but that didn't seem like an option here. Beyond that, what was there to offer? She didn't need his excuses or explanations. She knew why he hadn't told her it was him instead of Althea who'd betrayed her—that would have been difficult and Otto never liked doing the difficult thing. Maybe he'd even convinced himself that it hadn't just been him who had let the secret slip.

He'd seen the guilt in Althea's expression just as she had. Maybe he had told himself a pretty story that the truth he had sold had been superfluous.

And maybe he truly believed it would not change anything. She hadn't told him about Althea's letters, after all, the way the woman had continued to write her for years following their brief affair. What if Hannah had been able to open even one of those messages?

What would it have changed?

None of that mattered, though. At the end of the day, Otto had chosen what was easy over what was right. And Hannah had watched her entire country make the same choice time and again. Maybe there were countless others out there who would do the same thing. But she found she had no tolerance left for them.

Had he been simply drunk and careless with the secret, maybe she could have found it in herself to forgive him. But he had made the callous decision, had calculated what her brother's life was worth, and had made the most selfish choice he could.

"I want you to say goodbye," she said, just as gently as she'd said everything else.

But she might as well have slit his throat open, given how his face crumpled and then the rest of his body followed. On the ground, he hugged the decanter like it would offer him some sort of solace as he wept, tears turning him ugly for once in his life.

"Hannah." He sobbed out her name. "Don't do this."

She crossed the room, knelt before him, cradling his cheek in her hands. He nuzzled into it like a child seeking comfort. Swiping a thumb under his eyes to dry the wetness there, she leaned in to kiss his forehead. Then she sat back on her heels and made him meet her gaze.

"You have not asked for my forgiveness," she told him. "I will give it to you anyway. But I do not want to ever see you again."

A broken exhale was all that he could manage. She waited, giving him one more chance, seeing not him there, but Althea, apologizing for something she hadn't even done. Apologizing for hurting Hannah, even though she'd been innocent of the crime. The contrast took the broken pieces of Hannah's soul and stitched them together.

Not everyone chose themselves first.

When Otto said nothing, Hannah smiled sadly and stood and walked toward the hallway.

"He was going to die anyway," he called, in that same voice he'd greeted her with. Young, brash, defensive. Again, her fingers itched with the desire to slap him. But she restrained herself.

She turned, studying the mess of him. "I blamed myself."

He whimpered but didn't say anything.

"For telling Althea about Adam," Hannah continued, just in case he missed the implication. "I was never as angry at her as I was at myself. And you let me live with that for years."

His mouth moved, but no sound came out.

"Every single day you woke up and chose not to tell me was a day I could have hated myself a little less," Hannah said, no longer interested in pulling her punches. "Every single day you woke up and chose yourself over me. Life is made up of those choices, you are made up of those choices."

Otto curled further in on himself. "Now you can hate me instead of yourself."

"You already do that enough for both of us," Hannah said, letting her eyes drop to the decanter. "Goodbye, Otto."

This time when she turned it was final.

Hannah didn't let herself think, didn't let her mind wander or worry or obsess; she just took the familiar route home, the one she'd walked countless times with and without Otto.

Without realizing it, she found herself back in her apartment, her spine pressed up against the wall, cradling the box of letters she'd never opened in her lap, the copy of *Alice in Wonderland* resting on top of it.

Methodically, she slit each envelope and read each message. She'd been expecting accusations, apologies, pleas even. Instead what she got was a story she now recognized as Althea's second novel.

When she got to the last envelope, the one that had been

heavier than the others, the one with the scrawled *Don't be stubborn* on the outside, she found a visa to America, an open-ended ticket for ship passage, and one last single piece of paper.

On it was a dedication, which Hannah knew with certainty had never made it to the final copy of the book.

She swiped at tears as she read it.

To Hannah, for being the hero every story wishes it had.

Chapter 48

New York City
July 1944

Viv worried that Althea James might faint on her. The woman was far too pale, her mouth set, her hands clutched so that her knuckles were white.

"Breathe," Viv whispered as she shepherded Althea into the backstage room where actors would have waited for their cues when the theater was operational. The location ensured that Althea wouldn't be able to get a glimpse of the overwhelming audience before she had to go speak in front of it. "I've been told it's helpful to picture everyone in their underthings."

Althea's eyes flew to hers, and Viv couldn't help but be reminded of a spooked horse.

"Actually, no, absolutely not, don't listen to me," Viv said as she caught sight of Bernice Westwood in the hall. She heard the thread of panic in her own voice when she called out to the secretary. "Will you sit with Miss James, Bernice? Just for a few minutes."

The worst thing for Althea to do at the moment would be to stew in silence and worry. Bernice would take care of that.

"Course, sugar." Bernice leaned against the arm of the blue

sofa where Althea was perched and proceeded to play her role perfectly. "Let me tell you what I heard about two of the editors from *Publishers Weekly*. They just found out they have the same mistress . . ."

Viv grinned as she left the room to hunt down Hannah Brecht, putting out several small fires along the way.

Where Althea had seemed on the verge of falling apart, Hannah was utterly composed. She stood in the wings of the stage, watching the bustle with a vaguely amused expression. She'd arrived so early that Viv had plopped Hannah down in her office and handed over a copy of Fitzgerald's *The Great Gatsby*—an upcoming ASE that Edith had to fight to get included in the program due to its lackluster sales.

Once the audience started filtering in, though, Hannah had gravitated toward the action.

Viv paused and watched her for a second. She wore a flattering green shirtwaist dress that Viv had noticed brought out the warm color in her eyes and contrasted nicely with the dark curls that she'd let cascade around her shoulders. The stage lights kept her half in shadow and half illuminated and Viv thought that maybe that's just how Hannah lived her life. In the sun and the shade, both, sharing herself but keeping her mystery, as well.

"Are you nervous?" Viv asked as she came up beside her. Hannah didn't take her eyes off the audience.

"Not quite the right word," Hannah drawled with something that sounded close to humor but wasn't.

"Hmm," Viv hummed. She'd never gotten used to Hannah's reticence, with how she watched the world as a spectator rather than a player in it. The attitude threw Viv, who had never known a way to guard herself from caring too much. And so it made her clumsy at the small talk that Hannah didn't even seem to need.

"You said Miss James would be in attendance?" Hannah asked, finally glancing over.

Viv checked the slim watch she'd worn just for today. "Yes, I'm actually going to wait to fetch her until after most of the other speakers have gone. She seemed . . . nervous."

The corners of Hannah's mouth twitched, but she simply crossed her arms and watched as Mr. Stern strode onto the stage to introduce the first guest—a man who'd lost both legs in the spring and had been kept entertained in the hospital by the ASE books.

Viv hadn't limited herself to taking care of only Hannah and Althea when setting up the event—she'd enlisted librarians who served as volunteer readers for the council, a family member of a soldier whose last letter home had been about the ASE project, the GI who had discovered the books in a hospital in Italy, a war correspondent who'd been stationed with men in the Pacific. If Taft could hold out against the barrage, he was an even more cynical man than she had thought.

The people who mattered, though, were his constituents, and Viv felt fairly certain her fellow Americans would be won over.

As they neared Hannah's portion of the event, Viv looked around until she spotted Edith lingering nearby. "I'm going to get Miss James. Would you let Miss Brecht know when to go on?"

"Of course," Edith said, reaching out to draw Hannah closer. Hannah hesitated, watching Viv for a moment like she wanted to say something, before smiling that restrained smile of hers and turning toward Edith.

Viv paused, unsure if Hannah actually needed comfort before facing the crowd. But after an internal debate, she decided to take Hannah at her word and headed toward the waiting room.

Althea's eyes were still wide when Viv stepped into the backstage room, but Viv got the impression she was more intrigued by Bernice's gossip than scared.

"Ready?" Viv asked after Bernice sent her a small wink.

Althea had dressed in a crisp white blouse and red plaid skirt that might have been better for a taller woman. Still, she projected a serious aura that Viv knew would go over well with the audience.

"We still have one more speaker before you, but I thought you might like to watch," Viv said, stopping herself from enfolding Althea in a hug. But just because Viv had grown closer with the woman didn't mean she'd forgotten the way she'd slammed a door in Viv's face not long ago. Acknowledging Althea's nerves might not be welcome or appreciated.

"Who is it?" Althea asked in a way that gave Viv the impression she didn't care but wanted to focus on something other than her own upcoming speech.

"A woman I met here in New York, actually," Viv said, as they maneuvered their way into the wings. Hannah was waiting beside Edith as Mr. Stern introduced her. "She works at the Brooklyn Jewish Center, which has a library devoted to the books banned by the Nazis. Before that, she worked in a similar library in Paris."

Beside Viv, Althea froze, her eyes locked on Hannah's silhouette. "Hannah."

It was only an exhale, really, one that got swallowed up by the crowd's applause as Hannah stepped out onto the stage.

"Yes," Viv said, eyes darting between the two of them. If possible, Althea had paled further, her jaw wobbly as if she were trying not to cry. "She did mention that she knew you."

Althea's eyes closed as she huffed out a laugh. "Once upon a time."

Chapter 49

New York City
July 1944

It had been more than a decade since Althea had seen Hannah Brecht. And yet she'd known it was Hannah by her shape alone, by the way she held her head, by the fall of her hair and the sway of her hips as she walked.

Althea wanted nothing more than to give in to her shaking legs and sink to the floor. Hannah Brecht, in America. Not only America, but New York City, only feet away from her.

Hannah Brecht *alive* and not buried in some mass grave.

That hadn't been a certainty, Hannah being alive. Not after the Nazis had marched into Paris. Althea had still hoped, had still told herself that Hannah had opened her last letter. But the war was all but designed to crush any of that spark out of a person. Hope seemed worse than foolish, it seemed dangerous.

Sound rushed back in when Hannah greeted the audience, the microphone picking up the wryness in her voice, the one that spoke of many lives lived, of many horrors seen and survived, of people and speeches far grander than whatever she was about to say.

Vivian Childs was watching Althea, not Hannah, though, her eyes squinted in concern. Althea blinked at her a few times, not sure what to even say to reassure her.

"Did she know I would be here?" she heard herself ask.

"Yes," Vivian said softly, her expression uncharacteristically gentle. Althea wouldn't go so far as to say she knew the woman well, but they'd spent enough time together now that she thought she had the girl's number. She was young, vivacious, passionate in a way Althea could never remember being. So sure the world could do good, even when she'd seen how bad it could be.

After only a single long night of reading those letters from soldiers, Althea had been left gutted, torn open and bleeding. Vivian had to do that every day and still she strove to try to fix the injustices she'd seen.

Part of Althea had been ashamed, watching Vivian move through life. What had Althea done but hide away and lick her wounds for more than a decade? If it had been anyone else at the door, Althea would have kept it closed. But when Althea looked at Vivian, she saw what she wished she could have been when she'd been younger.

Althea James had always wanted to be a different version of herself.

She doubted Vivian Childs had ever had that thought.

Being around Viv made Althea believe again, believe she could change the world, just because she wanted to.

But had Althea known Hannah would be at the event . . .

What? She couldn't finish the thought. Would she have come? Or would she have been paralyzed like she had been for the past ten years? By fear and guilt and also anger. Because the anger was there, she wouldn't deny it. It burned like an infinite flame in her chest, reminding her every moment of the way Hannah had turned to her with wounded eyes, so ready to cast blame, so ready to believe Althea could betray her.

War had a way of making previous hurts inconsequential. But at the sight of Hannah, this one flared to life once more.

None of that mattered, though, because Hannah was speaking.

“Few people have to watch their country die,” Hannah said, her lyrical voice all the more captivating because she spoke softly. Althea found herself leaning toward her, and she imagined the rest of the audience was no different. “I have had that dubious privilege, and I can tell you that it comes not as a rebel shout but as a sly whisper. The cracks creep in, insidious as anything I’ve ever seen. It can start with rumblings about an unreliable press and rumors about political enemies that will threaten your family, your children. It can deepen with each disdainful remark about science and art and literature in a pub on a Friday night. It comes cloaked in patriotism and love of country, and uses that as armor against any criticism.

“When I hear people talk of Germany these days, it breaks my heart. Not many remember that some of the greatest thinkers and artists of our time came from my country. Einstein, Schrödinger, Mann, Arendt, the list goes on and on. Despite what propaganda posters may have you believe, those exiles represent the Germany I know far better than the madman currently at the helm. I grew up in a place that prized intellectualism, reason, and civil discourse, in a country that held a reverence for books. I grew up in the land of *Grimms’ Fairy Tales* and Goethe’s epics. I grew up in a democracy, fledgling though it might have been, that allowed space for radical ideas and uncomfortable discussions, that encouraged critical thought and free speech.

"When I tell people about the 1933 book burnings in Berlin, many are shocked to hear that it was students who led the charge, who lit the pyres and brought the books to the flames."

Althea closed her eyes, thinking of a light rain, of novels stacked high in wheelbarrows, of Diedrich's twisted expression as she confronted him.

"Because how could that have happened? Those students cherished books. Just like many Germans who burned their own collections all across the country after that night cherished books. But they loved their own beliefs more. And that kind of love? It can rot a person from the inside. Can rot a country from the inside."

Hannah held the crowd's attention easily, as if she could grasp the threads of it in her hands and pull.

"There are nights I lie awake wondering what the moment was that we lost the Germany I knew. Some might point to the invasion of Poland, the official act of war. Some might look at the Anschluss the same way. There are a million such moments. *Kristallnacht,* the Night of the Long Knives, the Jewish boycotts, the race laws, the opening of the concentration camps, the November treaty that brought about so much bitterness. But sometimes I think it was the moment right before the gasoline was poured on the books. The moment the most educated country in the world willingly, joyously, wholeheartedly turned away from knowledge."

Hannah looked down, not at notes, but like she was fortifying herself. "I was asked to speak today because a bright, passionate young woman believed that I have something important to say about the dangers of government censorship. Perhaps I do. I can tell you that there are people out there who want the world to only think as they think. In fact, long before Hitler had the power to incite countrywide book burnings, he wrote in *Mein Kampf* that a smart reader should take away from books only the ideas that support their own beliefs and discard the rest as useless ballast."

She emphasized the last phrase in a way that made it seem like it was a direct quote.

"I can tell you that banning books, burning books, blocking books is often used as a way to erase a people, a belief system, a culture," Hannah said. "To say these voices don't belong here, even when those writers represent the very best of a country.

"I can tell you many things about how men who crave power use fear and panic that's incited by certain ideas to get what they want," Hannah continued. "Just as Goebbels and Hitler did that night in May when they convinced a country that setting fire to words that you don't like or don't agree with will make you *right*. But I think, more importantly, I should tell you about that death I witnessed. Of the way Germany's democracy turned to ash under the weight of itself.

"I am here to warn you that it is so easy to let the fuel spill onto those pages. Once that spark catches, once the fire is lit and the flames begin to consume everything you hold dear, there is nothing in the world that can put it out.

"We cannot stop individuals who read for the sole purpose of confirming their already closely held beliefs." She enunciated each word, a delicate fist pounding on the podium. "But we can stop the dictators, the tyrants, the bullies who try to impose that method onto others. This may feel insignificant, this moment here, in this room, talking about a single amendment to a bill that was drafted with the best intentions. I can tell you, though, that history is built on moments that feel insignificant. We didn't know that night of the book burnings that the event was anything special. We pictured a few students with a few books. Even when we arrived and saw the stacks upon stacks of novels and research journals, we didn't realize everything that would come after.

"In 1928, my father, along with the rest of my country, was mocking Hitler. They saw him as a joke, someone who could be easily controlled, someone who would burn out after everyone heard his deranged spiels. Only a handful of years later, we had to flee Germany after my brother was dragged to a concentration camp, where he would be murdered for his beliefs.

"History is built on moments that feel insignificant," Hannah said again, and Althea marveled at how she could land each word as a punch. "And so in every moment you must ask yourself: Do you want to be the ones handing out the gasoline cans? Or the ones trying to put out the fire?"

"Yes," Viv whispered as the audience broke into applause.

Althea laughed, overcome and overwhelmed, her eyes wet, her soul aching, her mind back in that plaza in the one moment in all her life she'd been brave. If she did nothing else right in the world, she would always have that night. Viv grinned at her, with just a touch of mania. "All right, your turn."

Althea just blinked at her. "You want me to follow that?"

Chapter 50

New York City
July 1944

Viv melted back into the shadows as Hannah Brecht walked offstage, not that it mattered. The woman's eyes were locked on Althea.

From Althea's earlier reaction, Viv had gotten the impression there was more to the two women knowing one another than *once upon a time*. But the intensity with which they watched each other now confirmed it. Viv had the sneaking suspicion that if they'd been alone, they already would have been tangled up in each other's arms.

"You're here," Althea said on a whisper.

"Because of you," Hannah answered, not quite as shaky, her hand curled around Althea's wrist, the two locked in their own world.

Viv hated that she needed to interrupt the reunion, but the fact of the matter was that there was an audience waiting on her. And the show had to go on. She stepped forward, once again making her presence known, and two pairs of eyes snapped to her in surprise.

"Sorry, but . . ." She trailed off, jerking her head back toward the stage, where Mr. Stern was waiting in expectant silence. "Althea?"

Althea shook herself slightly, opened her mouth to say something to Hannah, but then closed it. She smiled at Viv instead. "Right."

Hannah didn't move until the last second, stepping out of Althea's way but just enough so that their shoulders brushed as she did.

Viv raised her brows at Hannah, who smiled back and shook her head.

One thing that Viv could be grateful about—however Althea felt about seeing Hannah, it had at least brought some color into her face. She no longer looked like a strong wind would take her down.

From Viv's angle, she could see the nervous breath Althea took before she started, but Viv doubted the audience would be able to. The audience that was on its feet, the raucous applause almost knocking Viv back on her heels.

Exactly what she'd wanted.

It took a few minutes for everyone to retake their seats, but Althea barely even seemed to note the commotion.

"I've been told my book was in the pockets of the GIs when they stormed the beaches in Normandy," Althea started, and the slight chatter that had lingered from the standing ovation quieted immediately. "I've now read countless letters from the men, their families, their leaders who assure me my book has saved them. And perhaps I should talk about that. How the Armed Services Editions change lives, entertain grateful troops, the whole song and dance." She paused then inhaled. "Instead, I'd like to tell you about the months I would have gladly joined the Nazis."

A rumble went through the audience at that.

"I was invited to Germany in 1932 by Joseph Goebbels, the man who runs the Nazi propaganda machine—quite effectively, I might add," Althea continued. "The night Hitler was named chancellor, I marched in celebration. I was naive, you see. I thought politics were all civil, I thought world leaders were constrained by norms, that while there could be and had been war, that war would be waged by rational men.

"I had never cared for politics before then," Althea said, with a careless little shrug. "They didn't affect me, I told myself. And what could I do, anyway? I could vote, finally. But why do so when the world would turn as it always had? Politics were something *done* far away from my life, a game that was played by men who had too much time on their hands."

Sporadic laughter covered up the insulted murmuring Viv could hear from a few of the congressmen in the front rows.

"When I got to Berlin, the Nazis used that apathy against me. They spun compelling stories about an economic recovery, a return to a Germany that was greater than it had ever been before, a movement that had been born from the young people's discontent. On the other side of that coin, they gave me a boogeyman to fear—the communists who they said would kill you dead in the street as soon as look at you. In fact, it was the Nazi thugs who had no compunction in doing that."

Beside Viv, Hannah nodded.

"What does any of this have to do with the ASEs, you might ask," Althea said, with a slightly self-deprecating smile. "I started paying more attention to politics in the decade since I had my eyes viciously opened in Germany. And my opinion on the practice hasn't changed much—it still feels like people are playing poker or baseball or football. Each side counts up their wins and losses without regard to the lives involved, and most of the time that's fine. Things swing left and things swing right, and we get a semblance of a government coming out in the middle."

The speech was a little sharper than Viv had been expecting, but as it was Althea James speaking, it seemed no one was willing to risk looking bad in storming out.

"Most of the time, it's fine," Althea repeated. "But it can also blind you to the occasions when politics isn't just politics. World leaders spent most of the years before Hitler invaded Poland pacifying the man. They treated him like he was any other politician who would play by the rules of the game, the unspoken ones that keep millions of citizens from being disappeared in the middle of broad daylight. The unspoken ones that keep the party's street fighters from murdering their opponents in the town's square. The unspoken ones that keep countries from brutalizing their neighbors and slaughtering their own people.

"Miss Brecht told you that you are sitting here in a moment that could be far more significant than it feels," Althea said, and Viv saw Hannah's mouth tick up. "As someone who was there that night with her at the book burnings, I have to agree."

A ripple cascaded through the audience at that, surprise and delight at having the two speakers tied together.

"I am no longer that innocent girl from Owl's Head, Maine, who had stars in her eyes that blinded her to cruelties because she just didn't care enough," Althea said. "Even if it's the elephant in the room today, I know why this amendment exists, I know the politics behind it. Roosevelt's fourth term is your boogeyman, Senator Taft."

Viv gripped her clipboard. "Not one for half measures, is she?"

"No." Hannah sounded far too amused. "Apparently not."

"And you want the numbers on your side of the scoreboard to be higher than your opponents'," Althea said, clear and decisive. "But if you walk away from today, from every testimonial about how much joy and relief the Armed Services Editions bring to our boys overseas, then all you are is stuck on a court playing games while the rest of us live in the real world.

"There are bigger things in this world than politics," Althea continued. "There are bigger things in this world than scoring a win for your side just to score a win for your side. This might seem like a melodramatic overreaction for some of you, maybe you scoff at the notion that there should be so much brouhaha over books. There were plenty of people who felt that way in May 1933, as well. And I promise you, if I've learned anything from my time in Berlin, it's this: an attack on books, on rationality, on knowledge isn't a tempest in a teacup, but rather a canary dead in a coal mine.

"There are moments in life when you have to put what is right over what party you vote for. And if you can't recognize those moments when the stakes are low—let me assure you, you won't recognize them when the stakes are high. Thank you."

"Jeez Louise," Viv muttered, but when she turned to grin at Hannah she found the space next to her empty. It threw her, but she didn't have time to dwell on it. Althea was there in front of her, and Viv couldn't help but throw her arms around the shorter woman.

"I'm proud of you," she breathed into Althea's temple, not caring that Althea probably gave about two figs if Viv was proud of her.

Althea patted her back awkwardly. "I hope I didn't get you into hot water with the senator."

"It doesn't matter," Viv said, pulling back a little. "Even if the papers run only some of your quotes, he'll look petty if he continues to dig in on the issue."

"And he'll look like he's a Nazi and on the wrong side of history if they run Hannah's," Althea said, her eyes slipping to the spot behind Viv. But Hannah wasn't there, and she wasn't anywhere that Viv could see backstage. Althea's shoulders sagged, but then her walls were back up. The smile she shot Viv was forced, but Viv didn't know her well enough to prod. "Congratulations. I do believe he'll yank the amendment after this."

"I agree," a voice came from the stairs leading out into the hallway.

Viv whirled to find Hale standing there, in his flawless suit and artfully rumpled hair, looking every bit the imposing congressman he was. But she could see the pleasure in his crinkled eyes, his repressed smile, the way he leaned toward her as if he wanted to gather her up in a hug like the one she'd bestowed upon Althea.

"You think it's enough?" Viv asked, a little breathless. She'd spent months trying to pull this off, and if she could actually claim success? That would be beyond her wildest dreams.

"Yes." He crossed the room and cuffed her on the shoulder, a light punch that had her grinning up at him. "I think it's enough."

And he was right.

The media had already been throwing itself behind the council's cause, but following the event in New York, papers across the country upped the ante. There were editorials in nearly every publication. The general message was: the men who were putting their lives on the line were quite able to decide for themselves what they wanted to read.

What Viv loved best, though, was the general consensus that books were not just books. They were stories that helped the exhausted men overseas remember what they were fighting for—freedom of thought, American values, antifascist sentiment. For a country that had been primed with anti-Nazi propaganda for years, the idea of being associated with Hitler and his authoritarian thinking was abhorrent.

It was Leo Aston who helped deliver the knockout punch. Not with his profile of Althea James and her time in Berlin as a guest of the Nazis, though that had been one of *Time*'s bestselling issues.

No, rather, he'd managed to overhear Taft as he walked out of Times Hall and told a staff member that if given the chance, seventy-five percent of servicemen would vote Roosevelt and that's why he was opposed to soldiers voting. After that quote started making the rounds, even Taft's allies began distancing themselves from him and his overbroad amendment.

And while that hadn't been the story Viv had been trying to tell, nor had it been what she'd poured all her hard work into, at the end of the day the event had helped get her what she wanted.

By mid-August, lawmakers were emerging out of the woodwork to support killing the amendment.

Moving faster than Viv had ever seen Congress act, lawmakers effectively gutted Taft's amendment by an overwhelming majority. The president quickly signed the legislation and just like that, the council was free to include whatever books they wanted in the Armed Services Editions program.

HALE TOOK VIV out to Delmonico's to celebrate with good red wine and a thick steak, in true politician fashion. She didn't mind, though; she liked it just as much as the lawmakers tended to.

"What happens now?" Hale asked as he contemplated the dessert menu.

"The world turns on," Viv said, sighing and sinking back in her chair. She had been sweat-soaked from the hot day, but in the cool, dark restaurant, she'd found exquisite relief and she wasn't looking forward to braving the weather once more. "We keep fighting the good fight when we can, I suppose."

Hale watched her from beneath hooded eyes, all sinful and dark and brooding. "What will you do when the war is over?"

"When?" she asked with a little laugh.

"You can read the writing on the wall as well as I can," he chastised. "Come work for me?"

"Is that a real job offer?" Viv asked, a little thrown.

"Yes and no," Hale said, putting down the menu to give her his full attention. "Yes, in that I think you would be a valuable addition to my team. No, in that I don't think you'll accept it."

Viv grinned. "If there's anything I've learned from this it's that I prefer almost anything to politics."

"You can't blame me for trying," he said casually, smiling at the waiter when he came over. He ordered a chocolate cake and two espressos. "But truly, what will you do?"

"Find some more good fights to fight," she said, nudging his foot with her own. He linked their ankles and she left hers there, caught.

"That sounds like politics," he said, with a half smirk.

"Everything sounds like politics to you," she shot back. Then she sobered, looking away from his intense gaze. "I think books, maybe? We've created a generation of new readers overseas. Publishing houses will be busy once they come back home."

"Telling stories," Hale said with a nod. It could have sounded patronizing but didn't. "People trust you with theirs."

Viv rested her chin against her fist. "I hope so."

He linked the fingers of their free hands together. "I would trust you with mine."

"You're biased," she said, with a teasing smile.

"Maybe," he admitted, rubbing a thumb over her knuckle. She didn't pull away when she might have a few weeks earlier. He studied her, the humor bleeding out of his face. "Are you happy?"

"Are any of us?" she asked with forced levity. When his serious expression didn't budge she fought the urge to retreat any further. And she admitted, "It's hard to be."

"Because of the war?"

"Yes, always. But also, I think I've been unduly influenced by novels," Viv said, dropping her eyes to their still-joined hands.

"What do you mean?" he asked.

If this were a book . . .

"There's a narrative that builds and builds and builds to a resolution," Viv said, trying to collect her scattered thoughts into something reasonable. "And then there's a denouement and then an ending."

"You had your resolution," Hale followed easily. "But now life goes on."

"Happy endings are for novels, not real life," Viv said, and then tossed her hair. "I would be angry if this was my ending, don't get me wrong."

Hale nodded like she was actually making sense. "But it feels strange to go to work and pay your bills and get your coffee just like any other day."

"Althea James said that she was guilty of too often thinking of herself as the protagonist of every story," Viv said. "I get that now."

"You were the protagonist of this one," Hale said, pressing his thumb into the vulnerable space on the back of her hand. "You fought like hell, and got the job done."

"But in the next, I might be a supporting character," Viv pointed out.

Hale laughed and it was a good look on him. Viv realized she wanted to be the person who did that all the time—the person who made him laugh.

"I can tell you," Hale said, bringing her hand to his mouth. His lips brushed against her knuckles, his breath hot, his eyes far too intense for the moment they were sharing. "You will never be a supporting character to me."

"Sap," Viv chided. But there was that warmth in her belly, golden like fizzy champagne that made her believe this really might be a happy beginning if only she could be brave enough to admit it.

"Maybe so," Hale said, with a quirked brow. "But you love me for it."

"I do," Viv said softly and when he beamed at her she couldn't help but grin back. "We'll make a knight-errant out of you yet."

Chapter 51

New York City
July 1944

Althea waved off Vivian Childs's offer to escort her around the city to see all the sights.

Instead, she let the woman bask in her victory and in her beau, who clearly had eyes only for her. Vivian had done something remarkable, and even if after all this she failed at her goal, she would have known that she had tried.

Wasn't that more important than victory itself?

Althea wasn't sure. She told herself it was, but the fact that she'd put herself out there and Hannah had walked away anyway was a blow she hadn't been expecting.

Hannah had been magnificent, inspiring, courageous, like she always had been.

For once, Althea had thought she'd met her there in that space that was worthy of admiration.

But when she'd stepped offstage, it was to find that Hannah had left. Had she even stayed to listen to anything Althea had said?

Would it matter if she had?

At the end of the day, Althea was glad she had given the speech, glad she had done something real rather than hide away in her cottage. Too long she had allowed a bad judgment call to dictate her actions. So what if she had believed the Nazis a legitimate party for a few months back in the early thirties? So had most of the world's leaders, who were far more intelligent than she.

It was long past the time that she shed whatever guilt had clung to her in the years since. She certainly hadn't earned a life sentence for her behavior.

She hated that Hannah had been hurt, but Althea realized now she had not been the cause of it. Adam's capture had been punishment for Althea's actions, yes, but the Nazis had never needed an excuse. If they'd known he was plotting against them they would have captured him regardless. The punishment was just a personal bonus for Diedrich.

For years, Hannah had been the judge, jury, and executioner over each move Althea had made, and she had no one to blame for that but herself. Hannah's ghost had permeated every aspect of Althea's life, because Althea had given it permission to.

And in the end, she knew that it hadn't really been Hannah's voice that haunted her every waking moment, but her own.

She had sided with the Nazis for three months and paid for that choice for ten years.

It was time.

It was time to move on. It was time to forgive herself. It was time to forgive Hannah.

Althea had been waiting for a moment when she could be the hero of the story. But she realized now that she didn't need to be. She had taken the spotlight, she had slain the monsters—or at least *helped* in slaying the monsters—and none of her problems had disappeared.

She had truly thought that if she did the right thing, if she fought the valiant fight, she could be redeemed. But redemption had never lived in one single moment. It lived in a thousand of them.

It lived in the times where she'd written about bigotry and hatred and the ways that it sunk into the soul with hooks and refused to let go.

It lived in the times that she'd taken groceries to a neighbor who, in Nazi Germany, would have been shipped off to a concentration camp because of his inability to walk; in the times that she'd challenged a friend's careless slurs; in the times she'd laid bare her own mistakes in hopes that others would learn from them.

She never again would wish herself a hero, but maybe she proved with each action she took that she wasn't a villain, either. She was just a person trying to live the best she could, trying to make sure no one else was hurt in the process.

Vivian had given Althea Hannah's home address, cautiously, carefully, in a way that had made Althea grateful that this was Hannah's secret keeper.

The big event at Times Hall had been three days ago, and Althea had yet to gather the courage to knock on Hannah's door.

Hannah hadn't written her, was the thing. Even though she must have opened Althea's letters, especially the one with the visa that Althea had pulled every string available to get.

Perhaps Hannah still blamed her for Adam's capture.

But why would she have smiled like that at Althea when she'd come off the stage?

Althea paced around the small park across from Hannah's apartment. It was in an up-and-coming Brooklyn neighborhood, the kind that Althea could see settling down in. Kids played stickball in the streets, women gossiped on stoops, old men played checkers on the sidewalk. It reminded Althea of home despite the fact that home to her had always been the cliffs and the sea.

It made her think that home might not be a place, but rather a person.

She stared down at the address and remembered that night.

Do people like us get happy endings? she'd asked Hannah.

They may be complicated, but that doesn't make them any less happy.

Althea sucked in a breath, gathering her courage.

And then she crossed the street, climbed the stairs, and knocked on the door.

Chapter 52

New York City
July 1944

Hannah fled.

She didn't often consider herself a coward, but for once she let herself be one.

Althea was stunning, powerful. With every word she spoke, Hannah's body trembled.

Hannah had fallen for the girl with the big eyes and big emotions, the one who'd worn her heart on her sleeve and blushed as easily as she breathed. That girl had ruined her, had sunk claws into a part of her soul and then poured salt in the wounds.

This woman in front of her, the one who spoke with such conviction, could be far more compelling. And that terrified Hannah.

She had used Althea's visa to flee Paris and everything she knew was coming. To flee Otto and his haunted eyes.

But she hadn't sought out the woman herself. Because she'd been scared about what Althea would say once Hannah told her that she'd been falsely accused for years. That Hannah had believed her to be a monster for years.

When Hannah had arrived in New York City, it was to a country that reminded her too much of everything she'd been escaping from. She'd seen the pictures, the ones that had Black Americans drinking from separate water fountains than white Americans; the ones that had signs proclaiming Jews the secret plague of the West. It had reminded her so much of Nazi Germany that she'd nearly thrown up after looking at them.

The land of freedom and equality had done little to roll out the welcome mat for her. Her third week in Brooklyn, she'd awoken to find slurs painted on her door. The Jewish Center regularly had to replace windows because of the bricks that were thrown through them.

Hannah had fortified herself, had realized that good people existed but so did fear and hatred. Most would do anything to protect their comfortable worldview and the status quo that helped them survive.

She had seen little in her new land to change her mind that humanity was worth fighting for. And so she'd holed up, lived her life, made friends with the truly kind people she'd found in her neighborhood, and tried to lose herself in books when everything became too much.

But seeing Althea again changed something in her.

Althea had no personal incentive to put a target on herself like she'd just done with that speech. Her book had already been sent out to the troops, had garnered praise and attention from the media and book reviewers alike. She had no need to explicitly call out members of Congress for being selfish and callous in the face of soldiers' needs.

And yet she had.

It wasn't always that strength of character was inherent at birth. Sometimes it came through strife and struggle and failure. Sometimes it came through growth.

Althea could have turned bitter. Falsely accused by a lover and used by a political party that had no scruples—Althea could have drifted, could have become mean. No one would have blamed her.

Instead, she used what little power she had to try to make the world better for men who were one breath away from dying in the trenches.

Hannah couldn't help but admire that.

Still, it was hard.

It was hard seeing someone you'd scorned, whom you'd believed the worst about. To look into the eyes of the person whose soul you destroyed—and to ask for their forgiveness.

Otto hadn't asked.

That fact had lived beneath Hannah's breastbone for years. Even after she'd gotten news of his death—suicide by opium. She'd mourned, she'd found a body of water and placed a ring of lilies into it. She'd said her prayers and her goodbyes and cried into the river enough that her tears could have changed the tides.

And yet still she would never forget that he hadn't asked for forgiveness.

Perhaps Hannah should have stayed after Althea's speech. Should have faced her in that darkened space, free of the baggage both of them had carried around for years.

For once, she felt sympathy for Otto. It was harder than she could have ever imagined to admit that she was in the wrong.

Still, she had been planning to do so, planning to get Althea's exact address from Vivian Childs. She just needed a few days to breathe first.

Then there came a knock.

Hannah stepped out of the kitchen into the hallway, her eyes locked on the door. No one visited her. Not here, not in her sanctuary.

Another knock.

Hannah crept forward, a washcloth balled in her hands as her mind conjured up a million possibilities. All of them ending in Althea.

She reached the door and looked through the peephole.

Then she rested her forehead against the wood.

Hannah thought of those letters, thought of the night Althea watched her with too-big eyes, thought of the way she'd sunk down onto the pavement. Thought of *Alice in Wonderland* and spring days exploring Berlin. Thought of the bed with warm sheets and fingers that liked to explore warm skin.

Thought of possibilities.

Thought of happy endings that maybe even she didn't deserve.

Thought of complicated ones that maybe she did.

Then Hannah opened the door.

Epilogue

Berlin
May 1995

Few people noticed the two women sitting on the bench watching from a distance as the Book Burning Memorial in Bebelplatz was unveiled.

But Martha Hale Schumacher had been keeping her eye on them since the ceremony had started. She touched her mother's elbow and jerked her head toward the women.

Vivian Hale's eyes followed the motion and softened at the sight of the two of them.

"They won't be able to see it." Martha pouted. The memorial would be so easy to miss, sunken as it was into the ground. Earlier in the day, Martha had been able to shoulder her way to the edge, to see the rows of empty white bookshelves beneath their feet with enough space to hold the twenty thousand books that were burned that night in May 1933.

Forever memorialized as a void.

"They don't need to," Viv said, wrapping an arm around Martha's waist. At seventy-five, her mother was still strong enough to tug her close, tall enough to press a kiss to the top of Martha's head.

The distracted gesture was so familiar that Martha let herself bask in it. Her mother was so tactile, her default way to comfort her children—and anyone, really—when she could. Martha had lived much of her entire forty-nine years of life pulled into Viv's side more often than not, it seemed.

Martha's father wasn't much better, and Martha had spent a good portion of her teenage years horribly embarrassed, and secretly pleased, at the way her parents couldn't seem to keep their hands off each other.

"Do you think they didn't want to come?" Martha knew she could be a bulldozer, just like Viv. And she had been the one to dream up this trip to Berlin once she'd read about the *Empty Library*. Her aunts had never been able to say no to her, and she had taken advantage of that a time or two or twenty.

"Oh no, darling," Viv said, patting her arm. "They wanted to be here. But they've heard a lot of speeches in their lives. They don't need to hear one more."

And that might be true, but the two women were the reason Martha had come to Germany. So she squeezed her mother's waist one more time, and then stepped away from the crowd, heading toward them, dodging tourists in American flag board shorts and flip-flops as she went.

Hannah smiled as Martha stopped in front of her, blocking the sun. At nearly ninety, Hannah was no less beautiful to Martha than she'd ever been. Her warm, golden eyes had grown cloudy, but the intelligence behind them was as sharp as ever.

"You're missing the activities, dear," Hannah said.

"That's my line," Martha teased, nudging Hannah's foot with her own, as she looked between the two. They were holding hands, looking relaxed and not at all travel worn despite the fact that they must be exhausted from the trip.

"We've been through enough activities in our lives," Althea said, with a wry grin teasing at the edges of her lips, unintentionally echoing Viv's thoughts on the matter.

Martha wanted to argue, to mention the weeks that both she and Viv had spent planning this trip for the four of them. To point out that they'd had to arrange passports and airline tickets and hotel rooms that would accommodate two older women who didn't have the best hips around.

But she took a moment to study their faces. Though both were serene, Martha acknowledged the tension in their postures. They were locked in a memory, the two of them, and it wasn't Martha's place to yank them out of it just because she wanted the touching moment she'd imagined while booking this whole thing.

She should have known, anyway. Though both could be called activists, they had never particularly enjoyed talking about their time in Berlin. They certainly had made sure the children who were part of their lives—including Martha and her two brothers—knew well how easily atrocities could happen when good people looked away. But it wasn't a subject they liked to dwell on in their free time.

They both spent enough of their professional lives on it, anyway.

After three outrageously successful novels, Althea had gone on to write several nonfiction books about how healthy democracies could easily die into fascism. She'd done speaking tours and had even been interviewed for a PBS documentary that they'd all dressed up in their Sunday best to watch. When she'd hit her sixties, she'd started writing children's books that addressed the same topics but in a way suitable for kids, replete with dragons and princesses and complicated endings that were never as pat as others in the genre. The series had become wildly popular and Martha had an entire shelf of signed first editions that she'd read to her own daughter.

Hannah had kept up a quieter war, working at the Brooklyn Jewish Center's library of banned books until it closed in the seventies, unable to persevere beneath the weight of Cold War–era sentiment. With help from Althea and Viv, Hannah had also launched her own little press, Through a Thousand Wonders, publishing everything from chapbooks on feminist theory to crucial educational pamphlets on the AIDS epidemic.

They'd run the press out of a little storefront in Brooklyn, only a street down from Martha's father's first campaign office. The front lobby that Althea and Hannah had set up as a gathering place for intellectuals and students and poets and philosophers was almost never empty. The only rule they'd set: no topic was off-limits.

Martha had been raised there as much as she'd been raised on the campaign trail. She'd learned about both the different systems of governments and how to get a bill into law before she'd turned seven.

But more than anything, Martha had learned that books were sacred, even the ones she didn't agree with or enjoy.

"Why didn't you like it?" Althea would ask, pushing Martha into forming an intelligent response out of a gut reaction. Martha maintained that the fact that her aunts had been relentless in teaching her about critical thinking was the reason she had been one of the youngest members of the House of Representatives ever elected.

Thinking about all that, Martha realized why Hannah and Althea didn't need the pomp and circumstance of today.

They themselves were memorials to the ideals that were being celebrated, simply by the way they'd lived their lives.

So instead of prodding them off the bench, Martha dropped down to sit beside the woman she had always called her aunt and burrowed up against her side just as she'd done since she'd been a child. "Tell me a story."

Althea stroked Martha's hair with her free hand and laughed. But, as always, she obliged. "Once upon a time . . ."

Acknowledgments

It takes a village to publish a book, and I'm so endlessly grateful for mine.

First, a huge thank-you to my agent, Abby Saul. For enthusiastically encouraging my desire to write historical fiction in the first place, for patiently helping me find the heart of this book through your incredible editing eye, for leaping off cliffs hand in hand and hoping we land on pillows, for champagne toasts and library celebrations and everything in between—I'm so eternally glad to have you along on this grand adventure with me.

So many thanks go to Tessa Woodward, who saw this book so clearly even before it was completely polished. From the very first time we chatted about your editorial vision, I was so excited for all the ways you could push this story to be the best, strongest version of itself, and for how I knew you would make me a better writer in the process.

To the whole team at William Morrow, thank you so much. Behind the scenes, there are so many people who put their heart and talent into getting a book into the hands of readers. I'm honored to get to work with you all.

To the #TeamLark group, you guys are the best example of how to be supportive to fellow writers. I'm so thankful for your wisdom and your puns and your friendship.

Everyone tells you when you start writing not to expect your friends to read your books, but the opposite has always been true for me. Some have even started recruiting their families and families' friends in their street-team efforts. I love you guys. Special shout-outs must go to Abby McIntyre, Katie Smith, Marissa and Jesus Carl-Acosta, Julie Volner, Teresa Goncalves, Tonya Austin, Jessie Silko, Kathleen and Kendra Hayden, and Katherine Kline, among so many others.

None of this would be possible without the support of my amazing family—Deb, Bernie, Dana, Brant, Raegan, and Grace. You're my favorite people, I like you and I love you.

When I say it takes a village, that includes you, dear readers. Thank you so much for taking a chance on this book, for spending hard-earned money and time that always seems to be at a premium these days. Like Viv, I think it's an author's job to help you escape for a few hours, to lighten your heart, and to make you feel. Thank you for trusting me to do so.

Lastly, I'd like to acknowledge all the wonderful, brave men and women who helped protect books from the Nazis. The world owes you a debt of gratitude.

About the author

About the book

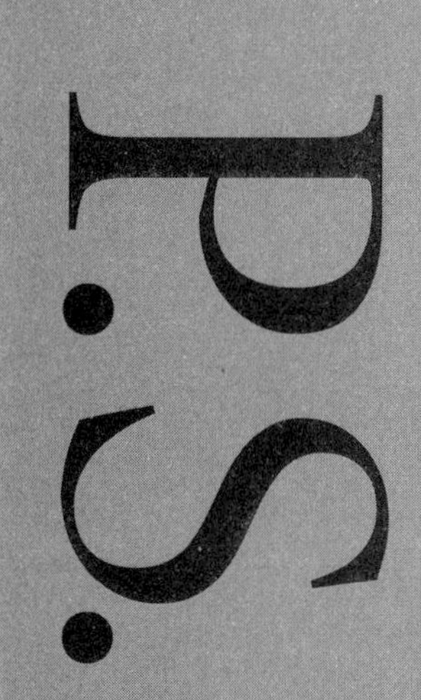

Insights, Interviews & More . . .

About the author

Meet Brianna Labuskes

Courtesy of the author

Brianna Labuskes is the *Washington Post* bestselling author of five thrillers. For the first decade of her career, Brianna worked as a journalist for national news organizations covering politics and policy. Visit her at briannalabuskes.com.

Author's Note

I was a book kid, the one who always had her nose buried in between the pages, who preferred the library to the jungle gym, who grew up to become the teenager spending hours of her free time browsing in Barnes & Noble and then the woman who never left her house without something to read.

Books have always been a foundational stone in my life, and I knew, if I ever could, I would one day write a love letter to them. Then I came across Molly Guptill Manning's most excellent *When Books Went to War.* (Yes, I'm also a history buff who reads about war in my spare time.)

Despite the amount of World War II content I've consumed in my life, though, I'd never heard of the Armed Services Editions. The idea of them captivated me instantly. What better way to honor the power of books than through an initiative that brought stories to soldiers in their darkest moments of need? Thus, *The Librarian of Burned Books* was born.

Now onto what everyone who reads historical fiction wants to know: what's true, what's made up and what's something in between. In *The Librarian* all of the main characters are my own creations, but the events they take part in, many of the historical moments that shape the novel, and several of the supporting characters are real.

The Armed Services Editions initiative was indeed an extraordinary undertaking by the Council on Books in Wartime. The amazing people involved revolutionized ▸

Author's Note ***(continued)***

books—making the paperback commonplace and creating a new generation of readers in the process. From 1943 to 1947, about 122 million copies of more than 1,300 titles were published and sent to soldiers stationed abroad. (And *The Great Gatsby* was, in fact, rescued from obscurity partly by the ASE program.) While any ASE book mentioned in this novel *was* a part of the initiative, I did tweak some of the dates to better serve my timeline. I'd also like to mention that the council had no knowledge of General Eisenhower's desire for each man participating in the D-Day invasion to have an ASE. The Army held back previous distributions and earmarked about a million books to distribute to the men in the marshaling areas days before they stormed the beaches.

Senator Robert Taft of Ohio did try to handcuff the program with his overreaching censorship amendment that he buried within the Soldier Voting Act of 1944. He remained stubborn in the face of countless editorials across the country calling for its removal, and only budged after a July 1944 meeting with the council. Here is where I took the most liberties with history to create my cinematic showdown between Taft and Viv. The council *did* launch a crusade against the senator's amendment—enlisting the help of newspaper and magazine opinion pages across the country—but the final meeting between the sides was a staid business lunch with a gaggle of press waiting outside instead of a rousing affair with emotional speakers. As Taft left the lunch, journalists overheard him making damning political comments about President Roosevelt and soldiers' voting rights. The misstep allowed his congressional colleagues to distance themselves from him pretty quickly, and the amendment was essentially gutted.

If you'd like to read more about the council, the ASE program and its predecessor—the Victory Books Campaign—along with real examples of letters the soldiers wrote to authors, I highly recommend Manning's work. The nonfiction account gives a much broader and more thorough look at all the ways books played a role as weapons in the battle against Hitler and the Nazis.

When you think World War II and books, it's also inevitable that one startling image comes to mind—the flames against the dark sky, students tossing books into the pyres by the armfuls, the audience gleefully cheering them on.

Anyone who loves books is haunted by everything that night in May 1933 came to represent. People often ask me if I put anything about myself into my characters, and the answer is almost always no. The exception is Althea's reaction to the sight of the bonfires:

"It's sacrilege," Althea whispered. If Althea had a church, it was within the covers of books; if she had a religion, it was in the words written there.

I began writing *The Librarian* back in 2020, when the current fervor for banning books in the United States was more of a rumble than a shout. But, as they say, if history doesn't repeat itself, it certainly does rhyme. The parallels to the time period I'd just thrown myself into researching were easy to see, and so I knew where we would likely end up.

Even in the darkest times, though, there is always light to be found.

For me, that was stumbling onto the ▸

Author's Note ***(continued)***

libraries in Paris and Brooklyn. Not much about them has survived the passing of time beyond a few articles from when they opened, a Wikipedia entry or two, and a handful of scholarly articles that I probably contributed about half the hits to. In fact, the libraries were often just throwaway mentions in the larger context of censorship efforts of the time period. They had famous patrons and supporters—H. G. Wells and the Mann brothers in Paris and Einstein and Upton Sinclair in Brooklyn, among many, many others—but they have been mostly forgotten by history. Still, I was immediately enchanted by the idea of them because they represent the very best of what we can be when we approach the world with empathy, curiosity, and wonder instead of fear, hatred, and intolerance.

It's easy to look into the past and see the impulse to destroy books as deeply human and inevitable, but so is our desire to protect them.

In 2022, both the New York Public Library and the Brooklyn Public Library launched programs to make commonly banned books available to people across the country who might not have access to them otherwise. A small island library in Maine made it its mission to fill its shelves with the books that have made all those banned lists. A group of moms in Ohio created a website with maps to track books being challenged across the country.

There is always light to be found.

It's hard to ignore that many of the challenges we're seeing are targeted toward queer books and authors. I didn't intend to write a sapphic love story when I first came up with the idea for *The Librarian,* and yet the moment Hannah made her appearance on the page—riding her bike, heartbroken and tough as nails, through the streets of Paris—I knew she had been in love with Althea.

Once that was decided, I went into a research spiral that landed me in inter-war Berlin and Paris, where, I joyously discovered, queer communities not only existed but flourished.

In Berlin in particular, there were the cabarets and night clubs, of course, but there were also popular films and hit songs and magazines that all featured the queer experience. Magnus Hirschfeld, the man whose institute was raided by the fascists before the book burnings, was decades ahead of his time with his research into the queer identity. People lived out in the open in a way that wasn't really seen again for decades. To read more about this time period in the city, I suggest *Gay Berlin* by Robert Beachy.

While Paris in the thirties wasn't quite at Berlin levels, there was a vibrant community there that was accessible to queer residents. Le Monocle in Montmartre was one of the earliest and most famous sapphic nightclubs in Paris, and lesbian Natalie Clifford Barney did, in fact, host a weekly literary salon at her house on the Left Bank, drawing the likes of Gertrude Stein, among many others.

We're often told that trauma and pain are indelible parts of any LGBTQ historical story, so much so that joyful queer romances set in the past are sometimes deemed unrealistic or fantastical. While our scars can't be denied, they shouldn't erase the fact that there was happiness and love there, too. Queer people have always been able to "curiously wander through a thousand wonders" and see more than just the banal at the end.

On to the broader points of history ▸

Author's Note ***(continued)***

mentioned throughout: Almost all of the events and historical figures are, to the best of my knowledge, accurately portrayed. But because I am very, very human, I am sure there are a few errors that I inserted by mistake. My apologies in advance.

I chose to set Althea's point of view in the first half of 1933 not only because of the book burnings, but because so much happened so quickly in that specific chunk of time that I've always been fascinated by those months. If I'd included all the ways they set Germany on the path toward the war and the holocaust, this would have become a textbook. But if you're interested in the early days of Hitler's rise to power, I highly recommend the Great Courses that I've included in the Dive Deeper section.

While much of the focus in history tends to be on Hitler's male enablers, I did want to include Helene Bechstein, of Bechstein piano fame. Helene and rich, powerful women like her tutored her "little wolf" on table manners and other etiquette, and helped him navigate Berlin's upper echelon—a crucial part of him being accepted by the high society donors who would help him into power. Women are so often scrubbed out of historical context that it's easy to forget the roles we can play in the crucial moments that shape humanity—for better, yes, but also for worse. We should not forget.

It should also be mentioned that Hannah's fears about Otto's assassination fantasies were based on real-life events that occurred long after Hannah would have fled Paris. In 1938, Herschel Feibel Grynszpan shot a German diplomat, and the Nazis used the incident as a pretense to launch Kristallnacht.

Now, while much of the historical backdrop of *The Librarian* hews closely to real-life events, one of the bigger alterations I made—besides adding a hefty amount of drama to the final showdown with Taft—was with Goebbels's cultural exchange program. While he *was* in charge of setting the cultural agenda for Hitler's Reich, I created that specific initiative as a way to get Althea into the grasp of the Nazis.

I do hope that some of the history in *The Librarian* has piqued your interest, but at the end of the day, more than anything, I hope the story moved you, resonated with you, made you laugh or cry or have that tightening in your chest that can only be described as a million different feelings at once.

As *New York Times* bestselling author Jewell Parker Rhodes says, "I love historical fiction because there's a literal truth, and there's an emotional truth, and what the fiction writer tries to create is that emotional truth."

My ultimate goal is to have done that for you.

Thank you so much for reading.

Books From the Book

Below is a list of all the books mentioned in *The Librarian of Burned Books*, besides the two fictional Althea James novels.

Armed Services Editions

Oliver Twist, Charles Dickens
The Adventures of Huckleberry Finn, Mark Twain
The Adventures of Tom Sawyer, Mark Twain
The Grapes of Wrath, John Steinbeck
Candide, Voltaire
Yankee from Olympus, Catherine Drinker Bowen
The Call of the Wild, Jack London
Wind, Sand and Stars, Antione de Saint-Exupéry
Tortilla Flat, John Steinbeck
Strange Fruit, Lillian Smith
A Tree Grows in Brooklyn, Betty Smith
Chicken Every Sunday, Rosemary Taylor
Vanity Fair, William Makepeace Thackeray
The Great Gatsby, F. Scott Fitzgerald

Others

The Adventures of Alice in Wonderland, Lewis Carroll
Reinmar von Hagenau's poetry collection
Too Busy To Die, H. W. Roden
Romeo and Juliet, William Shakespeare
Siddhartha, Herman Hesse
Of Mice and Men, John Steinbeck
The Ingenious Gentleman Don Quixote of La Mancha, Miguel de Cervantes
Parnassus on Wheels, Christopher Morley
Les Misérables, Victor Hugo
All Quiet on the Western Front, Erich Maria Remarque

Grimms' Fairy Tales, Jacob and Wilhelm Grimm
Ivanhoe, Walter Scott
Tender Is the Night, F. Scott Fitzgerald
One Thousand and One Nights

Dive Deeper into History

For more information on the historical events that inspired *The Librarian of Burned Books* check out some of the sources I used to research the novel below.

Books

When Books Went to War, Molly Guptill Manning
Books as Weapons, John B. Hench
The Book Thieves: The Nazi Looting of Europe's Libraries and the Race to Return a Literary Inheritance, Anders Rydell
The Berlin Stories, Christopher Isherwood
The Rise and the Fall of the Third Reich, William L. Shirer
The Death of Democracy, Benjamin Carter Hett
In the Garden of Beasts, Erik Larson
Gay Berlin, Robert Beachy

Articles

Leary, William M. "Books, Soldiers and Censorship during the Second World War." *American Quarterly*
Von Merveldt, Nikola. "Books Cannot Be Killed by Fire: The German Freedom Library and the American Library of Nazi-Banned Books As Agents of Cultural Memory." John Hopkins University Press
Appelbaum, Yoni. "Publishers Gave Away 122,951,031 Books During World War II." *The Atlantic*
"Paris Opens Library of Books Burnt by Nazis." *The Guardian* Archives
Whisnant, Clayton J. "A Peek Inside Berlin's Queer Club Scene Before Hitler Destroyed It." *The Advocate*

"Between World Wars, Gay Culture Flourished in Berlin." NPR's *Fresh Air*

More

The Great Courses: A History of Hitler's Empire, Thomas Childers
"Hitler: YA Fiction Fan Girl," Robert Evans, *Behind the Bastards* Podcast
Magnus Hirschfeld, Leigh Pfeffer and Gretchen Jones, *History Is Gay* Podcast
"Das Lila Lied," composed by Mischa Spoliansky, lyrics by Kurt Schwabach

Book Club Discussion Questions

1. Did you know about the Armed Service Editions or the burned books libraries before reading *The Librarian of Burned Books*? Was there anything you learned that was surprising to you about either?
2. Each point of view (Althea, Viv, and Hannah) is set in a distinct location and time period. What role does the year and city play in each character's development throughout the novel?
3. *Alice in Wonderland* comes up frequently. Do you think the themes in that story are reflected in Althea's time in Berlin? How so?
4. Did you enjoy the way book quotes were layered into the scenes throughout the novel? Did they add to the story for you? Was there any one in particular that resonated with you?
5. Throughout the novel, Hannah struggles with the idea of resisting the Nazis through the power of words versus resisting with violence. Is there ever a time when violence becomes necessary? Is everyone capable of being pushed that far?
6. In Chapter 5, Hannah tells Viv that the reason the Brooklyn library is so important is to protect the Jewish culture: "*Books are a way we leave a mark on the world, aren't they?" They say we were here, we loved and we grieved and we laughed and we made mistakes and we* existed." Do you agree

with that statement, and do you see that reflected in the kinds of books that have been banned in recent years?

7. Viv views her quest as essentially telling a compelling story to get voters behind her cause. How was that tactic used by both sides in other ways in World War II? Do you see it being employed in today's politics?

8. Was it uncomfortable to read Althea's early chapters when she was enchanted by the Nazis? Did you judge her for not realizing what they were sooner? Do you think it would be easy or difficult to break free from an ideology if you had been in her position?

9. How much did you know about Berlin's night life and its queer community? Were the scenes surprising in any way? Did you notice parallels to our current landscape in both the openness and acceptance of the progressive society and then the pushback that followed?

10. In Chapter 16, Hannah says, "*Burning books about things you do not like or understand does not mean those things no longer exist.*" Yet book burning has existed nearly since the beginning of mass-produced books themselves. Why is the strategy so common? And then, in the same chapter, Hannah says that it's actually the books that weren't burned that bother her the most because the Nazis used them to study the very people they wanted to erase. Which is more disturbing to you?

11. Is it ever morally justified to ban a book? ▸

Book Club Discussion Questions
(continued)

12. Were you surprised that the libraries included *Mein Kampf* on their shelves? Do you agree with their reasoning?

13. In Chapter 23, the women discuss how much difference one person can make, and whether small changes can add up to mean more than a grand gesture. How do you feel about individual politics versus collective action? Is one more effective than the other? And does the book reflect that discussion in the end or counter it?

14. Characters answer the question, "Do you have a favorite book?" differently throughout the novel. Does one answer in particular resonate with you? What is your favorite book (if you have one) and why?

15. Viv points out that it's not always an author's job to tell the truth. Rather it can simply be to entertain the readers. Do you agree or disagree?

16. Was Otto's betrayal unforgivable? Would you have burned that bridge like Hannah did?

17. What did you think of the final speeches? Were there any lines that stuck out to you—for good or bad? Did you find Hannah's and Althea's complementary to each other, and if so, why? Did anything make you think of what's going on in politics today?

18. Did you find the epilogue satisfying or do you wish you could have imagined your own complicated ending for the characters?